http://www.cherryh.com/

D0173397

C. J. CHERRYH
DEFENDER

DAW BOOKS, INC.
DONALD A. WOLLHEIM, FOUNDER
375 Hudson Street, New York, NY 10014
ELIZABETH R. WOLLHEIM
SHEILA E. GILBERT
PUBLISHERS
www.dawbooks.com

First Paperback Printing, November 2002.

1 2 3 4 5 6 7 8 9 10

To Asad, Barb, Harriet, and Irene,
and to Ann, Lawrence, Elaine, Elizabeth, Elinor
and Cynthia . . .
They found the missing pieces.

1

Firelight went up to the red figures of an ancient frescoed vault, smoke-hazed from the braziers on either side of the black stone tomb. In the dark congregation, watchful eyes now and again caught the firelight and reflected it, gold fire brighter than the sheen of light off opulent brocade.

It was an atevi place—and solemn tribute to a decades-dead aiji. Decades in the past, Valasi might be, but the association he had created had only grown wider at his death. It spanned the continent now. It reached around the world. It shared the heavens with strangers.

An atevi place, an atevi ceremony, an atevi congregation . . . but one human, one pale, blond, very small and conspicuous human stood in a crowd of towering atevi lords, some of whom had often and fairly recently entertained the idea of killing him. Under the court attire, the frock coat and the lace and the brocades, Bren Cameron wore ten pounds of composite that would stop most bullets, if any of these very adept gentlemen and ladies ventured an assassination without proper Filing of Intent.

The Assassins' Guild, on the living aiji's order, would not allow that to happen. The tall atevi on either side of him, Banichi and Jago, in the black and silver of that Guild—they knew the odds, they knew all the agreements and contracts currently in force—knew the likelihood of illegal risks as well. And while assuring him there was no contract Filed, and that no Guild actions but surveillance could be taken for days on any side of this gathering—they still insisted on the armor.

So Bren complied, uncomplaining, with not too many questions, and kept his head generally down, evading any too-direct stare that might draw attention.

Deference, respect, solemnity . . . in a place where humans least of all belonged.

Tabini-aiji had decreed this honor to his father's tomb, so the invitation declared, for a memorial and a reminder of the origins of the Western Association— well and good. Humans and atevi alike honored their dead, and they held memorials, particularly at points of change or challenge.

But what was changing? Or where was the challenge?

But predictably enough—they could hardly ignore the call to venerate the aiji's father—the loyal lords of the western *aishidi'tat* had come in with no trouble. Those from the south shore and from the farthest eastern reaches of the Association arrived in far more uneasy duty, surely with questions of their own. They had been Valasi's allies, most of them—and saying so had been unfashionable in the west for decades.

The aiji-dowager, too, had flown in from the east for this solemn event. If she hadn't, rumors would have flown.

Ilisidi, aiji-dowager, Valasi's mother.

Tabini's grandmother.

And the whole world knew that one of the two, Tabini or Ilisidi, had almost certainly assassinated Valasi.

Well, grant she came: no mere opinion of men perturbed her. If one was an atevi lord—and she was among the highest of atevi lords—one rigidly observed the proprieties and courtesies that supported all lords, whatever the circumstances. One consistently did the right thing.

And if one were the human paidhi-aiji, the official translator, the point of contact between two species, one also did the right thing, and came when called, and kept clearly in mind the fact that this was *not* human society. A paltry assassination by no means broke the bonds of an atevi *association*, no more than it necessarily fractured man'chi—that emotional cement that held all atevi society together. A judicious, well-planned in-house assassination only made the association more comfortable for all the rest—eased, rather than broke, the web of association and common consent—in this case, the family bond on which the stability of the world depended.

A well-chosen assassination might make unity easier, once the dust settled, and a species that did not, biologically speaking, *feel* friendship . . . still felt something warm and good when its surrounding association settled into harmony.

Were they here to meditate on that fact?

To renew the bond?

A human couldn't possibly feel it. Wasn't hard-wired to feel it. Tabini had called him down from the orbiting station for this service, which he'd taken as a simple excuse covering a desire to have some essential conference, some secret personal meeting which would make thorough sense.

But thus far—there was no meeting. There was going to be a special session of the legislature—and that had made sense, until it was clear he was dismissed, and would not attend. There'd been one intimate audience with Tabini on that first day, in which Tabini had entertained him in his study, a great honor, talked about hunting—one of Tabini's favorite occupations, which he never actually had time to do—and asked in some detail about the welfare of associates on the space station. They'd had several drinks, become quite cheerful, shared an hour with Lady Damiri, the aiji-consort, and discussed the weather, their son's education, and the economy, none of which he would have called critical—nor ever discussed with that much brandy in him if he'd thought it would become critical.

Good night, Tabini had said then, good fortune, not forgetting there *was* a memorial service involving, oh, the entire continent, and would he kindly sit among the foremost in attendance?

Not quite news to him. He'd known it would take place—hadn't quite known, before landing, that it was quite so extravagant, televised, or followed with a special session.

So he was on temporary display at the edge of the aiji's household, wearing that white ribbon in his braid that reminded all parties he was the paidhi, the translator, the neutral, not an appropriate target.

He represented to those present, among other controversial things, the full-tilt acquisition of technology over which Tabini and Valasi had had their fatal falling-out.

So Valasi died under questionable circumstances, and instead of declaring any decent period of mourning and reconsideration, Tabini had immediately opened the floodgates of change: television, trade with Mospheira . . . railroads. Valasi's paidhi, a human whose modest advocacy of airplanes, an expanded rail system and limited television broadcasting had scandalized the traditional-minded among the atevi—had quit, retired, and left the job to him.

Tabini had immediately taken—well, with atevi, a *liking* to him didn't translate, but certainly Tabini had sensed that he could work with him. Occasionally he had wondered if Tabini had spotted the world's greatest fool and thought he could get the sun, the moon and the stars from him. . . .

The stars—considering that not so long afterward *Phoenix* had shown up in the heavens, the colony ship returned to its lost human colony on someone else's world.

Things out there, *Phoenix* reported, hadn't worked out. *Things* had involved an alien encounter gone very wrong at a space station that never should have been built. And while the paidhi asked himself how he had ever gotten into this, Tabini's close cooperation with humans spiraled wider and wider.

It took atevi into space, into a near-unified economy with the human enclave on Mospheira. It took two species and three governments to the very edge of union.

And atevi had never forgotten the hazards of swallowing foreign answers to local problems.

Ilisidi entered the tomb, among the last, just behind Lord Tatiseigi of the Atageini, uncle of the aiji-consort. She walked with a cane, went in the company of Cenedi, her chief of security.

And *Cajeiri* was with her. Bren noted that—the boy, almost lost in the company of adults, took his place with Ilisidi's party.

There was a change. The aiji's heir took his place, not with uncle Tatiseigi, but one place down, still in the front row, with great-grandmother Ilisidi.

Cameras were discreet, but in evidence, and cameramen shifted slightly to get a good view of Ilisidi and the boy. This was going out across the continent: a ceremony of national unity and a memorial in respect for the past, it might be: but it was also a public function in which the alignment of public figures was highly significant.

So the aiji-dowager stood there now before Valasi's sarcophagus, just visible in the tail of his eye. She was diminutive for an ateva, white-haired with age, leaning on that cane . . . sharp eyes taking in every nuance of expression and surely conscious of the camera. The boy stood stock still, just visible past Cenedi's black uniform—Cenedi also being Guild security, oh yes.

Guild security was all through the assembly, despite the limited seating.

A war of flowers out there in the corridor: of colors, of position in here—and a sense of progress and opposition in delicate balance, with the Assassins' Guild to guarantee good behavior.

But far, far better than the alternative.

The aiji's immediate household filed in. That was Tabini, Lady Damiri, and *their* attendant security. Tabini-aiji was in black and red, his house colors. Damiri wore gold and green, the Atageini colors, and carried a lily in her hands, strong contrast to her black skin, amid the glitter of emeralds. They took their places, finishing the first row.

All seats were filled. There was a little murmur of expectation.

Then a bell sounded.

Utter silence descended. A camera changed focus. That was the only sound now, lamplight momentarily gilding an imprudent lens.

That stroke of the bell called for meditation.

Next would come a statement from the head of house—Tabini, in this case. Bren had read the program somewhat before he entered a shadow too deep for humans to read.

And whatever the aiji had to say, the gathered lords would parse it for every detail. It was important—an address that could, if it went wrong, break the union of lords apart. It always could. Any chance word, gone amiss, could break the Association at any time— and in this context, bets were doubled. Tabini had made deals with human authorities, sent atevi to work on the space station, admitting a flood of new technologies. He'd had to, for a whole host of economic and practical reasons that sliced right across the ordinary order of politics, throwing conservatives into alliance with the most liberal of western powers.

He'd had to reach across traditional lines, across ethnical lines—across associational lines.

And so the agreement with humans widened, policy deliberately blind to the causes of the last world war, dancing across the shards of old resentments, skipping over divides of opinion that had once swum with blood.

Most of all, the crisis in the heavens and the need to secure a voice in that resolution had shoved the whole economy into a hellishly scary rush, a fever pitch run that no one at first had thought would last more than a month.

No longer than three years.

Then no longer than six.

As yet there was no slowdown, no cooldown, no pause for breath—and no meeting of the associated lords—until this.

The silence after that bell was so absolute that breathing itself seemed a disturbance . . . and in that silence, of all things, someone dropped a program, a crack of parchment on stone that set a twitch—if not a killing reflex—into every hair-triggered, Guild-trained nerve in the chamber.

Every Guild member had to skip a heartbeat. Every lord present had to make a conscious decision not to dive below the benches.

But it was only the next aiji, *their* someday ruler,

diving almost to the edge of the flower-decked sarcophagus to rescue that wayward, unseemly folio.

In his haste it escaped his fingers on his retreat.
Twice.

Bren winced.

Three times.

The boy had it. Scrambled back to his place in the
standing line.

Cajeiri, Tabini's and Damiri's son, the hope of the
Association, Tatiseigi's grand-nephew—was the
height and weight of the average human teenager—
but not, by any means, average, human, or teenaged.
Cajeiri tried—God knew he tried, but somehow his
feet found obstacles, his hands lost their grip on perfectly ordinary objects, and when Cajeiri would swear
to all gods most fortunate that he was standing still,
everyone else called it fidgeting.

Now of all times . . . in front of the whole assembled
Association, the lords of the *aishidi'tat*, this was *no* time
for boys to be boys, or for a child to be—whatever
he might be.

Cajeiri was invisible in the first row again. Silence
hung all about him. The dignity of the highest houses
settled on his young shoulders. Tabini, Tatiseigi—now
Ilisidi, in whose care the young unfortunate attended
the ceremony—were all in question in that behavior.
Fosterage was the rule of the great houses, once a
child of rank left the cradle. Tatiseigi, the maternal
uncle, had had a go at applying courtly polish, in the
rural, rigid politics of the Atageini stronghold in the
central west. Now Ilisidi had him: in her district,

modernist meant someone who installed a flush toilet in a thousand-year-old stronghold.

God help the boy.

A second bell. Solemnity recovered. This was the second point, fragile second, unfortunate second: atevi lived by numbers, died by the numbers. *Two* of anything presumed there would be a third. There *must* be a third. The very note, echoing in the stone recesses of the place, on this occasion, gathered up the tension in the air and prepared to braid it into a cord . . . if the third bell, please God, would only ring without unfortunate omen.

Cajeiri held himself absolutely still. *Two* would ring ominously even in an atevi six-year-old's brain. *Two* always meant *pay attention: another will follow.*

Bren had been to Malguri himself. In a way, he wished he could go back there, have another try of his own at a life a human wasn't regularly admitted even to see. In a certain measure he so envied the boy that chance.

Ilisidi had her hands full. He did know that. The boy, thus far, with the best intentions, had destroyed two historic porcelains, set off a major security alarm, and ridden a startled mecheita across newly-poured cement in Tatiseigi's formal garden.

Finally, unbearably, with the least shifting of bodies in anticipation, Tabini, head of house, foremost of the Ragi atevi, aiji of the whole *aishidi'tat*, moved out of the row to the single lighted lamp that sat before the sarcophagus.

Tabini, tall shadow, took a slender straw, took light from one lamp and lit one of two others.

Two lamps lit.

Jago, armed and informed, nudged Bren's hand with the back of hers. *Pay attention. Be on your guard.*

Banichi, on his other side, didn't move.

Every bodyguard in the whole chamber must be thinking the same, prepared for anything. It was in all the machimi, the history-plays: in the feudal age, in Malguri's age, the time of bright banners and heraldry, assemblies thus invited had been murdered wholesale, slaughtered by hidden archers. Whole tables of diners had fallen ill at once. Ladies had perished in poisoned baths—name the death: someone had delivered it.

Hearts beat, atevi, and in one case, human, with utter trepidation.

Tabini, damn him, knew it. The third bell had not yet rung. And Tabini turned, in that terrible, unprecedented interval.

"*I speak,*" Tabini declared, in that resonant, still-young voice, "between the second and the third bell. *We live* . . . between the second and the third bell of our associated lives. *We live* . . . on the edge of decision and chance. *We live* . . . between expectation and fulfillment. Between the second and the third bell of our collective existence, I am Valasi's son, I am Valasi's heir . . . I *am* Valasi's successor."

After the hasdrawad and the tashrid, the bicameral legislature, had determined for the second time that Ilisidi would *not* be aiji, they had appointed Tabini to head the *aishidi'tat*.

And the whole assembly, caught between the bells and the lights, heard felicitous, redeeming *threes.*

Every atevi nerve rang as a human could only intellectually comprehend—not feel, gut-deep: felicitous *one*, then the two strokes of *we live*. Then *I speak*, disastrous two—felicitous *three* of *we live*. And now no resolution of the first *cahi*, the first proposal, at all, but the infelicitous *two* of *I am*. A human brain could short-circuit keeping up with the bracketing structures, but Bren swore he felt it in his own nerves: and he *felt* his knees go weak when Tabini gave the assembly that third, redemptive *I am*. The whole audience held its breath, angry as they must be at this tactic. *That*, in this audience, didn't matter. They were caught up, snared, and couldn't move. *Daren't* move. *Felt* the *aishidi'tat* threatened—and were drawn, unwillingly, to hope that it, and their lives, continued.

"*I speak* as your appointed guide into time to come," Tabini said. And delivered the *next* third stroke, that painfully wound-up, merciful third: "*I speak* for the unity of the assembly of us all.

"We do not forget," Tabini continued, as nerve and flesh all but liquified in relief and bodyguards stood down from red alert. Tabini swept on, in possession of all attention. Thank *God* no program dropped. Breathing itself was at a minimum. Tabini's oratory was all fortunate threes now, rapid, hammering into nerves still resounding to two strokes of the bell, still waiting for the resolution of their universe. "We do not break our strong connections with all that Valasi-aiji built. We do not abrogate our traditions. The more knowledge we acquire, the more we rationally comprehend the universe, the more we control our own destiny—"

Sensitive spot: the number-counters who so powerfully ruled the traditional world had long discounted the numbers of the heavens, meaning they had deliberately, scornfully dismissed the work of astronomers, who had failed to foresee the Landing.

But the modern-day Astronomer Emeritus, a genius of his age, brandished numbers that confounded the number-counters—those mathematicians who claimed to guide the less talented to understand the balance of the universe. The newly respectable Astronomer Emeritus was Tabini's. And with Tabini's blessing, the Astronomer Emeritus worked to understand the stars and make reliable paths through the heavens. The numbers flowing down from the heavens now ran a starship and promised to connect atevi to a rational universe that also accounted for humans—

To a universe, what was more, that brought them a *second* foreign species. That this new species happened to be hostile—well, well, but the soaring optimism of good numbers insisted the difficulties could be overcome, irresistibly so.

Atevi relied on a rational universe.

Humans on the island enclave of Mospheira had faith in miracles.

Humans on the starship over their heads had more faith in a second armed starship and a planetful of allies, in a universe otherwise sparse with life.

But atevi being an independent lot, fiercely so, and hating worse than poison to be handed a fait accompli involving someone else's numbers, had politely declined to make too strong a point that a human species that had misplaced its own home planet was not infallible. In the main atevi were impressed by what they saw going on in the heavens—what, at least, the dedicated and the suspicious alike, armed with binoculars, could make out as going on in the heavens. It was at least a personal enough contact with the presence up there to make it a national obsession, and binoculars and telescopes enjoyed a vogue at garden parties and secret meetings.

The latter—since a last die-hard cadre of the traditionalists wanted their world back the way Tabini had inherited it, *sans* telescopes, *sans* autographed roof tiles—*sans* the frantic push of atevi interests skyward. But the majority even of the conservatives had dropped the traditionalist fight over the very concept of Air Traffic Control: they'd lost that argument, long since, and scrambled to get aerospace industry in their own districts.

Yet did the builders of such facilities properly consider the numbers? They derived them from new-fangled *computers*, to the contempt of the die-hard traditionalists and the dedicated 'counters. Dared one trust them?

"The more numbers we gain," Tabini was saying to the assembled lords, "the more I myself appreciate Valasi's work. *Not*," Tabini added, before certain die-hard conservatives burst a blood vessel, "that I would argue less with my father, but certainly that I would listen more. *His* time was too soon to know everything: but in his wisdom he laid a foundation for the *aishidi'tat* that would assure a strong leadership . . . and now I know that he saw change coming. Now I know that he prepared for it. Now I know that my father was a wise man."

Oh, *that* was clever: generational authority was a tenet of the conservatives . . . while the aiji's increasing power over their lives as a central authority was a continual sore point. Now Tabini equated one with the other, wound the cord of their own argument around a strong young fist, and yanked.

Count your fingers when dealing with Tabini. His enemies and his allies both said that.

"My father warned me," Tabini said. "He saw us growing reliant on advances that we would never have the chance to make for ourselves. But *because* these inventions, like all real things, come of true numbers, he saw that they use the natural universe, he saw that they were good, he saw that if we did invent them they would be much the same. He had, however, every intent of shaping what came to us into *our own design*, he had every intent of maintaining sovereignty—" Another sore point. "*And because it follows from every previous invention—he clearly had every intent of going into space.*" The cadence dragged them right into it . . . and marched on, leaving the fiercest opponents to mull over a very strong point: if not that aim, what aim? "In the new numbers, our economy runs white-hot. We *have* no hunger, we *have* no feuds, we *have* no want of employment for the clans. We mine, we build, we distribute, and we have no scarcity anywhere. Thanks to our vantage from orbit we rescue a forest from blight. We warn a village on the coast to put up the storm shutters. We cure diseases we once thought hopeless. In the new numbers we send and speak and travel from one end to the other of every association, without wires or roads that blight the world. In the new numbers, we draw power from the sun's free light without smoke to obscure the sky.

"Never let us forget what is *kabiu*, or break the rhythm of the seasons, or of the wild things, or of our own bodies. Let us never forget how to build a fire, light a candle, or use our hands to spin thread. Let no single village forget how to weave cloth, shape a pot, or hunt its own food. If a machine made a pot, it serves for a while. But if hands made it, it is *kabiu*, and fit to pass to our children. This was the true understanding I learned from Valasi. This is what I now give to my son. This is what he will in his day give to his son. This observance of true value is what keeps *kabiu*. This is the source of things unseen. This quality, this *fitness* remains so long as we have the keen sense of what is real. And in a hundred thousand pots, one is *kabiu*.

"We *can* heal the sick, warn against weather, and supply common pots to every village in the world. But let us teach our children to make what is *kabiu*, and to recognize what is *kabiu*, and to value what is *kabiu*.

"This is the unity of one. This is the *aishidi'tat*. This is our heritage."

A bell rang. Tabini lit the third lamp in utter stillness.

The whole universe seemed to start again. A camera changed focus. Feet shifted. Breath came in and out.

Tabini turned, faced the assembly and lifted his

arms. "Go. Observe silence for this one day on the matters under debate. Meet with me tomorrow."

Silence on matters under debate. Tabini had just put *all* the burning issues in that category. He'd destined the whole damned basket of snakes for debate tomorrow—when the paidhi, who'd worked on all these issues, had to be at the shuttle site within the hour.

Tabini having put every issue under legislative seal—no one could talk. The doors at the rear opened, admitting the brighter light of the corridor outside, rendering all of them, human and atevi, old and young, easterner and westerner, as shadows.

With the opening of those doors the smell of flowers overwhelmed the slight petroleum scent of atevi bodies. The hush now was overwhelming. The outward movement, beginning at the back, proceeded, and row after row, kept going, participants likely wondering what they dared say—or think.

Dared he stop for a word with Tabini? It seemed chancy to Bren even to turn his head and look toward the aiji's household. He had a side view of Ilisidi and uncle Tatiseigi waiting in starched silence.

The outward movement reached the next to last row, the outflow proceeding with dispatch. At least there'd been no gunshots outside.

Their own row took its turn and moved out.

Bren followed Jago out, and Banichi followed him, the three of them, felicitous three, a unity differently destined than the crowd outside. The sarcophagus, the arcane secrets of death and the atevi's dealing with it, was at his back. Light was in the hall. The recessional suddenly felt to him like an escape toward life, toward a wholly different world, fleeing questions of eternity and mortality and Tabini's motives down here . . .

Tabini didn't consult him, didn't invite him to the most important legislative session in a decade—well and good. There was no call for hurt feelings. He had urgent jobs he *had* to do, up in orbit, and Tabini was probably wise not to embroil the paidhi-aiji in regional contentions.

He and his bodyguard went out those guarded doors among the flowers, into the outward flow of the elite and the powerful of the *aishidi'tat*, everyone on their way to the two lifts. There was talk, now, and there were guarded looks, brooding looks, satisfied looks—one could practically know the province by the expression.

He still didn't know what he thought. He didn't know whether what he'd been dragged down here to do had simply evaporated, and Tabini wasn't talking—or whether his mere appearance in the ceremony was enough to accomplish some purpose, and Tabini wasn't talking.

He could damned well bet there'd be conferences among allies who had been here. There'd be frantic opinion-seeking among the news services. He desperately wanted to avoid the newspeople, and they'd be swarming thick in the halls above.

He was due to be off the planet inside an hour now, and that, at the moment, seemed a very good idea.

They reached the lift, waited, in the murmurous silence of the hall. "Did you see the offering from Keishan?" one lord asked another indignantly.

Bren personally had not, nor wished to look, in this hazardous precinct where looks said it all. He had no idea which among the cloyingly perfumed flowers belonged to Keishan, but Keishan's neighbors clearly did, and were somehow disturbed by the placement, or the size, or the color, or a hundred other declarations someone could find improper.

"This way, Bren-ji." Banichi rarely pulled court rank to do his job, but they were late as it was, and with an out-thrust arm and a judicious eye, Banichi shunted him ahead of village nobility. Jago quickly blocked the lift door for him, and to Bren's dismay and relief, gave them the entire lift car to themselves.

Rude, to the lesser lords. Justifiable, but rude. Bren didn't know what to say—but when Assassins' Guild security indicated their charge should move, a wise man moved, and heaved a shaken little sigh of deep appreciation in the little time they rode by themselves.

"Is there a problem?" he asked them. But immediately as he said it the door opened onto another wall of flowers on the main floor—flowers, and lenses, and news service reporters who spotted a high source and meant to have it at any cost.

"What does the paidhi's office have to say, nand' paidhi?" was the loudest question, along with, "Is there a crisis, nandi?"

"I am apprized of none," he answered, his only safe answer. "I'm bound back to the station on the scheduled flight." He was relieved to let his security whisk him along to another bank of lifts.

The door shut.

"No particular difficulty," Banichi answered the prior question.

The lift rose up, let them out. They walked down a short hall in the restricted residency of the Bujavid and took yet one more lift, this one securitied and keyed, down again.

Down and down to the rocky core of this hill which was the Bujavid, the governmental nerve center, the seat of legislative authority, the state venues and the residence of the aiji and the highest lords . . . and the place of tombs.

"It should be a quiet ride, nadi-ji," Jago said on the way down.

He very much hoped so.

"Tabini never did tell me why I'm here," he said.

"It's a puzzle," Banichi said. And what puzzled Banichi decidedly puzzled most people. And gave him no better information.

The lift let them out in an echoing vault of concrete and living rock, a large, heavily guarded hall, a mostly vacant walk toward the Bujavid's internal freight and passenger train station—huge spaces, cut into the high hill, with guarded accesses for the trains.

Forklifts carried cargo to and fro. Security offices were constantly busy. Everything here was scrutinized—everything examined.

A red-curtained train waited at the siding—theirs, beyond a doubt, one of the short, well-appointed specials that sometimes had tagged them on to a long-range train, sometimes ran them straight to the airport.

It was the latter, this time, and Bren made a quick check of his wristwatch as they walked.

"We're just a little late," Banichi said. "No worry, nadi."

No worry.

"I need a copy of Tabini's speech, nadiin-ji."

"As soon as possible," Jago assured him, and he hoped that would happen before he was in the air. Absolutely no copies had been leaked, not even to intimates and staff, and he remained marginally uncertain whether Tabini, damn him, might have ad-libbed the whole thing. Tabini was capable of it, completely capable, but it was important enough he thought not. He himself wanted a re-read before the tone cooled in his memory, and neither he nor staff could take time now to secure one by ordinary channels.

They approached the red-curtained car—Tabini's private car, on loan to him . . . and he recognized the operations car that went next. It was arguably the tightest security on the rails. Banichi quickened his pace, entered the passenger car first to check out the situation there, then came back to signal him and Jago to to come inside.

A guard just inside surrendered a computer case, *the* computer, to Banichi, and Bren breathed a sigh of relief as Banichi handed it to him. The man was Tabini's, known to them. The car next door likely held the rest of that team. All of that was Banichi's concern. Bren took his precious computer—the computer he'd not expected to have to leave anywhere he wasn't, and had. He'd rather leave a newborn child on a railway track than have it out of his hands for five minutes—but if he trusted any staff as allied to him, it was logically Tabini's.

Not that Tabini wouldn't spy on him—excruciating to contemplate certain of the computer's files in Tabini's hands, but at least there would be no hostile use of them.

The red velvet bench seat at the rear of the car, beyond the bar, was his usual spot. He sat down on the bench seat, holding the computer in both arms. He felt violated, telling himself the while there was absolutely no reason to worry about Tabini's men getting into it, swearing to himself he was going to take off his personal files on the next trip.

The dark red shutters and velvet curtains at his elbow concealed bulletproofing. The body armor chafed under the dress coat and bound like a corset, and he longed to be rid of it . . . but not yet. Not yet.

"Fruit juice?" Jago asked.

"Yes, Jago-ji." His throat was dry. He thought he looked ridiculous holding to the computer as he was, and persuaded himself to turn it loose and set it on the seat beside him. He looked at his watch, trying to re-situate himself in the outside schedule, in his senselessly interrupted agenda aloft. There was Geigi, among others. Jase—Captain Jase Graham, who'd so badly wanted to take this trip.

Four minutes behind schedule, not his staff's fault. It took an unpredictable time to end a speech, move people through narrow halls, to wait for lifts. The shuttle might wait a little for him. It had some leeway. It didn't like to use it.

The train began to move. Banichi, communications

still in hand, had rechecked the situation with the pair who had handled the baggage. "The baggage is already aboard the shuttle," Banichi said. That wouldn't delay them. "They're advised we're on our way."

Moving the baggage was a risk. They didn't like to advertise their movements. With chaos inside the Bujavid, it was particularly risky.

As for missing the flight—Bren imagined to himself having to return to the Bujavid, to dodge news questions for days until the next shuttle—that was a political risk he chose not to run. Escape, on schedule, seemed to raise the fewest questions—leaving everyone only with the original question.

Why?

Why bring him down to the planet in the first place, hold a social meeting, a memorial, and dismiss him?

Jago gave him the requested glass of fruit juice, a sweet mixture. He took a sip. She had her own, and sat down beside him, a wall of living warmth and good will in what had been a chill day of vaults and lower level corridors.

Banichi sat down opposite, his large frame disposed on a seat the image of Bren's . . . a seat that fit Banichi.

Bren was young Cajeiri's size, used to finding his feet didn't reach the ground, used to standing in the shadow of his atevi bodyguards. Either could pick him up and carry him at a run . . . Jago *had* done it, to tell the truth. She and Banichi both could break a human arm entirely by accident. Atevi could jump higher, run faster, and see in what he called total darkness—all advantages to Banichi and Jago in their work.

All assets, on his side, in any dispute—assets that somewhat equalized the disadvantages of a Mospheiran on the atevi side of the strait.

The island of Mospheira, with its human enclave, very likely had gotten the broadcast of the ceremony simultaneously with broadcast on the mainland. The recent treaty said they would. But it didn't come translated, and Mospheira was incredibly short of talent in the Foreign Office since he'd left and taken the best with him. Kate Shugart and Ben Feldman were both aloft—so likely Mospheira would send the tape up to them and bring it down again before they put it on the air.

That meant the station—and his own staff up there—*would* have gotten the feed.

And of speeches this was an incredibly difficult one to render, with so much dependent on situation, nuance and context. . . . positional meanings meant headaches for a translator. Whatever they could put out needed footnotes. Whatever they rendered needed someone wholly fluent—

It needed *him*, when he could get his hands on it, to supply those footnotes, and he hoped the effects of human guesswork didn't ripple outward too far or generate position statements from human agencies before he had a chance at it. He rarely exercised his old function as a translator any longer—but there were moments when it was critical he personally do it, and this was one.

He still had Shawn Tyers' private phone number,

too, high though Tyers had risen—the presidency of Mospheira, at the moment, and a damned good president at that. He even reported to Shawn now and again, with Tabini's full knowledge, and Shawn's gratitude to Tabini for allowing it. Mospheira being the nation he *had* served until, in one of its prior administrations and in a bad moment in its politics, it had tried to kill him, remembering to report to Shawn did serve as a reminder where home had used to be, and it did make his service to Tabini far more comfortable, morally speaking, humanly speaking.

And what would he say this time? What had Tabini, that master of not quite saying what one thought one heard, given for specifics in that terrifying address?

Or was half he'd heard buried in context, which the best translator in the world couldn't quite fish out for safe human viewing? Threat, in Mospheiran context, could be toxic. Among atevi, it could be reassuring, a demonstration of stabilizing power.

The *aishidi'tat* built a starship in orbit over their heads. Don't forget, don't forget the old ways . . . that was the end of what Tabini had said.

But there were details . . . details so damned full of thorns a conscientious translator needed gloves. The atevi nervous system, the atevi body and brain that interpreted the degree of threat and promise in that twos and threes business and he couldn't guarantee that even Shawn Tyers would understand what it *felt* like in that room, the absolute terror, the threats, the resolutions, the business of an atevi association, an *aïshi,* being transacted in face-to-face encounter and gut-level emotion.

Where did humans have an analog—except a funeral among passionately feuding relatives?

And how to describe what it most *felt* like—

What it most *felt* like was the moment in a machimi-play when the holder of secrets divulged them, and set the fox among the chickens—so to speak—and sent things into freefall, all points of reference revised, usually with weapons involved.

And what did it mean, now, when conservative Ilisidi happened to be the highest-ranking ateva who had ever gone to space—and her pro-space, pro-foreigner grandson assembled the leaders of the nation to lecture them on anti-foreigner traditional values in *her* own words, while she was conspicuous in the audience and in new and conspicuous guardianship of the aiji's butter-fingered heir?

It could mean, on the one hand, trouble—that grandmother Ilisidi, newly custodian of *her* ally Tatiseigi's grandnephew, simultaneously Tabini's heir—was being outflanked by a maneuver that far outdid the previous dangerous push-pull maneuvers of that private relationship. If that was the case, it could more than get someone killed . . . it could remotely mean Tabini was about to shove Lady Damiri out the door.

Or, conversely, that Damiri and Tabini together had decided to push young Cajeiri out the door, effectively to disinherit him—

Was riding a mecheita through a formal garden *that* unforgivable an error?

He couldn't think it of Tabini or Damiri, or of Ilisidi,

but even this far along in his association with the atevi, he couldn't imagine he understood what the familial relationships were, or what atevi felt.

They didn't feel *friendship*, among first points. They didn't know *love*. They obeyed a different set of emotions. They herded. They flocked. They rushed to a leader in time of distress, and that leader was distinguished primarily by qualities a human regarded with suspicion: an atevi leader led because he *had* no higher emotional attachments, and flocked to no one.

A leader took care of his own. A leader preserved those he led. A leader became passionately distressed at a threat to what was his.

But the high leaders, the aijiin, didn't bring up their own children. They passed them around, fostered them out to high-level relatives and trusted associates to be tutored, taught manners—and to form associations with those same relatives on whom the whole structure depended. Cajeiri had been with his great-uncle Tatiseigi. Now he was with Ilisidi. He might not be with his parents again until he was nearly adult.

The boy would never, perhaps, forget this assembly in the tomb of his grandfather. That speech from his father would brand itself on a boy's memory. Even given species differences, that was likely true.

But how did a human understand the situation that might logically relegate a child elsewhere? Or even dispose of him? It happened in the machimi, in the hard, brutal feudal age. One *didn't* hear of it happening in modern times.

And there were some things he had always been a

little hesitant to ask even the atevi he trusted with his life. But the questions nagged him.

"Nadiin-ji," he said, as the rails clicked beneath the wheels, as the car took a turn he well knew, "Mospheiran humans regard their children very highly, protect them at all costs, and Mospheirans generally don't hand off their children to raise—" He supposed in that understanding his own father was not quite respectable, but he tried to simplify the case. And tried not to insult the people he lived with. "So I remain perplexed about Cajeiri's situation, to put it very delicately. Is there satisfaction with him? Is he in any way the focus of this ceremony? Why did Tabini ask me here, and why is Cajeiri suddenly with Ilisidi, when I thought he was with Tatiseigi, and has *that* anything to do with this event?"

They were mildly amused, and perhaps a little puzzled.

"Regarding the invitation," Banichi said—Banichi had had *that* question a dozen times in the last few days, "one still fails to understand the reason. We have kept a careful ear to the Guild, Bren-ji, and no one has given us a clue. Regarding the heir, Tatiseigi has *appealed* to the dowager to take the boy in charge: the dowager has received Tatiseigi, and the boy packed his bags last night."

"The dowager's plane has entered the hangar," Jago said. "Her crew has taken quarters in the Bujavid."

That was interesting: Ilisidi was not, then, returning to Malguri immediately. She was staying in the Bujavid with the boy in tow, and staying at least long enough to warrant a hangar for her private jet.

"One fears for the porcelains," Banichi said.

"His own parents would not—forgive me for a distasteful question—harm him?"

"No," Jago said quickly. "No, nadi-ji."

What do they feel? was the question he tried to ask, and wondered whether he ought just to blurt it out and trust his long relationship—but Banichi and Jago themselves were father and daughter: he had had a parent-child relationship right in front of him for years, and *still* couldn't quite decipher what they thought, or felt, except a strong loyalty—no, they existed within the same *man'chi*, and that was different: they'd served the aiji before they attached to him, still within that *man'chi*, and that told him nothing about their own ties to each other.

"I remain bewildered," he said to them.

"So are we all, Bren-ji," Banichi said. "So are the lords in the Bujavid. So are the news services."

"That's at least informative," he said. "They did broadcast it."

"To the whole *aishidi'tat*," Jago said.

"And the station, I'll imagine."

"One believes so," Banichi said.

"Curious. *Troubling*, nadiin-ji."

"Your staff is troubled, too," Jago said. "But we detected nothing aimed at you, nandi."

"Rather I'm aimed at someone else, perhaps."

"Yet we don't detect that, either," Banichi said. "And we gather nothing from usual sources. It's all very curious."

"What *is* the relationship of a child to parent?"

He amused them. Jago laughed softly. "It depends on the parent."

"It depends on the child," Banichi said.

"*This* child, nadiin-ji. I know I could never explain either of *you*."

"Cajeiri is bright, precocious, and the porcelains are in danger. If one could advise the aiji, best foster him to *our* Guild, to teach him where to put his elbows."

"Everyone has something to teach, is that it?"

"To the aiji's heir?" Banichi asked. "Very many have something to teach."

"Yet he has no security to speak of. When no one else draws a breath without security."

"He has a great deal of security," Banichi said, "in the *man'chi* of those in charge of him. He learns to rely on them. And they learn what he will do."

The train reached another curve. The protected windows obscured everything outside, but he had a vision of where they were, a brief stretch of wild land before the airport.

"Do you suppose this transfer of the boy to Ilisidi's hands, coupled with my presence, coupled with this honor to Valasi, and her attendance, and mine—all sums up to a declaration of peace in the household? Ilisidi supporting the aiji's push to space?"

"Her visit to the station did that quite well," Jago said.

"Yet something might be afoot in the east," Banichi said. "Or something might be brewing closer to Shejidan."

Never mind that atevi had no word for *friend* or

love. Enemy translated closely enough. *One who threat-ens my interests* applied on both sides of the strait.

What they thought of a human's prolonged associa-tion with the dowager as well as Tabini— Well, atevi had an untranslatable word for a person who bridged a gap and created an association they'd rather see in hell. *Troublemaker* was close. And that described him, for sure.

And Tabini made a point of having him down to the planet and then sending him back, dragging him like a lure past certain noses?

Half his primary security wasn't on the planet—couldn't therefore watch his computer, and Tabini's se-curity hadn't wanted people carrying packets into the mausoleum, a situation Banichi and Jago had *not*, in fact, been warned of, not until two of Tabini's staff showed up not only to assist and guard the baggage while the two of them guarded him, but to take charge of the offending object. On the one hand it could be simple indication they were being strict with the lords and didn't want to make an exception in his case. On the other—his stomach reacted—it could have robbed him of one bodyguard or set a stranger with him, which Banichi and Jago wouldn't allow, not even for Tabini's men—or it could all be a ploy to get their hands on the computer. Banichi and Jago were as nervous as he had ever seen them and, when that was presented to them, about as put out as he had ever seen them. One rarely saw them vexed with the authority that ruled them all—but vexed they had been. They'd been a week on the planet, and suddenly and without warning, *no*, the computer couldn't go with them into the service, even when they were told the service would run close to shuttle launch?

So here they were, having gotten through it, headed back to orbit with no more explanation than before, but at least back into his own security, back into the safety of a closed world, where such surprises wouldn't come up. Much as he missed the world, much as he pined for blue sky and the heave of the deep sea under him, much as he missed the people he couldn't take with him—he knew the world up there was safe. He *ran* his own section of the world up there, and he knew what was going on in it.

Down here he'd had to take the computer back, not knowing what might have been done in two hours. And he *wasn't* wholly sure Algini, the best computer wizard on his staff, had the expertise or resources to find out quickly—not compared to the resources Tabini-aiji could draw on.

The tracks clicked at a rate now that told him the engineer had clearance all the way, and that they were doubtless inconveniencing trains all over the system. They were late. But they were going to get him off the planet. If they were rushing like this, they were going to make it.

The train took a hard right turn, the last. Jago got up and restored the juice glass to the rack, untroubled by the motion of the car.

They had made the airport spur with that turn, not destined for the public terminal, but to the far end of the airport, which handled diplomatic cargo, space-bound cargo, and occasionally explosives, curious juxtaposition.

They braked. "Plenty of time," Banichi said.

Another exposure to daylight and the chance of assassins. Bren personally gathered up his computer, but willingly entrusted it to Jago's offered hand. The body armor chafed. He tugged at it, straightened his cuffs and saw to his pockets—ready for a dash once the train stopped.

"The packages made it into baggage?" He even hesitated to ask, amid more serious difficulties his staff had had to track.

"Early this morning, nadi-ji. No worry."

The video games for staff had made it, then, likewise Bindanda's request for two particular spices. And the treats . . . those were his idea. He wished he'd been able to think of something appropriate for Jase—something that wouldn't touch on Jase's longing to be down here and cause more frustration than it cured.

The car's doors opened on a daylight he had last seen from his apartment windows before the ceremony. The view beside the car was a vast tract of concrete, a clouded sky—blue-green foliage walled off by a high fence. A van was waiting for the train, but it would not be Tano and Algini backing Banichi and Jago up this time—no: two more of Tabini's own, stationed there to swear to the van's integrity.

He made the small jump down—a small atevi-scale jump that jolted his knees—to the siding. Jago brought all the hand-baggage, a trifle to her strength, and escorted him briskly to the waiting van—holding back just that small bit that let Banichi double-check that the driver and the guard were indeed Tabini's agents. Members of the Assassins' Guild knew one another socially, so to speak—shot at one another, under contract, that being their job, but exchanged pleasant words at other times.

Clearly everything did check. Banichi signaled them, and they boarded.

They *were* going to make it. Bren believed it now, heaved a long sigh as he hit the seat and the door shut. The van moved. Chain-link fence and blue-green scrub gave way to a wide panorama.

Then the shuttle came in view, on the runway.

Sleek and white: *Shai-shan*, oldest of the fleet, the first shuttle built and the one whose crew they knew best.

Fear of flying be damned, Bren thought—it was far safer than where he had just been. It was safer than the whole planet had become—in terms of schemes and plots, and those, in atevi society, were never without consequence.

They halted right at the bottom of the cargo lift . . . cargo lifts still serving for personnel, a minor economy in a program otherwise making progress hand over fist. They were in time. They exited the van in haste, walked up onto the platform.

One could hold a transcontinental airliner half an hour or so, but the calculations were made for *Shai-shan:* she rode favorable numbers, and her ground crew didn't like to revise them. Stewards at the open hatch door above waved at them anxiously.

A wind was blowing cold as, with a bang and a jolt of the hydraulics, they rose up and up to the open hatch. Banichi spoke to someone on his pocket com, confirming their arrival.

They'd made it.

2

Air inside was immediately warmer. "Have I time to shed the coat?" Bren asked, and the steward said there was at least that, yes, nadi.

Bren immediately peeled off the coat, with Jago's help—slipped out of the heavy vest and let the stewards, who were well accustomed to such precautions, stow coat and vest discreetly in baggage.

Hand-baggage went, too. All but the computer. Jago had that, and kept it.

In the democracy of the space effort—and a single, rear-boarded aisle—they passed alongside atevi station workers bound for their jobs in orbit—most back from leave, a few first-timers. Bren knew no few names, and a few rose, bowing under the cramped overhead. "Thank you, nadiin," Bren said. "Thank you." He found himself exhausted, after very little exertion for days—very little exertion, and a great deal of tension. He wanted his seat, which was always up in the front, where the steward was waiting. He made what haste he could.

"Nandi." The steward's position marked his proposed seat, not quite the first row, this time, but close.

The forward steward he knew very well—having shared with this crew and the shuttle team the effort that consumed their lives and energies. These were zealots, enthusiasts for the program. He was *in* their association; they were *in* his. Boarding, he was already home.

But there were, among atevi—not too unexpectedly— a handful of human passengers, too, in the middle batch of seats. They were going up, workers who'd flown over from the island to catch the shuttle up to their jobs.

And his own seat, forward, turned out to have a human companion—a surprise, and a very pleasant one. He *liked* Ginny Kroger, and had by no means expected her on this flight.

Not his age, not his field, no longer his country . . . unless one counted the station itself, which for purposes of allegiances, he did. Virginia Kroger was gray-haired, thin, a woman with a fierce sobriety, a mouth that gave nothing away until she absolutely astonished a novice with a grin. No fashion-plate: she wore a thick gray, ugly as sin cardigan and doubtless had an equally unstylish parka in storage: Ginny always complained of the chill on flights, and was usually prepared: count on it.

"Gin." He saw now that rank and courtesy had handed him this seatmate, and probably Banichi and Jago had foreknown that before they boarded. "Nadiin-ji," he said to Jago and Banichi.

They took his meaning—certainly had no need to protect him from Gin, and no need to spend the flight pretending not to understand a word of Mosphei', either.

"No difficulty," Banichi said. The two of them had their reading and their amusements, and the hand-baggage that contained them.

It was his first chance to talk with Ginny in half a year. The moment they reached the station, duty would take them to two different zones. And her presence on station was very rare. "How's the island?" he asked, settling in beside her.

"Wet," Ginny said. Of course. It was spring. Rain was a given. "How's the mainland?"

"Wet. Security-heavy. The aiji's holding a family ceremony—*that* was the must-see that brought me down to here, it turns out." He bet that Gin had had a briefing from the Department of State as well as her own wing, Science, and knew he was here; but without an understanding, he couldn't give her a reason. "But I suppose I agree with the call: I did need to be here." Grand negligence. Let Shawn be as puzzled as he was . . . until he learned something.

The hatch had already shut. The passenger comfort systems had come up. Now *Shai-shan's* engines roared to life.

"Welcome aboard," the copilot said over the intercom, and began the rollout litany, the set of instructions, the list of horrors that a nervous flier hardly liked to listen to, but needed to, no matter how experienced: what to do if the takeoff roll aborted, what to do if they had to evacuate . . . all the scenarios in which a passenger had any choice.

Mostly there was no choice: there were few runways long enough to accommodate *Shai-shan* if something went wrong.

"No time for drinks, nand' paidhi," the attendant said, pausing by his row. "I'm very sorry."

"I'll have a fruit juice and vodka when we get up." Launch usually had him a mass of nerves, and he liked to have a vodka beforehand to calm down, but he discovered he had no need for that, today. Sitting in his own seat was a victory. "Made it in time," he said to Ginny, and heaved a sigh, telling himself it was, after all, true, and he was safe. "That's all I ask."

"We did hold count a little," Ginny asked, looking at her watch. "But we're rolling on schedule."

"We hurried. The fortunate hours." A Mospheiran might take a shuttle launch countdown as overriding everything else, but the exigencies of a shuttle launch had nothing against the atevi sense of timing and fortunate numbers, and Ginny did understand that. There were times things were done, as there were days and hours when nothing began. A memorial service and a shuttle flight weren't remotely in each other's consideration—except that neither would take place at an infelicitous moment.

Shai-shan moved out, and made a ponderous slow correction onto her runway—she was not agile on the pavement.

Above the entry to the cockpit, the bulkhead had the black and white *baji-naji* emblem, that tribute to Chance and Fortune, the devil in the otherwise fortunate numbers. Below it was a screen that showed them the runway.

It trued up in the view.

"Baji-naji," Gin said, meaning, in human terms *here goes nothing.*

And in atevi—*here goes everything.*

The engines roared and the acceleration pushed them back. The thumping of the wheels grew thunderous, and abruptly stopped as the screen showed them blue sky.

A split-screen showed the gear retracting safely below, and the ground and all the city falling away under them.

Well, another few roof tiles would fall in Shejidan. The planners had thought they could cease using the public airport once the new dedicated spaceport went into operation, but this one, the *old* runway—crazy as it sounded to call it that, as if anything was *old* in this frantic, less-than-a decade push toward space—still was in use, if only for *Shai-shan. Shai-shan* was *Shejidan's* shuttle. The citizens of Shejidan, even after so much inconvenience, prized their broken roof-tiles, gathered them up when they fell, patched their roofs and took pride in their personal sacrifices for the greatness of their city.

Their shuttle. *Their* station was up there, too, available for anyone with average eyesight, if that person went aside from city lights, as atevi loved to do. Just ask them whose it was.

Their starship, too, was assembling in parts and pieces up there. It seemed mad to say, sometimes, but by agreement it was *their* starship when, a decade ago, rail transport had been a matter of fierce debate.

The wider universe, the universe humans had opened to them, had caught on with a vengeance in atevi popular culture. A passion for the stars and the new discoveries burgeoned in the very capital of the atevi world. Shejidan was mad for space.

And maybe, thinking of that, it was a good thing Tabini had held that remembrance of things traditional. Remember the old ways, before all that was atevi changed, shifted—abruptly.

They'd already had several dangerous moments in atevi-human relations. For a second time, atevi had become fascinated with humans and humans had become equally fascinated with atevi. Once before this, they had worked together, lived together. Humans had failed to grasp what was emotionally critical to atevi, and vice versa, and the whole system had fractured, catastrophically, with enormous loss of life— which was why humans were living on an island as far out of reach of atevi as they could manage at the time. The social disaster they called the War of the Landing had started on a critical handful of mistaken assumptions—because humans and atevi had gotten along just *too* well at first meeting, loved, associated, and nearly ruined each other.

Maybe remembering a little history was a very good thing, as fast as things were moving.

Or maybe Tabini just wanted his son to see the human paidhi, if not meet him.

Maybe Tabini had wanted the boy to understand the history behind the *aishidi'tat*, and to appreciate the official, paternal, national, even space-faring approval behind the hard, uncivilized lessons Ilisidi was about to teach him. It was too easy for a highborn youngster to think the whole world was what he saw around him.

Shai-shan reached her stage one altitude. Wings reconfigured themselves. Hydraulics whined. And *Shai-shan* kept going.

No word for friend among atevi, no word for love . . . no word for *man'chi* among humans, no word for *aishi*, either.

But maybe both species were wise enough now in dealing with one another.

Maybe this generation figured out how to treat the changes that ran amok through everything they touched.

Maybe kids like Cajeiri would figure out how to deal with situations that shoved biologically different instincts up against one another in what had been, once before this, a dangerous, dangerous intimacy.

"Penny for your thoughts," Ginny said to him.

And what was he thinking? That atevi were clearly feeling stressed? That the aiji, who ordinarily backed every change proposed to him, held a ceremony in tribute to the old ways?

"The ceremony," he said. "Just before I took off. Whole reason for the trip down, it seems. Pace of change. Atevi want to catch their balance. Remember the traditional things."

"Maybe *Mospheira* should have a ceremony like that."

Ginny surprised him with that sentiment. She wasn't the philosophical sort.

"Why so?"

"Kids," Ginny said. "*Kids.* This generation thinks it's all a given."

"My generation?"

Ginny gave one of those rare laughs. "There's kids tall as I am who were *born* during your tenure, paidhi-aiji. You've been too busy way too long. There are kids just about to vote who think there've *always* been jobs in space, who think the War of the Landing is a dull chapter in a big book."

"That's scary."

"Oh, damn right it's scary."

Appalling thought. Six years since he'd been on Mospheira. The better part of a decade. And she was right. A ten-year-old kid who didn't care that much about history so easily became a twenty-year-old who didn't think it was important, either.

"That's incredible," he said.

"Kids think there'll always be a new invention every week. That there's a magic fix for every problem."

"That's good and bad," he said. "Bad, if they think someone else is always going to solve it. I'm sorry—I plan to retire someday and leave the mess to them. I expect them to do their homework."

"Oh, but you haven't been there. We Mospheirans—we do love our holidays. We love our leisure time. We're too damn convinced it's all going to work, so if we choose as a nation not to have aeronautics, it doesn't matter. We need a new swimming center in Jackson. If we choose not to develop our own security, it doesn't matter. The threat from space, that's always been there. Just ask any sixteen-year-old."

"Damn scary."

Shai-shan roared on, climbing, still climbing, headed for that queasy moment when, far above the earth, perilously riding her momentum and betting their lives in the process—she would shut down one set of engines, switch on another, and transit to space.

"And damn labor," Ginny said. "And damn unions. *They* don't think the crisis is that urgent either. The aliens out there aren't coming tomorrow. They might never come. What does the average factory worker care, except they want their televisions, their beach-front homes, their boats and their retirement plans?"

Atevi and humans were reaching a kind of engine-switchover, too: that was what Tabini's ceremony said. That was what Mospheirans *weren't* commemorating. Having gone as far as they could on the old arrangement of separatism, atevi were working directly with humans again, this time in orbit, where it made no sense to build two segregated space stations. On mutually uncommon ground, isolated from everything familiar and historically contested, they tried to adapt.

And that meant the carefully channeled interface was flung wide open, everyone exposed to the same stresses that had brought them to war before. Now with more lethal weapons, more power at their disposal—but with strangers supposedly looming on the horizon, strangers with a grudge, a grievance, or pure native aggression: no one was sure, least of all the human crew of *Phoenix*, who had seen their handiwork—they waited desperately to be invaded, and their children lost faith that the invaders would come.

The cultural differences, the biological differences that had led atevi to attack the early settlers were continually with them . . . now known and laughed at, on both sides, but those differences still tweaked live nerves in moments of frustration.

A worker, human or atevi, who couldn't overcome his own biologically-generated anger and laugh at a situation, had to ship out—he got a quit-bonus for his honesty, but all the same, he had to ship out.

And thus far, years into the project, they'd only had to ship out—what, fourteen, fifteen, out of hundreds? Not too bad a record . . . thus far. The two species had changed their cultures to fit—somewhat.

They'd developed a stationside culture of inter-species jokes, that was one thing—some bawdy and some stupid. Mospheiran experts had wanted to silence them, but atevi had let them run, and the ship humans had contributed the framework and Mospheirans took to it. A human team and an atevi team had a contest, one such joke began . . .

There was a whole series of those, that usefully illustrated species differences, cultural differences, and made two species laugh. That was the good news. No one had gotten mad. That was the other good news.

We have to get along had become the common sentiment between humans and atevi aloft, at least.

Aloft, and being over sixteen, they still believed in the invaders.

They just tended to forget about them, for long, long stretches in which the company contests or the prospect of a machimi play took precedence.

The flight, bumpy for a while, smoothed out. The vodka and fruit juice arrived. Bren sipped it and drew a long, long breath. The screen showed nothing but darkening blue ahead of them.

3

The vodka was down to icemelt, they were on their way in deep vacuum, and take-off nerves were quieter. Banichi and Jago, in the seats opposite, were reading manuals.

With Ginny, there was at least a wealth of small talk—island gossip, some of it hilarious, some of it union spats, political maneuvers that only elevated Bren's blood pressure and tempted him to have a second vodka.

But he didn't have to go to the island and deal with the problems, these days, and given the rare opportunity of a trip to Earth, he didn't go there, not even with family to consider. He left island politics to Ginny and Shawn and all the brave souls who had no cultural choice.

And it didn't damned well matter to the space effort if the island politicked about the shuttle port, and took forever getting its own shuttle off the ground. Four atevi shuttles were flying—well, count *Baushi*, which was simply a lift engine for heavy modules: a freighter, a simple freighter, that carried passengers in a small afterthought of a module . . . a lot like the aircraft arrangement that had once, in simpler days, squeezed the paidhi into the regular island flight, ahead of dried fruit and pottery.

He supposed if he had missed the flight, he might possibly have caught a ride on *Baushi* in a few days. He tended to discount it as a passenger option, but it was. Using both spaceports, servicing two shuttles at once, one on the early and one on the late phase of mission prep while a third underwent systems-checks and cargo loading, they had a flight newly landed or about to go nearly once a week, with rare exceptions, and if Mospheira ever got it completed, Mospheira was building a runway out beyond Jackson limits to improve their narrow choice of weather.

That runway construction was a major victory for the pro-spacers like Ginny Kroger. Jackson Aerospace, moreover, was finally breaking ground for its new cargo-launch facility on Crescent Island, to the south of Mospheira.

And that, Ginny opined, meant it was really going to happen. Businesses were moving onto Crescent—not only aerospace suppliers, but companies like Sun-Drink and Peterson's, intending to feed and clothe the workers. Jackson Aerospace was starting up in place of defunct Mospheiran Air . . . still buying its necessary aircraft from atevi Patinandi Aerospace and concentrating its own manufacturing in narrow but profitable niches—

"But overall," Ginny said, "good news. *If* the aiji in Shejidan gives them formal permission."

Permission to expand out of their enclave and Crescent Island, that they had. There were other proposals for humans moving onto air-reached islands no atevi interest was ready to claim. For political reasons going back to the War of the Landing, that was a major, major concession that hadn't happened yet.

"I favor it," Bren said earnestly. "I think it will pass. I don't, honestly, know whether it's going to pass this year—" More difficult, if the legislative session in the offing now blew up. Or faster, if it didn't. "It's still on the table. It could move soon, if things go as well as possible."

Better news from Ginny, the Heritage Party was still fragmenting, its idealists taking off to space and its hidebound bigots still scheming and planning a human takeover, but now a national joke, with less and less real power in their hands. In recent memory, the Heritage Party had won the Mospheiran presidency. Now they struggled to maintain membership.

"Nand' paidhi." The steward brought sandwiches— a human notion long popular on the mainland—and melon, an atevi institution. "Nandi." The latter to Ginny Kroger, with the same offering.

"Thank you," she said, without Bren's having to interpose a special courtesy to cover for her. She'd learned—so much. "Very fine, very fine and much appreciated."

"Indeed," Bren said on his own behalf. "I do favor these. Well-chosen."

The steward was pleased.

So there was harmony in the heavens. Talk with Ginny drifted off to their former partner, Tom Lund, who had been downworld and office-bound for the last two months on the Jackson heavy-lift project.

"Tom has a real gift for persuading the corporations out of their funds," Ginny said. "He's frustrated, but they're moving."

"They're making money."

"Everyone's making money," Ginny said—then added the ultimate islander objection to travel anywhere: "You can make money on the island, too, and still be home for supper."

"You can make far *more* money running Crescent operations." The *other* Mospheiran passion: finance, and the beacon of a new colonial effort.

"Try getting low-level personnel who want to live out there. That's the thing. They've poured foundations. Getting the houses, getting the facilities—it's all chasing its own tail. Mospheirans won't go until there's advanced plumbing and phone service."

"Atevi would do it. *Will* build it, if Mospheirans want to sit in front of their televisions and watch it all pass."

"Mospheira knows that. The legislature knows it. But it's the old story: the heads of corporations don't *trust* the very ones that are willing to go out there and take charge. The psychological profile of any administrator who'll leave Mospheira worries the corporations immensely."

"Micromanaging from remote-control," he said. "Bad enough from one end of the island to the other. On Crescent, it'll be a disaster, mark my words."

"I think Crescent operations can possibly get toilet paper right now without a corporate requisition, but maybe not."

"SunDrink's smarter than Jackson Aerospace. They just move."

"Oh, but now Harbor Foods wants to buy Sun-Drink."

"Good *God*."

"Exactly."

A SunDrink concession on the station had become a wildly popular and successful venture, patronized by Mospheirans and atevi who had a thirst for their traditional fruit drinks—wildly popular, too, among ship-folk who had never tasted non-synthetic food in their lives.

But Harbor wouldn't trust the zealots who'd sell their souls for a ticket to work on-station . . . oh, no, no one who wanted to be up there could be trusted. More pointedly, they wouldn't trust workers to make a decision, a guaranteed collision course for labor and upper-tier management.

Well, Shawn would know it was in the offing. Shawn would see the collision of interests coming. Strikes were a sacred institution on Mospheira. So was corporate pigheadedness.

Ah, well, it wasn't the paidhi's job any more. The paidhi-aiji, who'd used to mediate trade between the island and the mainland, rescuing fishing boats caught in border disputes, couldn't prevent Mospheiran companies making bad decisions these days.

"Anyone mediating?"

"Oh, Tom's on it. Bet he is."

Tom Lund, however, who'd ridden out the station-side fracas that attended the Tamun coup . . . Tom knew. Tom was a Commerce man, and had the power, moreover, to seize Harbor executives by the lapels and get their attention.

"I'll say one thing: there's not going to be a station strike in SunDrink. I'll support an atevi industry up there in competition if Harbor starts playing tough games with Sun on the station. There'll be no strikes. No strikes anywhere humans are in cooperative agreements with atevi. It's this lovely agreement we have: atevi workers don't hire the Assassins' Guild to settle with management and human workers don't strike."

"Watch Tom declare Sun a Critical Industry . . ."

"Where they are, damn right it's critical, if atevi are in the interface. When did this piece of silliness with Harbor blow up?"

"Hit the rumor mill this week."

"Oh, good. I'm out of touch for a few days and the next War of the Landing is in the works." He didn't want another emergency. "I've *got* to call Tom."

"I'm sure Tom's ahead of it." Ginny's eyes held a curious smugness at the moment. "So am I."

"How's that?"

Definite cat-and-canary expression. "Didn't I say? We're shipping, with special inspection to be sure there's no quality issue."

Labor fuss, another strike, this most recent one stopping work on the quality checks—but it seemed Ginny's handful of robots had finally, after a dozen delays, gotten through.

"Who bent?"

Ginny grinned. The spare, seamed face transformed from long-faced researcher to elf when she did that.

"Management. They give labor what they want, *we* sign a contract for sixteen more units *and* get our independent inspector on their line, and it's all settled. The robots are here."

"In cargo? Right now? Under our feet?"

"Damned right. Not only that—the deal-maker— they've taken an open-ended contract, with minor options. We've *got* our robots, Mr. Cameron."

It was suddenly a very good flight. The path ahead stretched broad and straight—robots to be delivered, fuel and materials to be mined, and the effort— delayed by politics with the senior captain, by politics with island conservatives and unions, by politics with the mainland traditionalists and the ever-to-be-damned 'counters—stayed on schedule.

"I owe you dinner," he said. "Ma'am. I owe you—"

"The best vat-culture ersatz meatloaf on the station."

He wrinkled his nose. Laughed, suddenly in high spirits.

They talked about the island, about mutual acquaintances, island politics.

"And," Ginny said, suddenly, Ginny who never forgot anything.

"And?"

Ginny reached down for a strap and pulled up her personal kit, from which she extracted a plastic sandwich bag full of mangled green leaves and crushed stems.

"And this is . . . ?"

"Sandra Johnson said just give it to you and you'd know."

Sandra Johnson. Sandra Johnson. Good God, it had been years. Dark years, terrible times.

Green leaves, stems . . . plant cuttings in a sealed container.

Sandra named her plants. He couldn't remember the names. But for some crazed reason, out of the blue, so to speak, she'd sent him a special remembrance. Two kids and a house in the country, but she still thought of him, and sent him mangled greenery to brighten up his living quarters.

"Old flame?" Gin asked. Not a streak of jealousy, no, there never was that between them.

"Secretary. Lifesaver." Sandra never had become famous the way certain of the participants in the initial fracas had become household words in two cultures. But none of them would be where they were without her. Some of them wouldn't be alive without her. "Literally a lifesaver. —Where did you run into her?"

"Oh, she used to work in Science. She dropped by the office, enlisted my help to get the plants through customs. The Head of Botany cleared them, personally, said they're bug-free."

He saw the packet had the Science Department seal, official as could be, and he wasn't about to open it until customs.

So a spider-plant and a whatever-it-was emigrated back to their origins, to meet their distant cousins growing outside the captains' offices.

"Well, thanks." He put the packet away in his own kit. "Really, thanks. Old friends. Pleasant suprise."

"No trouble. Well, it *was* trouble, but Botany owed me one and I owed Sandra one."

The steward picked up the sandwich wrappings and trays before they floated. Meanwhile the worker crew behind them let a pen sail too far forward. Banichi captured it and sailed it back. It was the usual games, new workers, zero-g jokes.

And in the long flight after, he and Ginny eventually ran out of gossip, retrieved their computers—Ginny from under the seat and himself from Jago's keeping—and spread out their own in-flight offices. Ginny had work to keep her occupied, a screenful of numbers.

He had his own. He'd downloaded a considerable mail file, to add to the paper mail that his staff had physically culled for him to take with him—a heavy parcel of it traveling in baggage, paper that, recycled, fed the station's growing need.

He still got the schoolchildren's questions. Might the paidhi send a card from space for an honored schoolteacher? Did the paidhi think that the aliens would come before the ship was built?

He had his answer in file for that one, for parents and children. There was every reason to go on as usual. The hostile aliens had destroyed the station that *Phoenix* left out among the stars, along with all its records and maps. *Phoenix*, returning, had taken one quiet look at the destruction and left without a whisper to go find their long-abandoned population—here, at the atevi planet. It was good odds the aliens had no notion where *Phoenix* came from.

Until—so the captains and the president and the aiji in Shejidan admitted to each other in secret councils—the aliens began to listen very intently to the nearby stars, and look for evidence of planets in their vicinity that might be the origin of that ruined outpost.

There were reasons humans and atevi separately reckoned it unlikely there'd be an immediate attack: two species had a better chance of predicting the behavior of a third.

But after all their reasons for confidence, and in spite of what they told worried children—they dared not bet the world on it.

One atevi class had written him to ask, simply: *Will we grow up?*

That question haunted his nights. The paidhi damned well planned to see that they did, as far as it was in his hands.

While SunDrink and Harbor played financial games.

Lodged in the back of his mind, too, distracting him from rational estimates and international concerns— was the fact that he was one more time upward bound, on a shuttle flight as irretrievable as a bullet from a gun, and for the second time in a year, he hadn't called his family while he was on the planet.

No was a hell of a lot easier from orbit than from a few hundred miles away. *I can't visit the island* was more palatable than *I physically can, but won't.*

But what could he do? He'd told his brother—he'd tried to tell his mother that he didn't want to go onto the island for *exactly* such reasons as the SunDrink/ Harbor business. He didn't want another phone call from his mother saying some damned extremist of one stamp or the other had vandalized her apartment building, because *his* picture had been on the news. He didn't want his face in the news reports reminding every random lunatic in remote points of Mospheira that the object of a lot of local resentment had a vulnerable human family in their reach.

So he didn't come. He lied. He dodged.

But this time the news was bound to let them know he could have come. He hadn't anticipated the television broadcast . . . and that, this time, was going to be hard.

He switched over to solitaire, pretending to work rather than think. Ginny was doing useful work. The paidhi, who lived by mathematics and pattern arrangements, couldn't win a single game for the next two hours, not a one.

4

The stewards reunited coats and small bags with their owners during the last half hour of approach.

There was the usual advisement: "The dock will be cold, nadiin."

Understatement. Bren went aft, accepted his knee-length formal coat, bullet-proof vest and all, and wrestled it on in that slow-motion effort which was the only successful tactic in freefall. Floating fabric had to be maneuvered just so, and lace cuffs had to be extracted from the sleeves and allowed to float.

He also had to get back forward and belt himself back into his seat without wrinkling the coat-tails. Ginny Kroger, herself in that battered parka, gave a helpful tug on the coat-tail and smoothed it behind him as he drifted down.

"Not the most sensible dress for freefall," Bren muttered. "Didn't have time to change." On principle, he never changed half-and-half, no mixing, for instance, of a more practical casual crew jacket with the formal court trousers; and no mixing of Mospheiran clothing with atevi, either. When he was in court dress he was nand' Bren, paidhi-aiji. When he was in island mufti and speaking Mosphei', as he did aboard station from time to time, guesting with Mospheiran station officials, then and only then he was Bren Cameron. Never should the two confuse his often-drifting brain.

On this flight, to and from, he had been stiffly, doggedly nand' paidhi, and he dressed to exit that way, in the rib-hugging coat . . . apt to freeze half through on the dock, but socially very proper.

He searched his small carry-on for his gloves. In vain.

The stewards made their final pass, gathering up loose items and advising passengers to put away every item that could break or drift free.

The forward screen meanwhile showed them the station—then *Phoenix* herself, a huge, dust-stained wall of white. Tenders moved like dustmotes about her: robots. Ginny's robots: she watched them with proprietary interest, and pointed out to him one of the oldest models.

"A-4. We're upgrading the memory, refitting the grappling arm for the newer version. The frame won't go out of use."

Far, far different scene in Bren's memory, than the desolation at his first approach.

The stewards meanwhile addressed a novice worker who hadn't a clue that *loose item* applied to a pen in an unzipped pocket.

The imminent-maneuvering warning sounded, routine approach toward the docking mast. The forward screen showed them one of the unused sectors of the station, now, an unlovely, impact-pocked stretch of metal. It was nevertheless a sound section, if it was

21, which Bren was convinced it was—he could just make out the 2 and maybe the 1—but it was a battered and long-neglected section of the station, all the same, due refurbishment in the next scheduled expansion of habitable space on the frame.

They fixed what they could as fast as they could, and before it broke, pressed ahead on program. The concentration of effort lately was to get residential and systems operations sections repaired, assuring residences where the influx of workers could find accommodation. Every area opened meant more workers could come up from the planet, and that increased the speed at which they could work, but it also exponentially increased the need for services—

And that need got more companies involved, with their help and their own concomitant problems. Like Sun and Harbor, one of which was going to win, and the other, not. Development had been a snowball rolling downhill ever since the first shuttle flew. Now they were at work on the construction cradle that orbited independently—well, *cradle* was premature, and *orbited* was a little optimistic. But it *would* be a shipyard cradle: orbiting in a linked mass, herded by robot tenders and occasionally by human intervention in their few runabouts, they had pieces . . . modules, whole prefab cabins of the starship they were going to build, all mixed with pieces of the shipyard that was going to build it.

There was a lot of that, everywhere. If they had room, and it was built, they lifted it to orbit. They wasted not an iota of cargo space. They had elements of the exotic engines up here. None of them had a frame in which to function yet, let alone a hull to which they could attach, and they were not yet stable where they rode, but there they were, herded by robots. It looked a lot like the atevi-Mospheiran-*Phoenix* cooperation itself.

But with all the problems, he had to say both it and the threeway cooperative worked. Atevi operators ran robots designed by Mospheiran robotics experts—by Ginny Kroger, among others—using atevi-designed computer systems newly linked to *Phoenix* sensors and remotely monitored by crew. The plans for supercomputers necessary to run the starship were already undergoing analysis in atevi labs—God only knew what atevi would do with the supercomputers, or what politics that would turn up. Atevi *dreamed* math and patterns, and hadn't had human-designed computers and software in their hands for a week before someone was saying there were obvious advantages and obvious possibilities, and someone else was saying there was an obvious infelicity in this and that code.

Change, change, and change. But they built on a pre-tried design they'd drawn out of the newly-recovered archives. They'd had no need to invent their way to space. In fact some held that the act of invention shifted all-important numbers that had already proved fortunate, a scary, foolish and unnecessary modification—

That, they could have settled. But it wasn't only atevi number theorists who threw monkey wrenches into what might have been a smoothly-running production line. The whole station refit and the shipyard assembly could have run a damned lot faster if *Phoenix* command hadn't suddenly taken it in their heads that the ship refueling, which hadn't been done since *Phoenix* had arrived back in the system, had to be a priority.

He'd raised objections to that with senior captain Ramirez, pitched his only fit of privilege, but in the labyrinthine ways of stationside politics, he'd lost. And fueling had proceeded, monopolizing robotics resources, taking up precious station construction budget when the mining operation, as one could anticipate, developed bugs.

But it was good to know sooner rather than later. They'd worked the bugs out of their plans and their equipment.

And now that was a refueled starship out there . . . which might be smart. Maybe it was. He supposed it let everyone sleep sounder at night. It made the crew happy, knowing that they weren't sitting inert at dock while the station drew down power for no few of its systems. And could anyone blame them, when a Mospheiran union wanting a second annual vacation in the contract delayed critical components, or when an atevi launch manager delayed a shuttle five days to gain felicitous numbers for an engine?

Politics, politics, politics. Everyone won a little. Everyone made sacrifices and gained benefits from the collective effort. Mospheirans compromised their dearly-held comforts to come up here, and had the benefits of advanced human medicine, not to mention the whole library of human achievement—the fabled human archive that the ship had sent down to the island. Atevi meanwhile shoved the throttle wide on their economy and risked destabilizing the most stable government the world had ever known, but *they* drew down numbers from the heavens, too, mathematical certainties that could unify their number-loving culture in ways humans could only imagine, a delight that all but made toes curl.

So if *Phoenix* crew ate vat-cultures and endured the worst jobs and slept aboard the ship to afford better accommodations to their world-born labor force, then they wanted something tangible for that sacrifice, too. And what logically did they want? *We deserve to have our priorities addressed, too,* had been the general cry from the ship-folk. They wanted to know that their ship, their whole world—and the defense of the whole solar system if anything went disastrously wrong in their estimation of the situation—wasn't sitting dead at dock.

In that sense, the shunting of resources to that operation was a reasonable act.

But, God, *Phoenix* had an appetite: they'd spent as much resource on *Phoenix*, which they sincerely hoped would stay motionless at dock, as they'd spent on the station with a population now in the tens of thousands. Three whole damned *years* of high-priority labor, fueling that ship, with just enough left over for the station, while certain things fell apart from sheer lack of exterior maintenance and manpower. Ginny's new robots would help bring the station restoration back to speed, but they'd slowed the whole program to accommodate Ramirez's insistence on refueling.

The aiji had accommodated Ramirez. So had the President of Mospheira. That was the plain fact. Mospheirans and atevi alike owed Stani Ramirez for his level-headedness against bad decisions in his own command structure—they owed him for his clear vision and his continual smoothing of the way ahead. And they wanted to strengthen his hand in the Captains' Council, one supposed.

So, well, hell, if the ship-fueling kept Ramirez happy, Ramirez kept the ship-folk steady at their work.

And it was *done*, that was the best news. *Done*, as of this month. Complete. Finished. And *now* they got the robots they'd tried to get up here before last winter.

"*Nadiin*," the shuttle co-pilot said on the intercom, "*take hold. Prepare for contact*." He repeated it in Mosphei', for their one Mospheiran passenger, though by now Gin knew that warning in her sleep.

They'd fixed the balky docking grapple, among the very first station repairs they'd ever made, and now the docking procedure was routine. First *Phoenix*, then the station became a white wall in the cameras. The image on the screen came down to the crossbars of the docking guide, and, sure enough, bless that grapple repair, they went in with a grace and smooth authority that brought cheers from the passengers.

Thump and massive click. Engaged. Safe.

Home again, strange as it was to say. Well and truly home.

"*Prepare to disembark*," the co-pilot informed them. "*Thank you, nadiin. Please follow the rope guides and don't let go for any reason. We can retrieve you, but it's a large, cold space, and very embarrassing to be searched after."*

Laughter, from the workers who were on their first trip.

"My best to the team," Bren said to Ginny Kroger as he unbelted, knowing they would part ways at the lift—Ginny to the human quarter, himself to the atevi. He drifted. They continued null-G at dock: the mast had no rotation, and they simply loosed the restraints, gathered their small amount of hand-luggage and floated up out of their seats on the slightest of muscle movements.

"My best to yours," Kroger said as the world turned topsy-turvy. In that sideways orientation they met Banichi and Jago face to face: "Good day to you," she said in passable Ragi—and had a courteous answer, at least as far as security spoke to outsiders while on duty.

"Nandi." Banichi had taken the bulkier baggage from under the seats, and moved with the precision of practice in zero-G. Banichi took the lead while Jago glided hindmost, casually sweeping Kroger into their protective field for no other reason than that Kroger was in their way, harmless, and attached to their company. The workers squeezed aside, waiting to let an atevi lord go first, and only then drifted free of their seats, subdued and decorous in the presence of *aijiin*.

The inner hatch meanwhile opened. A gust of cold air came in, biting cold. Gloves were definitely in order, but Bren hadn't found his—and now he recalled where his were, not in the carry-on at all, but in his casual jacket. And *that* was deep in diplomatic baggage down in the hold. The onworld household staff had not been apprized of the fact he would go directly to the spaceport from the ceremony.

Station personnel, meanwhile, met them as they disembarked, cold-suited, masked, stationed there to be sure they used the lines and that no one went drifting out a hundred meters to the far recesses of the docking mast.

Cold—yes. It was cold, a cold so bitter it hit the roots of the teeth on the first breath. Bren used his coat-tail on the safety line, having no wish to lose skin; and Jago, seeing his predicament, simply took hold of his arm and drew him along. It broke no few regulations—but he arrived at the end of the safety line without frostbitten fingers.

The personnel lift that faced them was nominally sheltered, but it had been waiting a few minutes—it was bitter cold as they entered it. Atevi workers would have certainly understood if the aijiin had taken the lift first and all to themselves, leaving them to wait it out in the cold, but on his standing order Banichi held the lift door open once they reached it, packing the workers in as they never would do in the security-conscious Bujavid—workers *with* their cumbersome luggage, to the confusion and embarrassment of the protocol-sensitive novices. On the planet, common folk had no wish to mingle too closely with aijiin, who sometimes drew bullets. Up here, there were no bullets to fear—but there was the consideration of frozen fingers and power-conservation.

"A different world up here, nadiin," Bren said to all

and sundry. "Here we do differently. Pack in. Pack in close. Customs will meet you downstairs."

They all made it in, pressed body to body. Banichi pushed the button and the lift banged into motion, bringing the floor up under their feet.

Baggage settled. The air warmed with the body-heat of a packed elevator—the other reason for packing it close—and Bren, with his hands beneath his arms, drew breaths of air that no longer quite burned his lungs.

Atevi spring court dress was *not* adequate for this transit, even with the vest. Ginny was far more comfortable in the tatty parka, and had the hood up. Rime was on the metal as the car stopped at the station main deck and let them out into customs—a set of tables and low-level x-ray and sniffer apparatus easily rolled in to meet the flight—in what was otherwise an ordinary station corridor.

"Let the paidhiin out!" the cry was within the lift, and workers pressed back in an effort to give him and Ginny the scant courtesy they could manage. Those nearest the door had to get out first, all the same, and simply bowed as they walked out through customs— a privilege of rank they didn't decline.

There they parted, having their own separate welcoming parties waiting. For him, Tano and Algini were both there, welcome sight—tall, black figures in black-and-silver uniform. Kate Shugart, from Ginny Kroger's staff, had come to welcome her. The hellos were warm enough, and reciprocal between staffs, but: the cold above had set into travelers' bones, and the desire for a warm drink and home overwhelmed any inclination to linger for social pleasantries.

Bren and Banichi and Jago walked along with Tano and Algini—rare that those two simultaneously left the security station, but it wasn't likely to develop a crisis in half an unattended hour, if things were going as usual.

"And how are things?" he asked Tano. "Any calls?"

"Oh, very well here. No calls. Jase Graham will be your guest tonight at dinner, nadi-ji, unless you object. Bindanda is doing his utmost."

Bindanda, that loan from Tatiseigi, was a very creditable chef, besides having done double duty as security and anything else that came to hand. Narani, his head of staff, would have made the judgement call accepting Jase as a guest tonight, but that was no problem. His staff had standing orders that Jase might be his guest whether he was absent, present, or en route.

Besides, Jase had so wanted to go down on this trip, having found a rare quiet moment that he could take leave of his regular duties. It hadn't happened. Ramirez had called at the last moment, senior captain, and there it was: no trip.

"I trust there are no crises. Nothing *behind* this invitation."

"Not that we know," Tano said—which covered a very extensive information-gathering apparatus. "The priorities committee met on schedule. Lord Geigi sent word to our staff that there were no surprises on the agenda."

"Very good. I have to see him, tomorrow if I can. There's progress on the robots—they're *here*, in fact."

"Yes, paidhi-ji." Not only Tano, but Banichi and Jago were listening, absorbing, putting pieces together, the most competent staff any man could ask for. They knew instantly what it all meant. They swept up every crumb of detail he gave them and would bend heaven and earth to make things work on schedule.

"One trusts the broadcast of the memorial made it up here."

"Yes," Algini said.

"Curious, was it not?"

"Indeed," Tano said.

"Do we have any theory what it meant?"

"None, on the surface," Banichi said.

"What it meant," Jago said, "likely defines itself in meetings yet to come. Curious, indeed, nandi."

But not their meetings. Not their risk. He'd been of use, perhaps, only as a symbol of the space effort. Tabini surely knew about the robots his shuttle was shipping up off his continent . . . and *that* was something Tabini would announce, a triumph of persistence, if nothing else, a new phase in the construction.

Clearly space would be a topic in the upcoming session, and Tabini showed his cards—so to speak.

Home again, home in every sense, where he had his own information-gathering apparatus. He had considerable power onworld. It was nothing to the resources he had here, in what had become his office, his residence, his steel-and-plastics world.

Home, and setting to work with a whole new set of parameters, given Ginny's surprise. Home, where Geigi, who was nominally in charge of the atevi side of the station, was far less enigmatic, and where things ran more or less predictibly. He drew a deep breath, worked chilled fingers, walked a corridor he knew to a lift he knew and rode it in close company with his own staff.

There was a subtle anxious mindset that took over when he was on the planet, in the constant knowledge that at any moment, at any slight miscalculation, he could meet a bullet and end all the work he did or hoped to do—and with it, hope for lives that he had no right to risk. Visits down there, under any level of security at all, had gotten to be a calculated risk. Up here there was more and more to be done, and down there the pace of change pushed the planet's less stable residents to greater and greater agitation. There was simply no replacement for him, and he had to admit he had no right, no personal right to take stupid chances with his life. That meant downhill skiing was right out, along with bad-weather flying or boating, and he hadn't been on a mecheita's tall back in four years. Not that he didn't miss those things, dream of those things—but at least—at least, up here, things ran, and he could stop anticipating disasters.

The curving corridor apparently ended in a door like all the other doors, but Algini keyed open the security lock, let them through into a whole self-contained world. It was the door of the Little Bujavid, as atevi called it. Lord Geigi's residence was at the start of this new corridor, the paidhi-aiji's at the end, and two unoccupied apartments in the middle, ready for any atevi lord who found it necessary to be here on short notice: Ilisidi had been the first inspiration, and the Astronomer Emeritus had visited as recently as half a year ago.

It was atevi decor from the first moment they passed the door, a muted color here and there, a great deal of white or near-white. The hall-end had the baji-naji conspicuous, next Bren's own doors.

Baji-naji. Chaos and overthrow: appropriate enough emblems not only for the space program but for the paidhi-aiji's household and this whole section: they all found more than a little humor in the notion.

But the baji-naji had a table beneath it, a wooden table with a single river-rounded stone: chaos underlain with, comparatively speaking, the most stable thing in the universe, their own precious world, the place that sent them.

His major domo Narani had done that understated exterior arrangement for the hall. Atevi visitors had greatly admired it. A photograph of it had reached the news services, as a result, and Narani, his modest major domo, from a small rural estate, with a peasant-bred practicality to his designs, had accidentally created a widely copied fashion throughout atevi society, an entire artistic movement in Shejidan that found approval on both sides of the conservative-liberal battle. His back-to-basics traditionalism that harked back to country modes and primitive expressions—so the practitioners of *kabiu'tera* declared. Narani might have had a whole new career on the planet, a respected master—if he were willing to leave here, which Narani was not.

In point of fact, Bren thought, he simply *liked* Narani's arrangement. In stabilizing the chaos around the place, it did satisfy the heart—God knew what wonderful things it did to atevi sensibilities—and to him, yes, both the baji-naji and the stone were very apt, very reassuring.

Home for certain. The door opened. There were bows, there were pleasant, familiar faces . . . Narani was, of course, foremost, an older gentleman, kindly and very much in charge. There was Bindanda, a roundish fellow of great creative talent—not only in the kitchen. A handful of staff who chanced to be near, men and women who came simply to fill out the number and make a good showing in the hall.

"Nand' paidhi," Narani said. "There will be dinner with nand' Jase tonight. One hopes this is acceptable news."

"Very acceptable, Rani-ji." He shed the coat into Narani's hands, and the bulletproof vest with it. The temperature was perfect, the place was perfect. Here his staff would steer him into the right clothes and the right place at the right time and he utterly could stop thinking about schedules and protocol crises. Once he would have called it lazy. With the pace of decisions his job had become, he called it necessary.

"When my baggage arrives, unpack it. Packets. All labeled. I've bought gifts for all the staff. —Danda-ji, your spices should arrive. And yes, the video games. I'll deal with my messages tomorrow if there are none urgent. —Is there, however, anything pending from Lord Geigi?"

"Oh, indeed," Narani said, and signaled a younger servant, who presented the message-bowl for visual inspection: it contained a good number of small scrolls, one of which was Geigi's message-case: he knew that one very well. He picked that one out and read it on the spot.

"Geigi advises me he wants a meeting tomorrow. Noon would be excellent, if it suits him. Anything my staff arranges with his staff will do very well."

There were a handful of less formal cases: atevi disputes or atevi advisements. The messages were from departments, two, by appearance, even from common workers: certain mediations with humans might properly come directly to the paidhi-aiji, a right guaranteed by centuries-old law.

And a handful of human language printouts. His staff had rolled them into the traditional form—and he feared one of those *might* be a letter from his relatives, who any hour now might hear via the news services he had been in Shejidan and *hadn't* called—he'd catch hell for that, when his mother knew.

And at the bottom, an accident of shape, not priority, rested a couple of flat, sealed disks that were with equal certainty from various station departments—data he'd requested.

Besides those, still more letters would come flowing into the mail system from the planet, following the memorial service. He could forecast that as he could forecast a storm from the smell in the air. From down there, adding to the mail he'd brought up with him, would come letters ranging from the thoughtful, well-dispositioned observations of lords he did deal with on legitimate business, to less useful suggestions from the amateur but well-meaning, and so on down to the truly unbalanced, be they harmless or otherwise—

rather more of those than the real proportion, actually. He had a very large staff on the planet whose job was to filter the mail—but they did pass through the choicest crackpot letters. Such missives, however amusing, gave him a useful sense of the fringe element—and the things sane atevi might actually feel, but would not express or admit. The fears of shuttles puncturing the atmosphere and letting all the air out had diminished significantly, for instance: those were easy. The alien threat was not, and now second-class machimi had a whole new subject matter: alien invasions which came down on sails of flame, destroying cities, frightening children into nightmares. There was an ongoing machimi involving an atevi starship crew fighting off aliens that remarkably looked like other atevi dressed like humans.

He truly didn't approve of those, but that failed to stop them.

Well, but he was glad to have matters underway with Geigi . . . and could scarcely wait to inform Geigi about the robots, which really was Ginny's triumph to reveal first, to Ramirez and the ship council . . . but Geigi was more his territory, and discreet with the other two camps.

So he could be sure Geigi's business wasn't the robots. The urgency was more likely Geigi's precious fish tanks—not the decorative ones in Geigi's office, rather the big ones that were meant to feed the space-based population. That was the project Geigi was determined to build as soon as they could spare the labor and machinery from the refueling effort. After three years, priorities were being reset, and he just bet that Geigi was intent on getting his own project to the top of the heap—especially hoping he'd come back from the planet with some new sense of the aiji's next priorities.

He wasn't averse to Geigi's program. In fact he was in favor of it. But he wondered, on his way to the bedroom, whether he could get a reciprocal concession out of Geigi. They were close associates, but that never meant one couldn't look for advantage in a situation. It was simply the way negotiations happened in court.

A younger manservant appeared in the hallway to inform him, a formality, that his bath was waiting . . . never mind the shower was always available: it was the form, the welcome home. He went in, shed the clothes into the manservant's waiting hands, stepped into the shower and vigorously scrubbed away the residue of candle-smoke and incense that had come with him from the memorial.

Simply shutting his eyes reconstructed that vault, and the world, and the mourners all eyeing one another up and down the rows like predator and prey.

Poor Cajeiri. His first public ceremonial, and he'd embarrassed the house, and his present and past guardians.

But the diplomatic relations of the aiji with the East weren't his problem. The East-West problem all belonged to Tabini and Ilisidi now, and there was no one in the world—literally—better at handling those stresses and strains on the social fabric. The *aishidi'tat* stood firm. Tabini ran it; he intended it to survive, and its welfare, however habituated the thought, was just not the paidhi's problem any longer.

Neither was the heir to the *aishidi'tat* the paidhi's concern.

He *needed* to sift through the mail. He needed to solve the pressing problems up here in the heavens.

Not least among them the matter of a fish tank and the prioritization of Ginny's new robots.

He let the water course over him and laid his strategy for a visit to Geigi.

And for a phone call down to the planet, to give a hello to Toby, who'd want a reasonable answer as to *why* his brother hadn't phoned when he was in easy range of a visit. That had to be a very, very carefully given excuse.

He felt guilty about that choice. He really did. But the schedule *had* been rushed. He was tired from the trip as it was. Sandwiching a flying trip to the island into his other business . . .

Honestly, no, that wasn't it. Toby's letters were full of troubles he couldn't solve and his phone calls were harder still. *No, I can't* grew thinner and thinner as the years passed, particularly when he was in range, and *please* was so implicit in every conversation he had with Toby. *Please come down here, please don't be out of touch, please tell me what to do with Mother.*

Hell if he knew. There *wasn't* a good answer, not outside of their mother deciding to do something different than she'd done for the last forty years. Mospheirans didn't change easily. Their mother didn't change, period.

Most of all, hardest for him to deal with Toby's

queries on his marital crises: *What do I do about Jill? How do I keep her?*

Say no to Mother was the only answer he knew. *Don't try to stand in where I know damn well neither of us should be. Get out of there. Don't go when Mother calls.*

You think after all these years I'm going to have a better answer? Me, the unmarried one?

He scrubbed his face and his hair, hard, not even wanting to think about that next communication with Toby. He couldn't play part-time marriage counselor, or psychologist, not atop everything else. He had—

God, he had Sandra Johnson's plants in his baggage. And uninvited as they were, she'd gone to a great deal of trouble to give him that gift. He didn't want to account for their accidental demise in the letter he was bound to get.

He put his head out of the shower and spied Bindanda.

"Danda-ji, there are some plant slips with my carry-on baggage. Would you kindly find out how to pot them?"

In an orbiting apartment with no pots, no soil and no fertilizer. But his staff necessarily specialized in miracles, and he could do Bindanda the greatest possible favor not to drip on the floor when he made the request.

"Yes, nadi-ji."

Toby, on the other hand . . . Toby's problem . . . wasn't something Bindanda could make go away.

Well, he had to call Toby. He had to. He'd probably better call his mother.

He'd do it tomorrow.

The shower beeped: even the paidhi had a water-limit . . . one he'd insisted on having, and there it was, a one-minute warning, just time enough to get the soap off in decent order.

He rinsed, cut the water off and stepped out. The junior servant was right at hand to help him into his warmed, soft robe and equally warmed slippers.

After that, he sat on a bench, had his hair dried and braided in formal order, and afterward got up and dressed for dinner, not in the full court attire, this time, but atevi-style, all the same, for a dinner at home, among intimates: the lace-cuffed shirt, close-fitting trousers, a white ribbon for his braid. When he asked himself, he didn't know why he didn't call for human-style clothing for a dinner with Jase: certainly it would have been appropriate, maybe more appropriate, and in most regards more comfortable. But somewhere in the hindbrain he was still on the world.

"Nandi." Bindanda brought him a small envelope—no question it was human, no question it was Mospheiran, at first sight. It had a little residue of dirt. From the plants, it seemed.

A letter from Sandra Johnson. With photos of Sandra and smiling near-teens. Good God, he thought. Who are these kids?

> *Dear Bren, I was repotting today and thought of you. I checked and these plant slips aren't contraband where you are.*
> *The picture? This is my oldest, Brent, and this is Jay.*

Was she married? Had she told him she was married?

I'm working in Brentano now, for a law firm, well, you probably know, Meacham, Brown & Wilson. John and I are happy here. But when I thought about you up there in all that plain plastic, I couldn't just toss the cuttings. I hope they're no trouble and if they are, throw them out. I told Brent and Jay I once visited the aiji in Shejidan and that I know you, and I'm not sure they believe me, but I don't forget those days. I think of you fondly and thank you for all you've done up there.

Sincerely,
Sandra Johnson

John who, for God's sake?

But she was certainly due a letter, and he opened the computer that had magically arrived in his room, and wrote an answer.

Dear Sandra, absolutely I'll treasure them. Growing things are pretty scarce aboard.

I'm so glad for you. Fine-looking kids. Congratulations.

Bren.

Due two letters, in fact:

Dear Brent and Jay, believe your mother. She saved the whole world, once, and the aiji himself still owes her a personal favor.

Sincerely,
Bren Cameron
Paidhi-aiji

Just occasionally there were entirely delicious satisfactions to the job. And he did treasure. . . . what were the plants' names? Hell, he couldn't remember. Seymor and Fredricka, he decided—granted they lived.

Tough specimens. Survivors. Coming home to the realm of their ancestors.

That letter, however, had led him to think about his mail queue, and he connected.

A letter from the tax authority on Mospheira. He needed to file a paper, the same paper he filed every year. No, they couldn't possibly accept his secretary's signature. It regarded the immense amount of pay he'd accumulated and not spent, and which he used to pay his mother's bills and buy birthday presents for Toby's kids.

A letter from a charity wanted an endorsement, Society for Beachside Preservation, something of the sort. He wasn't sure how *that* had gotten through Mogari-nai and C1. He wasn't out of sympathy for the cause. It sounded like something Toby might favor. But he doubted Toby had sent it.

The letter from the State Department turned out to regard his personal identification card, which had expired. He could bring the requisite cash and his expired card to any courthouse he could reach.

Well, *that* was a fair hike.

And a letter—God, a short note from Barb.

He hadn't heard from Barb at all for two years, not since her divorce. She'd said then she was getting her life together—adjusting to life as it was—life, as, dammit, she'd chosen it to be. She'd said she didn't expect an answer, and gratefully enough he hadn't sent one—

But he heard *about* Barb often enough. Barb and his mother got along, consoled each other—they had a frightening lot in common and every time he thought of it, he told himself his instincts had been right. Run like hell. The Bren Cameron that Barb and his mother both hoped would exist didn't exist, couldn't exist, not since he'd taken on the job—and thank God he hadn't run back after Barb's accident, hadn't gotten involved in her life again. He'd only have provided the chance to let Barb lock on and mess up the rest of her life.

Last he'd heard, she was all right. She'd come out of the accident alive and whole. A rough few years, one hell of a mistake, but she was doing all right these days.

Being on a space station without a convenient way down seemed a safe distance.

> *Bren,*
> *Your mother's not doing well. The new medications aren't what we hoped. I hope you'll find time to come down as soon as you can.*

The bottom dropped out of his stomach . . . not hard, just a little twinge of guilt. His mother's health hadn't been good, but the majority of the crises had involved some scheme to get him to visit. What was the date on the letter?

The day he'd left for the planet, dammit.

And if he had visited—if he had, every damned

time his mother would revert to the ordinary list of complaints and the tally of his failures to care enough, visit enough, do enough . . . no, no, no, he *didn't* feel guilty.

But he went for the message-bowl, then, opened the messages, and found, dammit, one from his brother, not with the usual header that would have tipped off the staff as to its origin and sent it straight to him no matter where he was: no, this one was from Community General, from the hospital nearest their mother's neighborhood. Toby hadn't known there was a reason to put an official stamp on it. Toby couldn't have known he was actually on the planet and in reach, if he'd only put an official stamp on, to alert his staff.

Dammit.

Bren, Toby said, *Mother's in hospital, her blood pressure again. The apartment manager found her on the stairs and called the ambulance. The doctors aren't certain . . .*

It went on. Toby'd gone to the capital immediately. There was a second letter with the same origin. Their mother was in the hospital. The medications had taken a toll on her other organs. The doctors were working on the problem.

Toby had dropped everything, ignored all his advice, left Jill to go to the capital to be available.

Well, when hadn't he felt guilty . . . for leaving his mother on the island, for leaving Toby to deal with her, when what she wanted was him, the one of her two sons who didn't come running?

When hadn't he felt like a scoundrel, ducking possible visits?

Yes, his coming onto the island was a danger to his mother and to Toby and Toby's family; but they just weren't damned pleasant visits, either, and if he was honest, that was the real reason . . . and the source of enough guilt to turn his stomach. Toby, granted, had at least had the good sense early on to go live up on the coast, out of range—but when things had shifted and Toby had turned out to be the only one of them who could be there, Toby would come back—at the worst moments Toby would get on a plane at whatever hour, leave his promises to his wife and his kids hanging while he ran down there to deal with the fact some lunatic had phoned their mother's apartment and set off her heart condition. They were real troubles, always real troubles, but they had a knack for happening on birthdays and holidays and other times brother Bren couldn't show up to visit, and the coincidence was more than suspicious.

Did other sons board a plane every time a parent had a medical incident? No. But did they? Toby did, because Bren couldn't. He *told* Toby not to go . . . but Toby went; and once Toby got there, Toby got all the complaints—no thanks for his being there, just the complaints. *Where was Bren? When would Bren come? Why couldn't Bren come? Tell your brother this, tell your brother that. . . .*

And ask why. Ask *why* Toby ran off to try to be a better son to their mother than he could be, and oh, there was a dark spot in that answer. He and Toby weren't rivals, never had wanted to be, but their mother could look right past Toby without a blip on her radar, and say her sons never cared for her—meaning him, Bren, the one of the two their mother couldn't possibly have with her.

Was that what was going on again?

Or was this finally the real thing, a real life-and-death crisis?

And even if they'd discussed it, he and Toby, and unmasked what was going on and shone light on the cold facts . . . the reality of that tactic hurt so much Toby went and did it again, trying for some better outcome, some moment when their mother would just once look at him and say to his face, "Thank you. You're a good son."

He picked small details out of the second letter, something about Jill off on business.

The hell. Separate vacations for the last three years, one separation, a new courtship. Now Jill was off on business at the moment and Toby wouldn't admit to her he'd flown down to the capital. Toby was, in fact, actively concealing where he was, though Jill was due home tomorrow—to an empty house up on the coast. *Surprise her with it—God, Toby. . . . what are you thinking?*

The kids, at least—hardly kids now—were in school—likely staying with friends at the moment. While Jill—Jill had had all the crises she was willing to take. It wasn't *what* happened. It wasn't the bouts of illness, which were a real illness. None of those things were the issue. What was the issue was a battle between two women over a son and husband. Jill knew she was always going to lose, and that Toby couldn't win.

I know there are good reasons, Toby finished his second letter. *If I have to handle things here I will. But I think you'll feel better if you can get down here.*

And who knows? She's tougher than either of us. She's beaten the odds before.

You may get a letter from Barb. I know you don't want to, but read it all the same. I think it's time to make peace on all fronts.

Time to make peace. That was certainly the truth.

Would he have gone to the island, if he'd gotten that letter before he left the ground?

Would he have thrown all his good reasons to the wind, missed his shuttle flight and caught the next air cargo hop to the island?

He didn't know. He honestly didn't know that answer and it was too late now to know the truth.

Turn around and catch the next shuttle flight down, next week?

Maybe. He didn't want to think about that answer. Not until the shock had settled.

And it would settle, before the chance came.

Meanwhile he owed his brother a letter. But he couldn't write *that* until he honestly knew what he was going to do.

Going down there when Tabini was in the midst of maneuvers as critical as any in his reign . . . risk all that that entailed? It *wasn't* a good time for the paidhi-aiji to intrude his human presence into a rush trip onto the continent and on to Mospheira. Even going in at the other spaceport wouldn't conceal the fact that he had landed—again. A furtive visit was even more apt to attract attention from the news than going down officially at Shejidan.

The more dogged of the conspiracy theorists, atevi and human, wouldn't believe for a moment that the family emergency existed.

God, he just didn't see how he was going to get there. He didn't know if he wanted to get there.

But leave Toby to deal with things solo, one more time . . . *not* to be there the one time their mother, who was the world's best at crying wolf, really was on the brink. . . .

What he most needed to do was to grab Toby by the ears once and for all and say, Go home, brother, you have a right to your own life. But he'd done that and Toby didn't listen. Toby was so damned smart, but in matters involving their mother, Toby didn't listen, because somewhere in the tangled depths of family politics, Toby didn't ever like the answers he got.

A small commotion had reached the foyer. Narani came to the office door.

"Your luggage has arrived, nandi. Crates have been set in the kitchen. Those without labels are in the foyer."

"Very fine, Rani-ji." He rose from his desk and let the messages lie—decided against the coat, after all, and walked to the the foyer, where, amid dinner preparations, the smaller luggage sat, large, travel-worn lumps of diplomatic bags about which the servants gathered in shy anticipation.

He personally opened the sealed tie and passed out the bundles and packages. He needed distraction. He enjoyed the gift-giving, like a holiday.

Letters. Abundant letters from happy, sensible, long-bonded families, whatever the baroque nature of atevi parentage and fosterage. He gave those into Narani's care, and Narani ceremoniously handed them to junior servants to sort and distribute, all with fair dispatch. There were special treat packets from various homes, small, brightly wrapped presents from relatives . . . those were the bulk of the bags— besides the requested video games, which regulations did not permit in the general uploads from Mogari-nai, and which therefore had to be freighted up. For Narani, a great-grandfather for the third time, there was a basket about which he had been curious: it was very light. It proved to be simply curls of fragrant bark, and that gift passed from one to the next, with appreciative sighs and second sniffs: smells of the world of their birth.

Then his gifts: he had provided, gathered from the Bujavid gardens, a middle-sized box containing bits of natural wood and a few curious rocks and sprigs, which the servants prized for their own common quarters, for *kabiu*. That was his gift to them, which he had personally asked of the gardeners.

For his senior staff, he had another box—a very fine two hundred-year-old bowl of southern work, for Narani and an antique book for Bindanda.

They were far, far more than servants to him.

For Tano and Algini, books. Tano had, besides, gotten a letter from his father. The two had begun to correspond, and did so quite frequently, now that Tano was out of reach.

Banichi and Jago turned up, at the distribution of gifts, both fresh from showers and ready for dinner—they came to present Algini their own gift, a very, very florid shirt, to laughter and applause from the servants, because Algini had a penchant for his old black uniform tees, in his rare moments off-duty. Algini accepted it in good grace, shed his uniform jacket and put on the shirt over the black tee to general laughter.

The door beeped. Algini shed the gift quickly.

"What?" Banichi said. "Not wear it for Jasi-ji?"

Algini said not a word, only put on his jacket and looked quite proper before junior staff could open the door.

5

Jase turned up in station casuals, never, these days, his atevi finery. Bren was sure it was a political decision that led a *Phoenix* captain, however unwelcome the captaincy, not to dress as a foreigner to the ship. Jase kept his hair cut, too, and at his least formal, still wore ship-issue, plain blue that might as well be a uniform. He'd been given his captaincy for political reasons, after the juniormost captain, Pratap Tamun—there were four captains running *Phoenix*, by ship's custom—had led a failed mutiny. The ship had badly needed a reconciling symbol in the wake of that disturbance, and Jase had become that symbol—a captain not tainted by the divisive politics that had led to the mutiny. But beyond the immediate need for a figurehead and over Jase's protests, circumstances and the senior captain's insistence had kept him in the post. In self-defense, Jase had thrown himself into the requisite studies, and the requisite manners, and uniform—hell, he probably even knew the set of orders that could activate the ship engines. Please God they could put off *that* order for decades.

"Hello there," Bren said as Jase shed his jacket into the servants' keeping.

"Good trip?" Jase asked him.

"Interesting," Bren said. "Good, I suppose." He decided, on the whole, it had been a good trip, no matter what he learned once he got home. No matter what he'd not been able to do while he was there. "The whole business seemed to be a funeral."

"Funeral."

"Well, of sorts. Belated. A memorial service for Valasi. Tabini's putting on a show, called in all the television people. Don't ask me why. Days there and I still don't know. I think we got the feed up here. I haven't asked yet."

Jase gave him a look as they walked into the dining room. Jase had lived on the planet, knew Tabini, and well knew the rumors Tabini had assassinated his father.

"Curious."

"Baji-naji," Bren said. "Everyone who's anyone was there, and for some reason, *I* was, and it was important that I be there. I'm still trying to figure it out."

But that was the last word of politics, dinner being the matter at hand, and he would not insult his staff by violating that very basic rule of a noble house. Banichi and Jago joined him and Jase on some more convivial nights, but this being a homecoming, and his security staff having, it seemed, given Narani their regrets, dinner had been construed a shade more formally this evening—it was clear in the careful arrangement of the table, in the number of forks laid out; seven, to be precise.

Jase settled, and paid courteous attention as Narani supervised their juniormost servant setting out the appetizer, a pâté of pickle, seafood and nuts that was improbably one of Jase's favorites. The accompanying crackers were a Mospheiran brand, but *kabiu*, and plentiful in the station outlets.

"And was Ilisidi there?" Jase asked. It was not quite a political question.

"Oh, yes. I had supper with her. She sends her regards, nadi, most specifically. I gave her yours." They spoke Ragi. Jase liked to keep up his skills and Bren thought in Ragi, dreamed in Ragi these days—refused to slip into Mospheiran or ship-accent unless he had to: it fuzzed his thought patterns in the work he had to do. "Ah. There *is* some additional news. The Astronomer Emeritus is coming up two months from now. *He* should keep Geigi entertained."

"There's a treat," Jase said cheerfully. Grigiji was a favorite and intermittent guest—a delightful and curious old man whose greatest joy was the observation station that was supposed to report to them if there was any signal out of the deep . . . and that incidentally gave Grigiji information on the wide universe. "I'll arrange something for him."

From Grigiji and the mathematicians they went on to discuss the weather in Shejidan, the quality of the fishing—but at each new course, offered great appreciation for the dishes. Bindanda had provided his favorites and Jase's: the effort deserved applause, and one always showed particular reverence for the meat course, under any decent circumstances.

It was another of Jase's favorites, among items they could import, a meat that Bindanda's artistry turned from station staple to a very fine presentation.

It was a slow finish, then, a delicate cream dessert—atevi had only a dim compunction about animals kept for milk, though they would not tolerate animals kept for slaughter. But they had gotten the notion of cream cheese from Mospheira, and this was seasonal fresh fruit, one of Bindanda's specialties, with a nut topping.

How Bindanda had gotten the fruit up here, on the other hand, must involve high crimes and bribery.

"Very fine," Jase said. "Where did Danda-ji get *this?*"

"I don't think we want to know," Bren said, and called out the chef to compliment him—both of them praised the dessert, which pleased Bindanda exceedingly. But they had not a word from Bindanda on his sources, so they were assuredly not official.

After that they adjourned for conversation on more weighty matters, in the library-cum-study. Bren assumed his favorite chair, propped his feet up, slightly feeling the effects of pressure-change and long travel, and took a brandy. Jase took one, being off-duty.

"Funeral for Valasi," Jase reprised. "Didn't he have one already?"

"One isn't quite sure what the ceremony meant," Bren said. He suffered a little dislocation, a flashback to the vault, the shadows, the live fire of torches . . . and tried to think by what handle to grapple with all the questions at once. "I attended and I still don't know why Tabini wanted me there. The meetings beforehand were all social. I wish you *could* have come. But I'm afraid there wouldn't have been any fishing—

except for information—and there was precious little catch in that commodity, either."

"What's your best guess?"

"A patch-up with the conservatives. An overdue patch-up. I don't know whether Ilisidi's on the inside or the outside of the plan . . . but Tabini's spent a lot of political credit getting what he's gotten."

"The economy's running well."

"Oh, it is. But prosperity and electric toasters only mean the far lunatic fringe loses power . . . and the legitimate sane conservatives lose power. And the very fact he *is* succeeding only makes it worse, to the other side's view. They *want* him to fail. They *want* something to go wrong. And he's just gotten stronger."

"So he offers them a favor anyway?"

"So maybe he knows they're getting desperate. He certainly made the transfer of Cajeiri into Ilisidi's care quite public . . . that may have been the statement he was making. Which was and wasn't a towering success at the ceremony. Which is one reason I honestly can't figure it: the boy wasn't exactly the centerpiece of the event—wasn't really involved. My meeting with Tabini—well, fine, and social, but I expected more. I bounced from cabinet meeting to cabinet meeting, all courtesy matters and briefings, all the department heads wanting to get up to speed on what's going on up here. I answered a handful of southern concerns about siting a plant down on the coast—I happen to agree with the ones protesting. They can put the thing inland. They don't need coastline. It's a damned eyesore where they want to put it."

Jase sighed. "I did look forward to the fishing trip."

"If you'd been there you'd only have gotten caught in this affair. But hang on. You'll get your ocean. Next spring."

"Promises."

"Promises. We'll *try*, this time. We'll try damned hard. I'll do some extravagant favor for Tabini and see if we can't get a couple of weeks."

"Weeks." Jase looked glum. "I could use a month or two."

"Something wrong?"

"I broke it off with Yolanda. Again."

"I'm sorry to hear it." That relationship had been on-again, off-again. Partners, mostly successfully, on-planet. On-station, decidedly not the case.

"Stupid personal stuff. I swear, I think she's asking herself how can she tell she's got authority if she doesn't wield it? She's taken up with a computer tech, now, a damned bad choice, but it's *her* choice, and sitting where I do—I don't care."

What did a friend say? That that wasn't quite the truth?

"Quarrel?"

"Sulks and silences. I'm on the captains' list and she's not, and I think that's the crux of it."

"She doesn't want the job. *You* don't want it. Yet you fight over it."

"Doesn't matter what we want. Doesn't matter what I want. I have the office. Suddenly my advice is a captain's advice. Whatever I say to her is criticism. If I have an opinion, it just blows up: unfair, pulling rank. So what do I do? We don't talk any more. We tried being lovers. Didn't work. Tried being sibs. That doesn't work. I don't know what we are, but we can't live with or without each other. She's going back on main schedule. She's seeing her tech. What do I care? But some things you ought to know."

Jase and Yolanda had been lovers, in the same job, stuck on a planet they couldn't, at the time, get off of. They were shipmates, never sibs—in the biological sense. But they were, if being planned by the same man could make a kinship, if being born at the same time, for the same purpose could make one.

They were both Taylor's Children. Conceived out of the genetic material of the heroes from before the Landing. Conceived to *be* heroes. Conceived to be *above* politics, if it was possible.

Thus far it hadn't been possible, even between the two of them.

"I should know," he echoed Jase. "What should I know?"

"She'd been talking with Paulson, and I asked about what. It's my job, to ask."

Paulson. Head of Mospheiran operations.

"And she called Mospheira," Jase added, "and said it was personal."

She'd served there. But in the last number of years she hadn't called Mospheira. Didn't *know* anybody on Mospheira, that he knew of, not in the personal sense. And now he knew.

"Who did she call?"

"Don't know. I thought I ought to have asked. Maybe it was an old friend. But Paulson isn't. And all of a sudden I'm the villain. I don't figure her."

Yolanda Mercheson, the third paidhi, the one originally destined between the ship and Mospheira—as Jase was the ship-paidhi, translator between the ship and Tabini . . . and him.

Well, a fractured romance was one thing. But having Yolanda start making phone calls between Paulson and Mospheira, on her own?

He left for a few days and things *did* go to hell.

"Can you trace who she called?"

"I might. It's not my job, now."

"Does Ramirez know?"

A heavy sigh. "I told him. What he said to her, I don't know. But she was in a mood. Called me a few names. Hell of it is, I don't know if it's a personal matter, and I can't find out—and if *I* ask, it's personal and she's not talking." Jase gave a short, unhappy laugh. "You said, never let the job get into my personal life, and vice versa. You were right. It did. It shouldn't have. Now that I've blown the alarm on her, I'm wrong. She's broken regs for a personal call, she's in deep trouble and of course now it's all my fault."

Yolanda Mercheson was as glum and methodical a young woman as Jase was high-voltage. Small wonder that relationship hadn't worked, logical as it might have seemed at the time between two people effectively shipwrecked.

"A pickle."

"As in dinner menu?"

"As in a hashed-up mess."

"I don't want this job, Bren. Hell, Ramirez doesn't even need my vote in council. No one dissents. No one argues. I suggested he move Yolanda into the seat in my place. I guess my report this week didn't encourage that, did it?"

"And Ramirez said, then?"

"Didn't even look up. Said I was doing just fine: that I understood the atevi. Never mind I don't have any other qualification and I couldn't handle ops if the instructions were printed on the console . . . which they're not. `That's fine,' the old man said. `You're doing just fine. Yolanda couldn't do what you do. Stay put.' Not damned fair, I say, when the most *I* want out of life is to get on the ocean down there on a boat and just get out of this."

"That's not what you want."

"I don't know what I want, to tell the truth. I know I never want to handle ops. I don't want to handle command. I could live off a diet of fish."

"If we're really lucky, you won't ever have to do anything about ops."

"Or Yolanda."

"You're doing fine. Geigi favors you. You give him great confidence, just knowing you're in office."

"I'm glad he's confident. I don't like what's going on."

"Tabini isn't at all unhappy to have one of the paidhiin sitting as captain up here: that's an understatement. It gives *him* confidence. The whole *aishidi'tat* is pleased to have you right where you are. We don't need Yolanda making independent judgements."

"Damned right we don't."

"I'll talk to her. I'll keep your name out of it."

"She'll know. But at this point, hell if I care. Maybe *you* can get yea or nay out of the Old Man."

"I can. Trust me." He hadn't mentioned the thing Jase would most want to know. *"Ginny's back. We've got robots."*

Hopeful quirk of an eyebrow. "Movement on the robots?"

"No. Freed. Liberated. Strike's settled. The initial load's just come up."

"Damn!" It was an entirely cheerful *damn*.

"In the station's receiving area, by now. I imagine she's notifying Ramirez even as we sit here."

"When did *that* clear?"

"Evidently very fast. Didn't have any idea, either, until I met Gin on the flight. I think *she's* escaping from the planet before one of the company execs can ask a return favor."

"Oh, this is good news."

"Looks as if everything's going to move. We're going to open the next section, first we can. I've got the figures, labor and support. Geigi will get his fish tanks."

"And the Old Man's going to be in a *far* better mood all around."

He'd certainly made Jase's evening. The unlovely little autobots were the backbone of the fueling and refit operation, and Ramirez had requisitioned a crippling number of them into his refueling and mining the last three years. They were finished with that— and now that they were finished, able to divert the robots back to other priorities, finally, the labor dam broke, and they had the autobots' next generation.

But it wasn't too late. It meant they could accelerate

station operations, and accelerate ship-building: *everything* was going to break loose.

And damned if Yolanda Mercheson was going to conduct some personal business on official channels in the middle of it. Yolanda wasn't going to be happy with him, either, before all was said and done, not if she'd been carrying on some personal business on Mospheira without going through channels—or if she'd been running some deal for Paulson without telling her fellow paidhiin. There was no legal sanction for the latter, and she wasn't paidhi to the island any longer. He didn't know whether to go and talk to her on what was clearly a sore spot. Between them, these days, there almost wasn't a friendship, but he could at least make his displeasure known. He could talk to Paulson and make Paulson less anxious to go that route, if Paulson was making trouble—and a sad state of affairs if he was, and if he'd gotten Yolanda to do something that proved the final split from Jase.

"I'll be talking to Geigi after breakfast tomorrow, if I can arrange it," Bren told Jase. "I'll promise him his tanks . . . I assume he gets his tanks. Any reason against it, before I set that promise in motion?"

"You aren't talking to the decision-making wing of the Captain's Council. Remember?"

You're still one of the captains, Bren thought, but there it was: Jase flatly refused to wield the power. At times it was more than inconvenient, but it was Jase's notion of honor, and there was no getting by it.

They had a second brandy, all the same, and talked about Geigi, Geigi's boat—the object of Jase's daydreams of ocean sailing—quiet talk at the end of a long, long week of hurry-up and changed plans, homecoming, and, thank God, arrival of the robots, that solved so many problems.

Bren found his eyelids at half mast, apologized, and Jase excused himself: "You'd better get to bed," Jase said. The rigors of travel were, curiously, another matter ship-folk had to learn about, and most didn't quite understand: the notion of packing one's belongings in a suitcase and rushing breakneck from point to point was something Jase had only experienced on a planet.

"Good of you to come," Bren said, saw Jase to the door himself, and added, because he meant it, "Very good of you to come. Do it again soon."

Fact was, he missed Jase. Didn't know how he would manage if Jase ever moved back in, since the affair with Jago had gone beyond affair, and gotten to be the next thing to married routine. But there were times a human argument, a human conversation massaged areas of his brain that felt far too little exercised . . . that was what it was, he thought: too little stimulation of the human that was left in him. Not good. Not at all good, for the human organism. He didn't know, before Ginny on the shuttle today, how long it had been since he'd had a lengthy social conversation with another human being.

Immediately after that, the brandy hit him with full force, persuading him that bed was just about the last objective he could reasonably achieve. Sensibly, he *wanted* to talk to Banichi and Jago tonight about a number of things, and dutifully, he should have advised his staff and settled down for an all-night debrief. Jago waited for him in the security post, still official and still in uniform, well, down to the tee-shirt, at least—but debriefing wasn't what she'd been led to expect tonight. *Sleep* was reasonably what she thought she had coming, and she, who'd been on out-side duty for hours, took precedence over Tano and Algini who'd had only on-site duty, off and on.

He wasn't in condition to confer with anyone, as it was. The Jase conversation had been the last. Even without the brandy he suspected he would have opted for bed, being just too dog-tired.

But there was more than that business afoot, more than Jase, more than Ramirez, more than Tabini's dealings with the provinces.

"Is there any word from my brother?"

"No, nadi-ji. Go to bed."

"Good idea." Tonight he just wanted to fall over and be unconscious for a few hours. "I'm going to sleep, Jago-ji. Are you coming to bed?"

"Soon," Jago said, and added, because she knew how curiosity consumed him, drove him, made him crazy: "Banichi likewise says get some sleep."

At least they didn't need him. Some things, if they rested in safe hands, he didn't have to ask. He simply directed himself back to the bedroom, shed his clothes into a servant's care, all but fell onto the mattress and pulled up the covers. His body temperature was sink-ing fast.

But he didn't sleep. He shut his eyes, wondering where Toby was, in what situation, whether there would be a phone call before morning.

After half an hour he got up, went to the computer

and keyed in a message. *Toby, I got your letter. I'm concerned. Call.*

He sent it. It had to pass through the security station out there. His staff would know, and probably be distressed about it. But he didn't explain. He went back to bed, no easier in his mind.

Jago eventually came to bed, a considerable weight on the other side of the mattress, interrupting an exhausted haze that was not quite restful sleep. He knew she was there, and dropped back off, safe.

Safe. Companioned. All things local in their places.

He couldn't oversee the others.

6

No phone call in the morning.

Perhaps, Bren said to himself, amid breakfast, the health crisis was over and Toby was on a flight back to the coast. If Toby could possibly reach a phone, he'd likely call, and if he couldn't reach a phone, it likely meant he was traveling—which was as good news as a phone call.

In the meantime, morning courtesies included a hike all the way to the Construction Operations office to meet officially with their nextdoor neighbor, Lord Geigi—electric runabouts were available for the trip, but undignified, in Bren's island-born view of the universe—besides heartily cursed by walkers in the halls. Bren, for his part, preferred walking, for the exercise, if nothing else: he'd watched certain office-bound sorts put on the pounds, and fought the tendency.

Besides, in long stretches of hall where Jase swore on his life there were no bugs, he could talk at leisure with his staff, much as he and Banichi would talk in the open country down on the planet.

"So how has the world taken the aiji's address, by now?"

"In curiosity," Banichi said. "In great interest. Great interest and an expression of discontent in the East."

Hardly suprising.

"Any clues why he wanted me?"

Tabini, and the ringing of that bell that held every imagination entranced, entrapped.

"One is not satisfied," Banichi said. "We've reviewed the tape. But we haven't discovered the absolute answer, Bren-ji. We have not, not in the configuration, the seating, or in anything said during the ceremony. Legislative proceedings are under seal, down in Shejidan. And *that* is troubling."

"Something is very peculiar, nadi-ji."

They were coming into a more trafficked area now, beyond the limits of any secure conversation. Remarkable sight, atevi and humans in about equal numbers, coming and going on business, atevi and humans in office clothes and workman's clothes— regulations-wise unable to say more than a handful of words to one another—notably *please go, please come, please stop.... please call the supervisor immediately*, in the most meticulously memorized and numerically neutral courtesy. But by that means the common folk of two species did talk, if only in those approved, memorized phrases for known situations.

They tried to be careful. But at certain points they had to cooperate.

And sometimes it came down to things ludicrous on the surface—at least to one side of the question— but fraught with the most serious emotional reactions.

Fish, for instance, and the urgent reason he had to talk to Geigi about robots and a fish tank.

They reached the construction office, a reception area inside of course tastefully arranged: small scroll-paintings and a reception table, with a bowl for correspondence—and an inexpensive soft drink dispenser for human visitors. Geigi was nothing if not even-handed, though the split in decor made an atevi visitor look twice.

They were expected. The attendant rose and bowed, and immediately opened the door with a key push.

"Nandi." Security on duty just inside was as easy, as cordial: Tano had called ahead.

And in this easy place, Bren left Banichi at the security station to take his ease with Geigi's staff, there to have a soft drink, likely, and exchange information.

Meanwhile he went on into the inner chamber, where Geigi, in informal clothing this morning, presided over a desk well-littered with papers, beside a tank humming and bubbling and populated with color and darting movement.

"Bren-ji." Geigi rose—great courtesy, for a lord in his own territory. He was a jovial man whose whole attitude toward life was experimental—and, for an atevi lord, very spur-of-the-moment. He swept business aside, knocking two storage disks onto the carpet in the process, and personally dragged a chair up to the side of his desk. "Tea—tea, will you, Bren-ji? I swear I could do with a cup. We have this most amazing infuser—" Geigi himself went to a domed creation on the bookcase counter, put a plastic cup beneath, and created a cup of tea.

"Thank you."

Geigi hastily created another, stirred it with a plastic rod. "Not so fine as that, but hot."

"Very welcome." One was appalled. A tea-maker. A Mospheiran tea-maker. In an atevi lord's office.

"Back from the world and all, and a puzzling trip, I take it."

"I have no idea why I was called, nandi, I truly don't."

"What, pray, is the aiji doing down there?"

"Mystifying us all. I wish I knew. So does everyone."

"A requiem for Valasi-aiji, and not a whisper of ill intent to the living or the dead."

"Not a one. And I can't answer."

"Can't."

"Truly can't, Geigi-ji. I was down there. I came back none the wiser. But!" It was rude to change subjects on a gentleman, but Geigi was an intimate of long-standing, so intimate he risked his reputation with truly marginal tea. "I had a seatmate on the flight up, nandi. Gin Kroger."

"Gin-nadi. With news?"

"Oh, with more than news, nand' director! The robots are with us, and more certainly on their way."

"A wonder!"

"I talked with Jase last night, filed intent to have *some* of our windfall diverted to your fish tanks, my closest of associates, and *we*, you and I, nandi-ji, need to put our heads together, so to speak, and set priorities and requirements and a timetable before someone else gets a bid in."

"This is marvelous!"

"If the tanks can do as they need, Geigi-ji. If they can provide the needful food."

"I have every detail." Geigi leapt up and went to a central cabinet, among the other high, clear-doored shelves and cabinets that graced this very modern office. From it he extracted a stack of much-abused paper, brought it to the desk and spread it out, sketches of a circle containing many little circles.

It was an actual engineering plan, an exploded diagram of what he had last seen as a series of sketches on scrap paper: an aquaculture tank, with triple walls and heaters and solar panels and details he hadn't seen.

Another trip to the cabinet and Geigi laid something new atop it all: it might be another tank, or a tricky sort of valve—the paidhi had gotten fairly proficient at engineering over the last decade, but this one eluded him.

"This is my own invention," Geigi informed him. "And mathematically, baji-naji, I can say there are potentially sufficient variables to make the solutions for escape exceed the number of fish. This is an escapable trap."

"An escapable trap, nandi."

"It admits fish to an area where they may be caught. It revolves, see?" Geigi went back to a second cabinet and brought a plastic model, a somewhat taped-up and revised plastic model.

One began to get the notion.

Fairness. Mathematics that would prove to have harmonious numbers.

Atevi hunted. And fished. They did *not* raise animals for slaughter. The ship-folk's cultural divorcement from the concept of eating living things ran head-on into Mospheira's love affair with food and meat. The mainland's code of *kabiu*, fitness, meant eating no meat outside its appropriate season, and eating with ceremony—respect, even reverence: ship-folk began to take to that concept, though queasily.

But for atevi, reverence didn't mean processed meat, and it didn't mean domesticated herds. And that had been a major stumbling block in trying to supply food to the station.

Fairness meant going out to fish for wild fish, not scooping up everything that lived in one whole tank and processing it without individuality.

But this revolving trap, this remote-fisher, offered a statistical chance to the fish to escape.

"Ingenious," Bren said.

"Fry hatch along the bottom, where this grid—" Geigi pulled a sheet of plans from the middle of the stack, which showed a mesh smaller, one presumed, than the adults. "And a rapid current sweeps the young into the hatchling tanks, to what passes for shallow water. There are three outlets and one inflow. Of outlets, one offers this choice."

Absolutely ingenious. Roulette, for fish.

Geigi was self-pleased. "*Phoenix* engineers, who understand this floating in space, these no-gravity pumps, they do this sort of thing very well. But we can satisfy the objections of the most fastidious. Fish may become resident in this facility; we don't breed them. They breed themselves. And even from the fishing tank there is an escape back into the breeding tanks."

Bren examined the plastic model, asked himself why a fish would want to dive through those holes—a question the paidhi had never asked himself in his life.

Some fish, like the species they planned to have in orbit, were *kabiu* in all seasons, having no migration or well-defined breeding behavior that made them appropriate or inappropriate.

It was *not* like the introduction of high fructose sugars, which had addicted the crew and made SunDrink a wild success. To the bewilderment of the Mospheiran companies who had hoped for *Phoenix* to argue on their side and accept meat products, the human ship-crew did not take readily to meat . . . but did take to the atevi view of fairness and fitness and season. Fairness made a sort of sense to the ship-folk, while it vaguely disgusted Mospheirans, who preferred not to think of the fish on one's dinner plate as a personality.

"We can offer the fishing tanks for recreation," Geigi said. Bren had wondered how long it would take before Geigi offered that notion.

"At first, however, nandi, I fear we'll do well to have the fish reproduce."

"We need a game biologist."

"And the engineers." It all was, to Mospheiran sensibilities, an insanely grandiose plan. But insane things had been engineered before now, since humans falling in from space had landed in a steam-age culture. One had only to look at the Shejidan spaceport to know what could be done to accommodate atevi sensibilities. Fresh water fish, however, not salt. A sea turned out to be a very fussy, very complex environment to maintain.

And once there were the robots, they had the means to automate operations and increase the supportable station population at the same time. With an unlimited food source, they could envision full-scale operation, a station population adequate to any operation . . . *any* operation, and a food-source that wouldn't exclude atevi from orbit: *that* was the center of their plan.

"If we achieve this, nandi," Bren said, "and quit spending so much of our launch weight on food, we'll have the labor up here. No question." In the most logical sense of how to proceed, he supposed he should push for a Mospheiran style fish-farm to start into operation first, to feed enough Mospheirans to make the harder project easy—but getting more Mospheirans than atevi up here was the very last thing they wanted to do. "This keeps everyone happy. I'm quite convinced."

"Very good," Geigi said delightedly. "Excellent!"

It was concluded. It was only twice and three times the scale they had intended, but now two thirds of the population were in accordance with the other third, and *kabiu* could be satisfied for good and all, now that there was a positive abundance of worker robots.

"We have at least a materials estimate," Geigi said—and stopped, as the door opened and Geigi's chief of security slipped in with a quietly blank look. Security never intervened in business except on life or death.

"Nandiin," the man said. "An urgent message for the paidhi."

For *him?* And two lords' security agreed to interrupt a meeting? It was nothing good.

Might it be his call from Mospheira? Some message from Toby?

"Excuse me, nandi." Bren rose. "I'll deal with it quickly."

"Whatever you must do," Geigi said, rising, the soul of courtesy.

Geigi's man led the way outside. Banichi was there, to be sure, and Bren's immediate expectation was that Banichi had received a message, something relayed from Tano.

But Geigi's man opened the door to the general reception area, where an unlikely individual, in blue fatigues and with a blinking lot of electronics, waited for him.

Kaplan. One of Jase's aides, considerably out of formal uniform such as he mostly wore nowadays.

"Excuse me," Kaplan lisped in Ragi, and lapsed into ship-language. "Captain Graham's sending, sir, Captain Ramirez—he's had a seizure. They've taken him to infirmary."

"To *station* infirmary." Ramirez would ordinarily go to sick bay on *Phoenix*. The station infirmary was closer—for minor things or, conversely, for absolutely urgent care.

"Orders said find you wherever you were, sir. Captain Graham thinks you should come, right now."

"Absolutely." He changed to Ragi. "Ramirez has been taken to station hospital, a health crisis, I take it. I'm going at once to pay respects. Tell nand' Geigi."

"Yes," Geigi's man said, and went to do that immediately.

Which left him with Banichi and Kaplan.

"Kaplan. We're with you."

"Yes, sir." Kaplan led off, out the door.

Ramirez. He'd been subconsciously primed for grievous news to come from the planet, not from here.

But Ramirez . . . Ramirez had been in dubious health—and he was one of the three keys to the whole atevi-human partnership. The paidhi-aiji could suffer a personal loss and go on doing his job the same day. The paidhi could lose everyone he loved in the world, and the future of three nations would go unshaken.

But Ramirez stumbled, in the midst of all the agreements and programs that relied on that one man . . . and three worlds shook.

Lord Geigi, no less, overtook them at the lift. That was Ramirez's importance. Bren acknowledged the presence with a glance as the car arrived, and all of them got in together, bound toward a very small installation on third deck, which had only one virtue— its proximity to Ramirez's on-station office.

They didn't speculate aloud, he and Geigi. But it took no telepathy to know they shared the same thought, the same apprehension of disaster.

7

*P*hoenix security was evident in the infirmary corridor, two men in fatigues; and armed guards occupied the infirmary foyer as if the place were under siege. It was anxious security, worried security—security whose highest authority was behind those doors, incapable of command.

"Mr. Cameron, you can't bring them in here."

Kaplan was absolutely speechless. Bren swung a stark, forbidding look at the human officer, Jenrette. *Ramirez's* man, for God's sake, delivered a prohibition to an atevi lord and his retinue as if they were random tourists.

"Mr. Jenrette, this is Lord Geigi and *his* security." Bren spotted the personal guard of Captain Sabin and Captain Ogun present further in; and Polano, who was another of Jase's message-runners. "Captain Graham sent for us."

Jenrette took a deep breath and made that slight nod of the head that ship personnel had learned to use with atevi authority. "Apologies. Mr. Cameron, the captain . . . the captain's in a bad way. The other captains are with him and I can't let *anybody* in right now."

"We're here officially, sir, from the aiji's side. I hope you'll convey that to appropriate channels. We're here to help if we can, nothing else."

"Yes, sir." Jenrette's nerves were wound tight, but he let go a pent breath and looked grateful.

"I'm sorry," Bren said. Jenrette's whole life was wound up in Ramirez, and Bren sensed in the man's manner that Jenrette knew they were very near to losing the captain. After all the close calls, this might be the last one, and Jenrette was struggling. "I'm personally sorry, Mr. Jenrette."

"Thank you, sir." The last was a breath, heart-felt in expression.

Banichi and Jago, further removed, meanwhile, were in near-silent communication—likely with Tano and Algini, back in their residence. So was Geigi's security in touch with someone elsewhere.

As for Geigi, his solid, ordinarily cheerful face showed he well understood the heightened tensions . . . not in human terms, but certainly in practical ones. *Love* might not translate, but *man'chi* covered the situation. An association about to shatter translated into Ragi understanding very well, and Geigi's security was understandably on edge, considering their charge here in the midst of humans at a moment of transition. *Geigi's* men reasonably thought they were here to shore up order against impending chaos.

"One fears the worst," Bren translated quietly for Geigi. "Ramirez is alive at the moment, though the outcome seems very much in doubt. I don't think we have to fear a coup as Tamun tried to effect, not even a dispute of succession. Ramirez-aiji's chief of security is distressed, and only wishes to prevent intrusion." This above all else was not only understandable but commendable in a man in Jenrette's position. "These men all answer to the ship-aijiin. Doctors are with Ramirez. We may expect some sort of initial report on his condition."

"Understandable in all senses," Geigi said. "We will attend a decent time, and wait for the report."

Geigi's bodyguards meanwhile still looked uneasy. Their senior spoke to Banichi in low, worried tones. Banichi answered something, and there seemed to be some agreement, likewise some quiet communication to separate staff offices.

So they stood. They waited. There was little room in the place. The infirmary staff remained at the desk, looking anxious. A lone human worker came into the infirmary with a badly cut hand, and hesitated in dismay, but one of Ogun's security directed the man to the desk, and security escorted the worker quickly back into the patient care area. For the rest, quiet prevailed.

"One should set an extra watch on the survivors of Tamun's men," Banichi suggested quietly, in the wake of the worker, and it certainly was a worthwhile consideration. Tamun might be dead in the coup of several years past, but there were still a handful of crew under close watch, minor adherents of the Tamun affair who had had amnesty.

Bren hesitated; but critical as the situation might be, he went to Jenrette. "Mr. Jenrette," he said in a low voice, "my security expresses a concern regarding Tamun's people. I trust we know where they all are."

"At every moment," Jenrette said, and drew a breath and seemed relieved to find something within his capacity to say, yes, that was under control.

So they stood, over a period of minutes after the worker's passage, and the activity in the infirmary's central corridor increased in ways that seemed, from Bren's vantage, to center further up the corridor than the injured worker. Doors opened and closed somewhere in the depths of the place.

Then came a period of ominous quiet, no one speculating, no one saying a word. Jenrette, who had spent years of his life with Ramirez, stood barred from whatever proceeded with his captain, and Bren deeply pitied the man, who struggled valiantly to maintain his calm against evidence that something was wrong.

Then one of the doctors came out into the hall. Two and three others walked behind him, aides, all looking grim and defeated. The doctor spoke to them, then saw the gathering, and came up the hall with a glum expression.

"I'm very sorry. Captain Ramirez is dead."

There were no expressions, no outburst from the men. "Mr. Franklin is in charge," Jenrette said calmly, passing command to Ogun's chief officer. "I'll be reporting to Captain Graham, now."

Jase had wanted to resign his office. Instead—Ogun commanded first-shift; Sabin, second: Jase became third, a heartbeat closer to command, in a ship that had just lost a wealth of its experience and knowledge of very critical decisions.

"Ramirez-aiji has just died," Bren translated for Lord Geigi and for his staff, who kept a solemn silence like the rest. "Command has just passed to Ogun-aiji."

Now the captains emerged from the room down the hall—Ogun, Sabin and Jase Graham. Jules Ogun was a black man, white-haired, square-faced and solid as a basalt pillar; Sabin, a slight woman of grays and dour expression on the best of days, was no different in expression today: they were Ramirez's two contemporaries, both taking matters in grim-faced calm.

But Jase . . . Jase, who'd regarded Ramirez as a father, at least as much contemporary father as he had—looked shaken.

Jase . . . and Yolanda. No one had notified Yolanda Mercheson to be here. And she had lost every bit as much as Jase.

Ogun shook Jenrette's hand, first, then looked at Bren, and at Geigi.

"Captain Ramirez is dead," Ogun said. "Seniority rests on me. Captain Ramirez's policies and orders stand until specifically revised. Mr. Cameron, will you relay that to the alllies? We're on our way to *Phoenix*, to make the official announcement in about ten minutes. We ask you keep it off the com until then, even for your personal security."

"Our condolences and respects," Bren said solemnly. "We understand. —Banichi, the ship-aiji asks no communication until the official announcement."

"One hears," Banichi said. It wasn't to say word

hadn't already passed to his own staff and to Geigi's, before Ogun had requested otherwise, but transmission had been in Ragi, and not apt to slip those channels. Now Bren ordered silence, a respect to the ship that hosted them, as the captains left, Jase left with them, and the aides attended them out.

The foyer of the infirmary was suddenly only atevi and the paidhi, and the language became wholly Ragi, impenetrable to the infirmary staff.

"They're going to *Phoenix*," Bren explained, "to make the official announcement. We should go back to our own offices now, to answer questions as they come to us, Geigi-ji. Ogun holds Ramirez's policies and orders in place, at least for the while. I'll send a courier to Paulson."

Paulson was acting head of the Mospheiran section, Mospheirans having been utterly without representation and without information in this turn of events.

"A good idea," Geigi said. "I'll send, as well, to my domestic staff."

By courier, that was, which didn't breach their agreement. They left the premises and took quiet leave of each other.

"Call Jago out to meet us at the lift," he said. He didn't construe that as violating the silence. "She'll see me home. You go to Paulson. I'll write a note." He searched his pockets for a notepad, found it, wrote as they waited at the lift, a notification for Paulson. A gentler notification for Yolanda Mercheson. He wasn't sure Jase would find the moment, caught up as he was in the captains' council, whisked back to the ship under bewildering circumstances.

By the time you get this you must surely know the sad news, that Captain Ramirez has died. Jase is caught up in official proceedings and incommunicado, as far as I can determine. He was called there, and took it hard. I know he's still in shock, as I know this message must come as a great shock to you; but I am free to write as I fear he is not, under official order, and express, as I know he would, concern for you.

My staff will welcome you at any time and convey messages or provide a quiet rest as you need. Please accept my sincere condolences.

—Bren

Jago arrived before he was done. He gave her the messages, and their destinations. "No danger," he said to her. "But requirements of propriety."

"Yes," Jago said, and went, quickly.

The messages might or might not beat the official announcement, but they would salve feelings. Especially Yolanda's. That Jase was *under official order* might at least take the sting out of the likelihood that Yolanda had not been advised, not even in Jase's mind—he feared so, at least. The look on Jase's face had said that not much at all was in Jase's mind at the moment—nothing logical at any rate. And Yolanda *wasn't* as close to Ramirez as Jase was. Not that he'd ever observed.

The pace of everything had stopped when Ramirez's heart beat its last. Now the rate of decision accelerated again, a set of movements that had immediately to be performed and a set of facts that had to be confirmed, abraded feelings patched, nervous allies reassured even if logic and common sense said there would be no immediate changes in policy.

The announcement came over the general address in the corridors as they reached their own apartment foyer, as Narani was accepting his coat. The intercom light near the door began to flash, in case they might not have heard.

"It's reported," Bren said to the staff in Ragi. Tano and Algini had come out of the security station. "A call to Tabini-aiji. Use my personal codes. I'll speak to the aiji himself if I can reach him."

"Yes, nandi." Tano and Algini would have heard every breath and whisper in their vicinity for the last hour: they were rarely out of touch with their own internal security, and the same, he knew for a fact, for lord Geigi. And likely two messages were going down to Tabini, and Paulson would immediately call the State Department on Mospheira, at the very least.

Then, very quickly, the facts would hit the public news services—no overwhelming shock, because Ramirez was no young man, and his heath had been a serious question for a long time.

But the loss of Ramirez was going to shake everything from the legislatures in Shejidan to the markets in Jackson. Every lunatic who'd been halfway quiet would become agitated and full of speculations. Every paid publicity-seeker who wanted five minutes in front of the cameras was going to jump up waving his arms.

Crisis . . . under control, but yes. They had to get Tabini and Shawn Tyers fully informed, fast, and get a news release organized ahead of the fact.

He went into the security office to write one, and Tano hastened to open up the board and send as he was directed. Algini was monitoring, listening intently, likely to Jago. Banichi was talking to Narani, outside, likewise passing other details, and count Bindanda into that briefing, too. His security was operating on edge, not alarmed, but their nerves were wound tight, all the same. The passing of a lord was rarely without shockwaves, and somewhere in their atevi nerves was ingrained the belief that, species differences aside, some human might at any moment run berserk through the corridors. That it was not that likely to happen in a carefully selected crew was beside the point. If humans failed to do it, some ateva might do it for them, and Geigi surely had his hands full at the moment.

"Lord Geigi has made the official announcement to the staff," Tano reported, then, from his personal communications. "He's assured them that the transition is smooth. He's requested that non-essential staff go to quarters and official staff express appropriate condolences through official channels."

Get off the streets, that was. So to speak.

Get off the streets and be polite to the humans until whatever might happen had happened, simplest way to deal with the crisis.

Points to Geigi for simplicity: no explanation, just clear instruction.

Mospheirans, on the other hand, were likely to populate the bars—there were several devoted to Mospheiran taste—and speculate. Depend on it, there'd be a dozen conspiracy theories in the Mospheiran section by the end of shift, and they'd build on each other.

Among the crew . . . the conspiracy that *had* attempted to take control of the ship, however, was old business and quiet. Tamun was dead. Jenrette had his allies under watch . . . under close arrest, it was likely, by now, without explanation, knowing how thoroughly and quickly crew tended to deal with emergencies. Mospheirans might insist on due process and rights, but as Jase put it, *rights don't mean anything when the ship moves.* Meaning that acceleration and emergency overruled everything. And if it wasn't an operational crisis, it was close to one. Their security would already have a heavy hand on matters, and ship crew would not gather in bars or even talk on the job.

"I have sent to Mogari-nai, nandi," Tano said, seated nearby. "Fifteen messages are in progress to Mospheira . . . one other is in progress to Shejidan."

There was the difference between the cultures, in a nutshell.

Among atevi those fifteen calls home might indicate fragmentation. *Maogishi.* Breakdown of order. Among atevi, that rated attention.

"That's to be expected," he said. "Department heads and a couple misusing their business clearances. Likely corporate calls, too. No threat of fragmentation. Just informative calls."

"The halls remain peaceful," Algini said.

"Best, all the same, if the human work force stays at work—if nothing else, to be near official channels instead of sources in the bars. I hope Paulson uses good sense."

"It seems so," Algini murmured, hardly diverting attention from his console. "There is a request for a communications stand-by. Will the paidhi add an address to Lord Geigi's?"

"I hardly need to," he said. "Lord Geigi will do best."

"I have the aiji's line, nandi," Tano said. "I have Eidi, at least."

Tabini's head of staff. "Pass it to me, Tano. —Eidi-nadi?"

"Nand' paidhi?" The voice, the rational, known voice from the planet was very welcome, water in a cosmic desert.

"Eidi-ji. I need to speak to the aiji, utmost emergency."

"Nand' paidhi, I regret—the aiji is unreachable even to the utmost emergencies. I can bring the message myself, under my own office, nandi, as fast as I can run."

God. Was something wrong down there? Or was it simply Geigi's call, beating his?

"Eidi-ji, Ramirez-aiji is dead, of natural causes. Ogun is ship-aiji now, Sabin second and Jase Graham third. The station and ship are quiet. The transition is peaceful, policies remain in place, but unofficial calls from the Mospheiran district on the station are already going out to the island."

To the news services, one might as well say, and from there straight to the rumor mill. Of all times C1 had been the choke-point, inconveniencing the free flow of information, it failed them now.

"I will bring that message, nandi, as fast as I can, under-standing its importance. Please remain available."

"I shall," he said. "Thank you, Eidi-ji."

The contact winked out, but that was all right. The message would go as faithfully and as fast as the man nearest Tabini could bring it to him. Eidi understood the importance. He had no doubt on that score.

And now the adrenaline more or less ebbed out of him in disappointment and frustration, knowing he could not speak to Tabini and could not get an imme-diate resolution out of the situation. Things weren't going to be simple, not when the changes were this high up the decision-making apparatus.

A week ago, before Tabini's phone call, the whole world had been running more than smoothly. Now . . . with Ramirez dead and Tabini pursuing some arcane piece of internal politics with his predecessor and the legislature that he still didn't understand—and his own family having waited until precisely this week to have a serious crisis . . . things had gone straight to hell.

In the small nook of his mind he reserved for pri-vate business, he did earnestly wish Toby would an-swer his messages and take at least one crisis off the docket. He thought perhaps if their mother was in hospital Toby might be there, and not in touch . . . though Toby was usually better than that, and usually checked periodically through the day, if he'd put a call in . . .

Well, now things were worse on that front. He couldn't call Toby now, not in the middle of these goings-on. Every call he made to the island was going to be suspect as political in nature. He couldn't do *anything* quietly any longer.

But Toby must surely realize that the moment the news broke. Toby would learn what was going on and then figure out that it was all on him to make contact—that it had to be.

"Nand' Gin is calling," Tano said then, a seat removed from him at the console. "She wishes to speak to you, nandi. Will you?"

Ginny Kroger. The *unofficial* and far more competent human power on the station. "I'll take it," Bren said immediately, and picked up an ear-set. "Gin? This is Bren."

"Bren, I'm getting disturbing rumors. Are you hearing any?"

"Ramirez has died. Unfortunately that's no rumor."

"Heard that. But that's not the rumor I'm talking about."

Did he ask her to spill it, and risk the security of the communication?

But if it was a rumor, it was evidently loose, and a little late for secrecy.

"Something you can say here, Gin?"

"Talk in the halls. No secrecy here." Time for a breath. A big one. *"Talk says the lost station's not destroyed, Bren. That it's still crewed. That the captains knew it all along."*

That couldn't be true. It couldn't. His heart stopped a beat.

No.

His deepest instinct said he and Ginny damned sure shouldn't be discussing this over the intercom, but his conscious brain said that if it was in the halls, it was a little damned late for secrecy and about time someone official spoke to the situation. "First I've heard," he said—understatement. "Gin, at this point that's just a rumor. Report anything else you hear: talk to Jago, on my staff. She can translate somewhat." Best if Gin could get to Feldman or Shugart, the official translators, but they were both in Paulson's office, and probably going berserk at the moment trying to monitor atevi internal communications, granted they weren't stalled trying to figure the intricacies of Geigi's message down to Shejidan. "I'll try to trace the rumor through channels." He was in the political stream up here. Ginny wasn't. But Ginny had access to the workers. "You try to trace it through the tunnels."

"I will," Ginny said. *"Keep me informed."*

"Same," he said to her, and punched out as he swung around in his chair to face an apprehensive staff. "Tano, get Jase on com. Use the beeper." Jase carried a pocket beeper they had very rarely used . . . granted Jase had it on him at the moment. If he was in a security lock-down, they might have objected to the atevi beeper. "Send him a code one."

See me. Emergency.

"Yes," Tano said, and punched buttons. "Done, nandi."

"Workers in Gin-nadi's hearing," he said then, informing his security staff, who might not have followed all that transaction in Mosphei. "Workers are carrying a rumor that the ship didn't find the remote station destroyed, as they reported, and that crew remained alive aboard it. That this was something the captains knew."

"Then the source is reputed to be the captains?" Tano asked.

"It would apparently go that high—if it's true at all." Everything they had done here to secure their mutual future depended on the ship's assurances that the aliens that had attacked and destroyed the remote space station couldn't possibly have gained information from the ruin—that the destruction there was complete, and that no data on the location of their own station could have gotten to the aliens.

And if that weren't entirely true—if the conflict out there was still going on—

Banichi appeared in the doorway. "Were workers or crew the source of the rumor?" Banichi, with his earpiece evidently attuned to proceedings in the security station, was completely briefed, and had the salient question.

"I don't know," Bren said. "But I want to know. Jago's out in that section. Is she aware?"

"Now, yes," Banichi said.

There was an increasingly queasy feeling at the pit of his stomach.

Tabini unavailable, Ramirez dead, the newly-arranged captains off to their private councils, and now rumor cast doubt on all their agreements—*all* the ship's many promises and protestations, all oaths, all reassurances—

This was very, very bad news. And it wouldn't raise trust, among the Mospheiran workers.

"We'd better get an official answer for this one, fast.

Keep trying to get Jase. Contact C1 as well as the beeper—" C1 being *Phoenix*-com. "Put me through as soon as possible."

"Yes," Tano said.

"If it's only a rumor," he said to his staff, "it's still serious. If it isn't—we've been lied to. But we don't assume that as first choice. It may be more complicated than that."

Meanwhile Tano pushed buttons and tried to find Jase.

"C1 doesn't respond," Tano said—and *that* was more than troublesome. "I believe a recorded message is saying all communications are routed through station central until further notice."

Not good, not good at all. Bad timing, if nothing else.

"Use the operations emergency channel."

"The ship is fueled, Bren-ji," Banichi pointed out.

Phoenix, once all but helpless, was not, at the moment.

"Gini-ji. Get Paulson."

"Yes, nandi." Algini moved, then signaled him the call was through.

"Hello? Paulson?"

"*Mr. Cameron?*"

"Paulson." The relief was a cold bath. "Rumor's running the halls. C1's not responding. I think we need a little extraordinary security out there. Keep workers on their shifts. No shift-change, do you agree? Restrict the bars and rec areas. Call it a funeral."

"*You've heard the rumor.*"

"What have you heard?"

"*That* Phoenix *lied to us.*"

That wasn't the construction he'd like to put on it. But that was certainly a Mospheiran gut-reaction—a mild one, considering the history of lies the ship had told the colony from the beginning, and the distrust there still was, on the planet, among those whose ancestors had parachuted into a gravity well to escape *Phoenix's* iron grip.

"We don't know all of it. We don't even know a legitimate source, unless you've got better information than we do. As far as we know, it's just loose talk that's gotten started."

"*We've already put the word out: we're holding employees at posts, we've canceled all breaks until further notice and shut down private calls. Supposedly somebody overheard something in the infirmary. Some worker. When Ramirez died.*"

Paulson wasn't the sort of director who heard rumors. No one told Paulson anything. Except now it seemed as if someone had. Someone had told everyone.

A worker had come into the infirmary with a cut hand. And been treated in the area where Ramirez died.

"What did they hear?"

"*Ramirez told Graham that the station out there is still operating. Still has crew on it.*"

Ramirez himself. He was stunned at the indiscretion. But maybe a dying man hadn't had choices.

And what did he say to that?

"Can you find that worker? It's got to be in infirmary records."

"It's not all, understand. Ramirez ordered Graham take no extraordinary measures to keep him alive. Said that he wanted to die. The ship was fueled and he was ready to die. That's what's being said around."

He didn't doubt the details. Now he wasn't sure he doubted the central rumor. A deep and volatile secret had broken out of confinement.

At worst construction, they were betrayed—and not for the first time. His *own* Mospheiran heritage welled up in him, in deep, angry suspicion.

He shut it down. Tried to think instead of react.

"We don't have all the facts," he said to Paulson. "I'm asking, keep your workers exactly as you have, out of places where they can gather and theorize. I'm applying to ship command for a clarification. Talk to that worker if you can. Let's find out the truth."

"When you know what's going on, I'd appreciate a call."

"Deal."

Still no answer to the beeper, and no help from C1. Bren punched out on Paulson and looked at his security team.

"Did you follow, nadiin-ji? Ramirez-aiji in dying said to Jase-paidhi that there were indeed people left behind on the other station and that at that time it was operational. He said, at the same time that he had fueled the ship and that he was ready to die."

"Perhaps we should visit Jase," Banichi said. "Jago and I."

If they were on earth, they would have other recourses—they might well have sent a messenger from the Guild. They weren't on earth, and hadn't, and he didn't want to start a war with the ship-crew.

"We're going to have to advise the aiji," Bren said. "That on a priority. Put another call through, Gini-ji, to Eidi, to anyone you can get."

"Put on the vest, Bren-ji," Tano said ominously, meaning the projectile-proof one that restricted his movements and his breathing, and no, he didn't at all want it, one more ferocious inconvenience in an already maddening hour—but under the circumstances and with what was riding on the lives of a handful of critical personnel, he had no choice but agree.

"I shall," he said. "I shan't forget it, Tano-ji."

"Jase is calling back," Algini said suddenly, and Bren snatched up the ear-set.

"Jase?"

"*Bren. I have a page from you. I'm on my way to a meeting.*"

"Jase. I don't know if you know, but whatever Ramirez told you—it got out. That the other station *wasn't* destroyed, for starters. *Is that true?*"

There was a slight pause. Possibly command hadn't known rumors were flying. He had the impression that, wherever Jase was, he had just stopped dead in his tracks.

"Is the rumor true, Jase?"

"*Bren*—" A short pause. Desperation in the tone. "*Bren, I can't talk about this here.*"

He lapsed straight into Ragi. "You'd better know it's not secret. It's being talked about among the workers. My staff knows. It's being reported on the planet."

"*The* crew *doesn't know, Bren. We* don't know. *Don't let it out.*"

"It *is* out. I understand what you're telling me . . ." That . . . God, the crew had not a clue and the captains had lied to *them*. That possibly Jase had had no clue either, and that was why Ramirez had told him: he could believe that Jase was innocent. "Is that the truth, Jasi-ji?"

"*He said so,*" Jase admitted. "*I was afraid the techs had heard.*"

"I don't know if a tech heard, but a worker in for treatment overheard. It leaked to the *Mospheirans*, Jase, and there's no stopping it."

"*I can't say more than I have right now. Bren, I'm asking you, don't call Tabini yet.*"

"I *have* to call Tabini. Every Mospheiran with a phone link, every corporate officer and the communications techs—they've already been talking. If you don't want a bigger crisis than we already have at this point, Jase, don't cut me off from Tabini. If merchants know it on the North Shore waterfront, damned *sure* I'd better advise the aiji very soon that we have a problem."

"*Bren, I can't say—I don't know—I think Ogun has something to say about this. I have to get to the meeting. Wait. I ask you. Wait.*"

All over the station-ship hookup, communications that shouldn't get out of a security folder were flying back and forth like mad. "Jase, you know where my loyalties are. Tabini ignorant is far more dangerous than Tabini informed." Jase, damn it all, hadn't given an official order in all the years he'd warmed that fourth seat. And didn't want to start now. "You were fourth seat and maybe it didn't matter. But now you're third. Like it or not, somebody who knows had better make a decision. You keep channels open for me to Mogari-nai. You know Tabini. You know the consequences, dammit, if he should be surprised, especially now, especially now, with critical meetings going on. You know that."

"I know. I know. I'll hold your channel open. I can do that. But that's all I can do—I can't go rushing around giving orders right now, I can't, under these circumstances. Tabini misinformed isn't damned good either, Bren, is it?"

"Somebody in command knows the truth. Somebody in ship-command damned well *better* know, Jase, and—hear me on this—there had better not be any surprises."

"There won't be. Bren. Trust me. We're about to address the crew on intercom. Get everybody out of the corridors. Secure all stations. We're asking the same of crew. Wait for Ogun. That's all I ask. One favor. Communication silence until then. One favor. Please."

"You know what you're dealing with. You know. We're secure out there as we're likely to be. But don't lie. Absolute truth to these people. *They deserve it.* Once in several centuries, they deserve it. Hear me?"

A small pause. There was desperation on the other end of the link. *"I didn't know, Bren. I didn't know. Crew didn't know. I'm not even sure Sabin knew. Now I think we're going to find out. Be patient. I'll talk to you tonight."*

Historically, it wasn't only the colonists the Pilots' Guild had lied to, and lied to habitually, as if the truth was the automatic last recourse of any situation, the one commodity always to be kept in reserve.

"Tonight," Bren said. He at least believed Jase—

whose mangled Ragi had contained half a dozen egre-
gious and inflammatory mistakes. He filled in the
blanks, filled them in with knowledge of Jase, where
nothing else would serve.

And Jase punched out to go to his meeting.

He sank back in the chair, dumbfounded—speechless
for the moment.

We're going to find out, Jase said.

*Hell, Jase, worse for the crew this time than for Mos-
pheirans. They set up the station out there. Wasn't it their
ancestors who crewed it?*

*And assuring us the aliens couldn't have gotten any clue
to let them track the origin of that station back to this
star—oh, well, again, just a little cosmetic exaggeration.
Don't worry. It's not that likely.*

Likely they won't come here and blow the planet up.

Bloody hell, what excuse is Phoenix *command going to
tell us all this time, Jase?*

He couldn't let the distress reach his face—first lesson of diplomacy among atevi: never look upset. He
looked at the ceiling a moment, away into white-tiled
space, drew a deep breath, then faced solemn atevi
stares with as much calm as he could muster.

"Well, Jase and I have had a lively discussion. As
you heard."

"One heard," Banichi said.

"Jase says the captains will soon address the crew,
nadiin-ji. Jase says he didn't already know what
Ramirez is alleged to have told him, so I suppose if
we're patient we may hear at least as much truth as
the other captains have to admit. I'm *not* pleased, I

may say, and I'm doubtful how much truth we may yet hear. Jase says we'll have Mogari-nai available."

"What measures shall we take?" Banichi asked him—Banichi had to ask, in matters involving humans. On the planet, among atevi, Banichi was inclined to know.

This one, unhappily, was up to the paidhi to figure out.

But once lied to—*where* did people start believing again?

"One wishes one knew, Banichi-ji. One waits to see what *is* said, one supposes, and then one tries to determine whether we've now returned to the truth . . . or whether there's only a new lie."

"Does this entail a quarrel among the human associations?"

"One isn't sure where the lines are," he said. "One isn't sure whose side certain individuals may be supporting."

"The ship being refueled," Algini said, "they can choose to leave."

It wasn't the first time his staff had raised that point. The last time had been in deep concern when Tabini had agreed to the refueling in the first place.

"There would seem to be very little we can do about it," Bren said.

"We have studied the matter," Banichi said, "and there might be something we can do about it, if we take certain key points within the ship."

Why was he not surprised his staff, independently and quietly, had come up with a theory of how to do it?

And he had to decide, quickly, whether to let them try.

But what was next on Ramirez's agenda? Or what might Ramirez have known? What might be coming in?

Dared they risk damage to the only ship they had—when they couldn't, themselves, operate it?

"We know more than we did, nadiin-ji, but we don't know what Ramirez knew. Before we make such a move, I hope I have time to talk to Jase. And I hope Jase comes to visit us with answers."

8

"**S**hipmates: the captains regret to report very sad news, that Senior Captain Stani Ramirez has passed away suddenly of natural causes, much mourned and missed by us all."

Funereal music had prefaced the announcement. The meeting—Jase's meeting—had produced, officially, an official announcement on every channel, one, channel 2, given over to a captioned translation into Ragi—Jase's, Bren strongly suspected. There was one ill-omened error of numerology.

"*Services are set for 1800h in the crew recreation area stationside. All but critical personnel will have the choice to attend.*"

Phoenix froze her dead—for disposition later, the word had always been. At some time *Phoenix* would send her departed crewmen to a rest that forever escaped gravity wells, but it hadn't happened yet. One assumed that for Ramirez. But they were hurrying to hold the memorial, no preparation. They had an hour.

"*This concludes the funeral announcement. A security bulletin follows.*"

Damned well time, Bren thought.

"*A rumor has arisen which has raised alarm among our allies. The captains have accordingly released the following accurate information. . . .*"

Be truthful. For God's sake, be truthful, Jase . . . *and be accurate.*

"*Certain information regarding the station at Reunion was kept secret due to the necessity of duplicitous negotiation among the allies—*"

God, Jase, *actomen'shi*, not *eshtomeni!*

"*Reunion exists. It suffered extensive damage and loss of life during alien attack. A small number of survivors decided to stay on the station, maintain a general communications silence and effect repairs such as would give them the capacity to refit and refuel Phoenix for a further, longer voyage, only should Phoenix find no resource here.*

"*In the event of a second alien attack or imminent disaster to Reunion, Reunion staff is to destroy the station with all personnel and all records.*

"*Phoenix command has pledged to Reunion volunteers that Phoenix will return as soon as possible to their relief.*

"*A list of known survivors will be available via C1, appended to this bulletin.*

"*The Council of Captains reminds the crew that we have no information as to current conditions at Reunion. There has been no communication with Reunion since, for the protection of all persons.*

"*This is Captain Graham. I ask our allies be tolerant of my foreignness and make all utterances respectful and fortunate in your minds. It is the intent of the ship-aijiin to work closely and frankly with our allies.*"

Well done. Well done, Jase.

As well done as could be, give or take a few glitches

and one piece of accidental honesty—or maybe Jase had thought it best to tell the whole truth.

Jago was back. The whole staff assembled at the security station, leaning in the door, not venturing further into the small room.

The content was explosive enough with the crew—who couldn't be damned happy with what their captains had done in maintaining secrecy. No democracy on the decks, that was sure. No debate about a decision to leave Reunion personnel in place . . . but *Phoenix* wasn't a democracy and never had been.

The list of survivors rolled past. He didn't personally know the names to look for, but he recognized crew surnames. There *were* living relatives—how close, and how emotionally viable the ties that bound them to ship-crew might be debatable, but the names told him there were ties, and the list numbered over two hundred individuals . . .

Two hundred individuals to keep a station alive.

But ask, even so, whether *that* list was definitive or not, or whether even Ramirez had known all the list or all the truth. The history of lies and half-truths was just too old, too long, too often.

And in all his career he doubted he had met a situation as disillusioning and as disturbing.

"I think one may transmit to Mogari-nai," Bren said. Eidi still hadn't gotten back to him, or acknowledged the second call, which might mean that Eidi had had to leave the Bujavid to carry his message—or it might mean that Tabini had heard the first one and wasn't going to acknowledge a subordinate so disorganized as to chase one message with another within minutes. It wasn't for the aiji in Shejidan to beg details. It was for the paidhi to compose his information in logical fashion and send, and he sent. He dropped his information, piece by piece, into the gravity well and waited for some echo, any echo, to tell him how Shejidan was reacting, what Tabini was thinking, what Tabini wanted him to do about the unfolding situation.

Tabini wouldn't rush to judgement or to action. Not in this. Silence meant that the subordinate in question should act as wisely as he understood how to do, and silence meant if the subordinate fouled up—the aiji in Shejidan could change everything in a heartbeat.

Jase, sending, would likely get no better reaction.

So Bren let it be Jase—didn't package the information under his own name, didn't revise word-choices into felicity and good grammar—the aiji knew Jase, and he wasn't superstitious.

But two stations—*two* was one of those damnable numbers that ran cold fingers down atevi spines no matter how modern and enlightened the hearer: *two* hadn't even been in consideration when they were considering building another starship: *three* was the plan as atevi laid it down, and *two* was only a stage they would pass through on their way to three.

Trust atevi personnel to weld a piece of the next frame only to say there was a fortunate third under construction.

He sent his own commentary:

> *Aiji-ma, this is the official statement of the ship-aijiin on information overheard by a Mospheiran worker and*

*rumored afterward by crew and Mospheiran workers
throughout the station.*

*This forebodes policy changes of some nature. I have
received reassurances from Jase-paidhi—and will accept them in your name, aiji-ma—that the treaty
stands, pending further information.*

In everything that came out, he believed that Jase
hadn't known, or Ramirez wouldn't have had to tell
Jase on his deathbed.

And *where* was Tabini?

Engaged in delicate negotiations, and relying on the
steady progress of the space program to convince the
skittish east to add their earnest effort to the west. *Of
course we can trust the ship-folk. Trust me, I know what
I'm doing. I know what I'm asking of you. All of it will be
worth it. We have a firm alliance.*

If Ramirez had set out deliberately to sabotage
atevi-human relations and the *aishidi'tat* at one
stroke, he'd have had to study hard to pick a more
delicate, more telling moment—granted the paidhi
had any true idea what Tabini was up to at the moment.

Now Tabini had to be shown taking control of a situation with the ship-folk, strongly advancing atevi
positions, asserting atevi authority over the
program—all through the paidhi, who was supposed
to do something about it all . . . the way the paidhi-aiji
was supposed to have been a reliable source of information.

And in spite of the quick shut-down of private station communication, he knew the shut-down hadn't

been fast enough, and that it might be the worst thing to do: it might be better just to let the most stupid speculations go out, because at least information would flow. Rumors would be circulating through the island as fast as two cousins on north shore and south shore calling one another on the phone.

"Keep our line flowing to Eidi," he told Algini.

So the messages went down, minute by minute.

And the paidhi had acute indigestion.

Might *Damiri* somehow get a message, before Tabini did? Might he suggest it, if he could ever get hold of Eidi again? He was down to considering uncle Tatiseigi, and maybe blowing Bindanda's cover and asking Bindanda to contact *him* directly.

Damn the luck. *Damn* Ramirez's timing.

Other information was flowing. He had plenty of messages from station offices, from Ginny Kroger, from Paulson, from Geigi, the latter saying, *We have sent to Eidi, but Eidi seems to have left.*

He sent appropriate messages to those individuals on the station: yes, he was going to the funeral service on the station, yes, it was entirely appropriate for atevi to attend.

By all means, the most stringent adherence to forms and politeness, while everything that was going on at official levels stirred echoes—oh, very definitely the deception echoed in his Mospheiran soul—and he was one of the Mospheirans struggling hardest to make this alliance work.

"Is there any protocol in specific we should know?" Jago came to ask him on behalf of herself and the rest of the staff, regarding the funeral. It was given she and Banichi would attend, in their uniform best.

"Solemn faces and silence," he said, "will offend no one. Respect, Jago-ji. We still don't know any other course. I still haven't heard from Tabini. I assume Eidi got the information to him, but I daren't assume everything is all right down there at the moment."

"One might safer assume that," Jago ventured, "than assume things will be peaceful here, if Mospheirans are also in attendance. Tano advised you wear the vest, Bren-ji. All of us are in accord."

"I shall, with no argument. Assure Banichi."

Bindanda and his assistant had laid out full court dress, lace-cuffed shirt and brocade coat, boots and all, and he dressed, had his hair braided. It was a funeral held, to the suspicious Mospheiran mind, much too soon, but he knew it was the ship's procedure, supposed if it was the deceased's choice to be frozen, it certainly provided a corpse for autopsy if questions came later. Concealment couldn't be the motive.

Geigi would be there, with no less honor . . . probably, too, with bullet-proofing, and an urgent desire to get information out of the captains about future steps. So with Paulson. Ginny would attend, without official status.

At least Jase was now a third of that council, and Sabin, the cipher among the captains, the one he least trusted, could not outvote Ogun and Jase. And Ogun . . . Ogun could rely on Jase's vote, if he represented Ramirez's policies, at least until Ogun forced an appointment of someone of their liking to the fourth seat and enabled a tie vote.

It was toward suppertime, and he urged the household staff to eat. His own supper was a packet of crackers, a cup of tea and an antacid.

There was still no answer from the planet.

At 1740 hours he slipped the bulletproof vest on, put his coat on and exited the apartment with Banichi and Jago in their formal attire—in their profession, that meant armed and wired to the teeth, the formal attire made especially to accommodate the tools of their trade.

Safe, he told his nerves.

They met Lord Geigi and his bodyguard likewise leaving their apartment, and joined into a single delegation on their way.

They met Paulson and Ginny Kroger, with Ben Feldman and Kate Shugart, the translators, when they reached the appointed area. There were a handful of section chiefs, a few corporation heads who were probably chiefly responsible for the phone calls down to the planet.

Crew constituted most of the mourners, crew dressed in the blues that were the ordinary for work assignment and an unused set being the best clothing most common crewmen had. They gathered in the dimly lit rec hall . . . no benches, only tape lines marking the rows, and they found their own places, atevi and Mospheirans constituting two rows next to one another. There was no casket, no deceased. That, too, was ship-folk custom.

It was 1755h. They waited quietly, respectfully. The hall by now was packed.

There was a screen on the forward wall. The row of

lights on that end was on, the sole source of light. Ogun came from a side door, Sabin next, and Jase. Their images lit the screen, so that everyone in the hall had a view.

No flowers. No incense. But it came to Bren he'd *been* in this scene and learned absolutely nothing.

Ogun advanced a pace to the fore. Light from overhead fell on his shoulders, sparked on insignia, silvered white, tight-curled hair above a dark, grim face. "We're here to honor Stani Ramirez," Ogun said, and drew a breath as one might for a recital. "Born aboard *Phoenix* in Big System, the year we began Reunion. He saw Deep End, and lived through Good Hope. He piloted a refueler there, and ran operations at Hell's Acre. He took the fourth captaincy there, when Munroe died."

Bren listened intently, taking mental notes on events in the history of *Phoenix* as he'd learned it. His staff understood some of it. Geigi himself did, though the names and the imagery might elude them.

Sabin had her say. "He was an able navigator and a fair judge." Cold, rational praise of a man who had been a good administrator and a good captain. "He resurrected the station here and stood against the Tamun Mutiny." Sabin had backed Tamun's appointment to a captaincy. That small fact passed in polite if knowledgeable silence. "The details are in the log. Captain Ramirez always understated his part."

Last, Jase spoke, a quiet voice, hesitant. "Stani Ramirez knew there'd be critical changes here: and he created paidhiin for the situation without ever having met one. That's why I was born. That's why Yolanda Mercheson was born."

Bren didn't see Yolanda. Hadn't seen her in the crowd.

"If he hadn't foreseen there might be communication problems," Jase said, "if he hadn't trained personnel in languages we never even expected to meet, we could have been in deep difficulty. We could be fighting each other instead of working together. He saw things ahead and he laid a course and he saw the ship through it. Taylor did that to get us here."

Taylor. The pilot that had rescued *Phoenix* from its predicament.

"Ramirez made us able to survive here," Jase said. It was a daring comparison. If the ship had a saint, it was Taylor—and Jase's status, one of Taylor's Children—had the place very, very quiet. Nobody expected much out of Jase in decisions.

But he'd hit them with words. He'd said things no one else could.

He'd mentioned Yolanda, when no one else had remembered her.

And Jase was right. The man who'd refueled the ship and died leaving them a hellish mess—had had the foresight to create Jase and Yolanda to study languages and cultures that had no possible relevancy to the ship; and whether he knew it or not—to make themselves different-minded enough that they could bridge that soft-tissue gap between ship-thinking and whatever they might meet on the planet.

That was Ramirez's doing . . . when most of the ship's crew couldn't conceive that the colony they'd left behind could possibly look at things differently . . . and Jase was right, Ramirez was one chief reason they were standing here, because the alternatives, the pit-falls they could have walked into—were a guarantee of disaster.

For creating Jase and Yolanda, and for listening to them, Ramirez deserved a monument.

And that led to one difficult thought.

Would the man who was that foresighted, that aware of time, distances, and change—then do something so damnably stupid as to lie to them all about Reunion and plan to desert them?

Why? That was the question. *Why* had Ramirez held Reunion secret?

Why had the whole Reunion business not come out when Pratap Tamun tried a coup against Ramirez?

Had Ramirez—unlikely thought—been the *only* captain who knew?

Tamun, the newcomer to the captaincy—he hadn't known.

Ramirez had waited until his last breath to tell Jase—as if Ogun and Sabin couldn't. A way of putting a stamp of approval on Jase? The ticket to legitimacy in the office which Jase had fought every step of the way?

Well, for damned sure Ramirez hadn't intended to be overheard.

The paidhi, better than most present, understood Ramirez's position. Damned if he didn't. In that light, he understood every maneuver the man had made. As a sovereign cure between strangers, truth was vastly over-rated.

Jase finished.

"The company is dismissed," Ogun said.

"What about Reunion?"

The shout came from out of the crowd at Bren's back. Shocked silence followed—about two heartbeats.

"This isn't the place or the time," Ogun snapped, and Ogun had the microphone. The tone went straight to the bones.

But: *"Why?"* a female voice shouted out, and in that breathless hush, didn't need a microphone. Faces were obscured in the dark. Someone else, male, shouted: *"What happened out there?"*

"Nandi," Banichi wanted his charge out of harm's way, and wanted him to move to the wall.

But Bren stood still, even when Banichi nudged him. "I want the answers," he said. Geigi also stood fast, since he did, both of them being fools, and Lord Geigi's security was also hair-triggered and worried.

Ginny and Paulson stood still, wanting answers, too.

And Ogun stood under the light, visible to everyone on the screen, his dark face frowning. Jase and Sabin were at either shoulder.

"Why?" the crew had begun to chant. *"Why? Why? Why?"*

Ogun held up an arm. Held it until, slowly, there was silence.

"One of you," Ogun said, "one of you with the guts to step into the light—come up *here* and ask me."

There was silence a moment. Then a single man moved into the light. *Kaplan*, of all people. One of Jase's displaced guards.

"With all respect," Kaplan said, his voice breaking. It cracked, twice, and he managed to say, picked up by the mike, "with all respect to the captains, apologies from the crew. But—" Kaplan got a breath. "We're with you, captain, we always have been with you, and we go into the dark with you, no question, but here we're being told things different than makes sense to us, and we don't want to leave here with any doubts."

Kaplan had learned *something*, being with Jase. It was a solid piece of diplomacy, a door through which crew and captains could fit together, if Ogun would just take the invitation and pick up the olive branch.

And Kaplan wasn't alone. Polano and Pressman were discernible in the shadows behind him.

"Mr. Kaplan, is it?"

"Yes, sir."

"Phrase your question."

"I'd rather ask the captains if they can explain better 'n we can ask, sir, because we *don't* know."

"Better than you can ask," Ogun said. "Better than you can ask, Mr. Kaplan. Answers are in that list of survivors posted on C1, channel 2. That's as best we have it."

"*It's not enough!*" someone shouted from the back, and Ogun drew an angry breath.

"All right. You want to know the truth, cousins and friends, the truth is, we didn't make the choice, we didn't *have* the choice. Now there *is* a choice to make, a last piece of business from the Old Man, and what we do about it, that's a question before the Council. Every man and woman of you, get to a com station, personally, read the list. That for a start. Then if you can't take orders and accept the discipline that's kept the ship alive, get a parachute and join the colonists. But if you *can* take orders, if you remember who you are and what you are and what your job is, then you know why you don't question an order except through channels. Right now my mailbox is stuffed with *legitimate* questions, which I haven't gotten to, in the heat of the hour, and *no*, I don't have all your answers. The Old Man didn't, either. But I'll tell you flat, I'm not going to have answers coming out piece by piece and individual by individual to be speculated on in the corridors out of context and with half the facts. So, Mr. Kaplan, seeing you've asked a general question, I'm going to respond to those *legitimate* letters of inquiry right now, in full. Stand to attention!"

Human bodies stiffened, unthought, automatic. Noise stopped.

Visitors stayed still, whether or not Lord Geigi understood enough of what was going on. Bodyguards were ready for anything.

"First question," Ogun said. "Are there any survivors who aren't on the list? Answer: we don't bloody know. If there is any other name, and a few could have been born and half grown by now, Reunion's in a position to know. We're not.

"Second question: do the aliens out there know where we are now? Answer: we *hope* not, but you know and we know there's optics, there are antennae, and anybody looking in the right general direction could already have this star in their sights.

"Third question: why did we keep it quiet? Answer:

it wasn't our idea. But the fewer people that know, the fewer can tell—if we were so unlucky as to be asked by the intruders out there. So forget you know.

"Fourth question: why didn't we take Reunion personnel off that station when we had the chance? Answer: that wasn't our choice, either.

"Fifth question: what are we going to do next? Answer: that's an issue under debate. Written suggestions will be considered. Turn them in, cousins and crew. We'll listen.

"End of statement. I've disposed of a stack of memos. Don't expect a written answer. For the rest, consider Captain Ramirez in light of what I've just said, and honor *him* for saving our necks and doing the damn best he could.

"Dismissed."

There was utter silence. Ogun turned and walked off into the shadows. No one moved for a moment, and then crew began to murmur and to stir and to file out the doors.

Not our choice. Not our choice. Not our choice. Bren found his heart beating double time. Banichi and Jago wanted him to move. Lord Geigi was moving. But he felt his legs all but paralyzed.

Not our choice.

Damn!

He moved. He overtook Geigi, outside the door. "One can render what was said, nandi," Bren murmured, head ducked, voice down. "In essence, there's a hint there's a higher authority on Reunion Station that ordered Ramirez to keep quiet. There is more. Shall we meet?"

"Immediately," Geigi said. This most inquisitive, agile-minded of lords had seen enough to have the picture. "Will my offices suffice?"

Geigi wasn't the only one disturbed. There was Paulson. There was Kroger. He edged past Banichi to reach Ginny on the other side of the door.

"Ginny. We need to meet."

"Damned right."

"You and Paulson? About an hour? *Geigi's* offices?" It gave him and Geigi time for discussion.

But it wasn't only them he wanted. He dived down the hall, Banichi and Jago taking full strides to catch up. He'd hoped to catch all the captains. As it was, Jase saw him coming and waited for him in the cross-way of the corridor, all the while the outflow of mourners passed them on either hand.

"I didn't know," Jase said, first off. "I had no idea until the Old Man told me."

"I believe that," Bren said. "I'm meeting with Geigi. Do we get an official presence? It would be useful, Jasi-ji. It would be damned useful."

"I'm *not* one of the captains. I'm a fill-in. I've always been a fill-in, you know that. I don't know if I can get Ogun—"

"You tell me this. Why did Ramirez tell you the truth? Why were *you* on his list to inform? And did Ogun and Sabin know?"

"Ogun knew," Jase said, telling him volumes about relations between the captains.

But the point might finally, accidentally, have hit.

"Jase. Ramirez is dead. He didn't *let* you resign. At

the last, he told you because he wanted you where you are. Can't you figure it?"

"I can't make a decision for them!"

"You'd better," he said, and Jase looked desperate. "That's what you're finally *for*, Jase. It wasn't just a translator Ramirez wanted. You *were* paidhi. That wasn't it. That didn't satisfy him. He named you a *captain*, and navigation and administration damned sure weren't your talents. He knew that. But he wanted someone on the captains' council who could promote understanding. So will you do it? Will you come? Use your voice, negotiate with Ogun, finally *wield* what Ramirez handed you? Dammit, Jase, you're the swing vote when they deadlock. And Sabin backed Tamun. I'm betting they deadlock. *Will you come?*"

"*Yes*," Jase said, and on half a breath— "*Yes*. I'll come."

They all met around the conference table, behind three closed doors and under the watchful eye of Geigi's internal security in the reception area outside. Their own security stood around them, a row against the walls. Jenrette was there with his partner Colby, Jenrette and Colby just having seen their captain to rest. They came now in the service of the most dubious captain to hold the office, but come they did, dutifully and soberly: Ramirez's men, representing that policy. Polano, Kaplan and Pressman were there, officially displaced by Jenrette and his partner, but still in attendance on Jase—one assumed, at Jase's orders, maybe because Jase wanted them under his protection after Kaplan's speech in the assembly. Jase had learned his politics not only on the ship, but in Sheji-dan, and Jase knew the value of a supporting *man'chi*, even among humans.

Impressive contingent. From no power, all of a sudden Jase came in with a solid, determined presence.

So did the aiji's wing—tall, dark and armed. While Paulson and Kroger arrived with no more than Paulson's secretary, a nervous man in a suit, who set a recorder on the desk and ducked back. Paulson was evidently and touchingly anxious about his record-keeping. Everyone else, depend on it, was wired as well as armed.

Small use that was going to be in a mostly atevi meeting. But there was a keyboard, and Bren took it for himself, being a fast typist and the only one completely fluent. There was a single screen, above a low cabinet.

"You first," Bren said in Ragi, and tested the keyboard. "Jasi-ji, if you don't mind. You have the answers the rest of us want. I'll be translating, one language to the other, back and forth." The alphabets weren't at all the same, but the keyboard had a fast switch. He waited to see which language Jase would use.

"Nandiin-ji." Jase looked into infinity for an instant, then locked onto the here and now. It was Ragi. Bren toggled the Mospheiran symbol-set and typed. "I honored Ramirez-aiji. I continue to honor that *man'chi*. Ogun and Sabin may vote me out at this hour—and, nandiin-ji, let them. But Ramirez is gone, and I have to do now as I see fit. And I'll give you what I know, respecting the treaty Ramirez made with the aiji in Shejidan."

I honored Captain Ramirez, Bren typed concurrently in Mosphei'. *I continue to honor him. Ogun and Sabin may vote me out of my post at any time, and I will not contest that. But Ramirez being gone, I have now to do as I see fit. I'll tell you what I know, honoring the treaty Ramirez made with the aiji.*

There was the Jase he'd known on the mainland. Thank God.

"And the other captains?" Bren asked.

"Ogun-aiji will stay by agreements," Jase said, "and I vote with Ogun, generally. In that light, I don't think they will appoint a fourth until Ogun and Sabin can resolve their differences, because I can prevent it, if I vote with one or the other."

"And these differences, nand' Jase?" Geigi asked.

Jase considered. Bren tried hard to think, typing between species-separate languages. Hindbrain was completely occupied, and the rest of the brain just listened, hoping for peace in the room and no repercussions outside, down the line.

"Differences in style," was Jase's answer. There it was: stone wall. Jase *didn't* discuss internal ship politics. That was probably wise, Bren thought. And stopped typing to gather a thought, a necessary question of his own.

"What agreements, nandi?" he asked Jase in Ragi. "And what prevented Ramirez-aiji from removing station personnel from Reunion at that time?"

"I don't know," Jase said, and said it in ship-speak. Toggle-flip. Mental shift, to another world, another entire logic-set. And likely, at the core of his being, Jase hadn't wholly noticed he'd switched. He was thinking *ship* now, and spoke its language.

Bren knew that kind of transaction, at gut level, he knew.

"Ogun knows that answer if anyone does," Jase said further. "I don't."

"Are those remaining on Reunion . . . Guild?" Bren asked bluntly.

"It may be," Jase said faintly.

Pilots' Guild. Bad word with the Mospheirans. Very bad word. Kroger's face and Paulson's said it.

"It's likeliest that's who's in charge," Jase said. "Some portion of the old Guild, at least. Someone or some group of it. Ogun says he isn't sure what passed between Ramirez and station leadership. If he does know anything beyond that, I'm not sure Sabin does. Which is reasonable. She came to her post during the voyage."

"And Tamun didn't know."

"Logically, no. Tamun would have used the information in a heartbeat, if he'd known. He'd have torn the crew apart."

"One believes so," Bren said in Ragi. It was the strongest argument that Sabin hadn't known—Tamun having been her protege. He saw a frown on Geigi's face—perplexity displayed for Jase as an intimate, the dispassionate atevi mask momentarily dropped . . . perhaps on that very point. "Let me add, too, in explanation for Lord Geigi," Bren interjected, "that Ginji and nand' Paulson have a bitter history and an ancestral anger with this Guild, because of past deeds."

"Be assured I'm not Guild," Jase said, flatly, in ship language. "As for Guild being on the ship . . . if it didn't all transfer to the station at Reunion, if there's any vestige of it left on the ship, the majority of us aren't aware of it being here. I think Ramirez intended, by creating Yolanda and me—especially in appointing me where I am—that we break with the past. The whole ship has no illusions what the Guild did. We know the responsibility it bears for the way it dealt with the colonists. Guild leadership dealt badly with crew, for that matter. And for us, for us, in terms of our making our own decisions, the Guild's become just a name on a remote record. A thing captains might still belong to as a matter of course and never think about or reference when we're away from the leadership. What the *crew* wants right now is an answer why we went off and left people who probably didn't have any choice about being left under Guild authority. In that sense, they don't like or trust the Guild any more than you do."

"Second question." Bren interrupted his typing. "What happened out there at Reunion, Jase-nandi, and was it the Guild's fault?"

"The official story," Jase began—that story was in the reports out for years: probably even Paulson and Ginny Kroger knew it inside and out, but Jase laid it on the table, in Ragi, once for all and with recent events factored in. "We'd made some sort of tenuous contact—more a sighting—aboard *Phoenix*, in a certain solar system, and we left and reported it immediately to the station. We did set instruments to listen and watch in that direction, but did not attempt to contact these strangers. They turned up again, or what we thought might be them, at another solar system. We watched about thirty-six hours. We left. We looked at another near star, found nothing. When we went home to Reunion to report, we found it destroyed. Or what we thought was destroyed. We were there just long enough to take on a fast fuel load. *That* was still there, untouched. What we now know, of course—that wasn't all that was left there, and they'd maintained that fueling port and safeguarded the fuel, but crew thought then it was just simply blind luck the refueling port still worked. We thought we were just very lucky to get out of there and travel on toward this system as our refuge. We don't know why the attack happened. If Reunion did anything to provoke it, we don't know. The station couldn't have reached outside its area except by communications. It didn't have any vessel but mining craft available to it. We don't know what happened during the attack, and it turns out it wasn't the devastating blow the crew looking at the station exterior assumed it was. If someone survived inside and intended to stay, clearly they survived with enough resources to assure we could fuel, and they had enough food production to assure they could survive at least two years for us to come here and report back to them. It's been far more than two years, and we didn't show up, and Captain Ramirez didn't tell us there was any time agreed on for us to come back. So maybe there wasn't an agreed time, and they won't be surprised we've delayed here."

"Two years," Bren said.

"Travel time," Jase said. "Round trip."

Bren typed, in Ragi.

"One sees a difficult situation," Geigi said. "And a dearth of answers. Jasi-ji."

"Nandi."

"What of dangers to this station?" Geigi asked. "Is it only against eventualities that Ramirez-aiji wished the ship refueled, or does he foresee these aliens coming here?"

"I don't know," Jase said. "I truly don't know, nandi. I *don't* see that our interests have diverged that far. The crew does feel obliged to you and to this place. This has become—it's become our port. And that's a matter of *man'chi*. But at the same time, there are so many unanswered questions, questions they should have known. If Ramirez-aiji left instructions beyond what he told me, those records aren't within my authority to access. *Ogun* succeeds to Senior Captain. *He* knows, if anyone does. And he hasn't told me. But the gist of it is this—Captain Ramirez did want to go back. He *didn't* want to leave those people behind in the first place, but he didn't know what he'd find here. And when he got here, of course he didn't have the resources behind him that we have now. *That's* changed. Ask the whole planet to trust him, ask you to work so hard fueling the ship—to send it back to the other station in return for some unprovable promise given here—I think he saw from the start that that wasn't going to work. You had to have something of advantage in the exchange. And we had to have something for ourselves."

Among the human faces at the end of the conference room, Jenrette, and Colby, who had been with Ramirez for decades, who might have been with him that long. There was wisdom in shifting the oldest staff to the newest captain on the council. There was, in Jase's whole bearing at the moment, the burden of knowledge Jase might not have had an hour ago.

"The Guild, when it was in power here, wanted to establish this station to support the ship," Jase said. "And when the station rebelled, it wanted to set up elsewhere, at Maudette. When the rebellion became louder and more widespread among the colonists, the Guild wanted to go farther out, to a place they'd spotted only by instrument. That didn't work out. But there was a second choice. And there they stopped to mine and build, nandi. They called their station *Reunion*. *Reunion* of all humankind was what they meant. *Reunion* under one rule."

"Well, *that's* not going to happen," Paulson said, the first word from either of the Mospheirans in what was a deeply troubling—but not damned secret—admission. Mospheirans knew. Mospheirans had broken with the ship over that one point.

"As I said—we don't support it, either, sir," Jase said. "The Guild meant to build and multiply until they'd far outgrown anything that might happen here—and I suppose at the start they hoped to come back and simply absorb all the building and resources that might have developed at this planet, and have their way. They always wanted to have numerous stations, numerous colonies."

"And they would wish to take the mainland for humans without struggle," Geigi observed.

"They're not interested in planets, as such, nandi. They don't regard planets as important to them. They've long dismissed any attachment to any world except as a convenient way to aim and anchor their ship. The resources of a planet, if they can be gotten into space, they're quite keen to have—but only on their terms. Always on their terms."

"They believed they could get all they want elsewhere," Paulson said, "if they had population enough to risk in the mining. But we threatened their authority, and rather than see our ideas create a general disaffection, they left."

"And for this we build a ship?" Geigi asked, when that came into translation.

Jase looked as if he had something caught in his throat. "Ramirez-aiji wanted that ship built. And one also believes, nandi, that the aiji in Shejidan has been aware of the situation at Reunion and that he has other plans for that ship, himself. The aiji in Shejidan—*and* the President of Mospheira."

Geigi sat back, confounded, Bren was sure, both by the information, and that Jase laid it on the table.

Tabini knew. *Tabini knew.*

"And what," Bren asked quite calmly, remarkably calmly, "what do the other captains think?"

"Ramirez knew that the aiji had plans. I think Ogun and Sabin do . . . but I don't think they care that he takes the first other ship, nandiin-ji. I've said I don't think they take Guild orders any longer, but I couldn't absolutely swear to that."

"And you *don't* swear to it."

"I said I don't take Guild orders, nor ever will. I wasn't *born* to take Guild orders."

"Ship-aiji," Geigi said. Only aijiin had no upward *man'chi*—no attachment above themselves: among atevi, it was a biological imperative—only a very, very few had all association in the world flowing toward them.

Fewer still *felt* no upward loyalty. Even Geigi would not claim as much for himself, or not claim it in anyone's hearing—independent as he was, and capable of going into space and operating more or less independent of the whole Western Association *and* Tabini's authority.

While Jase, their modest, quiet Jase, claimed to have no authority above him. Still, he was human, and that maverick separation didn't mean the ability to use authority.

"Understand," Bren interposed, "nandi, his lack of *man'chi* is not innate." It was a debate even among atevi as to whether aijiin were born or taught. "But I think you understand that he's taken a strong position, bringing Mr. Jenrette here, and demonstrating Mr. Kaplan, who spoke bluntly to Ogun in assembly, to be within his *man'chi*. This is *not* required. But he's made that clear."

"What was the full gist of Kaplan's speech?" Geigi asked. "A challenge?"

"A challenge to the silence, nandi," Jase said. "To

the secrecy. And a declaration that Ramirez's policies go on and that they won't change them."

"And the aiji, and the Presidenta, Jase?" Bren asked in Ragi. That admission was what still rang through his nerves, and what he was sure was percolating through Mospheiran suppositions in very alarming fashion—if not through Geigi's atevi soul as well. "*What* did they agree?"

"That the world will have the next starship," Jase said with deliberate obliqueness, "and the ship would get the fuel."

Not quite the exact agreement they'd published. Not the reassurances they'd offered that there was no way the aliens could get information out of Reunion's wreckage.

"All those years," Ginny said. "All those years we've been led along with one story. And now what? What are we supposed to do about this situation?"

"Jase," Bren said. "What *are* we supposed to do?"

Leave the situation as it stood, just betray the people at that remote station, never come back—and coincidentally leave the Pilots' Guild sitting out there on the touchiest frontier imaginable, free to call the shots with an alien enemy, free to create situations that others here at this station had to deal with by their blood and their sweat.

Or find it unexpectedly on their doorstep. There was that possibility, that could no longer be dismissed with assurances.

That station out there had records of the ship's origin at this star. And given a decade or so, an enemy might extract all sorts of information.

There were certain understandings that never had gotten clarified—not as chance would have it, but as discretion would have it . . . little details the atevi establishment had never gotten around to discussing with their Mospheiran associates. But this one— Tabini *knew?*

Tabini *knew,* and the captains up here knew, and he hadn't heard of any agreement?

He had a lot of trouble—personally—dealing with that one.

"There will be pressure from the crew to go back," Jase said. "And Ramirez assuredly intended to. But I think he meant to take control of Reunion. That the aiji in Shejidan and the Presidenta ally with him, if they have ships—and if there was fuel."

He'd forgotten to type. He felt as if the proverbial ton of bricks had landed.

"What's he saying?" Paulson asked. Folly, perhaps, to have held this multi-language meeting. At the worst moments, the translator, personally involved, lost all his threads.

Not a single tit-for-tat, secrecy and refueling in exchange for a ship. It was a whole structured, years-old alliance. With an agenda that stretched from here to forever.

"He's saying Tabini and the President, and I assume the State Department, agreed to refuel *Phoenix* in exchange for title to the second, and I assume third, starship as they're built. I *assume* this is an alliance." He'd never felt what he felt at the moment, this charge of adrenaline that had his hands shaking. Anger, it might be. Humiliation, along with it. And where was his right to be so shocked? He should have known. Friend, agent, translator, diplomat, in whatever capacity, Jase or Tabini or even Shawn *should* have damned well told him, but he had the wit to have dug it out, if he'd been alert enough. "I *assume* this all happened without me."

"And without me," Jase said, exploding the single most natural theory in a word, denying he'd been the intermediary.

"Might you translate, paidhiin-ji?" Geigi requested reasonably.

"*Yes*, nandi. We're speaking of an extensive agreement between Tabini-aiji, Ramirez-aiji, and the Presidenta, an agreement that both Jase and I deny making, but which Jase says indeed existed."

"Yolanda," Jase said, as if it just occurred to him who had, if neither of them had.

Yolanda.

Damn!

"We seem to have agreements in place." Bren typed Mosphei', furiously, while he spoke Ragi. "Yolanda Mercheson is the most likely intermediary who could have done this without our knowledge. We have reasonable suspicion now that the Guild is out at Reunion doing as it pleases, and Ramirez-aiji, commanding the only ship, the only mobile human agency, decided to come here and gain a solid base before challenging Guild authority. As it now seems Tabini-aiji, Ramirez-aiji, and Tyers' office all concurred in this fuel agreement, and in an alliance the terms of which we still do not fully understand. Now we have the robots we'd been wanting, Ramirez is dead, and the ship's been fueled. Jase doesn't know how these elements intersect, but they do clearly intersect, and he and I are both taken by surprise by these events. Understand—I'm speaking without consultation. I haven't been able to get through to Tabini. But above all, in this situation, Mospheirans and atevi need to assert our share of control. We're not going to be dictated to, pardon me, Jase, by the Captains' Council. We want—"

An equal say? That wasn't the half of it. The whole vista spread out in his mind of a sudden, one of those dizzying downhill perspectives, safe spot to safe spot down a hillside while gravity tried to kill them all.

"We want," he said, "more than one more patched-up promise atop promises that didn't work the last time. Ramirez knew what he knew and he wanted certain things: he wanted the agreement. He wanted the station refitted. He wanted the ship refitted. And he created someone to contact the planet." Also the truth. "So the Guild doesn't have any desire for planets. Fine. We do. We care about our lives, the lives of the people we represent here, and the aiji in Shejidan. We represent the atevi, who exist only here in the whole universe—while, pardon me, humans have a homeworld somewhere none of us exactly remember. The atevi don't give a damn what Ramirez cared about and didn't care about. They came up here to take care of their own business, as Mospheirans did, because *Mospheirans* have also gotten fairly attached to the planet they live on. I'm speaking for the aiji, now, officially, and this is what I say.

"Number one, and not negotiable: this is *the aiji's*

planet—which he's chosen to share with humans on a lasting basis. So the ship can talk all it likes about *their* options, *their* choices and *their* problem, but they're doing it on the aiji's tolerance and inside the aiji's consent, and endangering the aiji's interests in this quarrel they've picked out there far remote from us."

"A year or so remote," Jase muttered, and Bren inserted that in the record without a flutter.

"The problem doesn't go away," Jase said. "You can't wish it away. You have to deal with it. We have to deal with it. Ramirez lied to us, but it turns out he *didn't* lie to the leaders of the planet. So it wasn't that he didn't care about the planet's future. But the ship is fueled, and we're supposed to go bring Reunion under our collective authority—"

"And disrupt our lives, our futures," Paulson said.

Bren stopped typing. Lost the thread. Found his argument, Mospheiran to Mospheiran. "Is it only our lives? It may not be our trouble now, but when their trouble spills onto our doorstep, won't the people you represent be very much in favor of having a say—and the power to speak for their own futures? I'm not that surprised to be left in the dark: the aiji has that power, and he's used it. But it's much harder to maintain secrecy on the island, Mr. Paulson, as you know—still the president managed it. Hard to keep a secret on a ship, I'll imagine, too. And Ramirez did. We were all hit. But you know what? In the last ten years, we very different people have developed the same interests, and we've come to work together, and thanks to that secrecy and not knowing any better, we've spent ten years together building resources we now have to use."

Paulson, by his expression, wished he were rather on the North Shore, fishing, at the moment. Paulson was essentially a labor administrator, a financial officer with a background in town planning, who honestly imagined if he did go to the North Shore and went fishing someone else would solve the alien problem. It was Ginny Kroger, the non-official, that he was talking to and hoping for.

And Ginny, rock-solid Ginny, God save her, simply nodded, thin-lipped and resolute—probably thinking of the politics of getting a phone call through channels to the president, past Paulson's legitimate right to do it first and officially.

Trust Mospheira to have trammeled up their lines of action. *Never* trust putting anyone in office who'd act rapidly, and never approve anyone who'd ever let responsibility for a mistake sit an hour on his doorstep. That was the wisdom of the Mospheiran senate, as long as there'd been a senate. They wanted a stainless manager who wouldn't do anything startling or sudden. They put in Paulson.

Ginny's job, in Science, wasn't a senate-approved post, which was how *she* survived. Why she'd come . . .

He suddenly had a bone-chilling surmise that Ginny was *Shawn Tyers'* catspaw, Ginny *and* her robots—not briefed on all of it, likely, but not as deeply shocked as he was.

"We will inform the aiji," Geigi concurred. That was, give or take a phone system that worked, a one-step process, and an atevi lord who *didn't* take quick responsibility for a situation would find Tabini calling *him*.

And what would either of them say? *We now understand, aiji-ma?*

No. He didn't. He didn't understand at all.

9

"**H**as any message come?" Bren asked of Narani, safely in the foyer of their own residence. Banichi and Jago ordinarily found business of their own to attend on a homecoming, usually in the security station, but not at the moment. After the funeral, after the unprecedented meeting they'd just attended, they lingered. Tano and Algini, who'd heard both the meeting and the funeral, had come out into the foyer.

"One regrets, no," Narani said to him.

Nothing from the aiji.

Well, but it reasonably took a certain amount of time for Tabini to ponder the situation, and Tabini was likely still in the information-absorbing stage and hadn't an answer for him yet. Tabini would have gotten his message by now—he didn't doubt Eidi would use his considerable resourcefulness, and very unorthodox channels, if he had to, right down to the several guards that stood between Tabini and a bullet, guards who were linked to Tabini's staff by electronics as constantly as Banichi and Jago were in contact with their own local system. And if everything else on the planet went wrong, it was reasonable to think Eidi might call him back on his own initiative.

"Banichi-ji. Both of you. Tano. Algini."

"Bren-ji."

The five of them went into the security station, and Bren found the accustomed seat by the door while Banichi and Jago disposed themselves next to Tano and Algini. In the background the boards carried on quiet blips and flickers, which his staff understood. He never pretended to know, and he assumed if any of them did involve the answers he wanted, they would tell him.

"It was a satisfactory meeting," Bren said first, for Tano and Algini, in case they entertained any remaining doubts. "It was an extraordinary meeting. But it left us needing answers we can't get, except from the aiji."

"Is there any threat you perceive, Bren-ji?" Almost without precedent that Jago had to ask him that. But they were in a thicket of human motives and deceptions, and on the station, *he* was the best map they had.

"What likelihood, for instance," Banichi asked, "that the ship-aijiin will take action against Jase-paidhi, or Kaplan? One hardly understood everything he said in the ceremony, and less of what others may have thought, but words, indeed, came through."

"Kaplan has qualities," Bren said. "I'm frankly surprised he was the one to stand up and speak."

"Might he have spoken for Jase?"

There was a thought. "I doubt Jase would have asked him to do it—risking Kaplan's personal reputation, if nothing else, though I can understand Kaplan taking the order if Jase asked. I can't explain what they feel; I'm not sure I understand it myself, but ship crew and ship officers are a family association, far closer to atevi in that regard than they are to Mospheirans: I just can't envision what you might call a filing of Intent inside the crew. Tamun—" He saw the question in their eyes. "Tamun was a rogue. He drew people *apart* from the crew. He struck at authority. And some went with him. Some weren't certain of the authority, whether it had integrity, or whether it protected their interests—and by all we've learned there may have been reason for crew to have that perception. There *is* a division of interests between command and crew—they're full blown sub-associations, so to speak, and that's how the schism could develop at all. Kaplan spoke very eloquently about that schism today. He spoke as common crew. He spoke as common crew who felt the aijiin hadn't seen to their interests and hadn't trusted them as they might have expected their own aijiin to trust them."

"True, is it not?" Jago asked.

"Quite true. And Tamun's reasoning did exist in the crew, and dissent and anger may still exist in a few places. That's why the aijiin didn't want to tell the crew the truth—as they reasonably ought to have done. Kaplan, not Tamun, is the man who stands in the breach now. Jase ought to have accepted Jenrette and Colby as his aides and let Kaplan and Polano go on to whatever fourth captain the council appoints . . . that's the way they traditionally do things. Instead, Jase took Jenrette and Colby and not only didn't dismiss Kaplan and Polano from his *man'chi*, he took on Pressman, who's actually a mechanic, not a security man at all. But a friend of Kaplan's and Polano's. This is a major disturbance of the way the captains have done things in the past. I chided Jase for not taking up the authority Ramirez-aiji gave him, but I may have been unjust in that assumption. Jase seems to have made preemptive moves of his own—whether Kaplan forced the issue, and spoke without Jase's foreknowledge, or whether Jase had a hand in it. I rather think the former. And Kaplan spoke passionately and as if it were his own argument. I think Kaplan represents a faction among the crew that's very upset, and Ogun-aiji was smart enough to see he had to answer it right then or see the schism between captains and crew open up again. Personally, I'm glad Kaplan spoke up. I think Ogun is glad he did—maybe even glad the issue blew up then, into the open. Because they aren't atevi, I doubt that the matter goes into a third layer of complicity, with Ogun setting Jase up to set Kaplan to what he did, but it at least turned out to be in everyone's interest for Kaplan to speak."

"Still," Tano said, "Jasi-ji has taken Kaplan *and* his associates, even Pressman."

"More true, I suppose," Bren said, "that he didn't reject Jenrette and Colby and wouldn't cast off Kaplan and his associates. One might ask him, I suppose, but here we have the least senior captain with a security staff outnumbering the rest. An arms race among the captains, one supposes. It's a delicate moment. And possibly Jase took Kaplan under official protection not to save him from Ogun or Sabin, but to keep him out of *crew* politics. Now I think of it, that's the most likely answer. Jase just wants him able to say, *I can't talk. I can't answer that.*"

"Very strange, these humans," Banichi said.

"Mospheira, on the other hand, working with Tabini—did *any* of you know?"

"We did not, Bren-ji," Banichi said. "I assure you of that."

"Do you know anything? Do you *guess* anything?"

"About humans?" Banichi said. "No. That Tabini-aiji might conclude a secret agreement . . . it would by no means be the first."

It would certainly not be the first. And much as the aiji prized initiative on the part of his officers, he would not welcome being found out by one of those officers. Most particularly he would not welcome the whole thing blowing wide in the view of outsiders.

"I don't see what more we could do," Bren said. His security staff was no happier in being in the dark than he was. "I don't see that we were invited to know this, and I have the uneasy feeling that if we walk about too much in the dark we may do damage. But we still have no contact with Tabini. And news has to be all over Mospheira by now. Leaks are bound to start on the mainland. *Something's* happening down there—that's what worries me. But I don't know that we ought to try too much harder to make contact. Things seem to have stabilized here, pending a decision on the part of the captains, and I fear that decision is going to take the ship, the pilots, and Jase and all his resources out of our reach."

"Back to this other station," Jago said.

He hadn't entirely assembled that scenario. But when he did, it either left Jase with them, on this station, and the ship going off to deal with a situation that had flummoxed it before; or, nearly as bad, Jase going out there with the ship and trying to deal with a Guild intransigent and without that sense of loyalty that held the crew together.

In historical times, people had opposed the Guild and met with accidents. A few had been shot, and declared mutineers.

He didn't like either decision.

"If they take the pilots with them," Banichi said, "who will keep this agreement and train ours?"

"Good question, in itself, nadi-ji." He'd fought indigestion for hours. He had a recurring bout. "I don't like what I see. But I don't know what I can do about it, except advise Tabini as I'm supposed to do, and advise Jase as much as I can, and right now I'd say sit for a year and let's think what to do about this. We've *been* here for years. It's not as if it's suddenly an emergency decision."

"Ramirez has made it so," Jago said. "Ramirez has pushed this thing by refueling the ship."

"We can do very little more to contact the aiji," Banichi said, "except to use our last resources—which I will do, if you truly wish to gain the aiji's attention. This is your decision, nandi. Shall we?"

"Contact through the Assassins' Guild?"

No one spoke, but since they didn't deny it, he understood.

"I think we have to move very quickly," Bren said, "and not for atevi reasons. For crew reasons. Most of all for Mospheiran reasons. Ramirez lied. He lied with reason, he lied judiciously, he went through topmost authorities, as atevi understand. Mospheirans accept being lied to in little things, but this isn't a little thing. They could take the Pilots' Guild being in charge on the ship. They almost suspect that's the case. But finding out the ship *isn't* under Guild authority, but that Guild authority survived on Reunion—the most universally detested authority that ever existed, as far as Mospheirans are concerned—that means Ramirez wasn't really making the decisions, or never really was in charge, as they see it."

"Is it true, Bren-ji?" Jago asked.

"Certainly his authority was questionable in direct confrontation with the Guild. And that puts Mospheiran authority into a game far bigger than they bet on. Now we learn the Guild gave Ramirez-aiji orders to come here, maybe to create a base, maybe to prepare a defense—or maybe to gather force to come back and fight some general war against some alien enemy we never wanted to offend in the first place. Who knows now? If Ramirez lied in one thing, in their minds, he could lie in another. Maybe Ramirez-aiji didn't follow all his orders, and didn't intend to. Unless Ramirez wrote his orders in the ship's records, or passed them to Ogun, it's possible no one under this sun knows what the Pilots' Guild wanted Ramirez to do. Jase doesn't know. Ogun hasn't appeared to know. And if Ogun and Sabin don't know— this whole crew doesn't even know that basic a thing—whether they've been following Guild orders all along—or actively rebelling against them. They

don't know the most basic facts of their situation—
and it's not sure to this hour that even Ogun or Sabin
has possession of the truth to give them. I say that on
one fact alone: Sabin backed Tamun into a captaincy,
and if she'd known what Ramirez knew and *told*
Tamun the truth, Tamun could have used it. Tamun
didn't, even when he was losing. So he didn't know.
He grabbed Ramirez. But Ramirez didn't talk. So either Sabin didn't know, or she didn't talk. If she knew
and didn't talk, she didn't back Tamun in the mutiny.
If she didn't know—she didn't have the chance to
back him, and backed out and let him take the fall. In
that case we can't really trust Sabin, and we don't
know as much about Ogun as we wish we knew. So
that's an ongoing question, one we're not likely to
find the facts of until we're far deeper into this mess
than we'd like to be.

"Second point: the longer we sit waiting for an official decision, the more the conspiracy theorists are
going to have a run at this, on the island and on the
mainland, and even up here among the crew, who ordinarily aren't disposed to speculate. If you can use
your contacts to get a message through, Banichi-ji, I
think this is the time to do it."

Ignorance, ignorance, ignorance. It was widespread—suddenly the most abundant commodity in
the universe.

"One will manage," Banichi said. "Will you compose
a message, nandi?"

As if he could come up with a clear, coherent explanation to give Tabini, regarding all the human mo-

tives and actions around him, when the last hour hadn't done it.

But he had to try.

Aiji-ma,

Information has come to light at Ramirez's death regarding the survival of personnel at the distant station, and agreements the gist of which we now possess. We request your immediate personal assistance. The Mospheiran leaders on the station agree to stand together with myself and lord Geigi. We regard Jasepaidhi as our spokesman and channel of information among the ship-aijiin and have confidence in him.

Regarding these agreements, we are at a critical point of decision and request your personal communication immediately, aiji-ma. I cannot sufficiently stress the urgency of this request.

Your silence has made me question the integrity of the channels through which my messages travel. Please relieve my concern, aiji-ma.

He notified Tano and Algini. They achieved a link through C1 to the big dish down at Mogari-nai.

He sent.

And while he still had a link with that dish, he made a scrambled phone call to his own absentee household within the Bujavid's walls.

There he reached an excellent and refined gentleman, Narani's second cousin, a man who moved very slowly, but who found shepherding a skilled servant staff in a long-vacant, perpetually waiting estate his ideal retirement job.

"Nadi-ji," he said to this elderly gentleman, "have you noted any unusual circumstances lately in the aiji's household?"

"*No, nandi.*" The old man was slow, but he had instincts honed in a very dangerous school. Immediately his tone was all business. "*Shall we take precautions?*"

"Rather a small piece of needful intrigue, nadi-ji. Have you been out of the apartment recently?"

"*Not I, nandi, but numerous of the juniors.*"

"I wish you personally to carry a message to the aiji's apartment. Insist to speak to the aiji himself, or to the aiji-consort, or to the chief of security, or to Eidi, in that order, in my name, have you got all that?"

"*Yes, paidhi-ma.*"

"Say directly to any of those individuals that I have not received any communications from official channels, nor has Lord Geigi. Tell Tabini that I have sent repeatedly and beg him call me immediately to consult on business that absolutely cannot wait. If I don't hear some response I must send a courier down on the next shuttle, and I'd rather use all my resources here and not expose my staff to hazard—do you have all that, nadi-ji?"

"*Yes, nand' paidhi.*" The good gentleman had never failed him in lesser responsibilities, and was no fool. "*I will go this very instant.*"

"I'll wait on the line." He had no wish for another of his messages to fall away into silence. And he added, "Be cautious. If your mission can't be accomplished in safety, come back instead and report the hazard to me immediately. I'll keep this link open, meanwhile. Put on one of the staff to talk to me."

"Yes, nandi!"

Another pebble cast into a pond that thus far showed no ripples. He sat, chatted nicely with a middle-aged servant whose knowledge of the estate was limited to the premises. This involved an inventory of linens and an incursion of worms in the kitchen—dubious flour—while the future of the planet followed an old man's lengthy trek down the hall, into the lift, down another hall to the aiji's residence.

"Have you heard any rumors, Dala-ji?" Bren asked the servant. "Any interesting gossip at all?"

Unfortunate question. It involved a bitter, complex intrigue involving the servant staff of lord Tatiseigi and the servant staff of a southern lord, an illicit romance and a threat of invoking the Guild.

It wasn't what he wanted. But the dramatic recital filled the time, step by step through a disastrous and in fact stupid encounter—an affair between rival staffs had to be potent to convince otherwise rational people to create an absolute imbroglio of rival and irresolvable interests.

"So have they resolved the matter?" he asked.

"I think they'll attempt to leave their employ, nand' paidhi," Dala said. *"Because their man'chi is confused. But where will they go? Where will these lords that don't agree allow them to go, since they do know details of the households? Neither will let the other have his servant. Neither will let an ally of the other have his servant. And I don't think anyone else will wish to employ them with these two lords at odds and not trusting them."*

It *was* a royal mess, that was sure, a tragedy for the couple, a disaster for the two lords, who didn't want to be villains, but who couldn't have privileged information spread to houses outside the bounds of *man'chi:* and he was one of a handful on speaking terms with both . . . one of those cases of a matter chasing up the stream of *man'chi* until it finally hit someone of ability to absorb it.

Did he want two lust-driven fools on *his* staff?

But at that moment, for good or ill of the fate of the two fools in question, the old man came back, a little out of breath.

"*Paidhi-ma, nandi—*" A gasp for breath. "*I delivered my message myself to the aiji's major domo, who answered that there is no answer at present.*"

To Eidi, that was. And Eidi replied that there simply was no answer for him.

Had Eidi delivered the content as he saw it, but not the specific wording?

Had he somehow failed to make himself understood?

He could hardly shout from space, *Your conspiracy with the President of Mospheira has come to light, aiji-ma, and the ship-council is in crisis.*

Or, *Aiji-ma, how am I to do my job when you go past me and keep secrets with unskilled persons?*

Am I in disfavor?

It by no means seemed the case when the aiji and the aiji-dowager separately invited him for intimate dinners during his sojourn on the planet.

Nothing made sense to him. Nothing at all.

He signed off with the good gentleman, remembering to say, "Dala-nadi told me a sad story, nadi-ji. It does occur to me that I include the two houses in good relations. If you can tender my offices in mediation, and find a place for two fools, perhaps on the country estate, it would be a good service to both houses." Meaning he would gain favor with both. That was his recompense for agreeing to support the two fools and make use of their labor. "Surmising that they aren't of highest clearance, or Guild."

"One knows the circumstances the foolish woman gossiped," the good gentleman said. *"We might solve it. Forgive Dala for bothering you with the matter, paidhi-ji."*

"I do. And I expect a good outcome. Work to keep you young and sharp, nadi-ji. An excellent job, at all times. Thank you."

He signed off and sat staring at the crisis-littered desk.

He'd saved two strangers and two allied houses from a difficult situation, if they'd accept it, as likely they would. For them he'd worked a divine intervention.

Less fortunate gods seemed to preside over his communications with Tabini, such that he had to ask himself if he had become inconvenient, if his persistent attempts to warn Tabini were only exacerbating a situation Tabini wanted to keep away from his assembled funeral guests.

When were they going home?

When was Tabini going to get back to routine answers to things like, It seems to me, aiji-ma, that the whole alliance is about to explode, and that aliens are going to come and destroy the lot of us?

He got up and went to the security station.

"I've sent. I suppose you followed that."

"One did, yes," Tano said.

"I've done everything I can think of. I confess I'm in some despair of getting through. I did try the staff in the Bujavid."

"We are trying elsewhere," Tano said, "and the message went down. More, we don't know."

"I keep telling myself Tabini isn't going to be pleased with my constant battering at his doors."

"That there is nothing," Algini pointed out, "and no quiet message from the aiji's staff, considering your repeated attempts, is extremely puzzling. Your security is now worried, Bren-ji."

He was not reassured to learn that.

If Tabini had directly ordered silence . . . why?

And at a hellishly bad time. Incredible timing.

Which circumstance in itself, after long dealings with atevi, nagged at the nape of his neck and promised no rest until he knew. Coincidence might operate freely down in the byways of Shejidan, but it only overnighted in the Bu-javid's well-guarded halls.

And what reasonably could Ramirez's death and Tabini's silence have to do with one another?

The Assassins' Guild—one of *their* operations?

Station security, the entire situation of station security, was a sieve. The world sent up workers by the shuttle-load, vouching for them, giving them papers that were as real and true as the two governments wanted them to be, with care and attention as intense as two governments had time and budget to apply.

But it wasn't only the two governments that could

slip some agent into a work crew. Any one of the dissidents, the factions opposed to Tabini, to Shawn Tyers, diehards opposed to the concept of space presence, old enemies against the atevi-human association—they could.

And could they eliminate some random lunatic in the work force, some individual from whom the Assassins' Guild would never take a contract, some lunatic Mospheiran of clever bent and demented purpose?

The thought, foolish as it might be, U-turned him from the study back to the security station, where now Banichi had turned up, with Jago—discussing the communications silence, it might well be: did they have another crisis occupying their attention?

"Nadiin," Bren said from the doorway, "I know it would be possible someone assassinated Ramirez." Assassination, for some of their enemies, was an art form, and infinitely various and subtle. "But what if *Tabini* did it?" He could see it happening if Tabini felt betrayed in his arrangement with Ramirez. And if *that* happened, there were two agencies besides Tabini's own that might carry out the order.

He was talking to one of them.

"An interesting theory," Banichi said.

"We have had assurances from the Guild as late as this day," Jago said, breaking that secretive Guild's rules left and right, "that no Guild member is here without our knowledge."

Unprecedented straightforwardness. He was glad *someone* gave him truth enough to work with.

No Guild member outside his staff.

And Geigi's.

But that *didn't* answer the central question. He was back down the hall toward the study before he sorted that out. For all he knew, the Assassins' Guild had established a regional office on the station, one his staff knew about. Once he thought of it he could not imagine the all-seeing Assassins' Guild failing to take that step.

Damn, of *course* that Guild was here. But how long they had been here and what their activity had been— or how closely his own staff had been in touch with such an entity—there was no use retracing his steps to ask that second question, which would only make his staff uncomfortable. There were some degrees of truth he simply could not expect.

He knew, for instance, that Bindanda was Assassins' Guild, one of uncle Tatiseigi's men, with him for years. He wouldn't be surprised to learn that Geigi's staff held such small, known, surprises. Such infiltrations kept the great houses informed, and *man'chi* stable.

But it was downright stupid of him not to foresee. He'd experienced the increase in number of workers and the increase in complexity of worker management so slowly that the increasing possibility of various atevi institutions making their way up here too just never had taken shape in his overloaded human brain.

Of course, of course, of course—his own security never had told him. If he were ever under duress, would they wish him to know *everything* they could do and *all* the resources they had?

But damned certain there would never be another Tamun rebellion, no more instances where the station dissolved in chaos and bloodshed.

So the paidhi shut up and asked no more questions, but he didn't think it likely Ramirez had died of Guild action. That wasn't the signal he was getting from a staff that *would* signal him if they thought he did need to know.

It still didn't answer the question of Tabini's silence.

Defeat. Just defeat. He wasn't accustomed to running out of resources. He wasn't used to being out of ideas.

He sat down at his desk, started to key on his computer.

Quick footsteps sounded in the hall.

"Bren-ji." Jago signaled him with a hand-motion from the doorway. "Toby-nadi. On the phone."

His brother. Finally. Thank God. He went to the nearest wall-unit and punched in on the lit button. "Toby?" His heart was beating triple-time. "Hello?" He tried to reorganize his thoughts into Mosphei', his mind into a different universe, and far more personal problems.

"I take it by the location I've just reached that you're not coming."

Oh, Toby was not happy with him. Not at all.

"I can't come. Toby, how's mother?"

"Dicey. Really dicey. I don't honestly know."

"Hospital?"

"Hospital? Intensive care since midweek. Since you were down here, damn it, and didn't call, or answer your mail."

It wasn't cause and effect, his presence on the

planet, their mother's crisis. Intensive care didn't take maybes, didn't take mothers assuring their sons were in reach.

And a weak, years-chancy heart did what it did for medical, not karmic, reasons.

"I'm sorry. I'm sorry, Toby."

"Sorry!"

"I want to be there. Toby, I *want* to be there, and I can't, the way things are." Incredibly, one conniving part of his brain said: *Ask Toby what's in the papers; take the temperature of the island; find out what's public—* while another, more sensitive voice, said, *For God's sake, Cameron, this is your mother, your brother. Forget the damn intelligence report and ask your brother the right questions.* "It's one of those bad moments, Toby. I can't explain. You have every right to punch me out when I get down there. I know that. Take me on credit right now. I have to ask it of you."

"Bren, Bren, it's not me. I'm not the issue. Have you possibly got that picture? Mother's really bad. Really bad. She's asking for you and I'm sorry, right now I won't do. She wants you here, and I can't deliver."

Toby didn't say, *You're her favorite son,* but that accusation was in there, right along with, *I've given her all I can give, and I haven't got any more.*

"What she says, Toby, is all well and good, but when I was there, *you* were the perfect son and *I* was the vagrant."

"That's not the point, Bren! She needs you, she needs somebody, and she won't be content with me!"

"If you were the one out of reach, she'd be asking for *you.* That *is* the issue. It's always been the issue, and when you've had any sleep at all you'll know that fact of the universe. I know what you're going through—"

"I don't care what the issue is, Bren. I don't care about those games and I don't care about mainland politics. It doesn't change. It's always something, and I'm not playing. The plain fact is, she's really sick, and she's not faking it. She's not faking, this time. You think I'd call you with a lie?"

Toby was losing his self-control. And in that realization the negotiator who dealt between Tabini and the ship-humans sucked in a breath and made himself hard and cold as ice. "That may be. It may be true. But you listen to me, Toby. You say you're not playing. I'm convinced. I believe she's not. But you listen to me. She has a way of getting all you can give. When she's well, she wants her way. When she's sick she shuts down to just one priority, and that's getting everyone she wants as close as she can get us. No, I'm *not* her favorite son when I'm there. Then you're the best and *I'm* the son that ought to quit my job, get a haircut, and settle down in reach—and you know that's the truth. Toby, brother, you know it's never going to be perfect and you can't ever make her happy. If you need that to satisfy you, you're in for a big hurt. She's just the way she is, and we do what we can, but there's a limit."

"Bren, I've given her my wife and my family. What more is there?"

Bad news. Repeated bad news. "Where's Jill?"

"I don't know." Toby's voice conveyed utter misery.

"At a certain point I don't give a damn. Some hotel some-where. With friends. I don't know."

"Damn. Go find her." He didn't belong in Toby's private life, but he'd had a front row seat for this dis-aster for the last ten years. And this time he said it. "Mother doesn't have a right. She doesn't have a damned right to your life. Let Barb take care of Mother. You get out of there. Go find Jill."

"If Jill wants to go off in a fit, that's her choice."

"Jill's had plenty of provocation, brother."

"You're talking about things you don't know about, Bren."

"And I'm telling you—you and Jill haven't put in all this time to lose it now. Fix it!"

A small, wounded silence. *"Whose the hell side are you on?"*

"Yours. Your life. Your *life*, damn it, which you had going right, and Mother gets sick and there you are." God, it was autobiographical. "I want you to get out of there and go find Jill."

"And I'm telling you I don't give a damn!"

"You listen to me. The kids probably know where Jill is. You know Mother—just make her mad: she'll go miles just on the adrenaline. It's *good* for her, just like medicine."

"It's not funny, Bren. This time it's not funny."

"I'm not in the least joking. Go find Jill. I don't care where she's gone or how well she's hidden or how hurt your feelings are. Just walk out of there, go find her—"

"There's just too much gone on."

"There are too damn many broken promises, Toby.

There's too much someday and not enough right now. I don't care if you get mad at me. You need to get mad at somebody besides Jill. Get mad at Mother. Get the hell out of there and live your own life. You want the truth, Toby? The absolute truth? I didn't call when I was on the mainland because *I've* resigned from the emergency squad. I'm not willing to have my emotions yanked left and right by my family, not by Mother . . . and not by you. I wouldn't believe in a cosmic connection, but it seems to me that this particular crisis happened right after I'd made a public appearance and just when Mother had to have found out I'd been there . . ."

"Bren, *this isn't something she manufactured. It's not a trick. The doctors*—"

"It may not be fake, but it's still something she does to herself. Now she's got you waiting at her doorstep and she's got me upset and pretty soon she'll get well, if she hasn't done it to herself for good and all this time."

"*Damn it, Bren, this is critical.*"

"Oh, I believe you. And you said it: if you divorced Jill and moved in with Mother, you know she'd only have half of what she wants—and so help me, Toby, she's not going to get what she wants from me, and I don't want you there, either. She's got Barb, hasn't she? They've got each other. Tell Barb. Tell Barb *I'm* calling in a favor. Then go call Jill, *call her!* I don't care what you have to go through to get to her or how much you have to take. Jill understands this situation better than you think she does . . . *believe me*, she understands. She's had this all figured out for the last ten years, long before we did. Now *you're* learning Mother's tricks, aren't you? *You* want me there. And I can't give you what you want. That's the truth, isn't it?"

Another silence, one of those absolutely unarguable, unreachable countermoves.

He let it sit there, well knowing Toby wouldn't breach the silence first, but waiting, letting Toby get past the family temper.

Then Toby pulled the only trump card, and simply hung up on him.

Damn, he thought. He was sure he was right, so far as facts went—but not sure he'd handled it at all well, least of all sure that he'd been right to take that last shot.

Damn.

Well, there was nothing he could do and the agenda stayed, his, their mother's, and Toby's, and only the last was still mutable. In the best of situations Toby would let the advice percolate through his hindbrain and get up and make a few phone calls.

Maybe *he* ought to call Barb. She'd written him a note. Opened the door. Maybe he ought to patch up an old friendship and ask his own favors.

He looked to the door of the study, and saw a row of solemn dark atevi faces.

"My mother is ill," he said. "My brother has left his wife to go to her—or his wife has left him." They knew. Little as they understood human customs from the gut level, they knew this was not the desired situation. "I urged him see to his wife. I have some hope that Barb-nadi will be attending my mother. Tano-ji, will you make calls and attempt to locate Barb? She may be at the hospital in my mother's neighborhood."

"Yes," Tano said.

"I'll compose a brief letter. Send it when you have her whereabouts."

"Yes, paidhi-ji."

Oh, so slightly formal.

Jago had offered to file Intent on Barb. But Barb had her virtues. A devotion to his mother was one. He tried not to figure it out. It led places he didn't want to imagine.

But the staff left him in peace, having a mission to accomplish.

He composed his letter at the computer, brief as it was:

> *Barb, I think you surely know Mum's in hospital. I think you know too that Toby's been with her but he's had a crisis. Whatever's between us, personally, I know you've been incredibly good to my mother, and Mum needs someone right now. I'm asking, without strings, on your friendship with her, and thank you for sending word.*
> *—Bren*

He sent it over to Tano, and tried to remember where he had been in business that involved millions of lives.

But that was an equally precarious wait-see. Fate wasn't going to give him a quick resolution. Things weren't up to him to decide. Maybe this time he'd lose his mother. It had been close, from time to time. He'd tried to distance himself from situations he couldn't help, but the grief was still there. He could still remember the woman who'd taken him and Toby on vacations and who'd backed him, however humorlessly, driving her sons in her chosen directions—he forgave that. When he most doubted himself, she'd say—You can do it, Bren. Don't be lazy. Just keep going.

Good advice, mum. Really good advice. Just keep going.

It saved a lot of thinking. Autopilot. Too stupid to kill. Too ignorant to see a defeat staring you in the face.

Sometimes you just ended up beyond the crisis-point not knowing how you'd lived.

Narani had said something about breakfast. Bren found his mind at one moment far, far distant, with a space station that ought to have died and hadn't—and local at the next moment, with a captain who shouldn't have died, and had; and then planetbound, with his staff's warning about Assassins' Guild activity on the station, and Eidi, who he believed had faithfully carried his messages.

And not to forget that incongruous ceremony for Valasi, a funeral years late for a father Tabini had probably had a hand in assassinating.

And the chance that Ginny Kroger was working for Shawn Tyers, who'd landed in the presidency after years of spy-chasing in the Foreign Office.

No. It was a chase around far too many bushes.

Ramirez had been in lousy health since the Tamun mutiny, had been downright frail for months. It took no outside agency to explain why a man with one foot in the grave—so to speak—tipped right over at a bad moment.

He hadn't had that much sleep.

"Nandi," Algini said from the doorway. "Jase-paidhi."

God, he thought. What else?

He'd slept in his clothes, doubtless to his staff's distress. He got up and took the call.

"*Bren*," Jase said.

"I'm here." He already knew it wasn't good news. Jase sounded exhausted. Far from exuberant.

"*The council has voted*," Jase said, and chose a slow, considerate ship-speech. "*We're going out to the other station. Imminently. I moved to delay for a month. I argued. I was voted down.*"

The ship was leaving dock. Leaving the planet.

Chasing after a problem they all, some less willing than others, had in common.

Deserting them.

"Without consultation? Jase, I still haven't been able to get through to Tabini."

"*The proposition's going to the crew in general council. In about an hour. Ogun's wasting no time at all.*"

With the crew suspecting a double-cross, fast movement on some course of action was the best thing. In that sense it was a good thing the council had decided—but the decision was far from the balanced outcome he wanted.

"I'm not upset they're going. But they're moving

without a response from the aiji. He may agree, but he has to give his agreement. I know he's stalling, but there are other issues down there. This is dangerous stuff, and it's going to create ill will."

"*I know. I argued that point. Ogun listened, and he and Sabin still voted together. Departure's imminent . . . granted the crew agrees. And they will. All they have to do is send essential personnel to stations and flip the master switch. They'll run tests. But the ship's in running order. There's not going to be that long a delay. Then there's no more debate.*"

"Are you going? Or are you staying here?"

A small pause. "*I want to stay. It would make some sense. You and I can work together. But on this one, I'm not sure whether Ogun will vote with me, either. I'm not sure he wants someone here who cooperates that easily with you and Tabini. I know Sabin wouldn't like my being left as liaison. But I'm damn little use in operations. I'm putting our conversation into the log, by the way.*"

If Jase was speaking his own dialect, overhearing was always a possibility, and he hadn't said anything he wouldn't say in captain's council.

"That's fine."

"*I'll be talking to Ogun and Sabin, if I can, trying to argue them into leaving me here. Here, I'm useful. It's the best outcome I can think of.*"

"It shows good faith to Tabini, for one other cogent argument."

"*That's a point. I'll use it. I've got to go, Bren.*"

"Thanks. Thanks for the advisement."

Thanks for the advisement.

Was he surprised? Not that surprised.

Breakfast was all but on the table. He'd upset Bindanda if he let it go cold. He saw the maidservant hesitating just beyond the door, an earnest young face, too good sense to interrupt the paidhi in a phone call: she advised him simply by her waiting presence.

"Yes, nadi-ji," he said. He was cold. "My indoor coat, if you please."

She hurried to the foyer closet and brought it back. He slipped it on, unrumpled, morning ritual, calming to jangled nerves. One day and the next. Routine. The cosmic carpet was about to go out from under them, but they observed the amenities. And he'd gotten about two hours' sleep.

Banichi and Jago had likewise turned up for breakfast, black-uniformed, informal and comfortable— armed. They always were. And they probably hadn't slept either.

"We may have to send a courier down to Shejidan," Bren said. "Can we hurry the shuttle? Immediate launch? There's reason to ask."

"One will learn, Bren-ji," Banichi said. "Tano?" Banichi had his earpiece in, and listened, and gave a little inclination of his head. "Tano will inquire during breakfast."

"The ship's going," he said to Banichi and Jago. "They're holding a vote of the crew, but I have a notion it's going to pick up and go. One has to ask still how much of a presence they're going to leave here. We need technical people to continue with the ship-building and train atevi personnel to manage it. So now we learn, one supposes, whether Ramirez-aiji meant us to have a starship at all, or whether it was all show, to get his ship fueled. *That's* why we need a courier. The ship is about to power up, preparatory to leaving. And the aiji doesn't answer me. Has there been any response from the Guild?"

"Nothing," Banichi said. "No answer at all. Which is unprecedented, Bren-ji."

So was all of it. Currents were moving. Big ones. "If Tabini won't answer our messages, then we have somehow to rattle his doors. If we do it in error, if we disturb what's afoot—well, that's a risk. The aiji knows us, that we're apt to try something. And I think now we have to take that risk."

"One understands," Banichi murmured. The two of them took their seats at table, fortunate three. Silver dishes were arranged. Servants stood by to serve, and began with tasty cold jellies in the shape of the traditional eggs. Bindanda had been very clever, and the quasi-eggs were very spicy, and good.

"Excellent," they agreed, and complimented Bindanda's handiwork as the next course proved to be a vegetable and nut pâté surrounding stuffed mushrooms with small split-nut fins. Bindanda put the station's synthetic cheese loaf far in the shade.

Could one even think politics over such a breakfast?

Bren did, and he was sure Banichi and Jago did.

Nor were they quite out of touch with Tano and Algini, having their quasi-fish in the informality of the security station.

Banichi murmured, quietly, urgently, at a hiatus in the serving, "A shuttle has just launched. This would be the freight shuttle."

His heart beat fast. *"Early,* isn't it?"

"A little early," Jago said.

"A courier to *us?*" It made a certain sense, when he was trying desperately to decide who of his staff to send down to Tabini.

It was about damned time, was what.

"One has no information," Banichi said. "Possible that we'll hear before docking."

"Possible that there's a security force aboard?" Bren had his voice down, trying to preserve propriety, but a shuttle: that was a two-edged prospect. "I wish very much that Tabini would consult, nadiin-ji."

Understatement, twice over. Tabini had tacitly demanded one simple thing of Ramirez in return for his support of the ship: control of the station. The ship maintained an iron hand over personnel's comings and goings, and over communications, but atevi were set at key physical points of the station. And to Bren's observation, *both* powers thought they ran things, while Mospheirans thought they ran the business operations and the commerce, such as there was—they did that fairly undisputed.

And everyone had tacitly agreed not to challenge each other, under Ramirez's command.

Now Ramirez was gone, taking all his secrets with him. And now they had their heaviest-lift shuttle arriving, nearly on routine, but just a worrisome little bit early—while the ship-crew was voting to pull the only starship out of the agreement and go off on a mission to stick their fingers into the most sensitive situation possible.

It took a degree of control to appreciate the next

course, and to make small talk with his staff and the kitchen.

And at the time when they often set about their day's business, Banichi and Jago had another revelation from the security station.

"They're reporting only routine."

He had a very strong feeling, all the same. He hated like hell to be taken off his guard.

"Do you know, I think we should arrange to meet the shuttle when it docks, nadiin-ji. I think perhaps we should prepare the third residency, in hopes of putting the aiji's official answer in a somewhat better mood. If we're wrong, we can always power the apartment down again. Tell the station and the ship we're doing some maintenance in there."

"A very good idea," Banichi said.

It took a long time to warm up an apartment once it was mothballed—not quite the chill of space, but certainly the walls grew cold and difficult to warm.

"One assumes, at least," Bren said cautiously, as they entered the study, "that Tabini has taken my advisement and Geigi's utterly seriously. If it turns out to be several hundred of the Guild, I trust they'll take care with the porcelains." Heavy lift as well as antiquity made the decor in the adjacent apartment extravagantly expensive. "But it occurs to me, nadiin-ji, that the *dowager* is available to him, if it weren't for Cajeiri."

Ilisidi had been on the station, understood the station, had met with the living captains, and knew Ramirez face to face.

More, she had authority. Vast authority.

And it was very, very possible, if Tabini had to choose someone for a quick personal assessment of the situation—outranking both the paidhi and Lord Geigi—Ilisidi would be a very astute observer. Very powerful. Surrounded by close, armed security.

If he were in Tabini's place, trying to figure how to get an invasion force onto the station—Ilisidi's prior welcome on the station might make her very valuable.

"Fosterage wouldn't stop her," Jago said. "One doesn't expect it would."

"Dare we think?" Bren asked. "I do think I should meet that shuttle, nadiin-ji."

Ogun and Sabin might take him and Geigi as ordinary obstacles. They'd be damned fools to try the same tactic on the aiji-dowager.

"It would be very bad," Banichi said, "if Ogun-aiji now decided to remove the ship from the station without staying for discussion with us. But we have only verbal persuasion to apply—without doing damage."

If the proposition the ship-council reached was to take the ship immediately out of range of negotiation, there was very little the station or the planet below could do about that decision—short of sabotage.

That wasn't, to say the least, practical—or useful at the moment.

"Dare we call the shuttle?" he asked. "Advise them at least that the ship might be moving?"

"One doubts, for security reasons, they would admit to any presence aboard. We have a number of hours. Is Jase-aiji a firm ally?"

"I don't doubt Jase. I'm not sure, however, that I

dare phone him again." He thought about that a moment. "Or maybe I'd better."

"One can carry a message," Jago said.

"Dare I tell him? Dare we risk there being nothing on that shuttle, after all, but flour and construction supplies?" His security had nothing to tell him on that score. "Maybe I should just tell Jase the truth." Novel thought. "And let *him* suggest what to do about the ship's schedule."

"Is there any doubt at this point the crew will vote to go?" Banichi asked.

"I don't doubt some will vote against it," Bren said. "I don't doubt, either, that enough will vote to go. And the aiji's sending some answer they don't understand could scare them right out of dock and complicate us into a confrontation. If we take the captains into our confidence, make them our co-conspirators, to give a reasonable answer and calm the situation—"

"Against the aiji?" Banchi thought about it.

"To get them to react the way we should hope they react, Banichi-ji. To *direct* their response."

"Assuming there's not flour aboard," Jago said.

"Do *you* think there's only flour aboard?" Bren asked.

"The shuttle disregards its former numbers," Jago said, that most basic of all considerations.

Something, at least, had changed.

There was one other individual he hadn't consulted, one who *might* have a clue to proceedings: Yolanda Mercheson, who'd gone past him and gone past Jase to make secret arrangements. And he thought about phoning Yolanda, inviting her in, asking her point-blank what those agreements were—but he thought he was very likely to find out without that confrontation, and without putting Yolanda in a position of breaching confidences of his aiji and her captains, which he very much suspected she would resist.

Touchy enough, his relationship with the third paidhi—touchy as Jase's, who was her ex-lover, and who hadn't gotten along with her.

Or maybe secrets had driven the wedge.

And secrets had been going on for years.

"I'll try phoning Jase," he said to Jago, and got up and did that.

"Mr. Cameron," C1 said. *"Hold on. You're on priority to Captain Graham."*

Well, *that* was improved.

"Bren?" A moment later.

"Jase, we've got a shuttle inbound. Anyone notice?"

A small pause.

"If you've called to say so," Jase said, being quick, *"I take it there's some concern."*

10

Time enough to prepare. Time enough to advise allies about a conjecture of a conjecture.

Time enough to open the aiji-dowager's former residency, set a vase with hothouse flowers on the foyer table, and arrange a welcome with a small flourish.

For once, Bren said to himself, he had gotten the edge on Tabini.

At least he hadn't been caught with the ship just pulled out and that armed starship facing the shuttle with a disproportional balance of power. The crew had voted. The foregone conclusion was concluded. The ship would move.

But Jase had presented a possible intervening fact—and Ogun, quite unexpectedly, had given a series of small preparatory orders, maintenance checks, numerous of them. And inventory of ship's stores. Dared one suspect cooperation?

The action of an alliance—in which Ogun might be better informed than any of them?

Ilisidi, if it was the dowager en route, had been figured out, anticipated, and factored in with astonishingly little fuss, considering all that was at stake—

Ilisidi, if it was she, having a considerable lot of credit with the ship's crew as well as the station.

No publicity yet. The shuttle wasn't talking about passengers and the ship, busy with its mysterious inventory, hadn't inquired.

Not even certain, while Bren anxiously figeted away the final minutes, that it wasn't simply flour and electronics.

But they were ready when the call came that the freight shuttle would use bay 1, which was personnel.

Time to put coats on, gloves in the pockets this time, servants from Geigi's household and his to give a final touch to the third residency.

Bay 1 was manned and ready.

And they had an entire delegation—himself, Lord Geigi, and Jase, with their respective security riding up in the lift, while station operations went through the customs routine, as if there might be simple workers to process.

Bren thought to the contrary.

Definitely political. Incredibly expensive in terms of fuel and wear on the equipment and the cargo the shuttle *ought* to have been carrying, on its regular schedule . . . but the aiji in Shejidan used what he had to use, and had with increasing certainty gotten his messages.

They waited in the warm territory of the third deck while the docking approach was in progress. Jase met them there, with his own escort, and brought communications tied to the ship.

"Ogun certainly thinks it's her," Jase informed

them. "Whether he's had a communication or not, I don't know, but there's every indication there's a passenger."

They took the lift up into the cold and zero gravity of the core, exited into that vast dock where light never seemed enough.

There they floated, hovering near the residual warmth of the lift shaft. Gloved fingers made patterns in the frost on the handgrips.

The doors down in Bay 3 were capable of receiving anything the freight shuttle could hand them—objects the size of a railway car, easily, and the big cradles were capable of receiving, maneuvering, offloading contents to various sorting areas.

As it was, if they needed more confirmation, workers had rigged the hand-lines for personnel. *They* had instructions from C1.

And they waited. Freezing.

Bren personally tried not to look up, or down, or whatever it was. For the sake of his stomach, he mostly stared at the railing near them and the yellow safety-ropes the workers deployed between them and the shuttle hatch. Jase cheerfully drifted slightly sideways to him, Kaplan and Polano and Colby loosely maintaining position along with him: lifelong spacers, confident of the lines.

"High-ranking," Jase said. "Definitely. There's been an advisement to customs for a wave-through. You're right, Bren. I think you're entirely right. The personnel rig is ready. Dockside has confirmed it. Engaged. They're in."

Jase moved out along the safety line. Bren followed

gingerly, with Jago and Banichi, and likewise Geigi and his company.

They were most of the way there when the shuttle's personnel hatch opened . . . a little in advance of the human workers reaching it.

There—there indeed was Ilisidi, in warm furs. Trust the dowager to devise something stylish for the event.

Elegant, she drifted in the hatch along with Cenedi's formidable, protective presence.

A smaller figure left the hatch past her right hand, too far—too fast—and drifted right off the platform.

And off beyond the lines. Trying to swim, in space.

A child.

A boy.

A protocol disaster.

Bren held his breath as workers scrambled, on hand-jets.

Ilisidi reached with her cane, and almost had the boy. But Tabini's son and heir, someday lord of the *aishidi'tat*, indignantly kicked free and attempted his own salvation. He twisted and kicked in an attempt to reach the door of the shuttle, and banged the edge of the hatch with an unfortunate booted foot.

He sailed off quite spectacularly out of reach—but not quickly enough to arrive anywhere useful any-time soon.

It was chilling cold. The boy was suited only for the brief transit to the lift.

Jase took a hand-jet from a worker and moved out among the rest, while the dowager, who cast an exas-perated glance at the boy's trajectory, glanced at Bren, maintained a grip on the line with the grip of her cane and lifted the other hand in a tolerant, benevolent welcome.

"Well, well. Bren-paidhi. So my grandson told you after all."

"Not exactly, aiji-ma." It was hard not to be distracted, with a desperate rescue proceeding above their heads, if there was an *above* in this steel cavern. But if there was one thing more hurtful to the situation, it was more notice. One only hoped it would not be on public reports. And what did one say, under the circumstance? *Did you have a nice flight?* "Welcome. Welcome from the staff and from the aijiin."

"Did you guess, then?"

"I learned of the early shuttle launch, and who else of such overriding importance would divert a shuttle to visit us?"

He managed to please her, in spite of the incident. An angry shout—the family temper—punctuated the icy air above them. No, Cajeiri had no wish to be hauled down ignominiously by human workers. No, clearly he wished to use one of the jets for himself, small chance there was of the workers or Jase allowing *that*.

Was it possible Ilisidi winced?

"Geigi-ji, too," the dowager said, however. "So clever, the lot of you. I trust I'm in time for the ship."

"For the ship, aiji-ma?"

"Do you think they may bring the boy to the lift in time for us, or shall I leave one of my companions?"

Bren gave a desperate look up—or out, or whatever it might be—since propriety forbade the dowager gazing after this youthful error. By now Jase had the boy by an arm and was towing him down.

"They have him, aiji-ma," Bren said, quite familiar with the dowager's iron notion of propriety. "Jasi-ji." He reached out a hand himself to steer Jase down, holding firmly to the safety line.

The boy was near enough. Ilisidi reached out with the crook of her cane and snatched the aiji's heir close, past her elbow, back into her chief of security Cenedi's hands and Cenedi very smoothly attached Cajeiri's gloved hand to the safety line. Jase braked, not showing off a bit, no, and stayed free-fall in escort of their party, workers hovering on the other side of the line—in event of other escapes, one surmised.

Cajeiri meanwhile was shivering—being smaller, and chilling even after his burst of furious exertion, but no one shamed him by noticing.

They reached the lift car.

"*That* will become the floor," Ilisidi said as they entered the car, and gave the proposed lift deck a stamp of that formidable cane. "Set your feet there, boy! Can you manage that? Thank you!"

Cajeiri turned himself as the adults did and youthful feet went there, just so, with no mistakes this time. It must be Cajeiri's earnest desire not to be noticed for hours and hours.

Court etiquette forbade noticing the event. Security forbade their discussing business of other kinds, so conversation simply and inanely regarded the dowager's flight, the launch weather, the weather in the far east of the Association, which was the dowager's domain—and, in one of those strange drifts of converse, to the hatch of wi'itikiin in recent years.

"Fourteen chicks," the dowager said proudly, as they rode down past third level, "this spring. All living. Those on the higher cliffs we surmise do as well."

"One is glad to hear it, aiji-ma." He truly was glad. It was amazing to him. Ilisidi came here turning their lives upside down even if they'd seen her coming, and told him chicks had hatched on the cliffs of Malguri, making what had been a cold, strange station feel the winds of the world. "One is extremely glad to know it." *What is this about the ship?* he wanted to ask, but this was hardly the place for it, in a lift that station security often monitored.

Cajeiri, likely, himself, destined for Malguri after this sojourn of Ilisidi's on the station, kept meekly quiet, family temper having had its expression—family survival sense having come to the fore.

Tatiseigi's being the boy's first lessons—what wonder the boy was grim, Bren thought to himself. No companions. No play.

Now diplomatic missions, God help the boy.

And what was this, *In time for the ship?*

And why did his heart beat double-time, and why did he reckon suddenly Jase should have heard, and hadn't, because Jase had been out of range.

"This is Jase-aiji, one of the ship-aijiin, who has extended you considerable courtesy. *This* is the paidhi-aiji, whom you surely remember favorably. This is Lord Geigi, whom you have yet to meet formally."

"Ship-aiji," Cajeiri said in meek tones. "Thank you. Paidhi-aiji, lord Geigi. I'm gratified you came."

"One is equally gratified by your courtesy, aiji-ma," Jase said smoothly, in the smooth tones of practice. *That* phrase he knew in his sleep.

"Young aiji," Geigi said.

"See you deal well with these men," Ilisidi said, and nudged Jase with the head of her cane. "Well done."

"Aiji-ma. *Thank* you for coming. We know it's an arduous journey."

"Nonsense. But from a handsome young man, acceptable."

As their feet found the floor with increasing solidity and a slight rotational queasiness.

"This isn't *right*, grandmother-ji," Cajeiri protested. "Are we safe?"

"Safe? Safe? Do you see these gentlemen distressed?" Ilisidi asked, and stamped the deck with the ferrule of her cane. "Conditions to become ordinary to your generation—one is certain, and far too soon. But well that you notice. Well that you notice, all the same."

"*Yes*, grandmother-aiji."

"This generation," Ilisidi said. "Will it be wiser, Geigi-ji?"

"One has hope, nand' dowager."

"Thus far, I doubt it. But I venture, hear? I do venture."

How did one query the dowager when she was in that mood? And where was there time for thoughtful conversation?

And what was this, *In time for the ship?*

The lift stopped, let them out in the ordinary station

halls, but instead of customs and station security, standard procedure when a shuttle with passengers came into dock—Ogun met them.

With *Mercheson* beside him.

Yolanda Mercheson, who avoided eye contact, bowing to the dowager.

"Dowager," Ogun said in the Ragi language. "Welcome to the station."

"Aiji-ma," Yolanda said. "We understand your quarters are ready."

Ordinary workers, mostly Mospheiran, passed by on their various errands—and stopped to stare at a meeting of the paidhiin and atevi aristocrats, and one the widely famous Gran 'Sidi, with her silver-haired chief of security, Cenedi.

And an atevi youngster.

Movement in the hall outright stopped. People stood. A few bowed.

Ogun took out his pocket com and spoke in his own language: "C1, clearance through the halls. Gran Sidi's in residence. Advise the council. Intentions as yet unspecified."

C1 answered, a simple acknowledgment of the orders.

"Nand' dowager," Ogun said then—he had learned that phrase in the dowager's last tenancy. But he gave only a passing glance to the boy—not in as much dismay as confusion, as Bren saw it. Ogun might have heard about the unfortunate incident at the dock, or not: he said nothing, simply bowed slightly, stiffly— never a shipboard or a Mospheiran grace—welcoming the aiji dowager to the station as if this was no surprise at all.

"Her discretion," Ogun said, passing everything atevi to the dowager and to them, and about that moment Ilisidi's cane came down smartly on the deck, the end of her patience.

"Translate," she said.

"A welcome, nandi," Jase said immediately.

"*She's* the representative," Ogun said.

Jase skirted an infelicitous mispronunciation rendering that. One forgave him: the dowager seemed to. She uttered a short, sharp hiss.

"Of course. Does anyone believe we sit in those wretched seats and come to such a frozen desolation in the heavens for our health? A chair. One assumes there will be a chair in a warm place. And supper. I insist on supper. When is the ship leaving?"

"The dowager says yes," Jase rendered it for Ogun, "and wants to know when the ship is leaving."

"Ma'am," Ogun said, a courtesy, "nand' dowager, we have to go through power-up."

This arrived in the Ragi language as *get it running.*

"Get it running," Ilisidi echoed the translation. "One hopes it runs, nadiin, with some reliability. We expect not to break down. Shall we move temporarily into our quarters?"

Not to break down. *We* expect not to break down.

Bren cast Jase a look and Jase seemed no more informed than he was. He cast one at Yolanda Mercheson, too.

"'Sidi-ji," Geigi said. "What is this? Are we informed?"

"Geigi," Ilisidi said, and laid her hand on Geigi's arm in a very intimate way. "Immediately. Your welcome is appreciated, Ogun-aiji—say so, girl! and be done. My bones ache. I want my chair!"

"Yes, aiji-ma," Bren said—she was *his* responsibility, not Jase's—and damned sure not Yolanda Mercheson's, if he had a choice in it. "Captain, she's anxious to be through the festivities and into a comfortable chair, and if there's anything going on I don't know, I hope I *will* know in short order." *What's this about the ship?* was what he ached to ask, but court proprieties kept him from asking outright. "With your permission, sir."

"The dowager proposes to be a passenger on this voyage," Ogun said. "With her entourage. The schedule is under construction at the moment. We'll notify her. We *will* inspect baggage: we have safety restrictions."

"I daresay you should have Cenedi there if you do inspect baggage, sir." He was accustomed to playing along as if he was utterly in the know, but this was the utmost, the most extravagant state of ignorance. A passenger on the ship, *hell!*

And Mercheson mediating when *he* was present?

"Well, he'd better come along, then, soon as the baggage is offloaded," Ogun said.

"Banichi, Cenedi will wish to supervise the inspection of baggage for safety. Jase, can you possibly attend that inspection?"

"I will," Jase said. No better informed, Bren was convinced—no complicity in what Ogun clearly knew. The lot of them acted as if, of course, no surprise, no concern, they'd known from the start; but he improvised at high speed, and disposed someone who knew station regulations, someone who spoke Ragi and ship-language, to attend on security checks to prevent armed conflict.

Meanwhile he kept close with Ilisidi, intending to stay close until he understood at least the general outline of what was happening. *Geigi* was as much in the dark as he was, he caught that from what outsiders might not perceive as an expression. Geigi himself was taken aback by this, and *Geigi* was deeper than he was in Ilisidi's confidence.

Mercheson and secrets and Tabini's silence figured in what was going on—he was sure of that. This *was* his looked-for answer from Tabini, and it was a potent answer.

But, God, send *Ilisidi* off to the remote station for a look-around?

Have her travel alone?

She couldn't speak to them. The ship's crew couldn't speak to her—except Jase. And *Cajeiri* had no place in a situation as fraught with danger as that. Was he supposed to babysit an atevi six-year-old?

What in *hell* did Tabini think he had set up? And with whom? With Ramirez, with *Ogun's* knowledge?

"Dowager-ji," he said, however, as blandly as if they were off to a garden walk, and showed Ilisidi and her party ahead down the corridor, leaving Ogun and Yolanda, Jase and Banichi behind—

Where Jase could find out something, Bren earnestly, desperately, hoped.

"On the ship, is it?" Bren asked, once they were clear of eavesdroppers.

"'Sidi-ji," Lord Geigi said at the same time, "this is a *reckless* venture."

"Perhaps it is," Ilisidi said. She had Geigi on the one hand and him on the other, Cajeiri safely in Cenedi's hands at the moment. "But my grandson has taken this silly notion that nothing will do but that he know what happens in this far place, and he needs someone of sense, I suppose, to make a fair finding. A great inconvenience, I may say."

"A very hard journey, 'Sidi-ji," Geigi said.

And Bren: "This is no shuttle trip, aiji-ma. This is far, far more than that."

"Pish." Ilisidi struck her cane on the decking twice in a step. "And a shuttle trip is far, far more than the inconvenient and uncomfortable airplane I use between here and Malguri. Everything is degree, is it not?"

"The scale of this, aiji-ma," Bren began. "If you please to—"

"Pish, I say. It has to be done. Don't complain for me, Bren-ji. *You're* going."

His heart went on quite normally two beats. Skipped one, as he believed he had heard what he had heard and the import of it came home. "Go with you? I've heard no such thing, aiji-ma."

"You hear it now."

"Yes, aiji-ma." There was, with official orders, only one thing to say, and he said it, calmly, with dignity, though he found breathing difficult.

Go from star to star, into a situation—

—this delicate?

It made a certain terrible sense. But—

"May I inquire, aiji-ma—I do trust the aiji knows your intention."

"And would you question my order, paidhi-ji?"

"Certainly I must, aiji-ma, to leave a post Tabini-aiji. . . ."

"Ha!" The cane stamped the deck. "Constant as sunrise. My grandson knows, I say. And he sends you to see to matters. *I'm* to be in the party to provide the requisite authority."

"Then I shall go," he said meekly. Scarcity of air made his head light. His hands were still cold from the foray into the cold. Now his whole body lost ground, inwardly chilling. "If I can arrange this with Ogun-aiji, who governs the ship, aiji-ma."

"All arranged," Ilisidi said. "I have my baggage. I do suggest you pack quickly."

All arranged?

He had to talk to Ogun. He had to talk to Jase. *Jase* was a fair representative of atevi and planetary interests with the ship's command. *Jase's* skills as an insider, able to deal with the ship authorities, the station authorities, the Pilots' Guild—that was indispensable. Jase natively had all the information, and the cachet as one of Taylor's Children. In Ramirez's intentions, he suspected—it was the other half of what Jase was born to do; and he couldn't let decisions remove that asset from the mission.

Tabini had clearly made his own arrangements.

Tabini had been dealing—with Ramirez—through Yolanda—behind his back.

He had a difficulty. He had a very great difficulty on his hands, if power was flowing into Yolanda's hands.

He had the aiji's heir and a parcel of very different culture being dealt with by a novice. As well send Kate Shugart to negotiate—with the best will in the world, but no resources. No experience.

"And I?" Geigi said. "And I, 'Sidi-ji?"

"My pillar of resolution," Ilisidi said, "the wellspring of my confidence. I shall see you privately. We have matters to discuss."

Geigi should meet with her. But he heard no word about the paidhi-aiji being privy to such a meeting—and in the rapidity with which events were moving, and in the dowager's agenda Bren doubted there was a chink left for an objection, or any change in plans.

At the last moment she might say—of course. Of course come with me. That had to happen. Surely.

Jago was taking it all in: no need to brief her. He was relatively sure Banichi had heard, and he was certain beyond a doubt that Tano and Algini had picked it up through Jago's equipment. They would be taking their orders through what he'd already said. They would be considering resources and making plans much as if they had overheard a casual order to run down to the planet for tea with the aiji. If he *didn't* get a further briefing from the dowager, or if he did, the one thing certain was that planning was already in progress among his staff.

But, God, what was Tabini thinking?

Send an elderly lady to deal with the Guild?

And what was Cajeiri doing here?

A transfer to Geigi's custody, it might be, leaving him on the station, a place of relative safety from assassination, where the boy might gain, instead of the antiquity of Malguri, the modernity of the cutting edge. *That* made a certain sense.

But to ask Ilisidi, at her age, to make this kind of flight—

He tried to calm himself—telling himself that the flight, however distant, was an ordinary operation of the ship, that the time it took, while measured in years, was measured in a year or so, not a decade, not a lifetime. Jase had traveled farther in his life. The ship was meant to do such things, and do them safely. It was routine for the ship.

And there was actually very good sense in sending the aiji's best negotiator, and backing him with the aiji's personal representative, to settle what a diplomat might be able to settle. If the ship-folk had a weakness in negotiation, it was their blindness to outsiders, their gut-deep certainty that the whole universe was like themselves. The ship had already had that illusion shaken, in dealing with atevi: they were a great deal wiser now than they had been when they came into the solar system.

But they weren't the only humans at issue. The station-folk at Reunion likely thought foreignness described the ship's crew, and that diplomacy and negotiation described an administrative meeting.

Not to mention—not even to mention the Pilots' Guild, which had been a thorn in the side of every colonial decision since the accident that sent the ship off its original mission—notorious in every legend of colonial operations since.

And *he* was supposed to deal with that situation?

Was, on the other hand, *Jase* going to deal with it alone? Or worse—Yolanda?

Ilisidi had said something. He sweated. One didn't ever ask the dowager to repeat herself.

But he had to.

"Aiji-ma? I was thinking on the necessities."

"Taken care of, I say. *Pay attention, nand' paidhi!*"

Pay attention. Pay attention. It meant everything. Use your wits. Use your resources. Hear what I'm saying and use your imagination.

"I rarely admit to confusion, aiji-ma." He knew her, at least. "Forgive me. This is an immense surprise."

"Surprised you indeed?" Ilisidi was not displeased by that notion.

"Yet your quarters are ready," he said, "aiji-ma, for at least a brief stay in comfort. Once I heard the shuttle had launched, I said to myself, well, I should be ready."

"Very well managed," she deigned to say, when he knew he had failed other marks—critical ones. "One expects it of such clever men."

As Jago opened the section door, admitting their party to a different, warmer light, and more humidity.

And a corridor within their own security.

"Ramirez is dead," Ilisidi said sharply, stopping just within the zone, the door shutting on the instant. "And this was anticipated. *Ramirez-aiji* knew he would not live to arrive at the remote station, and therefore made certain decisions: *unity of one*, that the ship-fueling must happen. *Infelicitous two and transitional three*, that the powers of the earth must be reckoned with. *Precarious four*, that the aijiin of the world must be admitted to plans. *Stable five*, that he must prepare a very difficult matter for other hands to deal with after his death. Prepare for change, nandiin. Geigi-ji. And you—" This with a thrust of the formidable cane toward Bren. "Your message is long since received, paidhi-aiji. *And* anticipated.

"That Ramirez *would* die," the dowager continued, "*anticipated.* That he would refuse medical help, *anticipated.* That he would likely do so before his aim was achieved, again, *anticipated.*"

"There was no assassination, then."

Cajeiri's eyes were wide, his face starkly apprehensive as he looked from one to the other. But the dowager was accustomed to such familiarity from the paidhi-aiji.

"An old man's choice," Ilisidi said. "Fully his choice. He knew it was likely. So he broached the matter with my grandson, if one can believe that part of the account."

Approached Tabini without him. Tabini had, years since, understood far more of Mosphei' than he ever admitted. And Ramirez had found his opportunity.

"Among essential matters," Ilisidi said, "my grandson demanded the new ship be under construction. I'm told that parts and pieces of it exist up here."

"You passed them while docking, aiji-ma."

A tap of the cane against the decking. "Ramirez wanted the original ship fueled, and this my grandson allowed, knowing Ramirez meant his successor to take the ship and do what he *should* have done in the first place: remove all inhabitants from the other station. This is essential to do. In the meantime," the dowager said further, sharply as the crack of a whip, "*in the meantime, nadiin-ji,* my indolent grandson proposes to accelerate production, *stir* the island's recalcitrant inhabitants to consider their own survival, and simultaneously hope for common sense in the *hasdrawad,* a wonder I shall regret missing, if it transpires. *Mercheson-paidhi* will become paidhi-aiji, as pleases my grandson. *She* will substitute at court and on the station, she and Kate-paidhi and Ben-paidhi . . . students, but adequate students, and Merchesonpaidhi has seemed adequate in these transactions. —Geigi-ji, my grandson has specific requests of you. You've become essential."

"'Sidi," Geigi protested. "Stay? I should stay, while you go?" Geigi was not happy.

"Do invite me in, nadi-ji." The dowager made a slight gesture toward Geigi's apartment, nearest.

"Of course, aiji-ji." Geigi motioned toward the doors, which his security hastened to open.

"Good day to you, paidhi-ji."

She left. She simply walked in. He was not invited. Cenedi, sending the boy inside, shut the doors himself, shutting Ilsidi's security inside with Geigi and his security, shutting them out in the process.

There was nowhere to look but at Jago.

"I am completely chagrined," Jago said. "We were outmaneuvered, Bren-ji."

"I think we were all outmaneuvered," he said. "*Yolanda* set this up. It must be. Ramirez's agent."

"At his instigation, paidhi-ji. We can't penetrate the aiji's closed communications."

"Nor would I ask it, Jago-ji." They were still outside their own quarters. "We should go home."

"Yes," Jago said, and they walked down the corridor to the end, where Narani welcomed them, without any intimation of having heard.

"Rani-ji," Bren said, "I think we shall be taking a trip."

"I have heard so, nandi, at least, so Tano-ji just said."

That fast.

"Pack for me." He made a quick estimation. "For Banichi, Jago, and staff for us. Tano and Algini will manage here, as if we were simply on the planet. But we will need attendance."

"And provisions, nandi?"

"Assuredly." Years. *Years*, and the exigencies of atevi diet. They more than favored alkaloids: they needed a certain amount for good health. "We hope the dowager, who is going with us, has taken some note of our needs, Rani-ji, but we will need a very great amount of provision—I don't know what we're to do." He tried not to allow distress into his voice, or his planning. "I suppose we can draw on station stores." The number of workers aboard meant a backup supply of goods. "Furnishings. There are so many things, Rani-ji."

"For the ship," Narani said.

"You *didn't* know."

"Not until Tano's information, nandi, but we shall manage, never worry."

Never worry. A slight giddiness possessed him as he slipped aside into the security station with Jago. Tano and Algini were at their posts. Surely Banichi was completely aware.

"We've been surprised," Jago said immediately, in a low, reasonable voice. "We need to move quickly. Tano, Algini, you will maintain here. The dowager is surely prepared, but we'll want our own gear."

"Yes," Algini said, and entered something on his console—which might, for what Bren knew, communicate with the kitchen, or Geigi's staff, or station supply.

Tano was sending, too. He was surrounded by staff with immediate objectives: secure, pack, provide. What they needed to know were the numbers. Who was going? Who was staying? How many, how long?

"Can Banichi talk to Jase?" he asked and, assured that Banichi could: "Ask him, in Ragi, nadi-ji, how long the trip, and how great the space allowable for us and for the dowager—and if he isn't now aware of the dowager's intentions to go on this voyage, make him aware, without setting objections in motion. Ogun seems to know the dowager's intentions, but we don't know how much he knows."

"Yes," Jago said, and proceeded to speak to Banichi in a rapid Guild jargon that Bren only partially followed, and that only because he knew the content.

There was a pause, in which Banichi perhaps spoke to Jase, or tracked him down.

All arranged, Ilisidi had said.

Ground . . . so to speak . . . was rapidly sliding out from under his feet.

But Jago had a message for him. "Jase says Ogun-aiji has called an executive meeting and Jase urgently wishes your attendance, Bren-ji."

One wondered if Ogun had contacted Ilisidi—or if Yolanda was not now the primary contact in the information flow he had always managed solo, and if certain things Ramirez had arranged were flowing one to the next, under a dead man's hand.

Damn Yolanda. He hadn't had to wonder about Tabini's intentions for years; but for years, apparently, he definitely *should* have wondered. Ogun might not be in favor of Ilisidi's arrival. Sabin surely wouldn't be. And both of them trying to handle that situation through Yolanda—*assuming*, perhaps, that they could argue with the aiji-dowager and the aiji once publicly committed.

Assumption, assumption, assumption—fastest way to lose a contest one *assumed* didn't reasonably exist . . . and this wasn't personal pride. It was global safety. Species survival.

The alliance could blow up before *Phoenix* ever cleared the dock. The *aishidi'tat*, if thwarted, could bring matters to confrontation, with all the station's supply at issue.

"We'll go," he said to Jago. "Banichi should meet us there."

The game had changed beyond recognition. He had to gather up the overthrown pieces off the floor and get some order in his universe.

Fast.

11

Banichi waited to join them in the executive zone, in that stretch of station corridor where *Phoenix*'s officers maintained executive offices. The captains' active presence was in plain evidence—the number of aides and security outside those offices, along the lighted row of potted plants—a number including Kaplan, Polano and Jenrette, at the end of the corridor.

Banichi, who'd followed it all by remote, didn't say a thing as they met. Only a look passed between him and Jago.

Our Bren's gotten us into the worst mess yet, Bren imagined that glance to say.

Had Banichi and Jago volunteered to be going where Tabini proposed to send them?

Could sane planet-dwelling folk even contemplate what they were now supposed to do?

The discontinuity of previous and future reality was so great it just made no sense to a reasonable brain, Bren thought to himself. He himself didn't yet feel the total shock—hadn't had time to feel much of anything but the pressure of a requisite series of urgent actions.

And he hadn't formed a position—in effect, since Tabini had spoken through other agencies, he found he didn't have one, except that of a subordinate taking orders. And he wasn't used to blind compliance. It didn't feel right.

"Mr. Cameron." Jenrette opened a door and let them in, all three. The aiji and the captains had hammered out the inseparability of a lord and his bodyguard in less pressured times, and no one questioned, now, that Banichi and Jago should enter with him.

Jase and Ogun and Sabin occupied three of the four seats at the end table—Ogun's dark face as glum and sorrowful as it had been during the funeral, Sabin's thin countenance set in the habit of perpetual disapproval. Yolanda was there, whether as staff or as interviewee. And Jase—

Jase didn't look happy at all—not happy to know that all he'd trained for was shifting, that was the first thing: Bren translated that from his own gut-feeling. Not happy to be dealing officially with Yolanda, either, Bren imagined—Yolanda was looking mostly at a handheld unit and not looking at anyone.

The other two captains, Ogun and Sabin, couldn't be happy about anything that had happened lately: not Ramirez's death, not the duty that had just landed on their shoulders; not with the information that had suddenly hit the station corridors.

And had Sabin even been in on the post-Tamun plans until Ramirez dropped dead and Ogun had to tell her? There was no way for an outsider to know exactly what had transpired between those two, or what the state of affairs might be. It didn't look warm or friendly, and Jase's expression gave him no warnings.

"Mr. Cameron," Ogun said. "I trust the dowager's informed you of the situation, and the reason for her presence here. We're not wholly content with it, but the aiji in Shejidan had an agreement with Captain Ramirez that's come into play. It was bound to, once certain information reached the aiji—shall I spell out the terms of it?"

Necessary to switch to ship-language. Necessary to switch to human thinking, to the captains' thinking, in particular, which might figure that *he* held special information *they* needed.

That might be true, if the aiji or the aiji-dowager were including him in their conferences. Perhaps he ought to say at the outset that they weren't including him. Perhaps he ought to admit that he was in the dark.

Pride trammeled up his tongue. And tangled up his thinking, which said, don't state any change to be the truth until you *know* it's true.

"What the aiji intended me to know," he said, "I knew. Apparently he wished me kept in the dark, captain, so I wouldn't make decisions outside my arena of responsibility. It's useful for you to know that, but it wouldn't be correct to extrapolate while things are in flux. The dowager says I'm going with you."

"Are you?" Ogun's tone was flat, but Bren judged that might have been a surprise to them.

"Decision of the aiji. I'm forced to abide by it, sir."

"Decision of our brother captain," Ogun said. Meaning Ramirez, who was dead and not available for argument. And Ogun was frustrated. "So the ship has you, and it has the dowager, and her staff."

"And it has mine, sir. I'll have a staff with me."

Ogun remained thin-lipped. Disapproving. "Sealed orders, Mr. Cameron. Mine to deal with. But by their terms, by what Ramirez set out, in this mission when it might come, the aiji chooses his personnel and his risks." Dared one think that the captains might have sneaked *Phoenix* out of dock without fulfilling Ramirez's pledge to include atevi? •

Certain of the captains might have wanted to do that. Jase would have surely said, in that meeting, that that would guarantee very serious trouble.

"We don't know what situation we have at Reunion," Ogun said. "We don't know but that it's gotten worse—we don't know the aliens haven't come back. We can't communicate, not knowing who's listening. We can't guarantee they've got the fuel for us, out there. So we needed robot miners to refuel us out at Reunion in case the situation's gotten far worse. And we couldn't strip this station of robots, either. That's solved."

Ginny's robots.

"We weren't prepared to have the aiji's *grandmother* as his agent. We'd asked, in fact, for you, or for his officer in charge of station operations. The word was— apparently—" A shift of the eyes toward Yolanda and back. Had communications been flowing freely even after Ramirez's death, through her, and not him? Probably, he thought in distress. "—the word was apparently that the aiji wanted family to represent him. We're concerned. We're extremely concerned about the choice that's turned up. What's *your* opinion of this choice, Mr. Cameron?"

"My opinion, sir, is that the aiji will do what he does. She has authority next to his. I understand that the travel itself isn't that strenuous . . . I hope it isn't."

"There's some strain. She's brought the aiji's *son*, as I gather."

"Cajeiri. Yes, sir. In her care." He dared not argue. It wasn't his place to argue.

"Captain Graham judges her health up to it."

"I'd defer to his judgement in that."

"He also says you can deal with Gran 'Sidi. That you're an asset."

Better than I've been here, evidently.

His own bitterness surprised him. And hurt feelings had no place. He jerked that reaction up short.

"I'll do what I can, sir."

"The fact is," Ogun said, "we have an agreement for atevi and Mospheiran participation in the station *and* in the mission."

"Mospheira has its representative on this mission?"

"Ms. Kroger."

Kroger. The ride up. The miraculous appearance of the robots . . . the president's personal intervention in the production schedule.

Dared one even think that Ramirez's death was timed?

Or self-selected . . .

"Yes, sir," Bren said.

"We have an agreement," Ogun said, "to maintain the station, to continue ship construction and training— and to provide for local shelters. Bomb shelters, Mr.

Cameron, on the planet. To provision them. To contribute advanced materials to be sure there's something left here if the situation goes to hell."

Bomb shelters. For the whole population?

He thought of the Bu-javid. Of the hallways of fragile porcelains and priceless work. Of the culture and civilization of two species. Thousands of years.

And Malguri's stone walls, reared against mecheita-riding invaders. Would there be bomb shelters to save what was there? The wi'itikiin on their cliffs—those delicate nesters, their hatchlings—the blue seas and bluegreen hills? Where were shelters for that?

"The situation remains what it was," Ogun said. "We don't know how safe Reunion is, and we can't risk communications to find out. Command considered an agreement to communicate in event of attack—or imminent destruction—but there was a general fear that if they did transmit, the enemy would know for certain to look for another site, and we don't want them looking. That remains the decision. There'll be no communication. If *Phoenix* gets into trouble—there'll be no transmission. We'll go there, get them to abandon the station and get out of there. That's the mission. *You're* along, Mr. Cameron, in case we encounter something other than the Guild. We take it you would be a resource."

Aliens, that was. He hadn't even polled his own nerves to know what he thought. He was numb—completely numb. "Yes, sir. Probably I would be." *Someone* at least would have the concept of thinking in another language, inside another, non-human skin.

"If it goes well, you'll have an idle trip. We'll depopulate the station, destroy any clue of the direction we've gone, and hope for the best. Unfortunately, of planet-bearing stars in the vicinity, there aren't that many. Of life-bearing planets, this one. Only this one." Ogun leaned back. "So if I were an alien looking for an origin-point for my enemy, I wouldn't have that far to look. And we can assume their optics and their instruments are adequate for starflight, which means adequate to find this star, this planet, if they haven't already done it. And this is our dilemma. If we go back there and pull back our observers, I doubt we conceal a damned thing. But we do send a signal. Don't we, Mr. Cameron?"

"Yes."

"What will we be saying?"

"The point is, sir, we know what we'll be saying. But we don't know what they'll be hearing. We won't know that until we encounter *them* and get a sample of their thinking."

"Ideally we won't encounter them. Ever."

"I'd agree."

Ogun considered that.

"If we're lucky," Sabin said, "they've gone off. If we go back there and stir things up again, we're likely to provoke what we're trying to avoid."

"Also possible."

"We're not ready," Sabin said. "Another hundred years at this star and we might be. But right now we've got two stations, one ship, and no defense. Bomb shelters won't save us."

"Nothing we've got will save us," Ogun said, "if

they take Reunion and come after us. Reunion is sitting out there as a provocation."

"We don't know what they think," Sabin said. "We're assuming."

Sabin happened to be right. Not necessarily in her conclusion, but in her reasoning.

"We don't know either way." Bren contributed his unasked opinion. "They may be waiting for a signal we don't know how to give. They may think they have peace. They may not know what peace is. They may not know what war is and may not know they may have provoked one. We don't know. But we shouldn't go into their territory looking for them."

"Cameron's said it," Sabin said shortly. "My vote is to put a stop to this whole thing and stay the hell out. If Reunion falls, we still have a fifty-fifty chance they won't come after us."

He couldn't swear to the math. But he agreed with the theory.

"We already have the crew's vote," Ogun said. "It's settled."

"It's *only* the crew's vote," Sabin said. "And it's not settled if we decide to the contrary."

"Reunion is almost certainly repairing," Ogun said, "and building. They'll get noisier over time, and they'll outgrow the situation as it is. They won't stay hidden. And whatever they do, they remain ours, *our fault*, whether or not they make good choices and whether or not they can deal with the aliens out there."

"Or if they build one ship, they can come here," Jase said out of long silence. "And they can come here with resources, and ships, and orders we don't want to take."

There was a thought. More than a thought—a nightmare none of them had talked about.

"We don't have to be idle here," Sabin said. "We're building ships of our own."

"So what do we have?" Ogun asked. "A human war on the atevi's doorstep?"

"We don't need to be sticking our nose into Reunion before we've built enough here *or* there to be able to defend ourselves against whatever that situation produces. I'm not saying don't go. I'm saying don't go yet. Ramirez's brought atevi and the Mospheirans in on it all, trying to force the issue, complicating the situation, complicating decision-making on what's *our* business, not the aiji's, complicating the issues, giving us these damned observers, and all of a sudden I'm seeing a hellbent rush away from patience, away from prudence and headlong into a decision to rip authority away from Reunion and try to bring it all here, under ours."

"We'd better," Ogun said. "Captain Graham has the right idea. We'd better bring the decision-making here, before they bring their decisions here."

"And I say wait."

"You're outvoted."

"I know I'm outvoted, as long as Captain Graham says yes on cue. I'm outvoted and we've got a mess. We've got the aiji's grandmother, and now it all involves prestige and power on the planet and could bring the government crashing down if we don't take this woman out there to interfere in our internal affairs. Am I *right*, Mr. Cameron?"

"Yes, ma'am. You're absolutely right about the going. But I resist the characterization—"

"And what the aiji thinks affects how efficiently we get supply. Isn't that always the threat?"

"The aiji's stability does affect things," Bren said. "Agreements made, are agreements, and have to stand. But the question is—and I'm asking, in the aiji's name, agreeing with *you*, Captain Sabin—is this the best decision?"

"Hell, no," Sabin said.

"It is the best decision," Ogun said. "And it's the decision we've already made."

"Sir," Bren said. "Captain Sabin. Excuse me. If we get two, then three, then four decision-makers involved here, pretty soon it can happen that they're not thinking *is this a good idea?* They're thinking, *how can I make sure my party's represented in the outcome?* That worries me. It worries me exceedingly. I wasn't consulted. Ramirez never consulted me . . ."

"That was rather well your aiji's option, wasn't it?" Ogun asked.

Score. "Yes, sir, it was."

"Stupidity," Sabin said, "and *I* vote for keeping quiet, building one, two, three ships, as many as we can—"

"Two, three, and four ships still won't match what a hostile species who's had the nerve to blow hell out of an alien outpost may have," Ogun countered. "We can't *know* what they've got. We can't ever know when what we've got is adequate to protect ourselves."

"We can't *know*," Sabin shouted at him, and pounded her fist on the table, "because you want to go out there and pull our damned observers out!"

"Observers who can't transmit to us without bringing all hell down on their heads," Ogun retorted in a quieter voice. "And who don't give a damn for us over them. As well not have them. As well get the provocation out of there, now, while it looks like *our choice*, an exit with dignity, and not us running for our lives. The decision's made. You can stay here, or you can take the mission."

"It's not official if Graham changes his vote," Sabin said.

Tabini couldn't go back, just withdraw his representatives and say to an already nervous Association—oh, well, we changed our minds. Jase Graham voted no, and we're turning back.

He looked at Jase.

Jase didn't look at him. Jase looked only at Ogun, then at Sabin. And voted. "It stands."

Dammit, Bren thought to himself. But not a wholehearted *dammit*. Only a sane wish this had gone differently—that he'd been in the loop a long, long time ago.

And how could Tabini do this to him?

He didn't know where Jase got his decision—whether obedience to Ramirez and Ogun, whether the sense that once the dowager reached here, there was no going back, but effectively—what could they do?

He tried to think of something. He tried frantically to think of something.

"In a nutshell," Sabin said, "you mean now crew's involved. They know command's lied—and we can't deny that. The atevi have gotten into it. The on-worlders have gotten into it. So the mission's launched, foolhardy as it is. Cameron's told you we're crazy. But we're going hellbent ahead with what never was a good idea, because it was Ramirez's idea, and he committed us to this mission. And now it's all mine."

"I'm sure you'll carry it out with intelligence and dispatch," Ogun said. "I've never doubted that."

"I'll carry it out. And it's going to be *our* decision."

Sabin. Who didn't trust atevi.

And, Bren thought, he had to work with her.

"Excuse me," he said. "Captain Sabin, somewhat to my own suprise, I've taken your side in this. I'm in a similar position: events have gone very far down a track that I can't retrace either. Since we're committed to getting what you now admit to be a Pilots' Guild authority off what you claim to be a wreck of a station, quietly, we hope they'll listen to reason. But let me ask *this* question: where do you stand, relative to them, in making future decisions? Bluntly put, are you going to defer decision-making to them, considering they outrank you—or are you going to retain command of the situation, over their objections?"

Silence met that question. Then: "You know I'm a bastard. I'm in command. And we won't surrender that authority."

"That's reassuring."

"We'll talk, if that's possible."

"More reassuring, Captain. Thank you."

"I'll be staying with the station," Ogun said, "to carry out agreements, to get the shipyard in operation. Captain Sabin will command *Phoenix* and the mission. That's the way it will be. Each to our talents."

Sabin's left eyebrow twitched. Sabin was brilliant with numbers, had a first-rate instinct in emergencies, and set off arguments like sparks into tinder wherever she walked into a situation. She'd backed Tamun. She didn't work well with people. Damned right she wasn't handling the station situation.

"I'll go with the mission," Jase said. "With your permission."

"Well," Sabin said, "well, well. So we *have* an opinion. And we want to be helpful. You want to stay with your atevi allies?"

"I believe I can be useful."

"Mr. Cameron?" Ogun asked.

His decision? God.

"I'm sure Captain Graham would be an asset in either post."

"Are you up to it?" Sabin asked. "How do you suppose *we're* going to get along?"

Jase—Jase with the devil's own temper—didn't blow. He composed his hands in front of him, as carefully, as easily as Sabin's laced fingers. "What I want and what you want, ma'am, neither one matters against the safety of all aboard. A second opinion might be useful. Someone is likely going to do something or propose something to the detriment of the agreements we have back here at this star. I know those agreements, I know the ship's needs, the station's needs, and I have an expertise that's more critical there than here."

"You have an expertise. We've got a translator, in Mr. Cameron."

"That's not what he does. As a ship, we don't see what he does. We don't *understand* people who aren't under the same set of orders for the last several hundred years. Diplomacy—diplomacy, captain. Negotiation. Mr. Cameron's good at it. So am I. And I can sit here on this station, helping Ms. Mercheson translate, as I assume she'll stay in that capacity, or I can go out there, giving you a backup, helping explain to Mr. Cameron and the aiji-dowager how the crew works and how the Guild works. And helping arrive at a reasonable conclusion."

Sabin didn't say a thing, only listened, hands still clasped, still easy. "We're not negotiating my orders, Captain Graham. We're not having any other orders."

"We don't know what we'll meet. And I know routine operations."

"Let's hope for routine," Sabin said glumly. "Keep the dowager quiet, and you'll be a use." Sabin's cold eyes shot straight at Bren. "So you're going. What kind of space allotment do you need?"

On the spot? Without calculations? "Myself, two security, four staff. The dowager—she has triple that."

"No outside equipment," Sabin said, "be clear on that. No electronics independent of our boards. That's a safety issue."

"We exist within the station without disruption and

my staff is well aware of the issues. I'm sure we can exist within the ship. These are extremely skilled personnel, captain. An asset, in the remote event diplomacy doesn't work. Of all else you leave behind, I'd advise you take all of our equipment you can lay hands on, along with our specialized staff and our weapons, that we know how to use with very great expertise. And they'll be at your service, should you need them."

Ship's security was electronically difficult to penetrate. Personally—ship's security had met Banichi and Jago, who were listening to scraps of all that was going on, and didn't prevent them doing what they did.

"Under whose orders?" Sabin asked. "I'll have *that* settled, Mr. Cameron. Yours? Or a planet-dwelling grandmother with a notion she gives the orders?"

"The dowager's security talks to my security, and won't do anything that risks the safety of the ship—or that contradicts a ship-aiji's orders. There *is* a respect for aijiin on staff, Captain. A profound respect for orders. Ship-safety is in your hands. Safety of outside accesses, while you're docked—I'd frankly recommend your people take advice from mine in establishing a barrier against intrusion. We're better than yours, at that."

He took a chance, but he'd spent significant time dealing with Sabin, and one couldn't insult a woman whose god was objectivity. She listened, absorbed, analyzed.

"Appearances," Sabin said.

"We can be discreet. Freeing other personnel on your side."

"Son of a bitch," Sabin said. Then: "The whole colonial residency's vacant on this mission. You won't be cramped. Your whole station residence couldn't even make a blip on the ship's fuel needs or add that much to its mass. Take anything you want."

"It won't be that extensive," he said.

"Kroger will have an establishment. *Technical* people. Certain number of robot support techs. Gear. A lot of it. *Her* staff has bulk."

He didn't, personally, want to spend the rest of a shortened life sitting at some remote star, reduplicating the plight of the ancestors. He was very, very glad Kroger and her robots were available.

"Station's fuel needs will be attended to," Ogun said, "with the older robots. We're committed to keep building here. Ms. Mercheson will be liaison with the atevi authorities, and with the president."

"I'd advise splitting that job, sir. Tom Lund would be very good on the Mospheiran side."

Ogun knew Lund.

"Reasonable recommendation. I'll talk with the authorities down there."

"It's going to be dicey with Shejidan," Bren said, took a breath. "I'll advise one thing, Captain Ogun, with all good will: that you take Mercheson's advice and tell the absolute whole truth at least to her." He saw the resentment building in a basically honest man, and plowed ahead. "Captain, if you make those leaders down on the planet look as if they don't know what the truth is, you'll not only *kill* any hope you have of dealing with those governments, you'll likely bring both governments down and have chaos down there that three hundred years won't fix, *no* workers, *no* fuel, *no* supplies at all, ever. I can't stress enough how precarious the situation can turn and how fast. And I am so relieved the ship is leaving you here to take charge of it. —Ms. Mercheson, you understand me."

He'd changed from questioning Ogun's expertise to praising it so fast that Ogun was still absorbing it. And wasn't coming to a conclusion. Yet.

"Yes, sir," Yolanda said, scarcely audible, and cleared her throat. "Yes, sir. He's right."

"We don't take threats," Sabin said.

"Captain," Bren said, "excuse me, but as the workers put it—gravity doesn't care. Gravity doesn't care, nor do the facts that govern the planet. If you want supply, tell the truth to your translators and let them figure out how to translate the situation in terms the people will understand. Conversely, listen when they say they can't say a certain thing, and suggest something that will be better understood. Most of all set a course and keep it. That's my condensed advice. Ramirez surprised us once. About one more lie injected into the situation is going to exceed the possibility of leaders ever explaining anything to them."

"Is the truth going to make them happier?" Ogun asked.

There was a deep-seated Guild-engendered conviction behind that question, a philosophy that had never done the ship any favors.

"You'd be surprised, Captain. Most Mospheirans—

most atevi, for that matter—won't ever care about anything political until their own supper's threatened. Once it is, you've got hundreds of thousands of people each with ideas and no disposition to compromise until their needs are satisfied. That's the way it's always been, and that's *why* my ancestors had rather trust an untested parachute capsule than trust one more rational argument from the Pilots' Guild. People don't give a damn what you're doing as long as they're confident where you're going. Atevi are fonder of intrigue than Mospheirans, but you've hit your limit of surprises with Tabini, no question. They'll accord you a certain credence as a new leader for the station, but they'll be watching. Both island and continent will be watching, and watching each other. You have to be even-handed, and you have to be right. Their belief that things must still be running all right because you two are left in charge is very important to their ability to work with each other. It's a confidence I share or I'd be telling Tabini and Tyers both to get the hell out of this arrangement and protect their own interests separately, and I'm reasonably confident that, even out of the loop as I've been, they'd both listen in a heartbeat. Instead I'm going to throw my support to you both and tell them both to trust you. You're both reputed as the absolute best at what you're each going to handle, so I haven't any objections, only my condensed, impolite, and urgent advice on things I think you already know. I'm done. I'm perfectly confident in both of you."

It was a piece of bald-faced flattery at the end, but was true, too. Ogun *did* have a knack for handling the truth with tongs and getting it safely delivered. Sabin could manage sticky operational situations and get out alive—related skills, but in completely different arenas.

Sabin was the hardest to reckon with. "You take orders, Mr. Cameron."

"On ship? I'd be a fool not to."

"Are you ever a fool, Mr. Cameron?"

"I'm alive. Most of my enemies aren't."

That struck Sabin's fancy. Delighted her, in fact. She almost laughed. And didn't.

"Chain of command, Mr. Cameron. Observe it. I'll take your atevi. *You* keep them happy. You keep their equipment out of my way. You keep them out of my way. I'm first shift, Captain Graham's third shift. Pilots will serve in the intervals. I want your primary hours on mine, Mr. Cameron. Say that I want the benefit of your opinions when they do occur. Or if I ask you."

"I understand you." No collusion with Jase. He very well understood that implication.

"Good," Sabin said.

"Any further words, Captain Graham?" Ogun asked.

"No, sir," Jase said.

Sabin's hands had returned to their interlaced calm. "Then make your arrangements, Mr. Cameron. That's all I need from you. That's all I hope to need."

"How much time?" he asked.

Sabin cast a glance at Ogun, glanced back again. "Three days to power up from rest. Three weeks to do this in decent shape. But three days will do."

Three days.

God.

12

"Three days," Bren said to Banichi and Jago on the way back to their section.

"Three days," he had them relay to lord Geigi and to the aiji-dowager even before they reached the security of their own hall. He wondered if Kroger knew, and if Tabini knew, and suspected the dowager already did.

He stopped personally at Geigi's door, and learned from Geigi's major domo that the dowager had already departed to her own quarters—small wonder, since she was straight from a long and difficult journey, and the place was warm.

He stopped there as well. Cenedi himself came to the door to take the message.

"One apologizes for the short notice," he said. "Cenedi-ji. The ship-aijiin seem to believe that the ship will somehow make that schedule." He fished shamelessly. "Perhaps their preparations were already advanced."

"One understands, nandi." Cenedi completely refused the hook.

"We hope it affords reasonable comfort for the dowager."

"Understood, nand' paidhi. We are not surprised."

Not surprised. No. And therefore prepared? Was that his answer? Three days' notice?

If that was the case, no one was surprised but those of them who lived here.

Meanwhile a small figure appeared to Cenedi's left, wide-eyed and apprehensive in the visitation.

Cenedi, too, had followed that minute diversion of his eye, as if someone in Cenedi's profession hadn't been aware all along of the boy's presence ghosting up on him, curious and likely wanting information.

"And the aiji-apparent?"

Cenedi gave a little lift of the brow. A motion of the eyes in the appropriate direction. "What of him?"

"Where will he be, Cenedi-ji?"

"The aiji's heir, nand' paidhi, accompanies the dowager."

"With all respect, this is an extremely dangerous voyage."

"Yes," Cenedi said.

What had he left to say or to object?

"I understand," he said, but he didn't understand. He wouldn't. Couldn't. He'd desperately hoped the boy would go to Geigi. And he'd hoped the dowager would have some sort of information for him, but nothing was shaping up as he wished. "Thank you, Cenedi-ji, if you'll advise her that I came as soon as I had news."

"I shall, nandi," Cenedi said to him—not coldly, but firmly.

So that was that. Feeling shattered, he walked on toward his own apartment, in Banichi's and Jago's company, asking himself how he'd let things come to such a state of affairs—and how Tabini could have sent the boy on such a venture even with other family members, and how Tabini could so have distrusted him as to go to Mercheson, or how he could ask his own staff to risk what they couldn't readily conceive as real—

Banichi hadn't known the sun was a star when the whole space business became an issue.

He had believed Tabini almost grasped the universe at large, but now, with Tabini's sending the dowager and the boy up here as if this was a short-term venture to another island, he was no longer sure Tabini did know.

He wasn't sure, among other things, that the aiji-dowager herself particularly cared about stars, or knew this wasn't the next planet over, despite her association with the Astronomer Emeritus, and he wasn't wholly sure Cenedi had a grasp of the geography—or lack of it—either.

Granted it *wouldn't* be that long a trip, at least as perceptions made it. The ship folded space—*folded space*, as Jase put it; and outraged mortal perceptions just didn't travel well in that territory.

"Nadiin-ji," he said to his companions as they walked, "understand, if the sun were a finger-bowl in the aiji's foyer, then where we're going would be as far distant as . . ." He didn't know. But it was far. "As far as another such bowl in my mother's apartment. Almost as far as a bowl on the dining table at Malguri. Do you see?"

"Quite far," Banichi said.

"And once we get there, there may not even be a station. This is not a mission to a station like this station. Nothing so comfortable. This is a ruin. This is an area of conflict and destruction, with unknown enemies that might simply blow up the ship before any of us know we're in danger. And Tabini's sending the dowager, and a boy who won't see the sun, won't see the sky, won't have any freedom aboard—" He was about to say they had sufficient time to make other arrangements and to persuade the dowager against bringing Cajeiri. But Banichi was quick to answer.

"Then he will learn the discipline of the ship, nadi-ji. He will learn."

"And risk his life, Banichi. Is it worth it? What can he learn? What can a child do?"

"If he were a potter's son," Banichi said, "he would learn clay. Would he not?"

Among atevi, yes. A child would, if he was among potters. If he were among potters he would not be fostered out to every powerful lord in the Association.

"Yes, one assumes so."

"So being the aiji's son, he will learn *this* clay, will he not? He will learn these leaders. He will learn these allies."

What was there for the paidhi to say to that? He foresaw he wouldn't make headway on that score.

And where *was* the proper school for an energetic, somewhat gawky boy who had thus far damaged an ancient garden—where was the school for a boy who would someday succeed the architect of the *aishidi'tat*, and for whom, all his life, even now, any untested dish on the table, any careless moment at a party could turn lethal?

Was he in greater danger here, where all the staff was vouched for? Or down there, in a time of Associational uncertainty?

"I'd hoped a safer life for him," Bren said forlornly. "For everyone on the planet, for that matter, nadiin-ji." They had reached the door. "I suppose the ship-children won't stay on the station, either." He'd held that discussion with Jase, theoretically, and in a safer time—how the ship had always voyaged with its children. How very fortunately they hadn't left them on the station, which despite appearances had turned out to be the riskiest place of all. *The universe isn't safe*, Jase had said at the time.

The universe seemed downright precarious for children at the moment.

But from the viewpoint in Shejidan, if the heir were absent, out of reach of assassins, and would presumably return—one hoped—older, backed by potent allies, and by that time possessed of unguessed true numbers, what was more, why, then dared any enemy of Tabini's make too energetic a move, with so many numbers in the equation unknown and unreachable?

In a sense—no. An atevi enemy was far less likely to move against a boy one day to appear out of the heavens with potent allies and gifted with mysterious new numbers.

Never say Tabini was a fool. Not in this, scary as it was—and not in other decisions Tabini had made. Neither a fool nor timid in his moves.

Never get in his way: hadn't the paidhi known that among first truths?

Jago opened the door. Narani was there, in the foyer. Of course Narani was there to meet him. Bindanda was. Several of the others attended, with worried faces.

"We have begun packing," Narani informed him with a bow. "One trusts court dress will be in order, to meet distant foreigners."

"Very good," he said, and felt as if a safety net had turned up under him. Of course information flowed on the station. They knew. "Rani-ji, there is a choice to be made, staff to stay, staff to go with me. I want this establishment to stay active. There'll be specialized needs. Mercheson, Shugart and Feldman will be operating out of the station. They'll be translating for the court. They'll need extensive expert help." Tano appeared at the door of the security station—Tano and then Algini, who had been following as much as they could, passing things along where appropriate. Thanks to them in particular, things ran smoothly. And he had to make a decision very unwelcome to them. "We have to have security staff remaining here, too." Narani, too, elderly and fragile, and very, very skilled at keeping the household running—ought to stay here, out of danger. "Rani-ji, I set you in charge of the household while I'm gone."

"Yes, nandi," Narani answered.

"Tano, you and Algini, you have to run matters here. You'll be in charge of Associational security on this station, right next to Lord Geigi's staff. Directly linked to the aiji, as I expect, too."

"Yes, nand' paidhi," Tano said quietly. He might already *have* a direct link to the aiji's staff—more than possible, that, all along.

"One hopes to be with you, nandi," Bindanda said, uncharacteristically setting himself forward: Bindanda, who made his own reports to the aiji's uneasy ally, uncle Tatiseigi. "I ask this favor. Who else can cook for you?"

"I'll weigh the matter, certainly, Danda-ji. You're of extraordinary value in either place."

Listening staff. Worried staff. They hadn't foreknown, at least, no more than he.

And he still hadn't personally absorbed the shocks of the day—he proceeded on automatic, doing what he thought had to be done, but he knew he shouldn't be deciding things on the fly, disposing of people's lives like that, treating their loyalty as something to pack or leave. . . .

But given three days, God, what could he do?

He stood there in the foyer, having shed his coat, and felt a distinct chill—the ship secretly prepared to move, Tabini aware of the mission for months, *years*, and bypassing him—

He questioned his situation, and realized he was looking at Bindanda, knowing at base level that his own household, like any household, had leaks to certain ears. He had to take the distress in stride. It was inevitable Tatiseigi and the conservatives would hear any faltering, any hint of weakness.

And did an ordinary human, however honored— set up for a decoy, perhaps—expect Tabini to tell him everything, once Tabini had gained a certain fluency in the language?

No. Not even reasonable. Everything in Tabini's character had advised him to watch himself.

And Ramirez.

Dared he say his human feelings were, personally, hurt?

That *he* felt cast aside?

So he made similar decisions regarding his own staff. Could he forget that?

"Your service," he said to Narani, when, immediately after, he caught Narani alone in the hallway, "your service, Rani-ji, is of inestimable value to me, either here—or going with me. I spoke just now in what I thought your best interest, in proper honor, and knowing the household will need a skilled hand. Or, Rani-ji, if it were your wish, you might also retire—with a handsome pension, I might add, and my profound gratitude. But—"

"Retire I shall not, nand' paidhi." Rare that Narani ever interrupted him. This was extreme passion.

"One hardly did ever think so," Bren assured him in a low voice. "But despite all I said, I urge you choose, Rani-ji, and settle the household either with yourself or another of the staff, and I trust that choice absolutely. I do want you to choose staff to go with me, to the number of four or five servants: I leave the fortunate numbers to your discretion. Security will be Banichi and Jago. I do think Bindanda might be of great use."

"Then if the choice is mine, nandi, I shall go with

you, myself, for one, and I shall prefer Bindanda, if you agree."

He was not sure he had ever quite, quite broached the subject of Bindanda with Narani. He considered, then took the plunge. "One knows, surely, Rani-ji, that he *is* Guild."

Narani lowered his gaze ever so slightly and looked up again with the most clear-eyed, sober look. "So am I, nandi."

He was absolutely astonished.

"In my *man'chi*, dare I ask, Rani-ji?" He almost asked now if there was anyone on his staff who *wasn't* in the Assassins' Guild. But he politely refrained from requiring Narani to lie.

The good gentleman lowered his eyes and bowed, ever so slightly. "As tightly so as your security is."

Dual, then, one of Tabini's own—it made perfect sense. As Bindanda was within Damiri-daja's *man'chi*, and within Tatiseigi's. And *that* bound up within his household the same potent alliance as bound very important elements of the Western Association.

"Who will be your third?" he asked.

"Asicho," Narani said, naming the young woman who attended Jago, at need. This was not the first young woman—and ask, Bren thought, in what merciless school Asicho had had her training, and to whom she was apprenticed.

"Accepted," he said, not even asking to what other power Asicho might belong; and he wished he had Tano's and Algini's technical expertise, but in the field, and this was, he rather relied on Banichi's. "Do as needful with the numbers. You have my complete approval, Rani-ji. You're impeccable."

"Nand' paidhi," the old man said, and gave a little bow and went to do what he knew how to do.

Absolute loyalty within the walls.

Betrayal straight from the top, from the aiji, it might be . . . and yet he was embraced by those in the aiji's *man'chi*, who didn't know they were betrayed. He tried to make that column of figures add, standing there like a fool in the hallway, and he couldn't.

Because, dammit, he was *feeling*, not thinking. Standing between species as he did, *thinking* was a survival skill, *feeling* was a useful barometric reading, and the job, the important thing wasn't the survival of Bren Cameron—it was the accurate reading of situations that enabled Shejidan and Mospheira to survive.

And whatever the ship did or arranged, he couldn't let it sell out those interests.

He took himself to the study to gather his wits, while his staff dealt with less abstract matters.

And, one world touching the other, a servant appeared, regular as clockwork, asking amid the necessary confusion whether he wished tea—he often did, when he ended the day.

"Yes," he said. A little routine was good for him— reassuring to the staff. So he agreed to the tea, and sat, and stared at the walls, the familiar shelves, the environment he had designed, he himself, with his own hand.

His place. His creation. It wasn't for him to resent being ripped out of it, sent off into danger as casually as he dealt with the servants.

Barometric reading? Betrayal was something he'd personally felt more than once with atevi. It was an emotion he'd most specifically learned to turn loose and forget, because the equations of behavior just weren't the same, and a human couldn't feel the tugs and pulls that made some decisions, for an ateva, logical and reasonable—even automatic, lest he forget. He'd been locked in Ilisidi's basement and beaten black and blue, and he'd forgiven that; he'd been handed over to an enemy, and set up for assassination, and he understood that. Forgiveness didn't matter a thing to an ateva who thought the decisions logical. *Man'chi* was *man'chi* and actions within it were all reasonable, when a lord needed something.

But there were puzzles.

Why would Tabini call him down to the planet for a completely empty mission? Why call him down for a small private talk that only discussed court gossip and then send him back again with not a word of what was coming?

Why, why, and why, when Ramirez was at death's door and events were sliding toward the brink?

Granted Tabini had known that, in specific—was the whole ceremony down there only cover? A way for the dowager to get to Shejidan and then board a shuttle—but for some reason not the shuttle that carried him, though he had become inconsequential to the aiji's plans?

Had his trip down and back been diversion, to attract the news services and raise empty questions, keeping the news away from Ilisidi? His presence was far more unusual than hers—and it had attracted notice.

Possible. Entirely possible. He could accept being used in that sense. It made perfect sense, and didn't at all hurt his feelings.

But the timing—right before Ramirez's death. *Right* before the news broke.

No. Cancel that thought. Assassination wasn't likely. The one thing, the one unintended event that let the cat out of the bag had been that worker with the injured hand, the one who'd overheard Ramirez giving Jase an emergency briefing. That had thrown everything public before the captains could move: *that* had brought the acceleration in the program, when a couple of thousand crew found out they'd been deceived, tricked, delayed and lied to. If not for that one accident, the surviving captains could have had a year or more to plan the mission.

Kroger had just arrived up here with the robots and the promise of an accelerated program; that was planned.

But Tabini had just turned over the management of his heir to Ilisidi. Then Ramirez died—and Tabini couldn't admit himself surprised or disarrayed, not even for a death. He'd already turned Cajeiri over to Ilisidi—and had to stand by that, or not send Ilisidi, who was the only choice that wouldn't create dangerous stress in the Association. Geigi would have been next most logical—but Geigi was western, and that was controversial.

So from the aiji's point of view, Ramirez had needed to stay alive.

Ramirez, who hadn't briefed Jase, which he'd clearly wanted to do, and did rashly at the last. The captains hadn't made provision for a successor, or for a full complement of four captains, acting or permanent, for the ship in operation. So as a group, the captains hadn't known. *One* captain might have acted to remove Ramirez, and Sabin would have been his immediate suspicion, but he saw no advantage she gained.

And the three day departure? He didn't know how long it took to prep a fueled ship for a mission from scratch. He did know that the ship never had been powered down, that it *ran*, continually, being a residency and training site for its crew, performing tests and operations the station couldn't provide—so in that sense it had never shut down. Maintenance was always going on. Galleys were active. Provisions were always going aboard, to what level of preparedness they had never questioned. The ship's machinery shops and production facilities, though micro-*g*, were warm, powered and in constant use, from the first days, when *Phoenix*'s manufacturing facilities had been the sole source of parts and pieces for station repair. They still were turning out a good portion of station foodstuffs, most of the extruded beams—there was very little difference, in that regard, from crew engaged in station manufacture and those on shipboard production, except that some operations went better in micro-*g* and some went better in the station, where things naturally or unnaturally fell into buckets. Crew came and they went, one facility to the other, and various aspects of the ship—including the power plant—had never shut down.

So maybe the ship-folk never had bet their lives wholly on the station or on the planet below.

Maybe the ship had *always* been three days from undocking and leaving, give or take the fuel to go anywhere in particular after undocking. He hadn't asked, and Jase hadn't told him what—to Jase—might be an underlying fact of life.

And now, in the paidhi's longterm ignorance of shipboard realities, *Phoenix* could just break away and go on a moment's notice. Three days might be the captains' notion of a leisurely departure. And the whole affair that had untidy strings and suspicious tags dangling off it—might not be the strings and tags of conspiracy, but rather of hastily revised plans, plans that had had to be changed in frantic haste . . . because the whole thing had been shoved into motion prematurely by Ramirez's failing health.

Well, *he* couldn't solve it. His staff didn't know the answer. As to whether Ramirez had explained the situation fully to Tabini, the aiji-dowager never gave up a secret, either, until she could get good exchange from it.

The simple fact was that they were going, and the dowager was going, and he was going, a headlong slide toward a cliff—beyond which he had insufficient information even to imagine his future.

And that meant he had to set his own private life in suspension; and it wasn't tidy. It never had been tidy, or convenient, or well-packaged; and now was absolutely the worst time. He didn't want to call the hospital and tell his mother—*Oh, by the way, I'm leaving the solar system for a couple of years. Good luck. Regards to Toby . . .*

He could send to Toby. He needed to. But he didn't know what to say: *Sorry you've been in the position you're in and sorry I can't help, but I've been kidnapped. . . .*

That was close to the truth, as happened, and he imagined Toby would be terribly sorry he'd hung up once he knew. Toby would be all sympathy for his brother, and he hadn't any expectation the spat they'd had was a lasting one—well, bitter because it touched on very sore topics—but Toby wouldn't think twice on his own misfortunes once that letter reached him.

But it wasn't a letter he wanted to write cold, either. He wanted to say the right thing, which he hadn't managed to do in the last few letters, or phone calls.

So what was there to do, then, while his staff packed and put together a suitable supper?

He answered memos from various departments, some incredibly mundane, one with a proposal for a new franchise for paper products, with a clever internal recycling option. On an ordinary day he might have been intrigued with it and spent energy chasing down advisors.

Today, he was sure the department in question had no remote idea what was on his desk. . . . and he didn't care if paper recycled or piled up in masses.

He couldn't call Paulson or Kroger with what he knew, not until there was an official announcement—and he wasn't in charge of the timing of that. Ilisidi was. The captains were.

He placed a call to Jase, on a small afterthought,

wishing Jase would join him for supper, and met, not uncommonly, a wall at C1: *"Captain Graham has your calls at top priority."*

Well, not too surprising, considering: Jase wasn't in a particularly festive mood and Jase had his hands full—besides which Jase had, at least marginally, family of his own to consider. Becky Graham was Jase's mother—and Becky's quarters might be where Jase had gone for an hour or two.

He hoped so. He hoped Jase wasn't up to his ears in meetings with never yet time to stop and realize he had lost the one father he knew—the one parent, in that sense. Jase was hardly more emotionally related to Becky than he was to the long-dead hero who'd contributed the sperm—but he and Becky had each other in common, little as they ordinarily acknowledged the bond. Jase was on duty, asleep, or talking to Becky—and least of all wanting to have to justify decisions or give explanations of Ramirez's actions to an old friend with problems of his own. Now that he thought it through, if Jase was on overload, and likely he was, it was hardly kind to add one more pressure—which was all it would be. He couldn't move a ship's captain back into the atevi domain where they could talk at will, as they'd used to; where staff could take care of him. He supposed Kaplan and Polano and now Jenrette did take care of Jase, in a subordinate sort of way, but when he considered Jase's emotional resources outside that, it came down to Ramirez, Ramirez, Ramirez.

No wide attachments among the crew. No close friends among the crew except Yolanda Mercheson, who'd grown up into a partner and now, cutting through every other fact, an ex-lover. It had been a bad mistake, that liaison. It had soured a relationship and laid bare realities of their familial situation that just weren't helpful.

And Yolanda being jealous and touchy of her professional prerogatives—justifiably jealous and touchy, since Ramirez had always favored Jase over her—man to young man. That had been hard enough; and ex-lover status seemed to put the coup de grace on the friendship. Ramirez had not only created two human beings, he'd monopolized their childhood, limited their associations, expected Jase to work miracles by his mere existence . . . and dropped him and Yolanda separately onto an alien world to learn to fit in. Then he yanked them off it the moment they succeeded, messed up their interpersonal relations by favoritism, having all his paternal notions fixed on Jase and being blind to Yolanda.

Then after advising Tabini he was having sudden, crisis-level health problems, he dropped dead, leaving his crew in a commotion, Jase and Yolanda bitterly wounded and generally messed up, and his allies pressed to act on a program he'd leaked to staff while he was dying. Jase was stuck in a rank he didn't want, in a job he didn't want. Yolanda had the job Jase did want. Not to mention Yolanda had wanted importance with the crew and never had had an emotional bond to her planetary responsibilities.

Damn Ramirez.

Hell and damn in general.

He was working his way into a piece of temper. He

typed a letter to Jase—in Ragi, to confound C1's perpetual snoopery:

On ship or on the station, our door is open at any hour. If you can by any stretch of argument persuade the ship council that having one of the captains closely resident with your atevi advisors truly makes good operational sense, you would be most welcome to reside here, among persons who would treat you most congenially, seeing to your every want.

Or if you simply have an overwhelming longing for pizza with green sauce, we would make every effort.

The Ragi language cannot convey every feeling I would wish to express: but Banichi and Jago would tell you that you are within this household, wherever your residence is compelled to be hereafter. Man'chi is not broken.

It was what they said at an atevi funeral, among those determined to maintain their ties when the essential link had gone. *Man'chi is not broken.*

Well, hell, Jase needed to know that. He decided he himself did, where they were both going.

He gave the letter to Tano to hand deliver to Jase, or to Kaplan or Pressman.

And he wrote to the ateva with the well-thought recycling program, and recommended it to Paulson. That was one problem off his desk.

He didn't know what he could do about his family, his staff down on the mainland—he didn't know how he could get hold of Toby, or whether he ought to try to talk directly to his mother. All the while he thought about the trip, with his irrational hindbrain insisting he was about to die.

And he wasn't brave, and he *didn't* want to know what it felt like when a starship played games with space and time and did things to human flesh and blood that nature never intended to happen.

What had begun as tension rapidly became indigestion.

"Banichi," he said into the intercom.

"*He's not here, nandi.*" Algini's voice, from the security office.

Surprising. He'd sent Tano out, but not Banichi.

"Jago?"

"*Jago has gone with Banichi.*"

"When everyone gets back from not being here," he said to Algini, "tell Banichi I asked, nadi-ji."

"*One will inform him that, nandi.*"

Get an answer, not inevitably. But one would ask, on this day when nothing was casual.

"Nothing's wrong, is it?"

"*Mospheiran crew is somewhat distressed, nandi,*" Algini said. "*They've announced the flight.*"

One could imagine *somewhat distressed.*

And it was headed, now, for the news services. His family would hear. And *he* didn't have the rank to get past Geigi, or Paulson.

"If news services call," he said to Algini, "I *will* talk to them."

The station was in increasing disturbance. His staff was ghosting about on mysterious errands. He'd almost expected a summons from the dowager this evening, but none had come. So Bindanda's preparations advanced. He heard muted activity in the dining room, service prepared.

The front door opened and closed. One of his missing staff was back. He took comfort in that, hearing the quiet tread that approached his door—Narani, with a report: he knew before he looked up.

"Nand' paidhi," Narani said, "Banichi is back. He has Mercheson-paidhi with him."

Yolanda.

There was a disconcerting surprise.

Yolanda—who stood to inherit his job, his place—everything he valued—everything Jase wanted . . . who wasn't the most skilled, where she was assigned, and where she had been operating. . . .

God—he was *jealous*.

Where had *that* come from? When had *that* happened?

Jealous that she was staying.

Angry that she'd deceived him and Jase.

Furiously jealous. Bitterly, painfully resentful. He'd kept the lid on his personal wishes so tightly and so automatically he rarely brought them out to look at, and *there* was a small, nasty surprise. He didn't want her under his roof—so to speak.

Not profitable to carry on a feud. No.

He got up, put on his jacket for manners' sake—atevi custom—and walked out to deal civilly with an unwelcome guest who'd arrived—unthinkable among atevi—uninvited, at dinnertime.

13

"Staff was about to serve," Bren said, meeting Yolanda in the foyer, intending to issue the polite invitation.

"I'm very sorry," she said fervently, in Ragi—which went a long way toward patching things with him.

"Do join me."

"Forgive me," Banichi said, having escorted Yolanda here. "Nand' paidhi, Mercheson-paidhi expressed concerns. One took the initiative to accept."

Yolanda's instigation, this visit, then . . . but not the way he'd expected.

"Mercheson-paidhi is an absent household member." He chose to regard it that way, which Yolanda Mercheson never had quite been, in his cold estimation. She'd been in the household for a time, on the planet, Jase's lover for a while, until that hadn't worked. Then back to Mospheira. Then back to the ship where she'd far rather live. "Staff will manage another setting. One trusts you have an appetite, Mercheson-paidhi."

"One is grateful," Yolanda said meekly, not quite meeting his eye—but then, an atevi caught in social inconvenience wouldn't meet his eye, either. Already there was a small flurry of service in the dining room, staff shifting chairs, not yet knowing how to arrange the numbers, or whether Banichi would join them.

"Banichi, will you join us?" Banichi's presence at least eased the unlucky numerology of two at table. *You brought her; you patch the numbers* was implicit in the invitation, and Banichi accepted, commitment of his own very valuable time—but there they were, Jago still absent—one supposed if something were wrong, someone would say so. Tano and Algini doubtless had their heads together, possibly assuring Jago's safety, or good records, wherever she was. That left Banichi.

He entered the dining room with Yolanda and Banichi, sat down, went through the formalities due any guest. They duly appreciated a fine, if informal dinner, the tone much as if Yolanda still were a member of the household.

And formal or informal, one didn't talk business—rather the quality of the food, the skill of the chef—the arrival of the aiji-dowager might have been a good topic, if the implications of it were business-free; but they weren't and it wasn't. The departure of the ship would have been a fine topic, if it were guilt-free and casual; but it was neither guilt-free nor casual.

So talk ran to the weather on the continent, the launch, the situation at the new spaceport, and the lack of news from Yolanda's former domicile on the island, which did actually skirt business topics.

Dinner came down to a delicate cream dessert—which Yolanda had always very much favored.

"One grew so accustomed to luxuries," was her only expression of regret.

He let that remark fall. That wistfulness, too, led to inappropriate seriousness. And Yolanda very clearly savored the dessert, and pleased Bindanda and the staff.

"Will you join me in the study?" Bren said at the end. "A glass or two?"

Thoroughly courteous. All business, now.

He had no cause to resent Yolanda—so he assured himself. Of course he and Yolanda should consult, and of course Banichi was absolutely right to have brought her.

"Jago's about business?" he asked in passing.

"One believes she's with Cenedi, nandi."

"Ah." A briefing. Information. One could only hope.

"Shall I attend you?"

"One might look in on that meeting." There was no reason to take up more of Banichi's time. Yolanda clearly had not come on a hostile mission. There were, among other things, pieces of ongoing business and certain addresses and numbers he had to hunt out of files and give to her before he left, and before he forgot to do it.

"Yes," Banichi said, and left them to the study and the brandy, the servants caring for the service and the numerology alike, quite deftly and silently. Brandies arrived, and chairs configured for three immediately found another fortunate configuration, ameliorated by a small table and a small porcelain vase empty of flowers.

"I have things for you," Bren said, for starters, and to let the brandy and a necessary task take the edge off his resentment before they reached any discussion.

So with a glass of brandy beside him and the computer in his lap, he did that, a few seconds' work, and handed her the file personally.

"This is a matter of trust," he said, "nadi-ji." It was the work of several moments to manage that intimate salutation, that particular tone.

She took it soberly and slipped it into a shirt pocket.

"I've given you the addresses of persons who will assist you, on the island," he said further, in ship language, "and I'd advise you to use those channels far more than the ones that tried to get close to you when you were down there. I can assure they *do* answer their phones. I've also included Shawn Tyers' private number, if you didn't have it." He wasn't utterly sure she didn't. "Several others." Barb's number was on the list. Toby's. People he didn't want remotely involved in any mess Yolanda might make of things, but he tried to have faith in her good sense, and they were resources she ought to know. "I've also given you contacts with my staff on the mainland, and you can rely on their advice. Some individuals aren't official. It's my personal list. Treat them gently."

"I understand," she said.

"You did surprise me," he said then.

"Coming tonight?"

"Dealing with Ramirez." He hit her with the question head-on, wondering what she would say for herself, whether her counter would be smug, justified satisfaction—in which case he meant to keep a good grip on his temper.

Smugness wasn't her response. "I'm sorry," she said. "I wanted to tell you. I wanted to tell Jase. I couldn't."

On evidence of the tone and the expression—he might believe that, but belief still didn't muster the personal feeling he wished he had for her. "Secrets are hell on a relationship, aren't they?"

He wished he hadn't said that. Instantly Yolanda's lower lip compressed, eyes showed wounding. Deep hurt, quickly held in.

"No question," she said in ship-speak. And she sat back and seemed to set the armor that covered all her soul, dealing with him, dealing with Jase.

He talked frankly to her after that, warnings, bits of advice about individuals and matters she did know to watch out for. Armor stayed. In a certain measure it made frankness easier. It always had.

Regarding Tabini himself: "I know you have a good relationship with him," he said, on that delicate topic. "I know you do, or he wouldn't deal with you. But take two warnings—infelicitous two. Don't back down from his baiting you. If he thinks you fold rather than argue with him, you'll be out of his confidence in a heartbeat."

"I've learned that," she said. "What's the other?"

"Tell him the truth." That she pursued the numbers—at least on a small scale—was encouraging. "Third point, fortunate three: listen carefully to what he advises. There's no one on the planet more dangerous than Tabini. Or smarter. Witness he's survived all the assassins aimed at him—partly by being so good and so steady in office that even his detractors find a use in his being there. *That's* his real success. I learn tactics from him—constantly. I hope you will. Quite honestly—" He made another real try at mending the interface he'd messed up, much as the effort seemed a forlorn hope. "Quite honestly I'm jealous as hell of your being where you are, and a little upset—well, a lot upset—at not being advised of what you were doing."

"His order," she said in a low voice.

"Tabini's? Or Ramirez's?"

"Both."

"But who initiated?" What she said tweaked something sensitive, something to which she might be oblivious. "Who contacted whom—first requiring your services?"

Maybe she'd hoped to get out of here without discussing that matter. Maybe it was something she'd been both stalking for an opening and dreading all along. But she answered seriously, meticulously. "I honestly don't know who did. Ramirez called me in. I don't know whether Tabini-aiji had called him directly or he'd called the aiji."

"It would be very useful to know that. But *not* to remark on, understand. I mention it for your safety. Always know details like that."

"There was no way to know."

Her perpetual defensiveness set him off. And he refused to let it do that, this time. There wasn't the leisure any longer to reform Yolanda. Only to use her services. "Some things it's necessary to know. Some

things it's unexpectedly critical to know. I'm not fault-
ing you, understand. I'm advising you to the best of
my own experience in this situation. In the interest of
everybody on the planet down there, I desperately
want you to succeed. I want you to do better than I
ever did at reading the aiji. I want you to so far eclipse
me that you'll never get caught unprepared. Which
means you'll never get anybody killed. And I'm not
sure I can claim that." Yolanda didn't understand him
or his motives any more than she understood the
minds of Mospheiran shop owners . . . and far less
than she understood Tabini, to his long-term observation. She was a spacefarer and if an event or an attitude hadn't any precedent on the ship—Yolanda
didn't see it. She flatly didn't see it.

"The aiji scares hell out of me," she admitted then,
the most encouraging statement he'd ever heard out
of Yolanda Mercheson. "And I'm not you, and I can't
deal with him the way you do."

"Be afraid of him. But don't show it. Stand up to
him, and show deference at the same time. Balance
the two. And you have my good wishes." God help
us, he thought to himself. She didn't show fear because she didn't always know when she *was* in danger. But she wasn't the only one with blind spots.
He'd come in that blind. He'd spent a night in Ilisidi's
basement learning that lesson. He'd had his arm broken, learning that lesson. "All right. That's your
province. You have to learn. You will learn. Turn-
about, advise me—what am I up against on the ship?
How do *I* make headway?"

She hadn't seen that question coming, either. She drew a deep, deep breath. "You mean with Sabin?"

"*And* the crew."

"Crew is easy. They know who you are. They approve. More than that, 'Sidi-ji is their darling and you're with her. Truth is, everybody *detests* Sabin. Granted they're both cold as deep space rock, the dowager and Sabin both—'Sidi-ji smiles at them. That makes all the difference."

"You know that smile's not necessarily a good sign."

"I know, but they don't know it, and they worship her. Besides, I think she likes it. Well, *like* isn't it, is it?"

"Like's fine with things. Not people. There's your difference. She likes their approval. She doesn't *like* them, because they're not in her association. Think in Ragi when you think about atevi."

"She favors their applause."

"She drinks it like good brandy. If they'd only worship Sabin, *Sabin* would warm up, don't you think?"

He saw the body language, disengagement from the very concept. "Not likely. Not ever likely. —But Sabin gets the ship through. We don't have to like her. If the ship itself's in trouble, I'll promise you, you want Sabin on deck."

"Next question. Do you want her in negotiations?"

Another long breath and a deeply sober thought. "Only if you plan to nuke the other side."

"Major question. Is she for us, or is she for the authority that sent you here? Does she *like* what we're doing here? Or is she against it?"

That brought another moment's thought. "Honestly, I don't know for sure. I don't think Ramirez knew . . . she doesn't like atevi, she doesn't like Mospheirans, and I'm not sure she likes the crew, for that matter. The best thing is, she won't be here, making decisions. Don't ever say I said that."

"Encouraging," he said. So he'd asked the questions. He'd had his answers, all he knew to ask for. Except one. "Did Ramirez tip Tabini off, that he was dying?"

The question scared her. She was far too readable. Far too readable, still, for safety in court.

"*Face*," he snapped, as he'd used to say to Jase, as he'd said to Yolanda more than once. And expression vanished from her face, well, at least that one vanished—quickly replaced with a frown.

"I thought I could be honest with you," she said.

"You can be. You'd better be, for about five more minutes. Then give expression up for the duration, except inside this apartment, with this staff. Damned uncomfortable pillow, the secrets on this job. *Did he tell Tabini?*"

"He told him. Therapy wasn't taking. He was having mental lapses—that's the truth, Bren. It scared the hell out of him, more than the heart condition, because he was forgetting things. And he told me to tell Tabini to get ready, that there *was* the alien threat, that the world had to get ready, that the ship had to be ready, constantly . . ."

"On three day's notice?"

"On three minutes' notice," Yolanda said. "We've been able to pull out of here at any moment for the last three months—with whatever crew could get aboard. But we haven't done that. We told Tabini the truth about the aliens and about the situation back on the station, and we asked for fuel so if some armed ship showed up we had some fighting chance against it. And, ultimately, so we could go back and settle what has to be settled back there."

"Meaning."

"Meaning to get that station shut down. Make the gesture. *Aishimaran to thema*."

Almost untranslatable: *sweeping the boundary*. Clearing troublesome disputed areas from an associational edge. Atevi neighbors would exchange property to achieve border peace, in a world with neither boundaries nor borders as humans understood the term—a process arcane and fraught with hazard.

"Tabini's word?"

"His word."

"Probably describes it very well. But that program in itself has an assumption—that the gesture will be read the way humans *or* atevi would read it."

"But we have to do something."

"Third assumption," he said. "You've already done something, in staying out of there. Now you think there's no choice but go back. But that's out of my territory, too. I can't claim I know what's wise to do. Two smart men, on more facts than I have, agreed it was a good idea. —Did Ramirez *intend* to die?"

"He was having attacks. The fueling being finished—he was talking with Tabini about breaking the news. About timing in telling the truth. Then the robots were ready. And the day he heard that, he had an attack. He worked past it. I knew." She tried to keep the still, dispassionate face. "Ogun knew he was in trouble. I don't think Sabin did, but I'm not sure. Then the last attack. And he wanted to talk to Jase, I guess. And he should have left it to me to brief Jase, because it wasn't secure there in the clinic, but there were probably other things he wanted to say, too."

"Like?"

"Things he'd say to us. Personal things. Like apologizing for having us born. For putting on us what he'd put on us. Not quite a normal life, is it?"

Bitterness. Deep bitterness. Maybe it wasn't wise to answer at all. But he did. "Most of us don't have normal lives," he said. "Especially in this business."

"But were you always paidhi-aiji? Didn't you grow up? Jase and I—we'd have liked to have known our fathers. We'd have liked to have something but a necessary, logical, already made *choice*. We'd have liked to fail at something without it being a calamity that involved the captain's council."

"I don't envy you in that regard. But you came out sane. And decent. And worthwhile. It's what we do, more than who we are, that makes our personal lives a mess. If we didn't do what we do for a job, ordinary people might figure out how to get along with us."

"Jase and I tried to make a relationship. We tried being teammates, we tried being lovers—not having any other candidates. We weren't good at it. Something about needing to be loved to know how to love, isn't that the folktale? We're kind of defective, Jase and I, in that regard. Really confused input, don't you think?"

"I don't think." Atevi society wasn't a good place

for a human with a problem with relationships to work it out. Himself, with a relationship in shambles and his own brother not speaking to him, he knew that. "You're all right. You'll *be* all right. Life's long. Hold out till we get back. You'll have a household around you. Mine. While I'm gone, I want you to come here. Live here in my household."

"I can't do that."

"Advice: do it. They're the best help you can get. And you won't be alone. Believe me."

Her lips went thin. He wondered if she knew where his comfort came from, or the situation he had with Jago. He was proof against anyone's disapproval, outside the household.

And he knew what he was asking of his household, to take her in, but he saw in her the signs that had taken other paidhiin down—the isolation, the sense of alienation, the burden of untranslatable secrets.

"Here is safe," he said. "For one very practical reason—you may become a target—take my offer. And trust these people. Completely."

"I don't trust. I don't trust people."

"Learn. With them, *learn*."

Deep breath.

"Listen to me," he said. "You can't debrief everything in your own language. You *need* atevi you can trust to talk to. If you'd had someone to ask about Tabini, in Ragi, it would have helped—wouldn't it?"

That made itself understood. Resistence weakened.

"All right. All right. I'll see if I can arrange it."

"You don't *see if you can arrange it*, Mercheson-paidhi. You do it. And listen to me. One more question, one more sweeping question: is there anything else I'd better know? Is there anything else you suspect that Ramirez might have told Jase, that you wouldn't have been able to tell him in a briefing? Anything you've suspected, or knew parts of?"

A shake of the head. "No."

One very last question. "Why in *hell* didn't you come to me?"

"*Tabini* might not have liked it. I didn't know what to do."

That wasn't quite the defensive answer he'd expected. It made sense; and that set him a little off balance. "I could have kept your question secret."

Hesitation. "The Old Man was pretty sure you *wouldn't* keep something from Tabini. That *man'chi* business. And I told him what I thought I ought to do, which was ask you, but he wouldn't risk it. He said that was why he called *me* in." A moment's silence. "He didn't ask Jase. I guess he thought Jase would tell you everything. Jase's attached to the planet. But I live *here*. He was the Old Man. My Old Man. That's all the logic I had to go on. I didn't want to be where I was. I didn't want to keep the secret. But I didn't know how to turn it loose or whether things would blow up if I did. And by then I *knew* we didn't have the time we thought we did."

"I know what you're saying. I appreciate you made a decision the best you could with what you had to work with. And I appreciate the line you've tried to walk, solo, trying to preserve your worth to the situation. But the situation's vastly changed. That's why I want you inside the household, so you're never confronted with an atevi question without advice. You know they could have advised you how to deal with Tabini—if they'd been yours to ask. And in time to come," he said levelly, "and when we get back, you can even tell me and Jase the truth. We'll all three sort it out. I think this has all finally become the same side."

"You trust Jase?"

Shocking question. It shook him.

"You don't."

Her doubt might be the aftershock of a relationship between her and Jase that hadn't worked.

"He loved Ramirez," Yolanda said. "He was wholly committed to Ramirez. And Ramirez didn't trust him—because of his relationship with you, I'm reasonably sure that was the whole cause. But Ramirez didn't trust him, in the end. You're upset with me, with what you found out was going on. Jase isn't. Jase is taking Ramirez's dying just too well. Too sensibly."

"He learned in Shejidan, maybe." But he didn't discount the question.

"But it hurts. It hurts, Bren. And he's not showing it. And I can't talk to him."

"You've tried?"

"I leave messages: talk to me. No answers. Jase didn't like what he heard. He's mad at me. Really mad at me. I think that I *was* working with Ramirez, and that Ramirez went to me—that stung."

Jase wasn't the young man who'd parachuted onto the planet. And that fact, perhaps, had foredoomed Yolanda to find her own way through the thicket he and Jase had made of their association . . . and foredoomed not to get answers, and to be even further on the outside.

Association, be it noted: *aishi*. *Aishi* had that troublesome word, *man'chi*, nestled right in the midst of it. He and Jase hadn't dealt with one another like two humans, in Mosphei', where *friendship* existed, where *friendship* might have swallowed down some of the problems in silence. Instead they'd dealt in Ragi, one of them with a *man'chi* on earth, the other with his *captain* in the heavens. They'd found a means of working around the *friendship* part, thanks to *aishi*, thanks to the organization of the household, where everyone under the same roof had the same set of motives, the same interests, the same imperatives and acted accordingly, in that clearly foreign matrix.

And Yolanda?

Yolanda had landed instead in that generations-deep nest of conspiracy and humanly seductive *friendships* over on the island of Mospheira, after living in her close-knit crew. On Mospheira she'd rapidly learned the finer points of being on no side, of being the one true outsider in a society where there *were* no outsiders. All the lessons of the ship to a factor of ten. And being in a matrix that wasn't as clearly foreign—that assaulted her human emotions with promises that didn't pan out. Always the outsider. Always the target.

"I'll try to patch things with Jase," he said. "I'll give him your message, for both your sakes. I hope you believe I'm on the level."

"I know what you once said to me. I said it to myself all the time I was working with Ramirez."

"What's that?"

"That if a side in a dispute doesn't have somebody they think is working only for them—"

"An honest broker."

"If they don't have that, they can do something dangerous to everyone. So that's what I always told mself I was. An honest broker. I was somebody working only for Ramirez, somebody who'd argue with him. The Old Man's dead, now. Now, I'm not quite working for Ogun. But Tabini's asked me to work for *him*. And I'm going to have to choose. I know I am. And you're saying go with the atevi, and maybe—maybe that's what I have to do, now. But I'm scared—"

"Good. Be scared. But don't be overwhelmed. That's where the household support will save you."

"It may save me. But what will save Jase? He's hellbent for going. He'll be with Sabin, trying to make her look as good as possible, trying to mediate her decisions—trying to keep the peace aboard. That's not good, Bren. That's not good for him, because he was Ramirez's, not hers, and he hates her. He really does. And on this mission is the last place he ought to be. Hear what I'm saying: he's alone. He's going to need help. You're what he has. Don't fail him."

He considered the equation. The warning. All of it. Was it after all, *love?* "I won't promise you. I won't." They'd gone about as deep as they could, each holding the other's interests hostage, each of them being where the other wanted most to be, each of the three of them given what another of the three most wanted to have. "Meanwhile you get to stand between atevi and humans until I get back. You'll have carte blanche with my staff they'll give you. I have the links, the communications, the staff, and the experts you need. Half my staff, understand, are spies, useful spies. Don't let on you know, even if they know you know: it's just not done and it'll make things impossible. Listen to me: wear the clothes, *dream* in the language; think in it. My remaining staff will see to your every wish. Down there, Tabini and Damiri will likely ask you to dinner, in which you have no choice. Staff will prime you on protocols. Observe them as you observe safety drills. Your life rides on it. The whole alliance rides on our survival."

"I don't need to be more scared than I am."

"You *can* be more scared than this. When you are— again talk to staff. That's why I want you surrounded by them. You're paidhi-aiji. You're most useful to Ogun when you take *Tabini's* orders and put yourself at his disposal. You'll be the honest broker—the only one there'll be for lightyears around."

A novice . . . but not a stupid novice, as it turned out and not without canny advice, either. Once he saw she was truly disposed to take that advice, he had no trouble pouring his resources into her hands and wishing her every piece of luck possible.

Yolanda said fervently, "I'm *glad* you're going on the mission. You want what I know about what's out there—if Ogun doesn't know, and he hasn't told Sabin, then there's two names to watch. There was a three-man exploration team that went in. I know that Jenrette was one of them; and two more got killed.

Tamun was trying to catch Ramirez during the mutiny, and they ran, and Tamun's mutineers shot them and Jenrette's still alive, but they aren't. I didn't used to think so, but now I ask myself whether Tamun suspected something, and if that was why he was trying to overthrow the council—but *Tamun* couldn't get at it, when he was one of the captains. He couldn't get the proof, or didn't release it. So we didn't know—and now Tamun's dead. And that scares me. All of that scares me."

God. Had they been on the right side, putting down the Tamun mutiny?

"Log record?"

"Common crew can't get into the log file. I guess not even all the captains can. There could be a tape—they always make one, through helmet-cam. But if there is, it's deep in log archives."

Jenrette. Two dead men who'd used to guard Ramirez killed when dissidents tried to capture them.

And possibly a tape.

"Tape of what?"

"Their going onto the station. Through the corridors. That's all I know," Yolanda said. "Which is what everybody in the crew knows if they'd think about it, which they probably haven't in years. That's the hell of it. We always thought the report was just what you'd think it would be . . . which it wasn't. But *I've* thought about it, since Ramirez admitted he'd deceived the crew. And now if there *was* a tape, or if Jenrette knows something—he's the only eyewitness alive. And he's attached to Jase."

Jase hadn't said a thing if he'd asked questions of Jenrette.

But possibly Jenrette hadn't answered those questions. Or Jase hadn't time to ask.

"I very much appreciate the briefing."

"Protect Jase."

"I will. I promise you I will." Jase, who couldn't handle the ship—Sabin, who could. They were in one hell of a situation if that relationship blew up.

And Jenrette—and tapes that might prove Ramirez's dealings with the station.

God.

"I want you here," he said. "Within our protection. Right now. Go pack."

"I don't think there's any hurry that extreme."

He left the last of his drink, pushing it back. Banichi was nearby. The room was bugged. He knew his security had followed part of it, as much fluency as they had. "I want you with our security, starting now, and I want to know you're safe and alive. I'm very appreciative, Landa-ji. But I'm not taking chances with someone who knows that many of the requisite pieces. You're paidhi-aiji. Accept it. Think like it. If human enemies, then atevi enemies, at all times, and sometimes before you, think they know what's critical. Here, you're safe. Come with me."

Was he surprised that when he saw her out to the foyer, the requisite persons were at hand: Narani, and Banichi, and Jago back from her conference?

"Mercheson-paidhi will handle affairs on the mainland, appointed by the aiji to take my post, with my approval. To that end, I set her within the household, in the care of the staff. She very much needs reliable people around her, and she promises to appreciate good advice."

"Mercheson-paidhi," Narani said, with a bow, and Yolanda made the requisite bow in return.

"One is grateful," she said properly. "Thank you all." She made the bow of someone departing, but Narani hesitated in opening the door for her—alone, no security, no escort. That was the way Yolanda had been moving about the station, and that wouldn't do, not at all.

"Banichi-ji, can you draw someone from atevi general security to attach to her? She needs her belongings. Landa-ji, I'd rather you just stayed here and let us collect your belongings. Is there anything you urgently have to have from your quarters?"

"Not that's a security rush, but yes, keepsakes. And my *mother*—" She was starting to think of consequences.

He was grateful for that. And had no good news. "We can provide reasonable security for your mother outside our perimeter. Within atevi protection, with a human staff—you can arrange that set-up, paidhi-aiji. You have the authority. You can authorize, you can build, you can order. It's up to you how deeply you need to pull her into this."

"I'll write a message for her. I don't know whether she's going with the ship, or not. We don't talk that often—but—"

"Frankly, I'd suggest she go. There'll be fewer potential enemies, and there she doesn't know anything, and can't pressure you with personal demands. Here, there's a danger, however remote, of hostage-taking, for someone else to pressure you."

Yolanda looked as if she needed to sit down.

"There are two reliable persons in general security, nandiin-ji," Banichi said, having been in communion with his personal electronics. "I have the names. By your order, we can assign them to bring the paidhi's belongings."

"Do so," Bren said, and to Yolanda: "We now have two agents to attach to you, to this household, as Tano and Algini won't be at your orders, nor should you ask. No matter the temptation, never stray out of this door without the two agents we assign to you. Same level of security as in the Bu-javid. No less hazard."

"Nandi," she said, the respectful form, and seemed utterly lost.

"The guest quarters," he said. It happened to be the library, at other times; but there were beds at need.

"I have a meeting with Ogun," she remembered, and added, gathering her scattered manners, "nandi."

"Advise your staff of your needs when they arrive," he said. "Go to your meeting on schedule, as you and they deem needful. But go with atevi security. Feldman and Shugart will assist her, too," he said to Narani. "They're Tyers' people. One believes one can trust their word, too. We'll want to provide them with residency here in the section. *Not* under this roof, however. They remain Mospheiran. Landa-paidhi's become paidhi-aiji, and she will stay here. Her staff will stay where she disposes them, in this household, starting now, if you can find a moment to advise her."

"Perfectly understood, nandi," Narani said. "We will make the arrangements."

In the midst of packing and everything else Narani had to do. Thank God for his staff.

Late evening. Long evening. They had a guest tucked in toward the kitchen end of the apartment. They had a new pair of guards, formerly attached to general security, undergoing a rapid briefing in what was for them a vast career advancement, and two servants with Tano and Algini quietly retrieving a teddy bear and the contents of Yolanda's closet from her on-station apartment. She had atevi-style clothing in her size, legacy of her days at court—a few years out of the mode, but adequate until the staff could manufacture something more current.

Yolanda had gone to her quarters with the look of a woman in shock by now, just too much change, too many decisions—the aftershock of too many secrets. She'd arranged certain matters and wandered off to her room, and the servants Narani had assigned her reported her asleep in her clothing, to their deep chagrin.

Bren knew . . . knew, he fancied, everything she was going through, alone: ultimately, alone, no matter how many people came and went; alone, the way each of the paidhiin was alone, in that sense, and maybe relieved to hear from another paidhi that the isolation had a name and a reason and a set of rules.

There'd come a time for him when he hadn't found the island safe, or comfortable, either. And he'd—not bullied her into the choice, but maybe narrowed the path on either hand, accelerated the choice, given it a shape for her. He felt guilty about that, or sorry for her, or relieved for her sake, or relieved because she was safer than she would have been—the forgotten paidhi, the paidhi who hadn't wanted the planet at all. He'd done the best thing.

Jase, now—Jase might or might not know where she was. Ogun did by now. She'd ended up postponing her meeting with the senior captain—informed Ogun she'd taken Tabini's request to heart, officially, and needed a few hours to rest, and by the way, was no longer functioning under Ogun's orders.

She'd already informed the aiji, the aiji-dowager and Lord Geigi, officially and in order of protocol—he'd helped her with the wording: *I have most gratefully accepted the aiji's summons to duty and accept Bren-paidhi's hospitality until such time as felicitous long-term adjustments can be made. I await the aiji's instruction, etc., etc. . . .*

He was as tired as she was. It was a decent letter. He knew he had to add his own. He wasn't, tonight, up to it.

The apartment was quietly, constantly, depressingly astir with servants packing and rearranging. He didn't ask special favors, not even tea near bedtime.

But Jago came while he was undressing for bed, to his great surprise. "News?" he asked.

"No," she said. "That's not why I'm here."

"Welcome," he said, and she lay down beside him. She was as tired as he was, he was well sure, but there was brief lovemaking, a release of nerves, a little rest for both of them.

The thoughts, the problems, however, wouldn't leave him alone. He slept briefly, then waked, fearing that that was all the sleep he could get. His mind traveled upstream doggedly, vexingly, back to complete awareness and a new assault on yesterday's problems.

Jago stirred beside him. Sighed. Drew a knee up, to judge by the motion of the bedclothes.

"Are you awake?" he asked.

"Yes," she said.

"Is there trouble with Cenedi? I never did ask, nadi."

"No, Bren-ji. It was routine." She kept things from him—she and Banichi did, being charitably aware that the paidhi's mind approached overload. The interview with Cenedi might encompass a good many things that would worry him, if he asked too closely.

Today there'd been a good many changes. Worrisome changes. And information shifted value. And he hadn't thought through the new configurations as far as he wished he had time to do.

"Have I done well with Mercheson-paidhi?"

"Indeed."

"Once she contacted us—she did contact us?"

"Yes."

"Once she did that, it seemed a good thing. Far safer for her to be here. I don't think her own people would move to restrict her. Or understand how to protect her. I *am* worried about Mospheiran influences. More—I'm worried about her own captains. I know I'm right to break her out of the crew."

"One does agree."

"You heard about the tape."

"Yes."

The conversation with Mercheson kept nagging at him. Her worries about Jase—worries approaching serious doubts—nagged at him.

And more . . .

"When I went down to the planet," he said, "that trip drew our concentrated attention there. Did it not, nadi-ji?"

She was a greater than usual warmth beside him— or he was colder than usual. There was only the least hint of light, to his eyes—but to hers, quite enough.

She rolled suddenly onto one elbow. He knew the pose, when his eyes failed to find her.

"It did," she admitted, increasingly keen and aware.

"We suspected nothing, then." There was no illusion of sleep, now. No possibility. "Persons might have moved up here, Jago-ji. Even Guild could have come aboard without us knowing. Is it possible?"

"We have a list of everyone on that shuttle that came up with you," she said. "And every shuttle flight previous. Thus far we've found no suspect."

His security had not been idle. Never, ever think it.

"So you have suspicions."

"It's our tendency, is it not?"

"Who will replace us here?" he asked. "Who is Cenedi leaving? I take it he's leaving some staff."

She named two men, Kalasi and Mandi.

"I don't know them that well," he said.

"They're very good," she said. "Of the *dowager's man'chi*, unquestioned."

"Not precisely Tabini's, that is to say."

"Hers, Bren-ji. Unquestioned."

Wake up, paidhi. Listen to your staff.

"Will Tano and Algini be safe, staying behind, Jago-ji?"

He felt Jago draw a long and thoughtful breath. "Cenedi's men will assist Lord Geigi. In that decision, we are outranked, Bren-ji. Our own staff—"

"We are Tabini's. Is that a difficulty?"

"One hopes otherwise."

Oh, he'd hoped for a denial on that score. "But the politics of it—"

"While the Association stays stable, our staff can ally with Cenedi's men. As Geigi's can. Under Ogun, things will likely change. Predictions fail us."

A low-level and chilling thought, often dismissed, kept nagging him. "*Lord Geigi* wouldn't have killed Ramirez, Jago-ji. Surely not."

"It's not his disposition. Although—"

"Although?"

"Lord Geigi has his own dealings with the aiji, Bren-ji. That isn't to discount."

"Through Tabini? Acting as the aiji's agent?" It wasn't a comfortable notion at all, that Tabini would have finally decided to take Ramirez out—but that theory satisfied so many other conditions, and filled so many holes, and agreed so well with things he'd found out from Yolanda. The timing. The horrid question of timing.

That trip.

Getting the paidhi-aiji *off* the station. Out of play.

Getting Banichi and Jago, what was more, off the

station and out of play—because those two were the most likely of anyone to detect critical movements of atevi staff.

"Or acting for the aiji-dowager. *There* is the close association, Bren-ji. Lord Geigi has long been in her association."

Ilisidi?

"Do you, even marginally, think it?" He almost asked—where is her motive to attack Ramirez? But he'd been thinking far too many hours in human terms.

"They *did* enter closed conference, the moment she arrived, Bren-ji. You have not been invited to her table tonight—yet Geigi was. *I* have been invited to conference with Cenedi, but at no time was I in position to overhear her and Geigi. One suspects something stirs there. But one still doubts her motive against Ramirez on her own behalf. There simply is no evidence."

"It might have been natural causes. There are coincidences. But one, unfortunately, has to suspect every direction *except* natural causes."

"Coincidence is the rarest beast, Bren-ji. Its tracks look like so much else."

"But with Tabini behaving oddly—oddly, Jago-ji. Oddly toward me. Oddly toward the whole association."

"Yes," she said, one of those enigmatic *of courses*, agreeing with him: *she* was puzzled.

So must Tabini have been—puzzled, or something like it.

By what Yolanda had indicated this evening, Ramirez, against all warnings from everyone who knew better, had opened direct communication with the atevi lord of the known world.

And while Tabini was the most enlightened, the most modern, the most interculturally aware of rulers, he was also atevi, and Ragi atevi, to boot—which meant he counted the expenditure of one man a very enlightened economy versus the need for troops, or wars, or invasions, all of which were as rare as coincidences in atevi dealings.

Tabini wanted a space station: he damned near had it. He wanted a starship: they were building it, and Mospheira had very few illusions as to who was going to get his hands on it once it flew. It *was* an atevi world, and rulers in Shejidan long before Tabini had been conducting a steady campaign, usually quiet and bloodless, to maintain atevi authority over it. If Ramirez had said the wrong thing, and if Tabini had become convinced that it would advance his interests to remove Ramirez—it was possible. And if Ramirez had been tottering near death, in Tabini's perception— if there was a real and increasing possibility of Ramirez's making mistakes and dropping stitches— far from eliciting the sympathy a Mospheiran might expect, that would have alarmed Tabini. It might have convinced an atevi mind accustomed to weigh one life against many that someone had to take charge smoothly and quickly . . . that it was the ethical, reasonable choice, even for Ramirez's own good.

There it bloody was. The whole reason for *man'chi*. Such things didn't happen in polite atevi circles because polite atevi circles *were* circles, inclusive, overlapped, interconnected.

It was *so* damned dangerous to deal with an atevi power from outside the circles.

He'd warned Ramirez. Shawn Tyers above all others knew the hazards, and hadn't been going past him, but Ramirez had engaged Yolanda as his own, wrenched her tightly into his orbit and played his own game.

Which meant—

"If Ramirez *initiated* contact with Tabini, he ignored numerous, very basic warnings," he said to Jago in the dark. "Tabini won't blame her for things Ramirez could have said, but she should be cognizant of them. And Ramirez may or may not have logged those conversations privately. As senior captain—he had the accesses to be off the ship's official record . . . I'm relatively sure that's the case. We don't know what they did. Only Tabini does."

"Affront would have brought him to you, paidhi-ji, I strongly think so."

Yet she reserved the chance she could be wrong. He picked that up. "Kroger's coming up here with those robots . . . that meant everything was done. The means to refuel, out there at the station, if the ship should go. Do you think that was the last stone?"

The last stone on the stack, that was. The one to touch off the slide.

"It is possible."

"Jago, I didn't see this. Of all disasters I could have failed to see coming—I didn't see this one."

"The aiji has taken the station," Jago said quietly. "One believes so, though Ogun-aiji may not think it.

Well to have Mercheson within these walls. It was well done, Bren-ji."

"Is that why Banichi brought her? Is that what you think?"

"We had not foreseen danger to Mercheson. But now we see movements within the crew that trouble us. We did foresee that Tabini would move when Ramirez died. And we did foresee that the dowager might come as his agent—but we by no means know whether we are correct in that assumption. We believe that *she* has demanded custody of Cajeiri as a condition for her help—a very potent symbol for the east, nand' paidhi."

Sometimes a human mind could think all the way around an object, feeling it all the way, and still come to wrong conclusions.

"That she's teaching the heir. That she's not being sent to her death. Is that the notion?"

"We suspect so. *I* suspect so, after talking to Cenedi. This voyage is difficult. She may not survive it. Cenedi has not opposed the venture, considering that Cajeiri is in her hands. If she should die, *Cenedi* will have custody of the heir-apparent, and be within that *man'chi*. More, this is a child, and Cenedi's will be the guidance and the instruction. There is the likely thought, Bren-ji. There is the reason the aiji's heir is with her. Tabini will be the power on the earth. Tabini will have his ship. Ogun will cooperate with him, if Tabini can take Mercheson into his *man'chi*, as seems likely to happen. It will all be subtle. Certain ones may vanish from the scene—as I foresee. Banichi considers Paulson in danger: I say no. Paulson is a fool, but a fool is safe in his office, if he's a Mospheiran fool. If Lund comes up here, Lund will know better; Lund may be in danger."

And he'd suggested Lund come, as a way to get Ogun better advice.

"You got the logs from Mogari-nai, didn't you?" Extraneous question, the answer to which he thought he knew.

"We did watch contacts. There were no records available to us. We did search Mogari-nai, at our level of authority, and at Guild level."

"But there is one higher."

"Yes. Always there is one higher."

"I think we know the truth," he said. "I think we know we were gotten out of the way, being called down there."

"One believes so. There will have been codes," Jago said, one of those rare revelations of her craft, "given to lord Geigi, or to his men, or even to independent agencies. This we always knew, that the station is very easy to infiltrate, with so many *man'chiin* involved. No different than the Bujavid. Anyone can send an unregistered agent—" Non-Guild assassin, that was to say—not lawful, but not utterly illegal. "Right now Banichi is attempting to trace atevi access to Ramirez's venues. But there are too many tunnels in this place, too many accesses, doors far too easy to penetrate, except here. Ramirez had gone onto the station, in a free-access area, observing a known pattern of activity when he had his attack. He ran such risks and heard no advice against it. There were very many opportunities. What happened, if it happened, caused a crisis which caused his death."

Next question. Next very scary question. "Human forensics might detect it, if they were looking. And Ramirez was neither buried nor burned."

"Troublesome."

"His body will go on the ship with us. If there ever is a question—if it matters—they can investigate."

"It is inconvenient," Jago said.

"And Ogun? His safety? He manages the training of pilots. He's a very vulnerable linch-pin, Jago-ji, in all the plans we have. If this place is such a sieve that random individuals can operate—"

"This Cenedi and I discussed. And there must be provisions made for his protection."

"Which will draw him closer to the aiji's hand."

"One can foresee such. Lord Geigi does think favorably of him. If he would draw closer to Geigi's *man'chi*, he might be safer. One is aware, however, that Ogun-aiji has no successor the aiji won't regard as junior."

The thought was terrifying. "I wish I was going to be here."

"Yet is there not danger where the aiji sends us?"

"Very likely."

"And should we let the situation out there arrive back here uncontrolled, unobserved, unmodified, nandi? You would not choose that."

He saw the deep void, and felt cold, and scared. Something in him insisted that an honest Mospheiran had no business going on ships into the dark, over unthinkable distances.

"One thinks," Jago began to say, further, and then Jago's hand rested on his shoulder. Someone was in the hall.

Someone turned out to be one of their own, from the foyer. And *one of their own* turned out to be Tano.

"Excuse me," Tano said. He was a shadow against the vague light from the foyer that permeated the central hall: no light touched within that outline. "Nand' paidhi."

Open as the household was, Tano would scarcely venture into his bedroom, not without an uncommonly urgent reason in the security station.

"Tano-ji. Trouble?"

"A handful of sudden matters," Tano said. "Your brother, nandi; also *Barb*-nadi—"

My God, Bren thought with a sinking heart. Toby. And Barb. Barb was not someone he wanted to hear from, but Barb, like Toby, orbited around his mother. He dreaded news from that quarter—especially together, in the middle of the night.

"Also," Tano said, "the aiji *and* the aiji-dowager have sent messages. All at once."

All at once.

Temper hit, hard after the first ice-cold shock.

"Either C1 or Mogari-nai has had a hold in place," Jago suggested softly out of the dark behind his bare shoulder, and, oh, indeed he was sure she was right.

Mogari-nai—site of the big dish that communicated with the station—or C1, the ship communications station—had blocked his calls, all the while assuring him there was no problem. And now, responding to some authority which could be only one of two, they released everything . . . all his personal calls, all his delicate family business.

And Tabini's message arrived.

Maybe Tabini had one to the dowager as well. And *that* had likely triggered something to him from the dowager.

No, the world below had not suddenly gone berserk. It was a chain-reaction, a dam-break.

A torrent of probable bad and worse news . . .

That the paidhi's mother was in critical care didn't matter, on the scale of nations and the future of two species.

"Find Jase," he said, furious, and trying to control both the temper and the shivers that resulted from the adrenalin hit. And no, one did *not* talk to a loyal atevi staffer that abruptly, ever. "Kindly call him, nadi-ji. Tell him I'm extremely distressed at what is clearly a mail-block from either C-1 or Shejidan, and I urgently ask its origin. You may explain the circumstances."

"One will do so, nandi. Shall I wait?"

"Ask now. Find out the truth diplomatically, nadi-ji."

Tano left at once. *He* got out of bed and searched the dark for his robe—ran his toe into the bed-base and smothered the yell of frustration.

Jago draped the robe over his shoulders. He felt it settle, thrust one and the other arm into it, belted it, all the while thinking, unworthily, but with a deep, sick feeling in his stomach—Jase knew, Jase knew, Jase knew about my mother. Didn't he know?

Did I tell him? If I told him, why in *hell* didn't he just let the personal messages through?

If not Jase—

Tabini. Who *didn't* know.

Unless the spy-net that surrounded him had told him. Which it might not have.

"Shall I wake the staff, Bren-ji?" Jago said, slipping on her shirt.

He reached one reasoned resolution. "I'll dress, Jago-ji." He'd sat shivering in his robe in the security station far too often in his career, dealing with some godawful midnight crisis. And damn it, it was halfway to local morning. Occasionally his comfort counted, and he could be inconsiderate pursuing it, when it meant having his very critical wits about him. Especially if he had to practice impromptu diplomacy. "I'll dress and I'll have hot tea, thank you, Jago-ji, if you'd kindly arrange that. I think our sleep tonight is done for."

14

It was the security station, but not without his cup of tea, and, of greatest import, with his security staff at hand, to keep current with what he heard and form their own conclusions.

He had showered, gathered his wits—dressed even to the morning-coat.

He had had half the tea, and set the cup down on the console near him as he sat down.

Jago sat down beside him. Banichi had thrown a robe about himself—no one had disturbed Banichi until now, in one of his rare chances at peaceful rest—and hovered behind his chair. Tano and Algini, at the far end of the room, worked in their Guild's equivalent of fatigues, with the addition of a light jacket—ready to fall onto the cots in the small adjacent alcove if they were so lucky—if this letter-flood proved an alarm over very little.

"Which will you wish first, nandi?" Tano asked him.

"The aiji's," he said, and immediately it reached his screen.

Bren-ji, the message said. At least it was still the intimate address.

Ramirez-aiji is dead. So I understand. This was by no means unexpected.

Your duties are removed, considered, and assigned to Lord Geigi's discretion. Worry no more for them.

I have honored you as a lord of the aishidi'tat. I have accorded you place and appearance among the highest in the Association. I have seated you among the household in view of all the great and notable of the world.

I have given you a lord's estate, a lord's title and position. You are Lord Bren.

What, preface to removing it? Dissatisfaction? He certainly saw the signs. He hoped it didn't unravel everything he'd done with Mercheson.

Now I make you my representative in the provinces and associations of the heavens.

I have instructed Lord Geigi, your close associate, to rule over the station during your absence, in particular to exert the authority of the aishidi'tat over the station's management and personnel.

Wait, there. *Representative in the provinces and associations of the heavens.* It at least wasn't a demotion. It did sound like one of those honorary titles to which elderly lords retired when they were due for honor, fancy clothes, long titles, but no power at all.

I appoint you chief negotiator to all you may meet, with all needful authority.

Not a demotion, one could say. God. Maybe Tabini
was perfectly serious. What did he get next? A request
to subdue that territory, the way the aiji had asked
him to take the space station?

*Understanding that great distances and long jour-
neys lie ahead, within your domain,*

Understatement, aiji-ma.

. . . nevertheless I send my son, heir to the aishidi'tat,
*to witness the conduct of foreign dealings, to be in-
structed in things which no ateva has seen, and to
grow in wisdom. I shall look forward to his safe return.*

To the best of my ability, aiji-ma.

*Regarding the surprise which this turn of events
may have occasioned you, I did not inform you of negotiations with Ramirez-aiji because I wished to provide you with no excuse on which to hang anomalous
behavior, therefore making it sure you would report
such small details to me, as you have routinely done.*

*If the ship-folk had done other than fuel the ship, I
knew that your suspicions and opposition would set
your agents immediately to learn the extent and reason of their actions.*

*I gave Ramirez-aiji his requested secrecy from sta-
tion and crew, but did so in the sure knowledge the
paidhi-aiji would never allow him to proceed beyond
his agreement.*

Damned atevi penchant for cross-checking, *that* was what Tabini claimed for a motive—keep everybody checking on everybody, and *not* trusting Jase, Jase being within Ramirez's *man'chi*. Of-damned-*course* Tabini didn't rely on Jase in any agreement with Ramirez.

And if he hadn't heard half of what he'd heard, he would have believed it was the whole truth: an ateva, however adept in human relations, couldn't get past the implications of an association, not on a gut level. *Jase* had been outside the pale, so long as he was promoted to a lesser rank of captain, so long as he was Ramirez's protege. Even the paidhi-aiji might have been under just a little shadow of suspicion in Tabini's reckoning—because of Jase, because he was up here, and out of Tabini's convenient reach: it was certainly a situation Tabini just wasn't used to.

And to an ateva mind—of-damned-course— Ramirez's death would free Jase from that *man'chi* and make everyone associated with him easier to trust.

Tabini had opened a behind-the-door communication with Yolanda—a double-check, very logical in atevi affairs . . . perfectly fine excuse, if, in accepting it, he followed the logic to the needful conclusion and took no detours past what he now thought was the truth.

There were facts, however, contingent on those assumptions that *were* pertinent. Even a master politician in atevi affairs could be mistaken about human loyalties. Jase was *not* more trustable now; quite the contrary. The captaincy settled on him would make him responsible to the ship *after* Ramirez's death in a way Ramirez had never been able to get him to be during his life. Now even Yolanda said—watch Jase. Rescue Jase from Sabin. And Tabini would believe him more. The old problems in the interface were *not* necessarily solved.

Ramirez-aiji came to me with the report regarding the survival of three hundred individuals on the remote station.

Came to *him*, was it? To Tabini? Interesting . . . answering what Yolanda said she didn't know. It meant at least there'd been a tight focus to the approach, one item, not a general fishing expedition on Tabini's part . . . he found that reassuring regarding Tabini's understanding of the hazards.

And three hundred alive. *There* was a datum to remember.

Three hundred individuals, however, was a damned tiny crew to try to maintain air quality, water, heat, and sustenance on a battered space station—read, a very tiny crew to try to keep the station power plant going for what might be decades, in some very small area of the station—he'd learned that by experience— all undetected by outside observation.

And *no* outside fuel-gathering or processing, not with that small a population: hence the absolutely critical matter of Kroger's robots. Certain priorities became more understandable.

He declared, Tabini's letter went on to say, regarding Ramirez, *that he has no* man'chi *toward the leadership aboard the remote station. More, he has declared them anathema and has joined as third in association with the Presidenta and myself, committing his successors to abide by this agreement.*

In effect, he has committed himself and this ship and all future ships to join the aishidi'tat, *considering the earth of the atevi his residence forever.*

God, was that *right?* Could what Tabini understood Ramirez to agree to possibly be the case?

If it was so, here was where the mistranslations Yolanda might have engendered on that topic could be very, very scary. Diplomats of two species and three governments used long-managed, absolutely precise language describing international relationship, lordship and ownership. And the juniormost paidhi, least fluent in Ragi, had been handling an impromptu interface between two leaders who spoke just enough of each others' languages to get into the very trouble generations of paidhiin had worked midnight hours to avoid.

Ramirez was dead . . . of what? Something he'd said? Something that had sealed his death warrant, because it contradicted what he'd seemed to promise?

Yolanda had probably tried to define her idiosyncratic terms, and she had the dictionary . . . but the interface could have blown up from that very effort to define terms. Anything could have been a trigger—a promise not fulfilled, an agreement seeming to be doubled back on—a death supposed to be imminent, but that didn't come off on schedule. Nuances were the devil.

And an amateur had tried her best, and preserved secrecy both parties wanted, and now one of the participants was suspiciously dead.

The same amateur who was going to have to take over his job.

But it wasn't the time to let his blood pressure rise, above all else. Calm. Quiet. Work with the situation that was, not trying to trace the dangerous turn from years back, not taking any hypothesis as true, no matter how many legs it seemed to stand on . . . but . . .

Damn. *Damn Yolanda,* that she hadn't come to him.

Damn her . . . but did he have the cold-blooded understanding of the situation sufficient to go to her and say, You may have killed Ramirez. Please be more careful, nadi.

There was more.

I entrust you now with the treasured past, the stable present, and the unpredictable future of the aishidi'tat.

Unpredictable certainly described it.
And Yolanda was the translator.

I think with greatest personal pleasure on our sojourns in the country, paidhi-ji, and will miss your attendance in court. I have consoled myself once more with the sight of your face, knowing that the time was short.

There had to be a better reason. Surely. Tabini had asked him down there and waltzed him right back to the station only to see him, saying nothing else?

Yet, knowing atevi, say all that Tabini would—and often—that number-counters were superstitious fools and the bane of his existence, Tabini was still atevi, did still look at the numbers of a thing. Gut-deep, maybe, for atevi sorts of feelings, dared he think Tabini had wanted to have a physical look and a little less theory behind his decisions?

Maybe he'd wanted to assure himself one last time of the qualities of the paidhi-aiji, before he did something so irrationally, impossibly foolish as commit the dowager out there, with his son.

What was he to think? That Tabini had made an emotional decision?

But the ceremony itself—facing change, change Tabini might have timed, that ceremony not only got him down there and Ilisidi in from the east, it also got various troublesome lords into arm's reach . . . where Tabini's canny security and direct access to the Assassins' Guild could insert agents onto their staffs, where he might make linkages that might be useful—who knew? Going to court was proverbially like visiting a plague ward: you might exit in apparent perfect health, but even the watchful and prudent were apt to have contracted a few unguessed contagions.

Trust that those lords knew that—but they were also bound to have seen both the shocking changes in Shejidan and the power—the evident economic and political power—of the aiji.

That would certainly bring some sober second thoughts on the part of any potential troublemaker.

Farewell for a time, paidhi-aiji. Prepared and strengthened by your services, I look forward to receiving you again at court and hearing firsthand the marvels of this new territory.

He took a sip of cooling tea, and cleared the letter over to the rest of the terminals with a *disseminate* command—for his security staff to read, and be entirely amazed. He'd read it. He'd have to read it a dozen times before he'd found everything buried between the lines.

Lord of the heavens? Paidhi to strangers?

He wasn't confident. He wasn't at all confident. But his authority . . . at least wasn't diminished. Tabini wasn't angry at him.

Dared he say the paidhi had had an emotional reaction to the thought that Tabini might have had an emotional moment toward him?

How tangled the relationship became.

"Did you contact Jase, Tano-ji?"

"Inquiry stopped at C1, nandi."

"One rather thinks the stoppage behind all these messages was not C1, however," Bren said. "And Jase may simply be sleeping, like reasonable people."

"Mogari-nai, then, assuredly."

"Almost certainly," Bren said. "Give me my brother's letter, Gini-ji, and read the aiji's."

Toby's letter went up on his screen—a letter straight to the point.

Sorry I hung up on you. You hit sore spots. Maybe you had to.

Mother improves and worsens day by day and I don't know what's going on. They're calling in a new specialist. That's all anyone knows. I sent some flowers in your name.

Damn it, Toby, if I wanted to send flowers, I would have.

But was that right to say? Was it right not to think that, this time, all matters of his policy about his family were suspended? This could be the last time. Ever. A bouquet of flowers—what was that, in the long battle they'd waged, he and his mother, he for his freedom, his mother for her concept of what the family was?

I sent her some in my name too, and in Jill's, and the kids. And I'm going on a three-day sabbatical . . . going to find Jill and see if I can explain one more time. Tell her the same old things, one more time. I don't think it's going to help, but I'll try.

Barb's with Mother. She wants to do this. Mother seems to improve when she's there.

But you're right: I have to go pull pieces together and see if I can get back what I had. That all relies on Jill forgiving me. If she does, there's something. I don't know if the kids can forgive me at this point. They don't have the perspective. But Jill might be my advocate with them . . . even if we can't get back to where we were

Don't go in expecting defeat, brother. Don't ask for half of what you need. You can't ever win like that.

But I can't help, either. I've done enough of that. Entirely enough. I've become part of the problem. Yours—and hers.

I know my troubles can't matter much on the scale of things you routinely deal with . . .

Oh, don't give me that, Toby; you damn well know you're pushing a button—a damned sensitive one.

I really do know that, Bren. And I'm glad you're out there doing what you do. Personally I don't know what to do with all the changes in the world. We agreed to the paidhiin to make change easier for atevi and maybe now we need paidhiin just to explain to the rest of us ordinary types where all this scary stuff is going so fast.

But you ride the wave, and the world's just going to change, isn't it? We have to cope with the station and space and the aliens and all of it and just carry on in spite of it all. I think that's one of Mother's difficulties, that the world just isn't the way she thinks it is—and now I'm not sure it's all the way I always thought it was. I'm not sure I like what's happened. I know I don't like you having to go off from the island and not being here, and I miss you. But that's not anything either of us can help, and I know I can't even imagine what you're dealing with right now. I guess I thought I could do the other things for you and take the weight off your shoulders, but that's stupid: the one thing Mother wants is her whole family, all the time, and she wants everything her way. I think you're right: it's not what she ought to have, even for her sake—it seems damned late to try to make that point, but it's not for want of trying, all these years, is it? You tried. Now I've tried. For a while I thought I couldn't be happy until Mother was happy, because I wouldn't have done my duty; and that's what's got me where I am and her where she is—and neither of us is happy.

So I'm going. I'm going to try one more time if Jill will believe me this round.

I left Barb there at the hospital. She wanted to, days ago, and now I've let her, and she's there, and I'm not.

You'll be able to get hold of me through my messaging.

You were right. I'm admitting it this time.

Forgive me. —Toby.

Forgive you? God. You still haven't gotten the point, Toby. It isn't forgiving you; it never was. There *is* no forgiving. We just *are*. That's all I ever asked.

He sat still a moment, finger crooked against his mouth, holding in the urge to say something, do something, intervene in Toby's life one more time. But that was right on the same level as *forgiving*. They needed to let go. He'd always needed to let go. In the end, he was like their mother, and he hadn't let go of her or Toby when he needed to.

His staff said nothing to him. But a silence had fallen in the room.

He composed himself, cool and calm.

"Next letter, if you will, Gini-ji."

* * *

Dear Bren, it began, the dreaded letter from Barb.

Dear Bren,

I've tried to write this a dozen times at least over the last three years and I still can't put in what I want, so here goes.

The short answer is, I'm with your mother. We're peas in a pod, aren't we, mother and daughter, all that important stuff?

I know you can't be here. I've learned a lot over the past ten years, and I know it doesn't matter a drop in the ocean that I understand anything—well, maybe it does matter a little, so I'm saying it anyway.

I know you are what you are, and that's all part of the package. I take the one with the other, and that's not all right, but it's what I've got and it's the bed I've made for myself, so here I am, still in love with you, still in a mess. What's new?

Out of the least likely source—a kind of understanding. It brought back one of the better evenings, one of the best evenings . . . the reason he'd thought he was in love with Barb, a naïve long while ago.

She'd married, suddenly, stupidly, bought herself a world of discontent and grief over his failure to be what she wanted—but over all, had there ever been anyone on Mospheira who understood him better?

Couldn't he have talked with her?

She'd developed a genuine tenderness toward his mother.

And wasn't there virtue in that? Didn't he owe her more than he'd ever paid her?

Toby's gone to the coast for the weekend. He's kind of in a state. I don't know whether he's heard from you since the phone call. He said you made a lot of sense, whatever that means, and I asked if he'd called you and he said he'd write later, so I hope he will.

And what about Mum, Barb? Can we possibly get to the damned news, for God's sake?

I told your mother I was going to write to you. I told her you were back on the station, and she said that was like you and she wasn't surprised. I asked her what she'd say to you because I was going to write this letter and she just said get here when you can.

How *is* she, Barb? Dammit, can you just say?

I know things are the way they are. So I've gotten to thinking how the station is part atevi and part human. And even if I can't handle the mainland, I think I can handle that.

Damn you, Barb. *No*, I'm not taking you back. I can't.

So I ask myself, kind of wistfully I guess, if I could find a place there, the way we used to be, just on occasional weekends, Bren.
Nothing formal or permanent. I tried the wife business and found out I'm not cut out for that, and I know you're not cut out to marry. It doesn't stop me loving you, whatever you think. I know about the atevi

woman, and I'm actually glad you're not alone. But whoever you're with, if she can understand, too, and if it ever gets convenient for me to be up there, maybe you can put in a word for me with her. At least say thanks and I understand. I've lived a lot of life in the last six years.

Meanwhile I'll argue your mother into understanding. I'm good at that. I practiced six years on myself.

Forever and ever,

—Barb

What was there left to say for Barb?

That Jago, exasperated and angered by the push and pull Barb had exerted on him before now, had offered to file Intent on her?

That she was, at least at the edge of his thoughts, his one remaining vestige of a human relationship neither birth nor the job had settled on him—the only lasting one he'd made for himself, for its own sake.

And, oh, by the way, she was divorced and free again. Never mind *his* whole world had changed.

There was a kind of tragedy in that. Desire for warmth and foreknowledge that she always stopped when the temperature passed the bounds of her own convenience. There was his mother in a capsule, the woman who'd taught him how to negotiate from the cradle up—negotiate for love, for career—for survival.

And if there was a member of his own species who could handle his mother, it was Barb; and if there was a human association he didn't want to rekindle to all its old heat, it was Barb.

Get here when you can. That his mother had said exactly what Barb reported—along with *I'm not surprised*—oh, that statement he believed. That complaint was so familiar it sounded warm and smelled of pancakes.

Well, it wasn't the nicest love a son could have, but it had kept him and Toby warm their lives long, and there was good news in the packet, after all. If Toby was off after Jill under these extreme circumstances, maybe Toby had finally gotten an inoculation of sorts.

And Barb was with their mother. *Peas in a pod,* and damn if she wasn't right.

And he was out of the picture. He might not ever see his mother again. It was a real possibility. But he could only think of escape, on that front.

Go, he wished Toby. Go with all you've got. Change. You can do it at that age. I did. Take Jill out on that boat and don't answer the damn radio.

"Put the files on my computer, Gini-ji. Thank you."

He wanted them, not for sentiment, but to remind himself of the facts of the situation every time he grew maudlin.

And to rethink Tabini's moves, if it became pertinent.

"None so bad," he said to the four of them. "It explains some things. I *can* assure you all that Barb's not coming with us."

Jago had a look on her face that defied translation.

He added, for her benefit, "Another solar system is too close."

The news would break soon, that the ship was going. The station and the ship were constantly observed by hobbyists. Its absence would make the news even if Tabini didn't announce it—and he was sure that Tabini would announce it first. His mother, Barb, Toby—perhaps the President of Mospheira to boot, though one rather thought that his old ally Shawn was a willing co-conspirator with Ramirez and Tabini—were about to learn that the world was, once again, not what they had expected.

"The dowager's letter," he said.

This one, it turned out, had come in by courier, not electronic at all—and not within the electronic system the ship could spy on. Tano leaned and gave it to him, a small, familiar message-cylinder.

The door had opened, and he and Jago alike had failed to know it. They *were* tired.

We will board a few hours before the ship leaves, the dowager's note said. *We have sent certain personnel to board and secure premises. We trust that you will find our arrangements adequate. We understand your mother is ailing. We express my grandson's concern, and mine.*

We understand you have taken Mercheson-paidhi into your hands and set her in authority over your household. My staff will respect that perimeter and assist her as necessary.

He showed that letter to Banichi, and it went from him to Jago, and on to Tano, and Algini.

"Will you answer, nandi?" Tano asked quietly.

"Before we leave," he said. He dismissed all thought of sleep tonight. He thought it might not be until tomorrow night. "Apologies to the staff, nadiin-ji. I'll have breakfast. Might as well take care of business that has to be done. Staff may have to get sleep as they can—if they *can* sleep, let them. Tea and cold cakes are enough."

In no wise would Bindanda permit that to be his breakfast, or the staff's. Tea there certainly was, and warm cakes, and a reasonable breakfast, an any-hours buffet in the dining room. The dowager's staff might find it scandalously impersonal, but his own staff had found certain useful compromises in crisis, in the breakdown of regular hours. Bindanda had recognized the signs, and quietly arranged an excellent table.

There was, in fact, very little for the paidhi to do physically, beyond sit at a keyboard and initiate communications to all manner of agencies that needed information and direction—agencies that had thought they knew who it was they were dealing with and now had to change their entire way of looking at things.

There were dozens of memos, this and that tag-end of information and transmission of contact names and communications channels, all to release as the ship undocked, and he had to remember the content, in case there needed to be changes.

There was a letter to the long-suffering staff on the planet, informing them they had to deal with one more set of requirements.

Please assist Mercheson-paidhi and amend her errors fearlessly, as you have done mine. Her frowns are only for her own effort: she has a good heart.

There was a letter to Geigi, wishing him good fortune. There was one to the dowager, stating he was in preparation to board.

And, among other things, there was a list, for Narani, of those things which staff might not think he needed. Certain picture files he wanted—if anything should happen out there, if they in fact were about to be taken by aliens, he could erase them along with things far more injurious. But he wanted the pictures with him for his sanity's sake, simple images of the coast, the gardens, of his residency in the Bujavid—and of people, oh, no few of people—Toby, on the boat, in that disreputable hat, smiling. Toby's kids, building castles in the sand . . .

He didn't look long. Here wasn't a good time to look. It called up far too many possibilities of things he could do if he could only get the time, the contact, the cooperation, and he didn't have the leisure of that much time.

He sought out reports on ship-status, which was 41 percent ready, whatever that meant—and he called Kate Shugart and Ben Feldman on C1 for a brief word, in essence: "You're the ones with University training. Mercheson outranks you and she's had immersion in the language, but you have the technical channels. Work with her and use them. You know the urgency."

"Yes, sir," the answer was in both cases, no question, no demur. They did know. That was their value.

Meanwhile news reports came in from Mospheira, and he saw the distress in headlines: *Alien Menace Revealed* from the seedier press and *President Reveals Pact* from the more reliable, neither of which made breakfast sit easy.

Shawn's public statement said, briefly, *We have cooperated with our allies in deliberation and preparation based on information now declassified. In accordance with plans made jointly with us and with Shejidan,* Phoenix *captains will, as agreed with us, undertake a carefully defined two-year mission back to their abandoned base, first to be sure conditions are as anticipated and secondly to retrieve certain personnel who have maintained the base as an observation post. They will then close operations there and return to us, to their permanent base at the station. No alien action is anticipated and none has been detected.*

One wasn't sure what the world expected to see at this distance, unless the aliens exploded a star or flashed a high-powered beacon at them. And in the limitations of lightspeed—an islander's mind still struggled with the scale of things—they *still* wouldn't receive the message for a number of years.

The planned operation has no bearing on station construction. Key Phoenix *personnel will remain on the station and actively participate in the program as planned. There is no change in agreements or schedule.*

So what else could they say? Shawn was no fool, either: Mospheira historically distrusted *Phoenix* crew. They were nervous about atevi strangeness on general principles and previous bad experience—but generally they knew what to expect with atevi. Distrust of *Phoenix*, however, had far, far more history with Mospheirans, and the very first conclusion anyone on the island would draw was, *It's all a sham. We've been double-crossed. They're stealing the ship. We've been conned.*

Still, the worst the seedier report had to say was,

The aliens could be looking this way at this very moment. The starship under construction is dependent on politicians for every bolt and panel. The legislature can debate day to dark, but the real threat is clearly out there . . .

They could have said far worse. The thread of trust was stretched very, very thin—but common sense prevailed. He took two antacids and drafted the most important letter of his career.

Aiji-ma, I stand in receipt of your letter and am honored by your personal favor.

As always, I will strive for the benefit of your household and the aishidi'tat, *and all allies. I will do my best, aiji-ma. All information at my disposal makes me sure that the other station is under Pilots' Guild authority. On evidence of past behavior of this Guild, I am determined that this Guild should by no means contact strangers in our name, and I will do all needful things to settle the situation in a stable fashion.*

He was certain that Tabini knew what was happening in the ship, as he was certain Ilisidi was far from idle in her apartments. But he reported, all the same.

—Jase-paidhi has been appointed one of two aijiin to go with the ship. If only because the other captain must sleep, I believe he will periodically have real authority over the ship's dealings, although he lacks technical skills and would by no means intervene in ship operations. I also predict he will not defy Sabin-aiji's will except in demonstrable need, but he is not without intellectual resources and resources of authority, and I know he will be a valuable ally.

Ogun-aiji will remain here, as you may by now be aware, and I strongly urge, aiji-ma, that the aishi'di-tat press forward in alliance with him in the building of the second ship, and the training of atevi personnel to manage it, as the most extreme priority.

Tabini who had had only rudimentary knowledge of his own solar system when he first came to power now had to understand the machinations of a human power at a remote station.

And he had to command and use a starship . . . considering the personally unwelcome prospect of losing Phoenix.

I have certain safety concerns regarding Mercheson-paidhi, who I understand will stand in my place, by your express invitation. I ask she also be allowed use of my apartment and all the resources of my staff in that service. They will save her duplicating my efforts in setting up and maintaining lines of communication.

Further, I am aware of certain areas where there may have been direct contact initiated by Ramirez, aiji-ma, and I am alarmed by the possibilities inherent in conversation unexamined for ambiguities. Mercheson seems a person of great competency and good will toward yourself and the aishidi'tat, and will perform honestly, I believe, but she is still a relative novice, not thoroughly conversant in court protocols and not as alert to nuance as she herself would wish.

I ask, therefore, that you yourself mediate where she is concerned, aiji-ma, no matter how provoked. I ask that you deal gently with Mercheson's inexpertise and that you impose calm on all dealings that may result from error. The sane and good actions of reasonable individuals may still be misinterpreted, but the good will between Ogun and the aishidi'tat is too valuable to let fall, as I know that you are earnest in your desire to preserve all parties from needless harm.

For that reason I believe both Mercheson and Ogun-aiji may be in immediate danger from various persons and agencies ill-disposed toward the treaty. I have taken Mercheson into my quarters and advised her to stay there. I am at present unable to surround Ogun-aiji, but am seeking ways to protect him. I ask that their safety be assured without diminishing their independent authority, so that they may maintain their utmost value to the treaty association.

For the rest, aiji-ma, I cannot predict what I may find regarding the alien threat nor can I do so until I see what the situation may be at the remote station. I *hope for the best outcome and will bend every effort to achieve peace.*

I have no doubt of the aiji-dowager and thank you for approving her participation in this extraordinary venture.

I look forward to our next meeting, baji-naji, aiji-ma. Remote as I may be, I shall turn my mind often to your generosity and your many good deeds toward me, and hope to bring you favorable news.

It wasn't a particularly brilliant letter. Humanly, he couldn't write to an atevi lord what he felt at depth. Professionally, he couldn't instruct the aiji how to deal with Mercheson in a single letter. Politically, he dared not say half he wished he could say: it was only a letter—and it might go astray.

He sent it the rounds of the staff. They praised it. Banichi and Jago would not flatter him, if it wasn't adequate.

By then he'd made several assaults on familial letters—and erased them in despair.

And there was no word from Jase, none from the aiji-dowager.

Yolanda waked, having overslept her watch for two hours, and emerged, ribboned and braided, in court dress appropriate years ago—walked about as quietly as she could, but he called her in.

"Jase is out of contact," he said. "Have *you* any means to call him?"

"I can go after him," she said.

"I want you safe, Landa-ji. Can you call him? Can you call Polano, or Pressman, or anybody?"

"I know someone who can get to Pressman," she said.

"Go try," he said, not even caring what channels communication ran to at this point. "Tell him to call me."

"Yes," she said, and went out to the foyer, to their communications in the security station.

She clearly had some resources of her own. Inside fifteen minutes she came in with a portable communications unit, and contact.

"Jase," he said.

"Bren."

"You all right?"

"No problems. I was downtimed in the tank. Trying to absorb some of the schedule detail. It's all right, Bren. Are you all right?"

"Going crazy here. I'm needing details of our accommodations. This came as a surprise to me."

"No one's contacted you."

"I think it's assumed I'm working through the dowager. This isn't the case. I'll be taking Banichi and Jago and four staff, felicitous seven, thank you, plus our foodstuffs, our furnishings, our belongings. What's our limitations?"

"Nothing. None. You'll be on deck five—they were going for four, and I explained there was no atevi going on deck four—"

"Thank you."

"You'll have five virtually to yourselves. It's operational, the plumbing works, the lights all work, and there's nothing on maintenance. That's room enough to swallow everything you've got in the two residencies. You could take the whole staff if you chose that . . ."

"I'm leaving an establishment for Ms. Mercheson, who's taking over duties here—who I think you know *is* here. Her service is at Tabini's request. It's not negotiable. She's detached from crew, to the paidhi's office. Is that going to be a problem?"

"No. That's accepted."

"I'd like to see you to go over some of this. Can we set a time?"

"Today?" Jase made the offer, the essential *is-it-critical?*

"When's convenient?" He made the matching counter. *Criticality's your call.*

"First off shift after undock. My breakfast. Your dinner."

"Date."

"You got a flood of mail, I noticed." That meant: *Is there anything wrong I need to know?*

"Yes, yes: the news broke. I'm up to my ears in it." It was all Mosphei' and ship-language, nothing hidden, and everything hidden: they passed information the way they'd learned to do in the Bujavid, where every wall had ears; and most of all he took reassurance from Jase's tone, and the simple fact that Jase was personally in touch. He knew about the tank. Jase had an immense amount to absorb; and he was utterly, terribly vulnerable when he did it. He wondered that Jase could find the courage, at the moment. "I'll take care of it. As things stand, I'll be packed in fairly short order; I understand the dowager is packed—"

"Her gear is already boarded, along with some few personnel."

"We'd better really get moving, then."

"First watch tomorrow is soon enough. If you wait until

*fourth, you'll be mixed in with crew boarding. Senior cap-
tain's expressed a preference to have all non-crew on before
the board-call goes out. We're leaving people. There'll be
partings. We want to give them room."*

We. Jase had finally included himself among the
captains, mentally. "Understood. We'll make it. No
problem. We're packed fairly light, considering. If you
need to contact me, don't worry about the hour.
—And if you just want to stop by before that for a
sandwich, we do compare more than favorably with
the crew lounge."

Jase seemed to be amused: at least he skipped a
beat, and since Jase's sense of humor usually vanished under stress, that response was reassuring. *"I'm
sure. Take care. See you after undock—maybe before, but
that'll be on business."*

"See you," he said, and gave the unit back to
Yolanda. "He can't get loose. But he seems all right."

Yolanda had stayed and listened, with never a sign
that he ought to extend the questioning.

"He seems fine," she said. He trusted her instincts,
at least on that issue. And his exchange with Jase—the
sort they'd learned to make in Shejidan—was like old
times, all the old signals, crisp on the uptake and easy
in delivery. Jase was fine, at least as regarded his freedom and his safety now.

Jase was attempting to gain an expertise he'd hith-
erto dodged and defied. In no wise could he bring
himself up to speed with this late start, but he could
learn what was going on, what was routine and what
wasn't—if schedules meant the technical minutiae of

ship-function, the things that should happen from un-dock to the moment they exited the solar system.

Jase wasn't idle. He'd never thought it, but he began to understand what Jase seemed to be under-taking, finally—not wholly surrendering to Ramirez's plan for him, no, he knew Jase's stubborn self-will. Jase hadn't given in. But Jase was far too clever to choose ignorance, either. Information came available to him, and Jase grabbed it while his feet were still—so to speak—on station decking, and be-fore his range of choices diminished. Yolanda wor-ried about his state of mind, and maybe a friend ought to worry about him battering himself against his own ignorance—but it was Jase: it was pure Jase, this headlong attack at a problem he could single out for his own.

Worry later, he thought. Right now Jase was doing things that made thorough sense to his longtime partner—if not the healthiest choice for a man who needed real sleep. There wasn't much of that going on in his own apartment, either.

By supper, his staff adamantly, with a flourish, pre-sented his favorite dishes, clearly determined that the paidhi should have a regular, sit-down meal and an hour-long hiatus in his problems.

After supper, better still, Narani reported their own packing complete, ready for boarding at any moment, while the ship-status showed 42 percent complete. The departure wasn't moving on schedule, he was sure, and he hoped for a reprieve—any reprieve, from any source. Tabini saying, no, he didn't have to go—

that would do ... though it wouldn't happen, and it shouldn't happen. There were worse things than going. Staying, while someone who'd make a mistake went in his place—that was worse.

He stayed up re-drafting letters until he knew he made no sense, and accidentally failed to store the right copies, three of them in a batch.

That was how things were going. He'd had two brandies, and sat staring at one of the pictures he'd chosen to take, thinking of camping on Mospheira's north shore, and Toby's yacht at anchor just off the cove.

Fire, fire on water, that night they'd fought off Deana Hanks' hopes of a war, around the beached wreck of a boat.

They'd had some successes ... the side of reason and interspecies sanity. They weren't out of hope. They'd won the big ones.

But to this hour he'd utterly, wholly, failed his family. He didn't have time left to do the things he needed to do, there wasn't a relationship he had on the island that he hadn't offended, and as things stood now, Barb had heard the news and learned he was on his way out of the solar system. He'd failed to send the letters he still had to send; he'd lost the draft, and his mother and his brother had to get the news the hard way.

So he had to get the letters written—again—not as good as they'd been before he lost the drafts, but the best he could.

On two brandies—he tried.

Dear Barb,

I have to thank you for your loyalty to my family, particularly in the last few years.

I can choose the right words for the job I do, but I never said the right things at the right time between us—maybe because I didn't listen that well, maybe because I had too much of my attention elsewhere, and presumed too far . . . all of which is behind us at this point. We still rely on each other in ways I have no right to ask—but knowing you're where you are, where I can't be, leaves me deeply in your debt. I hope, but have no right to ask, that you'll shed some of the good advice you've given me on my brother and my mother.

I count on you, without a right or a claim, and I can only pile the debt higher. With more good memories than bad—Bren.

He didn't send, not immediately. He slipped it into an electronic folder to send when departure was imminent.

The words finally came to him. The dam was broken.

Toby, by the time you read this you'll know the situation, where I am and why I can't be there. I can't ask you to explain this one to Mother. I just want you to know I couldn't have a better brother.

For your kids, for you and Jill . . . for all of you, I have to do this.

For all the rest of it,—

It was like writing a will. It might well be one. And he couldn't dwell on the situation, or grieve over it—the job didn't budget time for that. It never had.

I wish you the life you need and deserve.

Maybe after this there'll be time for me to pay you back at least a fraction of the favors I owe you. My fondest memory, the best human memory I have, is the sight of you at the rail of the old Molly *yacht, sailing in to save our skins. That, and you and the kids on the beach. I didn't get a family, except yours. I wish I'd been a better brother.*

I wish everybody my best.

At very least—forgive me the bad bits and be sure I'm thinking of you often.

He knew he ought to edit it. He knew there were two brandies on all that correspondence.

Dammit, what more could he say or do?

His staff was still at work—Jago, who had slept no more than he had; Banichi who, also, a certain number of years ago, had not cared whether the sun circled the earth or the earth circled the sun—it was, Banichi had said, immaterial to his job.

He supposed in a certain sense it still was immaterial to Banichi.

He tried to achieve that calmness of soul.

He took a deep breath and transmitted.

15

The ship, by morning, miraculously stood at 92 percent, which argued that elapsed-time had nothing to do with whatever the ship was doing.

With that, too, came a page of loading instructions for all the in-quarters equipment, instructions which—after the initial computer scan did the very rough translation—contained only minor glitches to send the staff into fits of laughter. *Don't have sex with inappropriate equipment* was the absolute favorite, which looked immediately to become a salacious proverb in the household. *Always be playful with officers* ran a close second.

It was a profound relief to laugh—if the paidhi hadn't a dire presentiment of a situation that might be all too frequent in Yolanda's tenure—which perversely brought hysterical tears to his eyes. He wiped them, and tried to steady his nerves, especially when Yolanda exited her quarters to find out what the laughter was about.

Handed the document in question, she looked at it. "Playful," she said, frowning critically.

Good for her. She'd caught that one.

And blushed at the other. "Oh, dear."

There was hope, Bren thought, and went off to the study to quiet his nerves. But there one of the servants gave him the routine message list.

Nothing from the planet. A vast, deep silence from that quarter.

Blocked again? It might well be. Tabini wouldn't want a smoothly-running operation distracted.

The fact that he had family in trouble—that didn't register, on an international scale. It didn't possibly register. He tried not to feel anything, not worry, not anger, not frustration: leave it to Toby, leave it to Toby, leave it to Barb.

Assuming his letters had gotten to them.

And still rely on them—because they were who they were, and they *didn't* need his advice, and it was only for their comfort that he wrote, not because they had to have a word from him. Wasn't that the point? Wasn't that what he had to rely on, ultimately?

He met briefly with the staff that would stay behind, Tano and Algini momentarily surrendering their posts to Jago. Narani attended to answer questions. The rest, those staying, were the youngest faces, including most of the female staff, the youngest over all—and given Yolanda within their care, Narani's choice of the oldest of the women as chief of household seemed apt enough.

"Staff will come up from the world to assist at your request," Bren told them. "If you request. In all points except courtesy to Mercheson-paidhi, you will still remain *my* staff, nadiin-ji, with senior authority over the premises, and I leave you a letter with my seal to make clear that you have that authority. You'll watch over my property and the integrity of security here, under Tano and Algini, who will be the ultimate authority in that regard, reporting where they deem fit. Please be circumspect in your actions, stay generally to the section, and consult with security in technical matters. *You* will act for Narani, and you will stand firm here. Only the aiji's own directives can override my orders. Not Lord Geigi's will nor anyone else's—not Ogun's, not even the aiji-dowager's staff—will take the place of my orders, and you will not consult other households except through Tano and Algini, who may use their discretion whether to take an order from those sources. Do you agree? Staff will obey senior security in matters remotely regarding security. Mercheson-paidhi will have reasonable authority in the house, but you may refuse an order long enough to consult with Tano and Algini as to that order's safety."

There were deep flushes, sudden extreme nervousness . . . the sort of young flightiness and uncertainty that he wished had a Narani in charge . . . he wished he could have two of that gentleman—indeed, two of everyone he was taking with him; but it wasn't possible, and he had to rely on Yolanda's honest intent and his servants' discrimination regarding hazards.

"Security may indeed resort to Lord Geigi or to the dowager's men with any matter that requires their attention," he said to them further, which was instruction mainly for Tano and Algini, "or that might suggest consultation. One trusts their discretion.

And as for the staff in general, don't ever hesitate to report a matter, however trivial, to security, at whatever hour. Better too much information than too little: you'll learn what's necessary. As for Geigi's staff, or the establishment the aiji-dowager may leave, one is sure they're very good, they're discreet, and one believes, Tano-ji, Gini-ji, you can rely on their advice . . . as you can rely on Geigi's or the dowager's *man'chi*, if the matter is of mutual concern. Also, Mercheson-paidhi is within your charge, not the other way about. Make her comfortable, advise her, correct her as you've corrected me. She's new to the office. She will make mistakes which will stem from foreignness, I am confident to say, rather than from fault in judgment." Please God, he thought, saying so. "Support her with advice. Leave critical judgments to Tano and Algini. They will know."

He rarely saw those two look worried. Even Algini gave him a look when he said that.

"I have every confidence," he said.

The ship stood at 98 percent. They had an advisement for all non-crew to board.

Whatever went on in the offices, on the island, on the continent, even in the apartment, stopped being his problem.

God hope the house of cards he and Tabini had built lasted long enough to provide a pattern for the girders of a whole new world.

God hope he got home sometime close to schedule.

Could he ever have dreamed he'd be making this trip, a decade ago?

Ogun had trained crew, a newly-refurbished station, brand new factories and the plans for a starship . . . if the people he left couldn't manage with those assets, he didn't know what more he personally could do for them.

He had already dispatched Bindanda and Asicho to board ahead of them, with his written authorization, which he trusted ship security had honored, and now sent two of the servant staff with another authorization, with two motorized trolleys loaded with all their baggage—those just far enough ahead of them to make it through the lifts and checkpoints and not impede their progress. The dowager's baggage was somewhat ahead of theirs, so staff advised him, also with authorized staff. Boarding for the rest of them—was down to the last minutes.

He and Banichi and Jago said their goodbyes to Tano and Algini in the security station, and again at the door—that was hardest.

One didn't hug atevi, not as a rule. He broke that rule, for his own soul's sake, and embarrassed them.

"It's the human custom," he said. "Indulge me, nadiin-ji, for my comfort, and take good care of yourselves. I value you very, very extremely."

"We are most extremely honored," Tano said, "paidhi-ji."

"Bren-ji," Algini said, and carefully, uncharacteristically, hugged him. Then Tano did. Bren all but lost his composure, and might have if, when he walked away, he hadn't been in company with Banichi and Jago and Narani and the chosen servant staff.

They had increased their estimate of those going. More had found an excuse this morning—*I wish very much to see this place*, was one, and: *My father would never forgive me if I left the paidhi-aiji* vied with *I wish to leave my mother's name in this far place*.

Ship authorities had said they had room enough for a few extra. For the whole apartment, if they wished. So the list grew a little, and Narani recalculated the numbers and ordered more compartments opened, which one authorized, a simple message to the ship—no fuss, no extraordinary effort.

Could a human or an atevi wish better staff around him?

And walking down that corridor, realizing how close they were to boarding and how close he was to letting loose the reins of the unruly political beast he'd ridden breakneck for his whole adult career . . . he experienced a certain momentary euphoria.

"Baji-naji," he said to Banichi and Jago in that giddy feeling. "Baji-naji, nadiin-ji, if it doesn't work now, if Mercheson-paidhi can't make it work, and if Geigi can't, on what we've built—" He said it to convince himself, after his dark night of doubt. "—I don't know what more I can do."

"Bindanda has successfully boarded," Banichi reported to him. "He reports the quarters are heated and lighted and he has set himself to stand guard at the entry, to establish a perimeter, pending arrival of the baggage carts."

"Jase-aiji has communicated with Tano," Jago

added—electronically connected as ever, "and given clearance for the baggage and staff to board. We're expected at our convenience, likewise the dowager, who will follow us."

It all felt completely unreal of a sudden, as giddily impossible as it had seemed possible a second ago. He was a kid from Mospheira. He was a maker of dictionaries in a little office in the Bujavid.

What in hell was he doing in the execution of an order like this one?

He had no business exiting the solar system. He felt the whole concept as a barrier, a magical line that, if he crossed it, would simply evaporate him, a creature that would burst like a bubble in the featureless deep of space.

Yet Jase had exited and entered several solar systems in his life. The ship did it as routine. Magic didn't apply. He had no business being scared of the process, or supposing that disaster would swallow them up without a trace or a report. Hadn't Jase had to have faith in boats, getting out on the sea for the first time, and figuring out that the sea was deep, and that he was balanced on a rocking surface high up—relative to the sea bottom. It didn't matter that a body falling into the water floated and didn't plummet straight to the bottom—it hadn't convinced Jase's gut. And knowing that this ship had done this again and again successfully—in atevi reckoning, were those not good numbers?

As the shuttles had good numbers?

Hell with that. He'd gotten more timid about airplanes, since flying the shuttle.

He'd begun to hold onto the armrests of airplanes, trying to pull the plane into the sky. Stupid behavior. Anxious, animal behavior. He told himself again and again what made airplanes stay in the sky . . . the way he'd used to tell Jase, who *truly* didn't like zipping along near a planet's surface . . . and didn't starships work on perfectly rational principles he just didn't happen to understand as well as he understood airfoils?

In the station's informational system, Banichi now reported, the ship had reached a mysterious 99 percent and holding.

"The dowager has decided to accompany us in boarding," Banichi said further. "Her party will overtake us at the lift."

So. So. A deep breath. Time to wait for protocols. He stalled his small party at the lift door.

In due time, at the dowager's pace, with her staff and with Lord Geigi and his men for escort, Ilisidi and Cajeiri arrived and joined them at the personnel lift. The dowager was of course immaculate and fashionable in a red fur-cuffed coat, and the heir-apparent, neatly pig-tailed in the black and red ribbons of his house, wore a modest black leather coat, red leather gloves, and a quiet demeanor vastly different than his arrival.

Terrified, Bren thought with sympathy for the boy.

Sent from Tatiseigi's ungentle care to Ilisidi's and Cenedi's, and now exiled to travel to the ends of creation in a human-run ship. Was ever a boy faced with more upheaval in his few years?

He was very glad Lord Geigi had come to see them

off . . . considerable inconvenience, all the bundling-up for the cold core, a disturbance in the schedule of a man who got only a little more sleep than he had, Bren was very sure. Still, the *man'chi* was very tight, very sure, and it would have been sad had Geigi not stirred himself out to walk with them.

Hug Geigi? Not quite.

"Paidhi-ji," Illisidi said with a polite nod, the intimate address, acknowledging her traveling companion.

"Aiji-ma." He bowed at the honor. "Nandi." For Giegi, with human affection.

Banichi had called the lift, at the dowager's approach. It arrived at precisely the grand moment.

"Young man." Ilisidi offered her arm to her great-grandson, and the boy took it ceremoniously, escorting his great-grandmother with the grace of the lord he was born to be. They boarded. Cenedi and his men, and the dowager's servants—small distinction between the two duties—held back. Geigi made a subtle wave of his hand, cuing *him* to move: *that* was the way it was, a difficult matter of protocols, and Bren moved, heart racing, thoughts suddenly a jumble of remembrance that, no, he was not demoted, and that Geigi, to whom he was accustomed to defer, gave place to him in the personnel lift—

As if he were higher rank.

Because he was leaving, perhaps, and numbered in the dowager's party, not, silly thought, that the paidhi-aiji, if he even retained the title, in any way outranked the lord of the station. Empty honors,

Tabini had paid him. The paidhi wasn't any lord of the heavens, and hadn't any claim to Geigi's *man'chi*.

God, no. He didn't want Geigi or the dowager to change the way they dealt with him. He didn't want a paper title. He supposed it augmented his rank in dealing with Sabin . . . no matter it was meaningless, but he suspected Geigi was, if charitable, amused. He hoped Geigi wasn't offended. He hoped the dowager wasn't about to make some issue of it all.

He didn't want any more. He *wanted* to retire to his estate on the coast for at least a month and look at the stars from the deck of a boat—Toby's boat, at that.

Instead, the lift arrived, and they all fitted in, the same procedures they used when taking the shuttle down to the planet. He hoped that workers would communicate and the baggage wouldn't stall in their path, and that it would all happen magically, so that the newly appointed lord of the heavens didn't end up in interstellar space without shirts or Bindanda's cooking supplies.

So much had to be a miracle. So much just sailed past his numb senses; and meanwhile he had to muster intelligent small-talk, in a station where the weather wasn't a possible topic.

"So much done so quickly," he said to the dowager as the lift rose.

"Did you hear from my grandson?"

"I did hear, aiji-ma." He feared he blushed. And it wasn't a topic he wanted to discuss, his elevation to mythical lordship. "One was very gratified by his letter."

"Ha," Ilisidi said, one of those ambiguous utterances. "Politics."

And Geigi: "My staff is in communication with your quarters, nandi-ji." Oh, he was glad to hear warmth in Geigi's tones. "Does Mercheson-paidhi favor fish, do you think?"

"She will be greatly honored by your attention, nandi." Fish was almost always safe. And he did remember. "She does favor melon preserves, extremely. All varieties of fruit."

"Ah." Geigi was pleased to have a personal knowledge. And his ability to get foodstuffs off the planet was scandalous. "One will manage."

The apartment might be awash in melon preserves. "I'll be in your debt if you can show my successor the refinements, nandi. One wishes she might have had the benefits of the dowager's estate, as I did."

"Ha," Ilisidi said again. "Benefits, is it?"

"I found it so, dowager-ji. It taught me a very great deal."

"The paidhi listened," Ilisidi said, and tightened her grip on the boy's arm. Gravity was at the moment only a function of the car's movement. "As some should! Do you agree, boy?"

"Yes, mani-ma."

"*Grandmother* will do," Ilisidi said sharply. "*Aiji* will do better. You have official rank here, if I say so, and we'll see whether those shoulders are strong enough, yet. So I say, today. Who knows for tomorrow?"

"Yes, aiji-ma." This quietly uttered, a young soul sharply keyed to the dowager's voice—

Mecheiti racing wildly on a hillside, breakneck after

the dominant. Reason had nothing to do with it. Bren didn't know why he flashed on that, of all moments when he'd nearly died. But it was the fact of native wildlife. It was the fact of atevi instinct: it was the nature of *man'chi*. . . .

He witnessed it, he thought. He didn't feel it. But he intellectually understood the boy had learned to twitch in certain ways to instincts that were life to his species, and held tightly to his grandmother's hand.

That was reassuring to everyone concerned.

They braked. The door opened in a waft of cold pressure-change that frosted metal surfaces.

This time, however, it was not the old familiar sights—not the shuttle dock, with the hatch leading to whatever shuttle sat in dock.

It was dock 1, and a long snake of yellow tubing, which led, he understood, to another, grapple-reinforced tube, where *Phoenix* rode.

Baggage must have cleared. He didn't see it.

"Well, well," Geigi said, "it seems this is the place."

"So one assumes," Ilisidi said. Suited workers now appeared in the tube, out of the bend inside it. "One assumes we have an escort. Go, go back to reasonable places before you freeze, Geigi-ji."

"Safe voyage," Geigi wished them. "Safe travel, safe return, aiji-ma, Bren-ji."

There were bows, such as one could manage, reaching out for safety lines strung along the wall.

Then Geigi and his men were inside the lift, they were outside, and the door shut at their backs with appalling finality.

Phoenix was surely at the other end—intellectual knowledge, but with no view of the dock, only the tube leading to the hatch, it felt rather like being swallowed by some giant of the fairy tales.

The workers beckoned them on. Ilisidi didn't question, rather proceeded down the handline in the only direction possible.

"One can't sail off here, aiji-ma," Cajeiri observed. "Are those the captains?"

"A sensible person wouldn't try to sail at all," Ilisidi retorted. "And those are workers. Don't gawk. Don't chatter. It burns the lungs."

Burn, it did. Breath seemed very short. Or the paidhi was breathing very rapidly.

"A small load of baggage was ahead of us," he said to the workers as they met. "It all should go to fifth deck, my possession."

"Yes, sir," the worker said. No argument, no delay, no fuss. "The tag was all in order. It's well ahead of you. Go right along. Sir. Ma'am."

Things went with frightening finality.

This is real, a small voice said to him, but for the most he felt numb—not as much fear of the trip itself as reason said was logical, rather more a sense of danger to the things he was leaving: fear of what might change while he was gone, family he might lose, people who might carry on their lives without him, and get to places and situations to which he was irrelevant.

I'll come back, he said in his heart. I'll make it back.

But that part wasn't wholly in his hands any longer. Now the unwinding of the yellow serpentine showed them an open hatch, and it swallowed them up, a large hatch, that had no trouble taking in all their party at once, with room left over for one of the workers, who punched appropriate buttons and threw switches. And bet that atevi security, his and the dowager's, recorded those movements, and the accompanying confirmation of lights.

The outer door shut. Then the smaller of the inner doors opened, and their chill gusted out with them into a corridor as bare, as purely functional as the access tunnels on the station: panels with steady and blinking telltales, gridwork deck, ladders going up and sideways—a puzzle to a ground-dweller until a ground-dweller's mind registered the obvious fact that he was drifting and didn't even know which way was up. The air smelled vaguely of paint and plastics and something that could be oil, or solvent. Fans roared.

It was a tubular corridor—ending in a pressure door, again, like the station accesses.

"A grim place," Ilsidi pronounced it, but alert to everything around her.

"This way, if you please," their guide said: his clip-on badge, on a close look, was ship security. "Captain Graham's compliments, I'll be your escort to your quarters. Mr. Cameron, if you'd please advise everyone watch the doors as we go."

"He presents felicitous greetings from Jase-aiji."

"Who is not here!" Ilsidi said, displeased.

"Who is managing the ship to keep it safe, aiji-ma, and sends security to direct us past hazardous equipment. I'm very sure it's proper."

"We demand Jase."

"Aiji-ma," Bren said, "it's by no means certain that Jase is physically on the ship."

"Are we to believe that planning is so slipshod, as not to include any inquiry from us? Are we to believe that this is the degree of care which attends our voyage on this chancy vessel? We do not budge from this corridor until we have assurances."

This very cold corridor, this corridor the cold of which had, after the deep chill of the dock, penetrated his coat and his gloves and started into his human-sized body.

But bluffing? No. Not Ilisidi.

"She demands Captain Graham, specifically," Bren said. "Protocol requires it. So we'll stay here."

"You can't stay here, sir. You're in a traffic area."

"I agree. I respectfully suggest this place is very cold, and I personally will be very grateful if Captain Graham is aboard, and makes every effort to get down here, so we can resolve this before we become a traffic problem."

Their guide had a baffled look, and relayed that fact on his personal electronics: "Gran 'Sidi's aboard and wants Captain Graham to take her to quarters immediately."

There might have been discussion. Or incredulity on the other end.

"They're in the corridor, sir, and won't budge."

"The aiji-dowager has suggested," Bren added, "that if he fails to appear this would be a major breach of protocol, not auspicious at all for the voyage. Downright unlucky for the ship."

The worker relayed that, too, as: "The aiji-dowager's upset, ma'am, and Mr. Cameron's saying it just has to get done. Something about unlucky for the ship."

Another silence. And if there was a superstitious streak left among the crew it regarded the ship itself.

"Captain Graham's in a meeting, sir."

He could suggest they get Sabin down to the entry corridor if Jase wasn't at hand; but he didn't personally want to deal with Sabin, especially Sabin disturbed from her work.

But still—setting a precedent with the dowager demanding Jase, dealing with Jase—it made sense. It was a means of getting hands on Jase at will. So he bit his lip, refused to shiver or to show any discomfort at all. "I'm afraid we'll stand here until he can find the time."

The security man relayed that. Meanwhile Cajeiri examined a panel with a mere glance, then an inclination sideways. And received a severe tightening of the dowager's hand on his arm, if the slight lift of his head was any sign.

"Captain's on his way," the man said then, with evident relief. "But he'd like to meet you on fifth level. It's warmer, Mr. Cameron, if you can persuade her to go on through."

Nerves twitched. Not polite, that unadorned common pronoun. But it wasn't time for a lesson in protocols, not here.

"Aiji-ma," Bren said in a low voice, "there's a reception arranged in greater warmth on fifth level, and Jase-aiji will meet us there, with your kind consent."

"Very good," Ilisidi said. And waved her cane forward. "Let this person lead, paidhi."

"Lead on," Bren said to their escort. The language had been clipped, moderate, but still touchy. "She says you may go in front of her."

Their escort gave a misgiving look at their party in general, at very large dark-skinned, black-uniformed atevi bodyguards, who drank up the available light in the forefront of the party, and who had moved closer: the paler colors of the household staffs were much to the rear at the moment. Their escort might not like it, and wouldn't at all like the weapons in evidence, and certainly wouldn't like the intransigence in the entry corridor. But there they were, ordered to fifth deck and their escort glided out, using the ladder for a handhold, into the first intersecting corridor and up to a lift.

The lift opened at a button-push and cast a bright, reasonable light into their shadowed steel passage. They boarded the lift and rode either up or down, a slightly startling set of paths and tracks, to a brighter area facing a seal-door.

Their escort opened it and led the way.

The atevi-repaired station corridors were still lighter than this, brightly lit and of felicitously pleasant tones: but here the green and brown paneling of the original station was indisputable, unhappy prophecy of the decor beyond. No one could invent those muddy shades on purpose: it was, Bren suspected what the extrusion medium tended to do with the dyes they injected to better a natural puce. The same kind of switches for lights and section-seals were ubiquitous, as if the master kit that had built the station had been applied here—or vice versa, and that meant their staffs could manage these panels without much confusion. He was sure Banichi and Jago had taken that in instantly.

One wondered if the service accesses also existed here, that network of tunnels that allowed service inside the station's workings.

Grim, human-style Malguri, it was, at least on this level, with moderate improvements in the plumbing and far worse to endure in simple inconvenience.

Ilisidi was taking it all in, stoically refusing to be appalled.

The aiji-apparent, however, looked around him as if he expected the walls to spew forth marvels—or to implode from age and decrepitude. Cajeiri hadn't seen the station at its worst—had lived in baroque splendor, among centuries-old porcelains, on hand-worked carpet, under gilt ceilings. He had seen, in fact, nothing in his young life more primitive than the new sections of the space station. He clung to the ladder rungs along the wall to keep from another ignominious drift, and tried not to jump when section door locks banged and moved, letting them through to another area, another corridor.

"Mind," Cenedi said as they went, "these doors are likely the same as on the station: they close without mercy, in the blink of an eye, to keep all the air from rushing out into the ether of the heavens, young sir. If you see red flashing lights, stand where you are. If yellow, run breakneck for the next section and hope not to be cut in half."

"Where do they steer the ship, nadi?" Cajeiri asked.

"Elsewhere," Ilisidi interposed. "Where boys don't need to be."

"But I want to see," Cajeiri said as they glided along.

"There may be supper," Ilisidi said, "and who knows, *I* may not wish supper tonight."

That was a threat. Cajeiri was immediately *not* happy. He still stared about him, head turning at every new door, every corridor they passed, youthful jaw set and the dowager's own glint in his eye.

Bet, too, if there was any similarity in the species, that every inquisitive bone in that young body longed for all of those emergency measures to go into effect at once—just the once, of course, just to find out.

Cajeiri had behaved admirably this far. One remembered, seeing the occasional look, that set of the jaw, that this was, in fact, Tabini's son, and Damiri's.

One well remembered, too, what it was like to be that young, that active, that under-informed. And on this excursion one was damned glad that no one less than the Assassin's Guild was in charge of the boy.

They reached a new section under their official guidance: three crewmen turned out to meet them— with a small presentation of cut flowers, no less, to the lady they called Gran 'Sidi.

"Welcome aboard," the head of the little delegation said in passable Ragi, all solemnity.

Ilisidi took the flowers like a queen, lacking a free hand, what with the cane—drifting slightly sideways at the moment. But she snagged the ubiquitous ladder-rungs with the head of the cane and managed a little nod, which greatly gratified the delegation.

"We are here to occupy our quarters," she said, of course in Ragi, complete cipher to the crew.

"She is pleased," Bren translated—it was not dishonest of a translator to meet reasonable social expectations on either side, in his practical and practiced opinion. "And she expects the atevi section is close— with Captain Graham, to be sure."

"On ahead, sir," their escort said, "and the baggage is ahead, too, and Captain Graham's on his way this very moment. Through here, sir, ma'am."

Very good news. Their escort opened a side door, where Bindanda had stationed himself—welcome sight. Cenedi quietly appropriated the flowers, incongruous but not unaccustomed accouterment for security, and they continued through, into a place not only populated by their own staff, but better lit and much warmer. The ship immediately had a more auspicious feeling, despite the mud-colored walls.

Cenedi had had staff aboard for hours, going over every minute detail of their accommodations, checking for bugs as well as inconveniences, one could be sure.

And Ilisidi's security had a camera live. As they passed the door, Bren caught the shine of an uncapped lens clipped to a uniformed, leather shoulder.

And what was *that* for? Bren asked himself in dismay. The lens certainly wasn't uncommon, but he was sure the lens had been capped during their trip up the lifts, possibly protectively so, during the intense cold—he had no idea of its limitations. He was sure he'd have noticed otherwise.

But if they'd uncapped it, bet that lens was live and they were transmitting. Was that for security review, privately, something relayed ahead to their staff, in the new quarters?

Something sent farther away, back through the hull, to Lord Geigi? He wasn't sure they could do that. Surely not. So there was a security set-up already active within their section—someone receiving.

He was not unhappy to know they had record of the route and the button-pushes that brought them here.

But for all he knew, Cenedi's men were making a video record for quite different reasons, a record perhaps to go out to Geigi, then to Tabini, who would be interested, to say the least.

Or—knowing Tabini—was it to go out to every household that owned a television?

Confirmation for the dowager's political allies that she was well and alive and in charge of her own armed security, on this ship, in this mission?

Atevi couldn't like the structure they saw—though atevi had gotten used to the concept of twos on the station. Everything in the corridors—doors, and window panels in offices, was configured by ship-culture, convenient sets of two, *pairs*, that anathema to the 'counters, more than vexation to the atevi sense of design: an arrangement of space that hit the atevi nervous system with the same painful reaction nails on a chalkboard caused for humans, and worse, he understood, if one were standing in it, experiencing it in three dimensions.

But some enterprising soul had painted two pastel stripes wandering the corridor, two, branching into five, then felicitous seven, right across the green tile.

Someone had arranged a spray of brightly colored plastic balls—seven—on strands of wire, from wall to wall, like planets and moons against the mud brown of the wall paneling.

The effect was less than elegant . . . the sort of thing that turned up in crew lounges. But seven. It was a valiant attempt at *kabiu.*

And colored paint. Where had *paint* turned up in their baggage? It had been at a low priority in station-building, wasn't manufactured on-station even yet: it had to be freighted up.

Had Jase had that stripe done? Had the dowager's staff prepared for the spartan environment? Atevi *couldn't* have done something as garish as the orange planets.

Staff drifted out from the offices, the dowager's welcome sight on both sides, and the staff who'd brought their baggage turned up from further on.

"Thank you," Bren said to their escort, with a little bow as automatic as breathing and quite impossible in null-G. "We'll be very comfortable here."

"I'm to show you temperature and emergency controls, sir."

There was a potentially explosive foul-up. "I'm sure you've shown the staff," Bren said, drifting slightly askew—difficult to maintain formality at odd angles—"and deputized *them* to show security personnel, who will show me and the dowager what's needful for us personally to do. That's our protocol, sir. *Believe* me, Captain Graham will confirm it."

Trust them, that the ship would not explode from *this* deck.

"Then is there any need of me further?" their escort asked.

"With thanks, sir, —one trusts Captain Graham is here."

"He's in the section, sir. He's on his way."

The door behind them opened at that very moment. He heard it, and when he turned, drifting, to look back, Jase *was* there.

Thank God.

"We're just fine, then. We'll all be fine. Thank you, yes, that's all we need."

"There will be *no* walking about," Ilisidi was telling Cajeiri quite firmly, in this place where, at the moment, *walking* was a euphemism, "no leaving your quarters without security escort, nadi."

"But this is all like a house, *mani-ji.* Surely—"

"Nothing is sure here!" This under her breath, with a hard jerk at Cajeiri's hand. "Hear me!" Bren tried not to notice the preface, as Ilisidi, disgusted, turned a sweetly benevolent glance toward him, and toward Jase, as Jase sailed to their side, and stopped.

Jase, in a blue uniform jacket, with the *Phoenix* insignia, the closest to captain's estate he'd yet come. The emblem looked like one of the wi'itikiin, the flying creatures of Malguri cliffs, rising from solar fires—atevi, having heard the legend, thought it very well-omened.

The inner door shut, making everything private, including Jase with them.

"Jase-aiji. How kind of you to come."

"Aiji-ma," Jase said quietly, distantly to Bren's ears.

The offices inside were all lit up, with atevi staff unpacking their own equipment.

And the stripes braiding their way down the corridor, past the windowed offices immediately in view, branched out to two side corridors in the section.

He'd approved the arrangement the dowager's staff had provided: numerous staff sleeping rooms, back near the kitchens, and two bedchambers, two offices/studies, for himself and for the dowager. They used a vast amount of room—they'd added staff, and only scantly advised the ship, which had, for all he knew, discounted the advisement: certainly there'd been no high-level reaction. Of room there was no shortage, so instructions said, and their baggage requirements remained negligible to the scale of things.

"I hope everything's in order," Jase said. "I hope you'll be as comfortable as we can provide, aiji-ma."

"Acceptable, ship-aiji." This, from the mistress of ancient Malguri, the dowager who slept on bare ground and still outrode two humans. "But association and *man'chi*. How stands that?"

"Firm," Jase said. The reassuring answer. "Still within the aiji's *man'chi*. And my ship's." One could have two *man'chiin*: the whole *aishidi'tat* was a webwork, and two and three and four associations at once was a benefit, not a detriment.

"Accept this," Cenedi said, and handed Jase one of

the pocket coms, "to keep us in close touch. The dowager relies on you especially, nandi, in this voyage. She will call on you whenever she has a personal question. She wishes to have this clear."

Jase bowed his head—the rigorous instruction of the court made that act the simplest, most basic reflex. "I'll endeavor to answer the dowager's questions."

"So what will the schedule be, if you please?" Ilisidi asked.

"If the dowager please—" Court expression for a brief stall, a gathering of words. "We're transient."

"Moment to moment," Bren muttered, on autopilot.

"Moment to moment." Jase scarcely blushed, seized on the apt word, and the omen fell unremarked. "Reliant on the numbers, aiji-ma, as crew boards. We have to have a precise calculation of mass. We'll leave dock and calculate, we hope, in about four hours. Crew boarding has begun. It can be very fast."

"Very good. And we will then walk decently on the deck."

"As soon as we're underway, aiji-ma."

"Is this where we stay, *mani?*" Cajeiri asked, sounding disappointed. "It looks like a warehouse."

"This is manifestly where we stay," Ilisidi said sharply, "and one will be *grateful*, great-grandson, that the facility will soon be operative and that the lights require no lengthy and laborious fire source, *not* the case everywhere in the world, as you will one day learn to your astonishment, I warn you. *Apologize!*"

"One regrets, nandiin." Meek response.

"One accepts," Jase said.

Ilisidi steered her charge onward, toward her own side corridor. Cenedi attended. Staff bowed, such as they could, adrift.

He and Jase had a moment, then—a solitary moment, after Jase's quick, confidence-establishing trip to this deck. At times, Bren thought, when he could do his old job, merely translating, correcting Jase's small lapse, he could sink into flow-through, not paying attention to what he said. At such moments he became a device, not a thinking being.

But he wasn't merely a recorder. And he knew he was close to panic, in zero-gravity, amid universal reminders they were all but launched. His eyes tended now to dart to details, and to miss all of them. Thoughts scattered. What became absolutely necessary eluded him, at the very moment he needed to gather the facts in and make sense and use the brief chance he had—like this one, to talk to Jase, to have things firm—to make requests, demands on Jase that might break an association, break a friendship, see disaster overtake them . . . he wasn't at his best. But time and the hope of remedy was slipping away from him.

"Jase." He got the word out. "Office." He changed languages. "Need to talk." Remembering that Ragi was the most secure code they could use, he shifted his mind back into that track. "A moment only, nadi."

"I haven't got time," Jase said urgently in ship-speak. "I left a briefing—"

"Jasi-ji." He snagged Jase by an arm, gripped the ladder with the other, and pulled Jase loose from his handhold, hauled him bodily into the right-hand office, the one Cenedi and his staff weren't occupying.

Jago attended him in, braked with a gentle toe touch on a cabinet.

He'd kidnapped a ship's captain. And he was gripping too tightly, too urgently.

Jago made a signal to them. *Wired.* Meaning Jase.

"In private," he said to Jase.

Jase hesitated, looked down at the grip on his arm. Bren let go.

Then Jase reached to his collar and pinched a switch.

"Can't be out of contact long," Jase said. "Sabin's not happy with how much time I've diverted here. Silence is going to be noticed."

"The paint down the hall. Your idea?"

"My orders. My sketch. Crew's execution. Caught hell for it."

Jase, practicing *kabiu.* He didn't ask about the orange plastic planets.

"Damned good," Bren said. "Excellent move. Impressive."

"You didn't hold me here to discuss the paint."

"Speak Ragi. Jase, I have a question. Not a pleasant question. —Jago-ji. The meeting with Mercheson. I have it keyed up." He had his computer. He opened the case, sailed it gently to her. "Play it."

"Nandi." Jago simply pushed the button, the computer floating in her grip.

"*So will you,*" Yolanda's voice said, that sound-clip, right there. "*. . . where you are—and I'm glad you're going. All I know—all I know of what's out there—if Ogun* *doesn't know, and he hasn't told Sabin, then there's two names. There was a three-man exploration team that went in. I know that Jenrette was one of them; and two more got killed."*

Jase's lips had become a thin line.

"Tamun was trying to catch Ramirez, and they ran, and Tamun's mutineers shot them. Jenrette's still alive, but they aren't. I didn't used to think so, but now I ask myself whether Tamun suspected something, and if that was why he was trying to overthrow the council—but Tamun couldn't get at it, when he was one of the captains. He couldn't get the proof, or didn't release it. So we didn't know—and now he's dead. And that scares me. All that scares me."

"Shit," Jase said.

"Log record?" the tape went on, Bren's own voice, alternate with Yolanda's.

"Common crew can't get into the log file. I guess not even all the captains can. There could be a tape—they usually make one, through helmet-cam. But if there is, it's deep in archives."

"Tape of what?" he'd asked.

"Their going onto the station. Through the corridors. That's all I know. Which is what everybody in the crew knows. But didn't know they knew. That's the hell of it. We thought the report was just what you'd think it would be . . . which it wasn't. And now if there was a tape, or if Jenrette knows something—he's the only eyewitness. And he's attached to Jase."

"When did she talk to you?" Jase asked, appalled.

"Does it matter?"

"It bloody matters. Is she all right?"

"You have to ask that?"

Jase wasn't pleased. Jase had a temper. But right now Jase looked stark scared.

"I put her into my apartment," Bren said, "with my staff, with instructions to protect her against the consequences of telling me the truth. —You didn't know I'd done that."

"I heard she was there. I didn't hear the circumstances. Obviously I didn't."

"But you're scared."

"I'm damned upset! This isn't a small affair, Bren. This is explosive."

"It took Yolanda some thinking, I imagine, to see past the obvious. *I* didn't see it, first off. Did you?"

"See what? What are you talking about?"

"*Ragi*, nadi-ji. Give me the benefit of your thoughts, if you will. Dare we say you know what I'm talking about, and we're both distressed about what Mercheson said?"

"I didn't expect Yolanda was involved any longer. I thought she was out of this, once Ramirez died."

"*What* was she out of?"

"Ship politics."

That covered the known world. "You were personally involved with her," Bren said, determined on confrontation. "Then, surprise, nadi-ji, you weren't. You couldn't face each other. —I could have predicted that breakup, forgive me. It's the job."

"It was *her* job, as it turned out." The job she'd done for Ramirez, the job she hadn't told either of them about. "Wasn't it? Or do we know something else?"

"You didn't know what she was doing when you

broke up. But it was there, nadi. Secrets are bad bed-fellows."

Ship-speak. "They're killers. None of which is here or there with what she's charging."

"And you're still mad. You were *damned* mad when you found out what she'd been doing with Tabini and Ramirez. But you were mad before that. You canceled her out. You didn't deal with her. You didn't talk. That was bad business, and I didn't know how to patch it. Our conversations stopped, too. She avoided me as well as you. I attributed it to the severance of relations with you. As it turned out, she needed help, and I was blind."

"She could have asked for it. Weren't *you* mad, when you found out what she was up to?"

"Damned mad. And jealous. I confess it. Confession's good for the soul. Isn't that what they say? Maybe hers is quieter now."

"I suppose it is. I don't know where the hell this is going."

"Well, for one, nadi-ji, I think she still cares and I know what bastards we are to live with under the best of circumstances."

"None of your business, and thanks for the vote of confidence."

"Listen to me, nadi." Back into Ragi, under cover, into a different framework of thinking, before think-ing spiraled out of parameters in ship-speak. "The *man'chi* underlying is the same, hers and ours, differ-ent than the ship. There's a human truth in that, like it or not, and I suggest you listen to the whole conversa-tion, in which she expressed deep concern for your safety and your welfare and the reasons—there were reasons—why she didn't feel free to come to either of us. I'm sure jealousy exists in your feelings toward her, but not professional jealousy. I think jealousy of Ramirez doomed your relationship."

"That's nonsense."

Right back to Ragi. "You aren't related by blood, but you are by father—real father, not the centuries-dead heroes. Ramirez was the head of *man'chi*, and like any aiji, he worked with secrets, he kept secrets, he nourished them, bred them and crossbred them. There's a reason he could deal with Tabini, whose whole instinct is secrecy. In that, I'm sure, nadi, that they damned well got along. And in the process, he made you and Yolanda jealous as hell of each other."

Jase didn't deny it.

"So he put her in an untenable position," Bren said, "made her privy to his deception of both of us. And she couldn't share a bed with you or a pot of tea in my household, not then nor after he died. No, she's not the most agreeable. She detested the planet. But now she feels safest not in the society she knows from birth, but inside my household, watched over by my staff—being paidhi-aiji and dealing with Tabini. This isn't the course either of us would have predicted for her. But she hasn't *been* where either of us thought she was, nadi. She's been in a very frightening territory, while you and I were living comfortably, building the future we thought was relatively safe. She knew. I doubt she slept well, these last few years."

"The hell! She could have come to me."

"Could she? And what would Ramirez have done, nadi? And what might happen with Tabini?"

Tabini had to give anyone pause. And Jase paused.

"His dying grieved you," Bren said, "and set her adrift, nadi. Now I hope she's found a harbor a little more calm than where she's lived. But while we've been comfortable these last years, she's had years to think, and to assemble the pieces Ramirez necessarily gave her. As translators, we're not quite machines, are we? We do bring in bits and pieces of our own knowledge. And there she sat, a member of the crew, hearing all this about the contact, knowing who went, knowing now that there *was* a secret, knowing it was lurking at levels we didn't deal with—what was she to do? *You'd* been taken into a captaincy she might have expected for herself. *She* was passed over, and still sat there, in Ramirez's company, a repository of his official secrets—and *why* didn't he appoint her to the office?"

"I've no idea. I wish to hell he had."

"But she was with him, nadi, day and night; she was subject to his calls—she had all those skills. Was he going to appoint a new captain who'd have full knowledge what was going on? Who had close ties to me, and who might gain access codes? A new ship-aiji who'd be with him so often she'd unbalance the relationship with other officers? She *lived* in his office. Wasn't that the point of your own jealousy? And what if that had played out among the other ship-aijiin?"

Jase had let go his handhold, so still he stayed in place, adrift. The pain and anger that had been part of his dealings with Yolanda seemed to have gone elsewhere, redirected, reflected.

"Maybe it was," Jase said. "Maybe a lot of things were poisoned in the process, nadi."

"Then Ramirez died and left you Jenrette . . . one assumes to advise you, where matters come up."

Anger gave way to intense worry.

"He was aboard the station," Bren said. "All the others that went aboard the station out there, I suppose, were Ramirez's men. What bothers me—all of them just happened to die in the Tamun affair. All but Jenrette."

"Defending Ramirez," Jase said.

"Like Yolanda, I'll tell you, I'm beginning to ask myself what Tamun was doing that blew matters up and started the shooting."

"I can't believe there was anything more in it than Tamun's ambition."

"He was already at highest rank," Bren protested. "What more was there for ambition to go for?"

"Control. Authority. Real authority."

"And what could give it to him, better than information? Jase, Jase, I'd like you to find out what Jenrette knows. I'd like you to get a copy of that tape, if you can do it, before we leave dock. Before we commit any further to this mission."

"I can't do that," Jase said.

"You can, nadi. Just ask him."

"No. You don't understand. It's not possible. Jenrette's transferred to Sabin."

"When did *that* happen?"

"When we made out the staff assignments. When

we divided the crew, and said who was going and staying. I wanted Kaplan with me, on my staff—I trust Kaplan. I wanted to keep him and Pressman and Polano as my aides, and most of all, I didn't want to leave them behind on the station, where Ogun's going to appoint a fourth captain, which was the regulation way things work. That's where they were supposed to go: they weren't going to be aboard, the way Ogun had drawn things up. But Jenrette and I—I don't say we don't get along, but everything I do, it's obvious in his opinion whether it's what Ramirez would do, or the way Ramirez did things: he second-guesses me at every turn, I'm not easy with him, and it's not the best situation, nadi. When I want something done, just done, cheerfully, I ask Kaplan; but I never was going to push Jenrette out. I respect his advice. So I said why didn't Ogun and Sabin just increase their staffs, which they could use, and I'd have Jenrette and his team *and* Kaplan and his. That's when it blew up. Sabin said I'd insulted Jenrette, which I was trying hard not to do. So with Sabin's famous tact, that fairly well put the personnel question into an hour-long, angry argument—all the principals being present, including Jenrette and his unit, and Kaplan and his."

God.

"And in the upshot of things, I exploded, I got my way and I kept Kaplan, and Ogun and Sabin increased staff by three, but by then there were hurt feelings, and Sabin said she wanted Jenrette's experience, if I didn't value it. I said I did want it, and it wasn't like that and I wanted him to stay; but Sabin said if she was going to increase staff, she was senior on the ship and she got the pick of staff on the ship. She wanted him, and insisted he transfer, and there it was."

Disaster. And worse. "When was this?"

"About six hours ago."

Not good news at all. He shot Jago a look and had one back.

Appalling news, considering that Jenrette's name had become an issue inside the residency, and Yolanda had just dropped out of Ogun's reach, not by Ogun's orders. And could a bug possibly get past Algini's countermeasures? Could distant listening devices have been hearing, if nothing else, the proper names at issue?

Were they doing that now?

"Coincidences do happen," Bren said. "Sometimes they really do happen, and merging staffs is always a mess. I can't see how the ship could get a bug past our surveillance. But this is worrisome, besides inconvenient."

"A breach could happen, nadiin-ji," Jago said quietly. "In our craft, once a countermeasure exists, one innovates. We don't know the ship's limits. They *are* the fathers of technology."

Constant warning. Constant caution. On truly sensitive matters, they talked on the move, in the corridors: harder to pick up. Inside the apartment, they talked behind an electronic screen, in the security station, in a very small safe perimeter.

Hadn't they warned him? And he'd talked to Yolanda in the study.

"I want that tape," Bren said.

"You want universal peace, too, nadi, but I don't know I can deliver it."

"They *have* universal peace, and they can lose the aiji's cooperation, and ours, and the island's, none of which will help them at all in whatever they're up to."

"We don't know that they care. If they're over-hearing us, and I don't think it's happening, but I don't know everything—they could be forewarned, even now."

"I'm saying if we're going to trust Sabin enough to bring members of the aiji's family into it, we're going to have to trust Sabin." He said that sentence in ship-speak, in case. And lapsed right back into Ragi. "And right now and until we know more, we won't drink a cup she pours. The tape."

"It won't be a tape," Jase said. "That's an expression."

"How does it exist?"

"Deep in log archives."

"Can you reach it? Can you get access?"

"I'm not senior. Ogun can," Jase added. "We could ask him. We could outright ask him."

"And, as you say, if we ask him, it could vanish in a moment. Permanently. And Sabin's senior on the ship. I'll take for granted she has the codes, nadi."

"I believe she does."

"It's worth a certain risk of diplomatic difficulty, Jasi-ji, to know in absolute detail what this ship met aboard the station. Can you call your former aide for a conference, some unfinished business?"

"I can't do that to him. Bren, I can't."

"I didn't say we were going to make a move."

"I don't know what it could entail with things as they are. And you aren't in command of this mission, Bren-nadi. *Ilisidi* is. Am I mistaken?"

"No. You're not mistaken."

"And if her staff finds out what you suspect, you can't tell me what she'd stick at."

True. He drifted back against the counter, took a solid grip. Air currents had taken Jase away from a hand grip and Jase reached and drew himself back before he lost easy contact.

"I'm not going to give this up," Bren said.

"I can try to talk to Jen—"

"Names," Bren cautioned him, and Jase cut it off.

"I can try to talk, myself, nadi."

"We have how long, reasonably, until the ship breaks dock?"

"Six hours at minimum. Not above twelve."

"I want the tape, Jase-paidhi." At a certain point in emergencies, all common sense seemed to cut out and priorities became very cold, very remote from the consequences of failure: downhill, breakneck. "I can't claim to have created the *aishidi'tat*, but I created the situation, the whole structure of twigs that supports it. So I know the alternatives. I know what we had before, and I know that there can be worse outcomes than a breach with this mission. I can imagine those very well: betraying the dowager, alienating the aiji— us finding out that our allies came here to get control of our resources."

"No."

"Maybe a war that devastated the mainland would suit certain purposes just very well."

"That's not so, nadi!"

"Prove it isn't. Prove to me your ship didn't come here with exactly that purpose—to find out the conditions in this solar system, to fuel the ship, and go home to report, preparatory to a power grab. We have only your word that the situation you reported out there even exists. We're betting the whole planet on details we don't know. You've insisted all along nobody on the ship knows better. But now that Landa-ji, out of her private hell of the last few years, points out the obvious, that there *would* have been a tape record in archive, well, *yes*, I'd rather like to see it before I step off the edge."

"What do you think? That the whole crew is in on a conspiracy?"

"No, I'm suggesting they're the last to know. Either get me the tape, or say you can't, or don't want to know, and *we'll* do it, but *don't* ask me to assume everything's all right."

Jase's eyes made an eloquent shift toward the door, the windowed wall. "I take for granted Banichi's heard what we've said."

"I'm sure."

"Has Cenedi?"

It was a question. Jago's face gave no hint at all.

"You may answer, Jago-ji," Bren said.

"Yes to both. We are within the dowager's household, of allied *man'chi*, nadiin-ji."

"Then this is my answer. You're within *my* household," Jase said in a brittle voice, "under my roof, as *my* honored guests . . . and so is the dowager. I don't think if it were Geigi's house we would contemplate breaking the historic porcelains because we had a suspicion."

"Not in the least. Nor do we here."

"Or endangering lives."

"Nor shall we."

"I wasn't aware of movements I should have known, because I was submerged in my own efforts at a very dangerous time—trying to memorize everything I could, as hard as I could, as fast as I could, after years of saying I wouldn't. And that's my fault."

"We're not speaking of fault, here, Jase."

"For the record, it's my fault. I know a mistake when I see it. But I won't compound that fault by turning one of my own over to you for an open-ended set of questions, or failing to take command of operations in *my household*, Bren-paidhi. Let's have that clear."

"You're saying you'll help us."

"I'm saying if this file exists, *I* want it, myself. I assume Sabin can get it, but I don't know that. I assume she knows it's out there. If she knows and hasn't told me, or if she doesn't know and I find out something she needs to know, I'll decide then what to do with the information. No. I won't help you. *You'll* help *me*, and I'll share information with your side."

Jase had his moments. On the planet—he'd had a lot of them, once he'd gotten his land-legs and understood the situation; but they hadn't seen Jase at full stretch since he came aboard and under ship's authority.

And he had no trouble accepting Jase on a slightly opposed side of the issue.

"I'll put that proposition to the dowager," Bren said. "But she'll know. What's your advice? Do we let you go out of here, when we suspect a remote possibility that security's been recording us, and that with half an hour's concentrated work on the part of people your ship could have been training for a decade—assuming they're about as fluent as the run of the University—they might translate enough to know what you're up to?"

"Letting me leave is a real good idea, Bren. As to asking me to stay and talk to the dowager—I assume you're going to offer—I've got a meeting I'm supposed to be back to, up there, that's going to ring alarms if I'm not back. Sabin's already suspicious."

"Why are you afraid of her?"

Jase looked at him as if he'd lost his mind.

"No," Bren said. "I'm dead serious. *Why* are you afraid of her, under the rules that are supposed to apply?"

Now Jase heard him. Thoughts raced.

"Where can you access the log?" Bren asked. "Jasi-ji."

"It's only two places. It's a read-write on the bridge and it's a read-only in the nav office. It receives and logs automatically from the sensors and the cameras, on a loop—automatically stores alarms and alerts, queries the officer store or no-store on the outside camera input on an interval the officer sets." Jase's eyes had a slightly glazed look. "I've been memorizing this stuff."

"It's not wasted. So Ramirez-aiji had to order a store on that camera info."

"It's possible he erased it. Possible."

"In his situation, at the time, considering there could be something to prove to colleages or successors to the situation—would you?"

"I'd keep it. I'd definitely keep it. But there's one other source. There's the men that saw it. Let me talk to Jenrette, under the guise of an apology—he has one coming—and see what he knows."

"Let *you* give *me* a call every hour on the hour to tell me you aren't languishing under arrest. Or better yet—suppose you take *me* on a tour of the operational areas and we both get hold of him."

"You want to know what I'm afraid of," Jase said. "She can do it. She *can* order security and I can't—she's the only legitimate authority, legitimate in that she knows what she's doing. And I can't replace her. Ogun can't replace her. If she says jump, people jump."

"One may have an answer, nandiin-ji."

Not Jago's voice. Banichi's, from the doorway.

And not just Banichi—Cenedi. And the aiji-dowager, drifting slightly sideways and attached by her cane to the ubiquitous ladders.

"We will see this ship-aiji at our table," Ilisidi said.

"Aiji-ma, I don't think she'll regard an invitation."

"*At our table!*" Ilisidi said.

"In these conditions?"

"The crew is boarding, is it not?" Cenedi asked. "And will gravity not exist once they turn the engines on?"

"In essence, Cenedi-ji," Jase said. "But at that point the ship will undock, which will necessitate securing all personnel to safety positions, where movement about the ship will be impossible."

"And then, ship-aiji?" Ilisidi asked sharply. "And then? Do we shoot off like a rocket? Or glide away like a yacht? And are we not expected to eat and sleep, or do we starve and languish for the duration of this voyage?"

"Rather well like a yacht, aiji-ma, if things go well, as they ought, but for safety's sake, one shouldn't be about, or setting tables."

"And when will there be supper?" Ilisidi asked.

"The schedule, aiji-ma," Jase said on a deep breath, "calls for crew to board and settle into quarters, then check equipment and turn on the engines, as you say. And then for about an hour, a little less, as we release we will be like the shuttle during station undocking—possible for us to move about, but strongly discouraged, for the same safety concerns. By the end of that period we will have set our bow toward our destination, aiji-ma, and then there will be two hours in which it will not be safe to move about. That will cease, crew will move about and assure that everything is working as it should, and persons in charge of navigation will be taking finer measurements and assuring that we are on course. There will be another two hours during which we must be secure in our places, and then it will be possible to move about again, for about six hours—by then we will be quite far out from the station."

"Pish. Infelicitous two, two, and untrustworthy six,

chancy ten. Clearly we are not at that point beyond return."

"No, aiji-ma."

"And one might *demand* to be taken back to the safety of the station."

"Aiji-ma, if one has any doubts—" Jase was clearly appalled. "It's no small thing to turn this ship around."

"If we say this ship must turn around, it must."

"It's possible . . . theoretically possible. But I'm not sure Sabin would agree to it."

Ilisidi waggled thin, elegant fingers. "This is a major point, is it not, Bren-ji, whether we can deal with Sabin-aiji, and whether reasonable requests will be heard. We have no desire to travel with unreliable persons. We will see this ship-aiji. We will estimate the reliability and good will of this person and invite her to our table. Or this agreement is abrogated. *Do we agree, paidhiin-ji?*"

Dared one say no? Dared one ever say no? And what was this *agreement is abrogated?*

What agreement? Bren wanted to ask.

"We shall see her in person," Ilisidi declared. "Now."

"Aiji-ma, crew will be boarding," Jase said. "Sabin will be busy."

"Busy?" Ilisidi snapped, and a whack of the cane at the ladders sent echoes through nerve and bone. "We will see her, I say. If she is busy, as you say, we shall do her the honor of visiting *her.* This very moment!"

"Bren," Jase said, turning an appalled appeal in his direction.

"The dowager will see the captain," Bren said in ship-speak.

"And if she gets up there and Sabin won't see her—"

Where had the whole situation mutated so thoroughly—from missing records to a confrontation over precedences and authority? One thing was a given: that Ilisidi *didn't* take well to *no*, in any language.

"We're diplomats, aren't we?" Bren said, with great misgivings. Jase might be a dozen things, but he was one of a few paidhiin that had ever existed, and some things there wasn't any resigning. Ever. "That part's *our* job."

16

The lift had room enough, Banichi having to bend his head a little; but there they were: Ilisidi, Cenedi and three of his men, with Banichi and Jago—and attendant hardware—two humans and seven atevi, fortunate nine, in fleeting contact with the floor of the lift.

Bren hadn't even been to his cabin yet. He hadn't changed his coat. He'd passed a message to Narani to advise him of a supper invitation, for his household's sake.

The lift stopped: instantly, they floated. So did stomachs. But the door opened smoothly, with a hiss of hydraulic seals. Jase had passed a message to his staff, too; and Kaplan, Polano and Pressman were right there to meet them, on what the lift buttons indicated as A deck, in a short corridor.

"Sir," Kaplan said. "Ma'am. Mr. Cameron." That was a damned rapid sort through the protocols: the eyes were near frantic, trying to take in this upheaval of natural order in the universe, but Kaplan asked no questions.

"Captain Sabin's on the bridge?" Jase asked.

"I don't know, sir. The bridge, her office, I don't know."

"Adjacent," Jase said in a low voice, and drew a deep, audible breath. "Stay with me, Mr. Kaplan. The dowager's asked to see the senior captain. —Aiji-ma, Bren-ji, kindly come and kindly don't touch weapons."

Kaplan, who didn't understand the latter slightly pidgin statement, looked as if he wanted to do something or stop someone and didn't know where to start. Polano and Pressman looked no happier as Jase shoved off his handhold and sailed down the null-g course to a wall-switch.

Bren followed Jase, desperately trusting atevi to stay with them—Banichi and Jago, and the dowager and her party. If anything went amiss up here, with armed atevi security, armed humans—

The switch opened the door. Bren expected another corridor, and offices: every other door led to the like.

This one opened on a wide technical zone: consoles, displays, flashing lights and readouts, and a number of busy technicians, some of whom looked their way in shock.

More did. Work stopped. Computers didn't.

It was that area that *Phoenix* never opened to visitors—that area *Phoenix* had never permitted to be photographed, even if Mospheira and Shejidan both had plans of such a place: the configuration, they'd always said, the precise configuration was as secret and classified as the interior of Tabini's apartments, the inside of the presidential residence on Mospheira.

And here they were in the control center, heart of

the computers, nexus for communications. The bridge itself was that open space just beyond the array of consoles that, in effect, ran everything above the planet's surface.

They were in it now. Up to their necks.

And that was Captain Sabin in the brightly lighted bridge section, under a light that sheened her gray hair like a spotlight. Officers and technicians floated at fair random, this way and that, oriented to their work or their convenience. But Sabin, not the tallest, not even the fanciest-dressed—she was in a long-sleeved black tee—was unmistakeable.

"There is the ship-aiji," Ilisidi said with satisfaction, pointing with the ferrule of her cane. "We'll talk."

With all the profound courtesy that implied, of who had come to whom.

And Sabin had seen them.

"No weapons!" Bren said immediately, and repeated it in ship-speak, loud and clear, with the gut-deep fright of a slip on ice. "The aiji-dowager has honored the ship's captains by coming to *them*, in their residence, and comes here in courteous deference to rulers in their own domain. This is a high honor paid the ship's command on this auspicious occasion."

Sabin's pitch, now. Please God, Bren thought. He'd cued her. Let Sabin once in her life moderate her response.

There was a four-beat silence. Everything froze.

Then Sabin lashed out with a booted foot and sailed toward them like a missile: techs hugged panels and got out of the way as Sabin flew from bright light to dim, from command to operations—and stopped, suddenly, with a reach to a handhold: a crisp, expert halt and a strength astonishing in a thin-limbed old woman.

"This is the bridge," Sabin said. "This is *restricted*." From Sabin that was utmost restraint. "Captain Graham." *That* was utmost restraint, too. Say one thing for Sabin: she didn't light into a brother captain in front of crew. But the anger was palpable. "I'm not going to speak to Mr. Cameron. I can't speak to the dowager. Kindly straighten this out."

"You're not speaking to me," Bren said and shot right ahead: "Through me, you're speaking to the dowager, captain. She's delighted to be aboard and pays you the signal honor of coming to *you* in your premises rather than requiring you to come to her in audience . . . *therefore* she came to present her compliments, making you a head of state, captain, and a very favored person."

Sabin's eyes were hard and black, still in attack mode, not a bit dissuaded. But she didn't call security to shoot the lot of them. "That's all well and good, sir, but I'll call on your good offices to be damned sure this doesn't happen again. Now if you'll get the woman out of here, we have work to do."

"Captain." Jase was going to try.

It wasn't a good idea, in Bren's experience. He drew a breath and kept going across the ice floes. "The dowager's come here to pay respects. There's a reciprocation expected."

"The hell!" Sabin kept going, but Bren rode right over the top of the outburst.

"You want your supplies, captain—I assume you want your supplies—perhaps we'd better continue this discussion in your office."

"Here's good enough." But Sabin had lowered her voice, and applied her version of conciliation. "I'm damned busy, Mr. Cameron. Get her the hell out."

"She does understand some Mosphei', captain. Please use restraint."

"I am using restraint. I want her off this deck. I want you and her and these people down on deck five and I don't want to hear from you again until we're at our destination, at which time I'll tell you where we are and I don't want to hear from you after that until we're back in port at this star. Is that clear?"

"Let me convey for the dowager that she may demand to leave this ship, and if she leaves this ship the diplomatic fallout will be extremely disadvantageous to everything we've spent the last number of years building—which I assure you won't help this ship."

"Don't threaten me."

"Far from it. The dowager's come here to invite you to supper this evening."

The look on Sabin's face was astonishing. An expression. A moment of utter, unguarded shock.

"Economical to accept," Bren said rapidly, before Sabin formulated a reply. "Establishing a cordial tone aboard, bringing the very expert services of her security harmoniously into *your* service, and the services of the paidhiin, to boot. We're *good*, captain. You *are* hearing me, and I don't think that was your original intention. We'll be very pleased to apply our talents to your opposition if you'll oblige the dowager, win her good will, and make our jobs easier. Besides, she sets a very good table."

Three expressions from Sabin in rapid succession: shock, outrage, and targeting calculation.

"You're the damned cheekiest bastard I've met in a lifetime."

"Yes, ma'am, and you're no pushover, on the other side. If our interests really did diverge, I'd be worried, but I happen to know our best interests and your interests are the same. Besides, you deserve a good dinner, and it won't be wasted time. You'll score a relationship that'll make a big difference out there ... that will outright assure you come back here to a working station with resources."

"Is that a threat, Mr. Cameron?"

"No, captain, it's a pretty good forecast. If this relationship goes bad, everything goes bad; if it goes brilliantly, everything becomes easier. Let me add my personal plea to the case: accept the invitation and you'll have my assurances I'll do everything possible to persuade her of *your* points. I can't stress enough how great an honor the dowager's done you by coming here: she's put her dignity on the line so as to make clear how greatly she respects your authority. Now it's very useful for your side to respect and accept her hospitality."

"*Damned* cheeky bastard, Mr. Cameron."

"Which I trust refers solely to me, captain, and I hope signals your gracious acceptance."

"There's nothing gracious about it."

"The traditional supper hour, for these affairs. Full dress. She'll spare no effort to honor her guest."

"How long am I expected to be honored? I've got a ship in the process of boarding."

"About three hours."

"Flaming hell."

"You'll find it worth your while. Eighteen hundred hours, senior captain. She'll very much understand if you don't reciprocate with a dinner of your own, given the pressure of events; but she'll be pleased to entertain you to the utmost." He switched to Ragi. "The captain, though pressed for time, is inclining to accept, aiji-ma, understanding the great honor you give her."

Ilisidi inclined her head benignly. "Very good, paidhi-ji. At the fortunate hour."

"She's very pleased," Bren said, regardless of Sabin's not-quite-expressed consent. "She honors your good will. Understand, as a great lord proceeds about necessary courtesies even under fire, proving one isn't at all harried. She views you very favorably."

"Damned nonsense." From Sabin it was a moderate response.

"My personal gratitude," Bren said. "Eighteen hundred hours, at our section: staff will meet you there. The aiji-dowager's good will and good wishes in fortunate number, ma'am."

He turned. He managed to include Jase in the sweep of his arm toward the exit, but Jase declined the refuge and drifted there slightly askew from them.

One trusted at least there wouldn't be bloodshed on the bridge. Sabin might have plenty yet to vent, but if appearances were an indication, Sabin was in control, and if she was thinking, she wouldn't let fly until the two of them were in an office with the door shut.

Under those circumstances he trusted Jase could hold his own and keep his head.

"Mr. Kaplan," Jase said calmly, "see them below."

"Yes, sir." Kaplan opened the door which had self-shut.

"And where is Jase-paidhi?" Ilisidi demanded.

"Preparing to account to Sabin-aiji for bringing us here, aiji-ma," Bren said, "which I trust he can do."

"He will suffer no detriment!" Ilisidi said, and turned and addressed Jase. "Assure us this is the case!"

"Aiji-ma, without a doubt."

"Well!" Ilisidi said, and by now the door had shut itself again. Kaplan scrambled to open it, and they left under Kaplan's guidance.

It wasn't that easy, and Sabin would have words of her own, but Ilisidi expected her below, and Sabin had accepted that.

Amazing, Bren thought. Astonishing.

He could imagine several scenarios to follow, in several of which Sabin decided not to come after all, and precipitated an atevi war. Jase, if he could make the point, would faithfully inform her there wasn't any change of plans possible, not at this point—not without the attendant war, at least.

He'd been steady enough during the exchange. Now, in the stomach-wrenching reverse of the lift action, he found his knees weak. If there'd been a floor to stand on, he thought he'd have felt them going. As it was, he simply tried not to twitch against his escort, and not to shiver as Jago cushioned their arrival on deck five. That brought a little moment of contact with the deck, and if not for Jago, he thought he would have stumbled, if nothing else, from the welter of confusing directions.

Not the dowager. The lift door opened and she emerged with Cenedi, perfectly in command.

"We shall see you at supper," she said, "paidhi-ji."

"Honored, nand' dowager."

What *else* was there to say? He didn't plan to eat. His mind was off into a dozen more scenarios, frantic in its application. War or peace was a hell of a dessert choice, and somehow in his management of affairs, his nudges this way and that, his quest after a piece of tape had ended up in a confrontation between aijiin.

Well to have it now, if it was going to happen, while they were still at dock and had options. The thought of Ilisidi pent up in a ship with a captain whose murder she fondly wished—a captain who was the *only* captain capable of running the ship's operations—was unthinkable.

God, he wanted to stay on the ground. He wanted to go back down to the planet and go back to his estate with his staff and wait there for it all to be over . . . but that wasn't a choice he'd given himself.

He had to get the authorities through this set of formalities, and he had to ask himself if Ilisidi thought she was going to *ask* for the ship's log or if his search for the records had become a complete side-channel to the dowager's intentions of running matters wherever she was. Certainly no one had informed Sabin she was second to the aiji-dowager on her own deck.

If anyone did have to convey that information, he knew all too well who the translator had to be.

They arrived into a scene of managed chaos, the midst of null-g preparations for the invitation . . . preparation which their constant communications net had already set into motion.

Bundles were everywhere in the paidhi's quarters, soft bundles, in general, which floated where they were not jammed tightly in, bundles that should give forth their contents and then fold down inconspicuously and with little mass.

Bundles were lodged up near the ceiling and a few were tucked into the narrow passage between bed and bath, rather like the egg-cases of an infestation of insects; and the bed itself—fortunately extendable—had a transparent half lid of sorts, which had not come down, and behind which a few smaller parcels were tucked as if for ready reference. Bundles were secured in the bath, bundles were stored in the shower stall, besides one that seemed to have exploded, strewing far more wardrobe into the zero-g of the premises than it could reasonably have contained.

Amid it all, Banichi and Jago had cases of electronics yet to set up, two of which they immediately emptied, donating them to Narani's urgent demand for a flat surface. They were still searching for the pressing-iron, and exactly how they proposed to use that in null-g remained to be seen.

"Press cloth in these circumstances, Rani-ji?" Bren objected. "The second-best shirt will do. I'm sure it will do."

"Paidhi-ma," Narani objected, "I beg you allow us to try. For our pride's sake, nandi. The coat has gotten rumpled, among other calamities. And the captains are invited."

Staff continued their unpacking, cursing the insistence of ship security on inspecting certain of the items in an entirely unacceptable fashion, and at the last moment, of stowing the contents of the baggage cart in a haphazard hurry. Things had gone askew from plan, and it wasn't in any way the atevi-ordered arrangement of rooms that let the staff do their duty in an orderly way. The staff was entirely distressed.

Meanwhile there was the scale of things. Banichi and Jago had quarters adjacent to his, and communicating by a door between as well as their own corridor access. A suite of rooms, the charts called the arrangement, each with clear floor about four strides long and two strides wide, which turned out to be, when occupied by atevi, human strides, if they were able to stride at the moment—and entirely too small. Niggling minor problem—storage for atevi-scale clothing was impossible in the tiny lockers provided for the original colonists. Greater problem: low human-scale ceilings made it very scant clearance for tall atevi such as Banichi even to stand up, once they were standing, and made a room in which four or five atevi were drifting askew a very small-seeming room indeed.

Those were situations for which they had been moderately prepared—at least in planning, before they tried to maneuver past one another. The closet and the food-storage closets were both what the ship called suites, and those were full, at the moment, Bren was told, of floating bags. The unpacked clothing would ultimately fit on lines to contain and order the wardrobes, once there was gravity, which now there was not. The unpacked security equipment had clamps and braces which did not mate to the room, rather to more gear that itself had to be fixed in place under these conditions, and which had to stay in place once there *was* gravity.

More, the galley stores and the security equipment included heavy items, and in the grand scale of things, even the dowager's invitation took second place to the need to get the heavy equipment and bundles sorted to the bottom and secured before undocking—before the simulated gravity sent the heavy things crashing down on the light ones. And on that score, there had been argument. Crew had advised them in a written communique not to take things into quarters, to leave them in cargo until after undock, and he had said no, they would take them in nevertheless. So doubtless crew who had shoved things into the cabins were quite smug about it all. So a jaundiced suspicion could guess.

And here they were, everything in their own control, if one could call it control—with a formal dinner unexpectedly at hand and baggage everywhere.

His luggage, however, was bulk rather than mass, and at least posed few breakage hazards.

"Just pad the equipment with *my* bags," he told Banichi and Jago, when there was question of bringing Tano and Algini aboard for a few hours to do the installation while they pursued Ilisidi's notion of formal entertainment. "We aren't going to be able to get this installed before we move. My shirts won't break. And we shouldn't pull Tano and Algini off internal security. I truly don't like that notion, Banichi."

"One can try to secure things," Banichi said. "Or we can draw personnel from Cenedi, perhaps before launch."

"I'm sure I have enough clothes. I'm sure I have far too many clothes. Do it, Banichi."

Meanwhile the domestic staff, which had expected a decent interval to do its necessary arranging, now searched to find, among other necessities of life, old-fashioned vegetable starch, which they intended to boil—one asked—in a sealed bag in the microwave . . . which also had to be unpacked and secured. One did not want to imagine the zero-g consequences of a burst bag of starch.

They had, however, located the pressing-iron—which fortunately *was* electric, not a flatiron as the old arrangement had been.

Plugging it in, however, required a unit and a small, unreasonably mislaid adapter to mediate between its three-pronged plug and the ship's power clips. That was well enough: they needed the adapters for the microwave, too.

The staff oh so rarely missed a social forecast. Narani had so carefully had his less formal second-best pressed, protected, and ready for what had, to Narani, seemed likely: an informal dinner with the dowager.

They had certainly been sandbagged. Caught out, half-prepared—excusable, under the pressure of their sudden departure; but now there was no margin.

"I could *surely* make do with the casual coat, Rani-ji," Bren reiterated, foreknowing the futility of that protest; and, no, no, even yet, absolutely not. Narani would perish of shame if he sent the paidhi-aiji to a state dinner in his second-best coat and trousers, and he would not admit defeat, yet, no matter the lack of adapters.

Not to mention that Banichi and Jago had to have *their* formal uniforms and everything of their individual spit and polish, and the equipment that went with them. That necessity had Asicho in a dither, because those hadn't been readied, either.

There was at least time to bathe, once Asicho shifted the baggage out of the paidhi's shower, and Bren simply turned over the clothes he was wearing, trusting no crew would be floating by in the common hall, and took refuge in the anemic fog-shower, which at least was unaffected by lack of gravity.

It was fifteen minutes of comparative peace until the shower beeped a warning, sucked up the moisture and turned itself off.

Asicho waited with a soft, sweet-smelling bathrobe, zero-g and all.

Meanwhile the adapters had turned up, and staff, having microwaved their starch to slimy perfection, prepared his shirt for ironing.

There was something remarkably tranquil about the aroma of fresh ironing. And Banichi and Jago reported one emergency solved and their quarters secured: they had unmade their beds, corralled the fragiles in small bundles of bedding and secured them under the lowered transparent bed-lids.

Bren settled to dry his hair and check last-moment messages.

Of mail, there was none but a parting well-wish from Lord Geigi, which he answered fondly, and with kind thoughts for the one atevi in all the world who probably wanted most to be here:

I shall attempt to secure pictures to show you . . .

Then, in that momentary pause, somber and thinking of very far places indeed, he composed a letter to his mother, hoping Barb would read it to her.

> *Aboard now, and thinking of you.*
>
> *I wish I could be two people, one to do things a son and a brother ought to have done, especially in these last years that I haven't been in reach.*
>
> *I think of winter in the mountains, the cabin we used to use. I think of the seashore we visited. I think of the kitchen and sitting in the morning drinking tea, and I want all that to be there when I get back. I have to go, for the safety of all we work for—but I'm coming back, and I want you to bake that really spicy teacake, and I want a few mornings to spend just like that, sopping up tea and teacake and telling you everywhere I've been.*
>
> *Then I want to take a good few days of the vacation I've got coming to fly you up to the mountains and see if that cabin's still there. It's the good memories that sustain me.*
>
> *I need you. Take care of yourself. Give my love to Toby.*
>
> *With all my heart, mum. Take care and be good.*
>
> *Bren.*

He nerved himself and sent, a button push that necessitated a reach after the retreating computer.

He trusted C1 and Mogari Nai at this point. He had to. He had to trust very many people for everything.

He left the computer fairly securely parked against the wall, near his bed, and concentrated on the hair-drying, Asicho being busy with Jago's uniform, and Banichi's.

His shirt when it arrived had lace so crisp it rattled, lace inserted through the coat-sleeves *before* he put his arms in, which was the secret by which the court achieved true extravagance of dress. Bindanda snugged up first the shirt and then the frothy, razor-edged collar while Narani supported the coat from behind and kept his hair out of the lace points.

Fashion, fashion, fashion: a little out of current, he knew, but a statement, nonetheless, a declaration, a respect for the dowager and her table.

He took a strange reassurance from the lace and the excess, like some ancient warrior of the archives putting on armor, some sense of atavistic participatory extravagance that declared a class, a club, a secret society to which the dowager and he belonged. Which was in a sense the truth. It meant that she would know him, she would read him accurately, and perhaps, if things went badly, listen to him much more reasonably than if he had arrived, as he had argued to do, in less than his absolute best. Narani was right. Narani's instincts said find the damned starch and steam the silk coat to rights, for the sake of all of them.

He anchored himself by a handgrip to have his hair

dressed: Asicho spread a silk scarf across the brocade coat shoulders, and her skilled, fine fingers rendered the braid with little tugs that tried to pull him loose from his mooring.

She accomplished the ribboning immaculately, he trusted, not taking time to find a mirror: white, for the paidhi's professional neutrality in a minefield of heraldries, associations and rivalries.

After that, in that coat of silk both fine and thick as armor, he could drift slightly askew from the ceiling and floor, let his computer drift in front of him on voice-command, and gather his thoughts over his notes and charts of ship structure and space allotments. Not a pleasant contemplation, but he had before him an assembly of his accesses, his resources, in the not-inconceivable eventuality of the dowager creating a breach with Ogun and with Sabin.

And a hostile collapse of the entire political structure.

Hadn't Tabini said from the beginning that he intended to rule the station, that he intended there be an atevi starship?

Would *this* one suit Tabini—to get a force aboard, outright *take* the ship for himself?

God, no. There was the boy. Would Tabini send his only child into an arena of conflict?

Damned right, if it set his enemies off their guard, he thought, not wanting to think it: yes, Tabini would, and he would do it without many second thoughts, expecting success *and* the boy's survival, because Tabini expected extravagant things of the extraordinary people he gathered from all across the world.

Tabini routinely sent his *grandmother* into situations like that—granted his grandmother was the greatest threat available.

It was possible.

Not advisable, not what he wanted to think about—but possible.

"If we need to get out of here in a hurry," he said to Jago as she drifted by, "do you have account of the route?"

"Always, Bren-ji," was Jago's answer. She anchored herself by a hand against the ceiling, a very easy reach. "Shall we plan?"

"Possible," he said. "Remotely possible. I'll do all I can to assure it doesn't happen."

"Yes," Jago said fervently.

"You're in touch with Cenedi?"

"Constantly," Jago said. His staff, ordinarily entirely independent, had attached themselves and him to the dowager's—convenient, until it came to him doing anything independent, or establishing his own priorities. Like preventing a war. Or theft of a starship.

Which, God, he wasn't sure he wanted to prevent. How could they *run* it, without Sabin?

"I have every confidence in Cenedi," he said to her. "But I have utmost confidence in you and Banichi, nadi. Utmost. You are *not* to accept a rear guard position, or to desert me at any time."

He conflicted *man'chiin* in that statement, and knew it. Theirs flowed up to Tabini himself, and by small detours, to him in the main, and to the dowager as Tabini's representative: there was no time at which that *man'chi* to Tabini wavered.

"I *know* this place, these humans, and these circumstances," he said, revealing his logic in the statement. "And the dowager ought to take my advice, but, infelicitous pair: may *not*. I fear a move to take the ship itself. And I will *not* lose from the household the two of your Guild I most trust to know and understand and defend the interests of the house, all to save some other man of the dowager's household. I will *not*, Jago-ji. If any such infelicitous thing should come about, I most assuredly will need my most experienced staff around me."

That at least occasioned Jago a moment's consideration . . . possibly because the paidhi was an utter, forgetful fool and the communications she wore was live and directed to Cenedi's staff; but it was late to moderate that statement, impossible to call it back, and, on a third thought, if it penetrated Cenedi's consciousness of a dangerous situation, *good*.

He touched his own coat, in the same position in which his bodyguard wore their electronics. It was a question.

Jago touched the same spot. "It isn't," she said. "We don't communicate with their staff, when we're inside. Paidhi-ji, we would tell you."

That was a relief. And in itself, that statement told him where *man'chi* lay.

"I will protect the dowager," he said, to ease their uneasiness, "but will *not* sacrifice myself or my guard or my staff that I have trained up here for very important work. I feel no call to do that. And if they were to attempt to take the ship—I don't know what we would do with it, nadi-ji."

"We completely agree, paidhi-ji."

This was *not* Jago off-duty, who slept with him. No, this was Jago in official relationship, and for atevi officers, instinct-driven to take such orders from the highest in the household, it was a profound, a revolutionary statement, with implications for the rest of the voyage—if they had a voyage.

"I'm sorry to have placed you in such a position. But in my estimation, we have no choice but to maintain my independent judgment."

"The aiji gave you very great authority. I speak for Banichi as well," Jago said. "And our *man'chi* flows through *you* to the aiji, nandi; it takes no detours. I think I speak for the staff, except Bindanda. And *his* is more aligned with us than otherwise."

Revolution, indeed.

A paper lordship.

Or was it? His staff had read it. And *they* took it seriously.

A lord in his own province—and his was the heavens themselves—could say no to very high-rank.

He was astonished. Appalled. "Jago-ji, keep me from foolishness. Say so to Banichi, Jago-ji."

"Oh, he knows," Jago said. "But I will tell him, nandi."

She went on her way. He folded up his computer, finding his hands trembling.

Absolute novice's mistake, that with the possibility of interconnected communications, and he'd made it. But gut-level, too, he'd relied on his staff, and wasn't disappointed.

Lord of the heavens?

A rival to Ilisidi?

From a carefully insulated center of his brain that might be mostly atevi, or mostly human—he honestly didn't know what he thought.

He'd been blindsided. He'd made one mistake. From now on he had to be flawless.

He had to *think*, was what Tabini expected of him. To keep the tempers on this ship in check he had to be neither-side and both-sides for at least this evening, examining everything, taking nothing for granted.

He didn't need a computer for that preparation. The tools he needed were inside himself: calm, and ice-cold, experienced analysis of motives.

Those things, and complete, professional objectivity in his view of participants.

There was a hard one. He didn't *like* Sabin.

And how was he going to keep everything restrained and reasonable at *that* table?

He stowed his computer inside a locker where he knew it would be safe when down became down again. He had no intention of having a literal crash.

Tabini *hadn't* set him up on this mission with Ilisidi without the cachet to go with it. His staff answered the situation, and made him put on this coat and take up the authority.

So *that* was what Jago and Narani and his whole staff had been saying when they scoured up starch and an iron? When only the best would do for Bren-paidhi?

He was a reasonably smart mender-of-the-interface. It had only taken him a half an hour to figure it out.

Near time to go down the hall and do his job.

Near time for them to go down there and try to prevent the calamity that thus far was headed for them.

His escort appeared in the door, Banichi and Jago in their court finery, shining silver and polished black leather. Their Guild remained efficient, while the lords rendered themselves incredibly baroque.

"A moment, nadiin-ji," Bren said, settling on one preliminary item. He was near a communications unit, in major points like the one he'd had on station, and he punched in the same authority he'd always contacted for people behind the ship-folk's communications firewall. "C1?"

"This is C1. Is this Mr. Cameron, on five?"

"It is." Clearly C1 had some indication where the call originated. "Contact Captain Graham. He has an appointment. Tell him call me regarding that."

There was a pause. It would be complete calamity, if Sabin decided at the last moment not to show, and to keep Jase incommunicado. More, if he was serving as diplomatic safety net, he had to avoid mistakes and missed appointments, and his heartbeat began a slow climb to panic as the silence on the other end stretched out longer than an ordinary transfer of communications.

"Captain Graham is en route," C1 reported, *"and says he'll see you in 5 B."*

That was their sector. Thank God.

"Thank you, C1." He broke the connection and drifted gently toward his security.

So things *were* on track, Sabin hadn't thrown Jase in the brig yet, and the situation at least wouldn't blow up before they even got started.

17

Cenedi had a security presence in the corridor, providing two men to open the door and admit them to the cabin designated as the dowager's dining room. It was a matter of pride with a lordly household: on the world or here above, a lordly house managed its own doors, however strung out down a common corridor, and no one else touched said doors, or did so at their peril.

It provided a homey, comfortable feeling, that formality, even if they were floating. Things were *right*, or at least more right than they had been a few hours ago.

And Jase *was* coming. Thank God.

The outer door shut. Cenedi met them inside, in a little alcove made by stretched fabric—very ingenious, Bren thought, separating the designated dining room. "Jase is on his way," Bren said in passing, and reached out to anchor himself and not to bump into the curtain as he drifted in.

There was a table; there were chairs. They were anchored quite firmly; and the dowager sat, or approximately sat, to welcome them, tucked into a chair and braced with pillows. She had that formidable cane in hand. By her, also tucked in with pillows, was Cajeiri, quite proper, considering; and beyond another fabric screen, the second doorway to the suite, which was, one was sure, the area from which dinner service would come.

"Aiji-ma." Bren launched himself from the wall with fair accuracy and grace, aiming himself toward what should be the seat next the dowager on her right. He grabbed it before he overshot, and the dowager graciously bade him to a seat.

"There, there, will you care for a pillow, paidhi-aiji?"

Staff had drifted in from that farther curtain, having pillows in hand.

Pillows seemed a good idea, a clever way to wedge oneself in, and he accepted the amenity. The athletic young man immediately shot away toward the door—tracked by Cajeiri's estimating, all-recording gaze, as every movement gained Cajeiri's fascinated if erratic attention.

"Jase is on his way, aiji-ma," Bren said, tucking pillows snugly. "One hopes that Sabin-aiji is with him."

"One *expects* so," Ilisidi said. Usually by now there was a drink service, if there were late arrivals; but just then, and to his relief, Cenedi opened the doors and admitted their two missing guests.

A little delay at the door: Sabin hadn't intended to leave her guard, but that matter was settled on a glance inside. Jase and Sabin both came drifting in, Jase assuring Sabin of the situation, that neither Cenedi nor Banichi and Jago would sit here.

So bodyguards had *their* conviviality across the hall, or the corridor, or however they arranged it, in whatever area—a prime venue for exchanging informal intelligence and gossip, if it were associated houses, as it was not, in the captains' case.

But there would be no stint of food over there, to be sure.

Jase indicated a seat of preference to Sabin, ceding that honor to his senior, when Ilisidi beckoned an invitation to them, and Sabin and Jase both sailed accurately into place, and into a chair.

"A pillow?" Ilisidi inquired, the servant standing by to offer it, and Jase accepted.

"Pillow," Sabin muttered in mild disgust. Clearly this wasn't the style of Sabin's table, such as it might be, or however ship-folk managed under similar circumstances. But Sabin took it nonetheless, a nice, brocaded pillow, with fringe, and secured herself at the table.

"Welcome, welcome," Ilisidi said. "We appreciate that these are busy hours for the ship-aijiin."

Bren translated.

"Damned busy," Sabin said. Sabin had been scowling when she came through the door and hadn't improved the expression since. Clearly her interview with Jase had been heated.

"We held a conversation," Jase said in Ragi, in the lowest possible whisper, "and the captain understands this is critically important, paidhi-aiji."

Passing information right across the table. In Ragi.

"I have a statement," Sabin said, jaw clenched. "At the appropriate time."

"A welcoming statement?" Bren asked.

"Call it that. Ready?"

"The ship-aiji wishes to make you welcome to the ship, aiji-ma," Bren said.

Ilisidi gave a modest wave of the hand.

"You can tell the aiji's grandmother that whatever arrangements Ramirez made were Ramirez's arrangements. They're not mine. I won't renege on her being here, but I won't tolerate your native types breaking our regulations or undertaking independent operations."

"Aiji-ma, the ship-aiji does not consider herself bound by Ramirez's arrangements, and states strongly that while she will not disapprove your presence aboard, she does not favor it and wishes you not to initiate operations that may infringe regulations or startle ship's officers."

"How elegant of her," Ilisidi said and waggled fingers. "Say that whatever the custom on the ship, business at the table is not our custom. And since she has made a demand, broach the matter of that tape Jase wants."

"Aiji-ma." This from Jase. "I beg you let me finesse that matter."

"You wish to translate, ship-aiji?" Ilisidi asked.

"Jase," Bren said, a caution, a strong caution—a plea on both knees, if there'd been an up or a down, for Jase to stay out of it, for the whole topic to wait.

"Oh, serve the drinks, nadiin-ji," Ilisidi said, losing interest in it all, and immediately a servant entered the room from behind the curtain, bearing a closed container. The servant *flung* the contents, startling them all with blue and red, yellow and orange and clear and amber globes that sailed all about the premises like so many moonlets on independent courses, to collide and carom and go on moving, sloshing liquid contents. Sabin stared in incredulity and looked alarmed, as if they'd loosed so many bombs. Cajeiri clapped his hands in glee.

"Oh, mani, may we take them?"

"The red or blue for you, young rascal of a grandson, indeed. Bren-ji, the clear or the yellow. Jasi-ji, the yellow is your favorite. Let our guest suit herself." She reached up and snared a fist-sized amber one on its way past, pulled out the recessed straw, and sipped.

Bren reached obediently for a clear globe . . . the likes of which they had proposed to use on the shuttle, for emergencies. "Captain, the clear globes would be vodka. The yellow, vodka and juice. The others wouldn't be safe for us."

Sabin picked a clear one, pulled her straw and drank. "Inventive."

"Sabin-aiji applauds the ingenuity of the service, aiji-ma." This, as the staff loosed another volley of planetoids, these white and yellow, which drifted more slowly through their midst.

One trusted the appetizer was safe. It was pureed, to fit through the straw, in internal sacs that collapsed, and sweet, and sour, and could be enjoyed in alternation, while one parked one's drink—if not in orbit—at least in convenient proximity.

"Delicious," Bren said. "My compliments to the

cook." Sabin had made a cautious trial, but Jase took to his with evident pleasure.

"Curious," Sabin said dubiously.

"Sabin-aiji views this as novel, aiji-ma."

"We are pleased," Ilisidi said, the full-blown royal *we*, when *one* was far more modest. Modesty was rarely Ilisidi's bent. "One hopes that our table will be the aiji's frequent recourse. Do you favor the eggs, then, Jasi-ji?"

God, the minefield of royal *we*, self-deprecating *one*, and that damned familiar *Jasi-ji*.

Do you hear it, Jase? Do you understand how to answer? She tests your fluency.

"Nand' dowager," Jase said with a little—a very little—nod of his head, "a great delicacy in space. I have so missed them."

Bang. Right back, dead on. Authoritative, lordly, dignified *I*, not *we*, not *one*, either—with no insult about it.

Bren let go a pent breath.

Sabin had, meanwhile, emptied her globe and reached for another.

"What are these?" Sabin asked, forcing a total, appalled shift of viewpoint.

Embryonic lizards hardly seemed a good answer for a ship-bound palate. "An organic delicacy, captain."

"Different," Sabin said.

"Translate, paidhiin-ji," Ilisidi requested of them.

"Sabin-aiji remarks on a novel taste," Bren said. And added: "Ship-folk are quite restricted in palate, aiji-ma. She is experimenting with new things, not unfavorably."

A servant had to retrieve Cajeiri's drink, and sailed it past him. Cajeiri dislodged an appetizer reaching for it, and accidentally fired the drink off at a tangent trying to recover the nudged globe.

"Gently, gently, young man," Ilisidi said. "Haste only startles what you wish to catch. Stalk your desires. Don't snatch."

The servant had secured the escaped drink, and put it into Cajeiri's hand.

"Yes, mani," Cajeiri said.

"Learn, rascal!"

"I do, mani."

"This is an exchange regarding the accident," Bren murmured by way of translation. "The aiji's son is, of course, inexperienced in zero-g."

"Still no place for a teenager," Sabin muttered, and Bren masked startlement. Now that he realized it, the ship had never seemed to connect this child to Damiri's fairly recent pregnancy, and on evidence of size, Sabin clearly had not a clue that the boy was six, not sixteen.

"My definitive statement, among others," Sabin said glumly. "But collective decision prevailed."

"Yes, ma'am." Far too late to change that misperception, or to renegotiate personnel. They dared not let the captain find it out at this juncture.

"I trust," Sabin said, "there's a watch on this boy."

"Yes, captain."

"Let me add another statement to the first: no atevi wandering about outside this section without contacting the bridge for permission, until further notice, and this young fellow stays on this deck, period, under any circumstances."

"Captain, I'll happily relay that at the appropriate moment."

"Now, sir."

He tried to think whether to lie, or whether to proceed; but lying—had its own problems soon to appear. And things could only escalate. Ilisidi, at least, was calm. "Aiji-ma," he said, "with personal apologies from the translator, the captain considers this urgent. She wishes us not to leave this section without direct contact with her, for a period of time that seems to be impermanent, one gathers until she's more certain of us, and wishes you not to allow the heir to leave this section under any circumstances."

"This ship-aiji is very persistently rude, is she not? I never detected this in *you*, Jase-aiji. It can't be custom."

"Aiji-ma," Jase said, "this aiji is reputed for direct statement and attention to agriculture."

"Business," Bren interposed, and Jase blushed.

"To business," Jase said. "Forgive me, aiji-ma."

A waggle of fingers. Ilisidi had emptied three of the white globes—empty ones sailed off to be captured and whisked out of sight—and she sent the fourth away.

"We are not mentioning to the captain that Cajeiri is six," Bren said. "She believes sixteen."

"Sixteen?" Cajeiri crowed, delighted.

"Hush, rascal," Ilisidi said.

"It's a convenient misunderstanding," Bren said, "saving argument. And there would be argument about his presence otherwise, in a dangerous place. Human custom is against it."

"Do you hear?" Ilisidi said. "You must pretend ten more years, young scoundrel, to satisfy the ship-aiji's expectations of your wisdom, your sense and your self-restraint."

"I think the ship-aiji will suspect me," Cajeiri said sadly, and the Ragi-speakers could not but laugh a little.

"There's a problem?" Sabin asked.

"The boy regrets his youth," Bren said. "And amuses his elders. I should urge you, now, captain, in the very strongest terms, to delay further business discussion. We're now approaching the heart of the meal, which atevi hold entirely sacred. Particularly should there be a meat course, which may, under these circumstances, be soup . . . be most respectful of it."

"I don't eat meat," Sabin said.

Sabin was pushing. Hard. Deliberately. And the translator himself was losing patience.

"One will relay that, captain. —Aiji-ma, the ship-aiji reminds us of the customs of ship-dwellers, and requests all others enjoy the offering of the season, but she is unaccustomed, and requests exception."

"One has indeed remembered this intelligence," Ilisidi said lightly. "Advise our guest that the sole white globe will be an offering for her taste." This, as servants glided forth and very deftly, very respectfully, placed globes before each of them—four light gold, veined with steam between the plastic and the globe walls; and one white globe, with cold condensation, which the servant placed before Sabin.

One . . . white globe.

Oh, my God, Bren thought, just this least, small apprehension.

"Aiji-ma," he said, and received a short, swift gesture in reply.

Should he defy that warning? Should he *do* something? Could he betray Jase, among other considerations?

And should he open his mouth and have security opposed to security and the whole mission aborted and the whole ship-human/planetary association come crashing around their ears—with Tabini's son and grandmother up here in the very heart of the ship?

He could keep his mouth shut, and trust Ilisidi to respect his honor, and play by the rules of the culture he'd devoted his life to preserving and advancing in good season—or he could assure a war.

He looked straight at Ilisidi, who looked straight at him, not smugly, but in sober intent.

"Not bad," Sabin said, sampling the offering.

Sabin, whose bodyguard, outside, in the company of his own, likely included Jenrette.

"Jasi-ji," Bren said, resolved to tell Jase, knowing after all else he had been through with Jase, that frankness was the only safety. "One should be prepared. The ship-aiji has challenged the dowager. There will undoubtedly be adverse results."

"Aiji-ma," Jase said, not, Bren thought guiltily— *not* having twigged to the source of the hazard. "One wishes, however inexpertly, to advance the cause of my senior, who is not a wicked woman, and who is accustomed to give orders for the sanity of the ship. . . ."

Safety of the ship, but it was within reason: Bren forebore a distracting correction.

"If she has offended you, aiji-ma," Jase said, "it was not intent to do so. Great respect for your authority has brought her at a very busy time."

"We accept that. Let her give us the tape. Ask her."

"Captain," Jase said, on a deep, deep breath. "There would have been a tape record—covering the entry of personnel onto Reunion."

"What's that to do with anything?"

"The aiji would like to see that tape. It *would* be in the log. Wouldn't it?"

"What's in the log or not is our business. When did this come up?"

And is Sabin wearing a wire? Bren asked himself, calmly taking a sip of an excellent cream soup. *And is it feeding to someone with at least rudimentary knowledge of Ragi?*

And are we in deep water already?

God, what ought I to do?

"It occurred to me," Jase said, leaving Yolanda innocently out of it, "that if we had security aboard, electronics would have recorded that excursion aboard the station."

Sabin had half-emptied the globe, and took a drink of vodka besides.

"And of course you went straight to your atevi friends with that theory."

"Friends, captain, can't apply with atevi. But I assure you they'd think of it for themselves once they

familiarized themselves with the ship's general prac-
tices, and it wouldn't be good to have them think of it
before we'd said, and it wouldn't be good to spring a
surprise on them after we're out there."

"So of course you spilled it on *your* watch."

"My watch is my watch, captain, and when I'm on
the bridge I do my job. This is the best thing to do."

The captain took another long drink of soup, one of
those imposed silences, in which she needn't speak,
needn't answer. It took the globe down to a quarter.

We're in it now, Bren thought. *And if she'd honestly be
persuaded to reason, on her own, and we've done this . . .*

"Mr. Cameron," Sabin said, utterly redirecting to
him, on the other side of the table, "what do you
think?"

"I think the presentation of those tapes would be a
gesture of good will." He should say something. He
should.

"I think I made my position clear. You're passengers. Not command personnel. Evidently you've received a briefing from my brother captain. But this is
an internal matter of ship's records, and no more is
forthcoming. You can convey *that* to the aiji's grandmother."

Or maybe not.

Cajeiri had lost a drink globe, and reached suddenly to retrieve it. Bren's nerves jumped. Jase's
surely did. They were the only ones who might understand both sides of the conversation—give or take,
Banichi, Jago, and the chance of one of Ilisidi's young
men understanding; and he didn't put it past her limits. His advisors knew at least sketchy details, and

hadn't intervened, hadn't given him a signal—
nothing.

"I can't urge enough," Bren said, "that we are a resource to the ship, a well-disposed one, and it would
be a very, very bad decision to breach agreements that
brought her into this mission. Is that what I understand you're doing?"

"Mr. Cameron, the Mospheiran delegate will be
boarding about now. And I'm sure *she* has her
expertise—hers happening to be technical, with the
robots; and if things don't go well, and possibly if
they do, her expertise will have its moment. And at
that time, with the thanks of us all, she will do her
job. Now that is a useful talent. Exactly what the
dowager does besides observe isn't exactly clear to
anyone, but she will be free to observe to her heart's
content. I'm sure it's a useful talent, but it's not one
I need underfoot right now."

Absolute reversal of agreements, Bren thought in
dismay. He saw Jase's distressed frown, and knew if
he did translate, all hell would break loose.

"Surveillance and security, captain, *and* command-
level decision-making equal to the ship, equal to the
island. As for Jase's expertise, and mine, *finesse* with
those who think they're going to have things their
way, to assure that we don't miscalculate and make a
mutually regrettable mistake. I urge you, I strenu-
ously urge you to cooperate with your allies, captain."

The air was chill, even yet. But a sweat had broken
out on Sabin's face.

"Well, you haven't persuaded me, Mr. Cameron.

And I don't need your aliens underfoot. So you're not that good, are you?"

"Captain," Jase interposed.

"No, no, no," Bren said. He'd been horrified a moment ago. Now, heart and soul, he stood back from himself, took a sip of his yellow globe, and told himself it wasn't at all human to be content with what he knew. Or it might be. And that somewhere in Sabin's mind there was a serious difficulty with their program. "The captain's quite right. We aren't able to persuade her that there's a difference between aliens out there, or people defending their planet. So let me propose that you and the senior captain view the tape together, and determine what's on it, and then let us reach a reasonable decision."

"Mr. Cameron," Sabin said, "let me break some news to you. You don't control what happens on this ship."

"A modest proposal," Bren said. While the sweat increased.

"It's cold in here," Sabin said suddenly, distracted. "Is this the temperature your people prefer?"

"It doesn't seem cold to me," Bren said. "—Does it to you, Jase?"

Jase threw him a look. It became a stark, a comprehending look. "Face!" Bren said in Ragi. And Jase did what Jase, over years on the planet, had learned to do, and totally dismissed expression.

"Aiji-ma," Jase protested. "*Bren.*"

"Aiji-ma," Bren said evenly. "Jase-aiji expresses grave concern for this accident. As do we both. And most earnestly assume it isn't lethal."

"The tapes," Ilisidi said. The dreaded cane had been at rest. Now she banged it hard against a table leg. "The *tapes,* nadiin-ji."

Sabin attempted to leave her place, to drift free, not quite in control of her limbs. Cajeiri froze in place, young creature in a thicket, as Jase sailed free of his chair to overtake Sabin, to seize her in his arms.

Bren pushed free as well.

"I've been poisoned," Sabin said. "Damn you!"

"Not lethal," Bren said to Jase in Ragi. He wasn't that utterly confident, but he said, in ship-speak. "I fear it's a reaction to something you ate, captain. The sauces. The sauces can be particularly chancy." Sabin was passing into shivering tremors, angry and incoherent in the chattering of her jaw. "Not generally fatal. It happened to me, once." On purpose. At the dowager's table. For just such reasons. "I'm very sorry."

Sabin reached for her communications unit, but her fingers had trouble with the button.

Jase took it, about to use it himself, but Bren shot out a hand onto Jase's and prevented that.

"You're in charge," he said to Jase in Ragi. "Not likely fatal, nadi, believe me. But you and I and our security are all going up there, to attend her to sickbay."

"We can't have done this!"

"Insulting the dowager at her own table? You can't have done that, either—which I assure you is far more dangerous to the peace than the soup. Disabling the opposition is a moderate response, a limited demonstration, in this case."

"Demonstration, hell! *Not likely fatal.* You don't know that. She's not young. She could die."

"Then stop talking and let's get her up there to the medics."

"Your agents going all over the ship—" Jase tried for composure, and Sabin had by now fallen into a tremulous semi-consciousness. "Damn you," Jase said hoarsely. "Damn you, Bren. *I trusted you.*"

"You *can* trust me," Bren said. "Move. Fluids are going to be a very good idea, very soon now."

They were floating mostly above the dining-table. Ilisidi had drifted up, dislodging a stray drink-globe, formidable cane in hand. Cajeiri followed, very, very cautiously, eyes completely wide.

Somehow, meanwhile, Cenedi had arrived from the serving-room, the back way—Cenedi, and then Banichi, together: a number usually unfortunate, but it was a pacifying unity here, with lords at loggerheads.

Perhaps even a human returned to ship-loyalties could feel that shift in the odds.

"She *isn't* Tamun," Jase said. "She pulled back from the coup."

"That's all very well. You changed the agreements, *you* wanted us confined to quarters, *you* started imposing conditions on the atevi representation on this mission, conditions I'm not sure would be quite as extreme on our still-to-board *human* delegates—"

"That's your suspicion, Bren."

"I'm afraid it is. But the odds have shifted. You know what's at stake. She's not dead. She's in reach of medical care you're keeping her from, nadi, and I'd suggest we get moving right now, no conditions, no maneuvers on your side. Let's see she stays alive, nadi, before we have the association blow up in our faces."

"All right," Jase said in ship-speak. "All right."

"One recommends fluids," the dowager said, "a great deal of fluids, very soon. A blanket, for wrapping. Quickly now."

Servants moved.

"We shall visit our guest," Ilisidi declared. "We are of course distressed."

"Let's go," Bren said. "Your security's outside. Calm them. I'll go with you. We won't let this break wide open, Jase."

"You're not taking this ship." This, in ship-speak.

"I earnestly hope not." And in Ragi: "We're sitting here at dock, we haven't gone anywhere, and I'm not letting you pull this ship out of dock with the dowager and Tabini's son aboard until we have some kind of cooperation and until the dowager is satisfied. Atevi act for their own interests, and it's their planet, their sunlight you've been borrowing. If you want admission, Jase Graham, negotiate, because the way Sabin-aiji's gone at it is shaping up to a disaster."

The servant had come back with a wrap, a wonderfully hand-worked piece, no common woven sheet; and very tenderly that young man helped Jase wrap the shivering captain in its tightly confining embrace—far easier on the captain, far more comforting than a hand-grip. "Get the light out of her eyes," Bren said, tucking a fold across Sabin's brow. His own gut recalled the misery, and he had every sympathy for what Sabin was about to endure. "Captain. We're getting you upstairs. Do you hear me? Hang on. This was surely an accident, an unfortunate accident."

With Jase he moved Sabin toward the door. Jago was outside. So were Kaplan and Pressman, and so was Collins, Sabin's man, with his team.

"The captain's reacted to something at dinner," Jase said. "Mr. Kaplan, alert the infirmary."

The dowager followed, with Cajeiri trailing close, the very image of the concerned host, servants adding a cloak to the dowager's formal attire.

"You'll stay here," Collins said to them, as if Jase were one of the passengers.

That, Bren thought, was a tactical mistake.

"Mister," Jase said, "they're going where I say they're going. That's up to the infirmary, where we can pass information to the medics."

"Cenedi-ji," Ilisidi said. "Have the area secure."

They moved. Cenedi and four men attended the dowager and Cajeiri. "Banichi-ji," Bren said, intent on going with them, and Banichi and Jago opted to leave security to Cenedi's men.

That added up to nine atevi, seven of them very large indeed—a boy and the dowager, and a handful of worried human security, with Jase and Sabin—Sabin being still conscious, but quite, quite beyond coherent expression.

They reached the lift together. "Second deck, Mr. Kaplan," Jase said, and Kaplan punched it in, Sabin's security crowded in with them so that there was very little space left at all.

The lift shot up, opened its door onto pervisible

walls and a waiting escort in blue and white, medics who received the captain in greatest haste and concern and wanted to eject them all back into the lift in the process.

"The dowager expresses great concern for the captain's welfare and will attend," Bren said. "Such incidents happen with native diet—rare, but they do happen. Her staff has a pharmacopeia of remedies."

"We have our own expertise," the chief medic said. "Captain."

"The dowager does know what was administered," Jase said, with no trace of irony or anger about it. "Mr. Cameron can translate. —What will you recommend, nand' dowager?"

"A purgative," Ilisidi said. "A strong purgative. The body will continue to throw it off in every possible way, and administration of fluids will be very helpful."

Bren translated. "Purge the system. Get her to a small, dark room. I've suffered a similar situation. Fluids will help the headache. I assure you there will be headache. Severe headache."

For the next several days. He didn't mention that. Sabin would want to kill them by degrees. And wouldn't want to see bright lights or raise her head above horizontal—however that worked in zero-g.

"*This is Captain Graham.*" Jase's voice came over the general address, and from Jase, in stereo, via C1's offices, Bren had no doubt. "*Captain Sabin has had a food reaction, and is recovering in sickbay, full recovery expected. We're close to shift-change. It's become my watch, and first-shift may stand down as relief arrives. Second-shift, report to duty immediately."*

Sabin began to try to speak when she heard that, and was, predictably, suffering nausea. Medics, atevi security and human, moved to assist. In zero-g, it was not a happy situation.

"Atevi personnel will move about freely during crew and passenger boarding," Jase continued on the intercom. *"Report any question to me via C1."*

A hovering grandmother, a vitally important child with security attendant, a handworked and expensive cloth—none of these were the ship's image of a coup, Bren hoped. It would hardly be the image of such an event in Shejidan, if one didn't intimately know the chief participant.

They'd rescued the precious throw and substituted infirmary disposables. And Sabin was both semi-conscious and miserable.

"We shall stay personally and assure ourselves that the captain is well, nadiin-ji," Ilisidi said. "We have antidotes, which I have ordered be at hand during any dinner."

"Aiji-ma, in case there should be any fatal outcome, one would hardly wish to have supplied a drug—"

"Translate!" Ilisidi said. Bren translated, and subsequently accepted a vial from one of Ilisidi's young men.

"This may be of use," Bren added, passing it to a medical officer, hoping to very heaven it might not be a fatal dose. "To be taken by mouth." He knew this one. "The dowager's medic provides it, out of years of experience with such accidents. It should be minor, except the headache. These are complex substances. I advise taking this remedy."

"It should be safe." Jase said at his shoulder, and in Ragi. "Stay here, Bren-ji, and keep matters quiet. Don't have it look worse than it is. I'm going to the bridge."

"There will be time to discuss," Ilisidi said, silk and steel, with a tender smile, "ship-aiji."

Jase didn't say a thing. Ship-aiji. She'd just made him that, in very fact.

Ogun hadn't necessarily wanted Jase here. Now he was. Now he was in charge, with power to abort or delay the mission. Ogun hadn't necessarily wanted Sabin in charge of the mission, either—hadn't liked her, and possibly hadn't trusted her associations, to put it in Ragi.

Possibly far too many of his thoughts came in Ragi these days; but he believed in what he saw. He believed that, all evidence accounted, Sabin was a potential asset, only a potential one; and that things trembled on the brink of very bad mistakes.

He saw Jase board the lift, taking Sabin's men out with him, leaving Kaplan.

Very bad mistakes. Which couldn't be allowed to happen. He intended to go inside the treatment room, but Ilisidi and her escort came, and they crowded into the room to the evident distress of the medics.

"There's limited room here," the chief medic said angrily. "Sir, if you'll persuade them outside . . ."

"This is 'Sidi-ji." The crew knew the dowager, knew her manner—and respected her. "I doubt I can. We're here to see the antidote given. She feels personally responsible, and it's a matter of honor."

"We've no intention of giving the captain another unidentified alien substance. . . ."

"You're the aliens, sir, by way of precise accuracy, and I do urge the dowager has a far more exact knowledge of native chemistry. This is a medication I've had, and if I didn't think it would ease the symptoms I'd never urge it. —Captain? You're offered an antidote. I'll vouch for it, on my personal honor. I've had such an incident myself."

Sabin was just conscious enough, and she'd had it on far more alcohol and a far better cushion of previous dishes: the one might accelerate, the other cushion the effects of the substance, and for all his assurances to the doctors, Ilisidi *hadn't* had that extended an experience at poisoning humans.

"At this point," Sabin said, teeth chattering, eyes clenched rapidly after one second's attempt to look him in the eye, "at this point, hell, it can't be worse."

It could.

"Captain," the doctor said.

"I said it can't be worse!" Shouting was not a good idea. Not at all a good idea.

"Just let her drink it," Bren said. "Hang onto it as long as possible, captain." Sabin's heaving stomach knew exactly what he meant.

"Give it," Sabin said.

Clearly the medics weren't in favor of native medicines. But one uncapped the vial and offered it, stoppered with a gloved thumb.

Sabin sucked the black liquid down between shivers.

"I don't know whether it would help or hurt to get gravity aboard," Bren said. "At least dim the lights in here."

"Listen to him!" Sabin said. "He's the only one who knows anything!"

The headache had hit. It was probably a good thing. They were pumping fluids in via a tube.

The attendance of atevi had taken position not just in the corner, but stacked rather as if seated in a theater, a black and brocade wall of watchers, Banichi and Jago among the foremost, Cajeiri's solemn young eyes staring amazedly at the goings-on.

Things settled. Sabin drifted with her eyes shut, medics monitoring, making notations, conferring in low voices among themselves. Bren watched, having learned in his mother's crises and in a precarious lifetime somewhat to interpret what he heard, which at least indicated to him that vital signs were solid. Sabin's pulse was racing—he remembered that effect—but not badly so. It went right along with the headache, which by Sabin's determined, jaw-clenched quiet was indeed what Sabin was feeling.

"Poisoned," Sabin said during one of her moments of lucidity. "Damn, I knew it."

"Yet you came to dinner," Bren said, from his vantage near the troubled medics. "You were willing to risk it. And it may have happened completely inadvertently." He much doubted that. "The dowager is here, captain. She is concerned for your welfare, and at this moment you might ask her for high favors, to make amends. She is, I'm sure, very willing to make amends . . . to make peace."

"Brooks." Sabin turned her head to appeal to the chief medic, a movement which brought nausea. She made a grab for a suction bag, and nausea replaced thought for a moment.

Bren felt pangs of his own—the memory of that illness didn't go away.

"Damn you," Sabin said behind the bag, face averted.

"Yes, captain," Bren said. "Damn me as you like. But I'm very sure you'd walk through fire to an objective. I suggest this is the fire, and there is an overwhelmingly important objective to be won. I came to a like conclusion once. I suggest you very well know what that objective is: their respect and their cooperation . . . and that you've been tested. Favorably tested, I might add. Do you want the objective? Do you want their cooperation, unmediated by me or by anyone else?"

Sabin beat the nausea, dismissed the attending medic, put up a hand that trailed tubing and wiped sweat from her face. A medic started to dry it with a cloth, and she batted it away.

"Don't touch me," she said. "*Don't anybody touch me.*" She added a string of profanities, and breathed heavily for a moment. Bren knew. Bren utterly knew, inside and out, the war going on in Sabin's gut, and in Sabin's very intelligent brain.

Sabin—slowly, this time—turned her head in Bren's direction, not without a sideward glance toward the towering mass of atevi. Sabin's eyes watered tears that stood in globules and blinked into small beads on her lashes. It was physiological reaction, not weakness, not—Bren was quite sure—abject fear, no fear of man, atevi, or the devil.

"Damn you," Sabin said. "You're in *our* ship, and you're alive on our tolerance."

"Captain," Bren said, "you're wanting supplies from *our* station and *our* planet."

"Your planet," Sabin scoffed. "You're *human*. Or were. Or ought to be."

"I am. And I still say *my planet, my people, my government and my leaders*. We're not your colonists any more. And through your character, your skills, your actions over a lengthy acquaintance, you've won the planet's agreement, not only in this, but in everything you could want. Everything you came to the dowager's quarters to get, you've gotten—if you're not such a fool as to let a cultural misunderstanding blow up the deal." He knew Sabin's temper—that it was extreme—but always under control. And he'd been on the station long enough to know two more things about Sabin, first that the crew's dislike of her did get under her skin, and that she did make occasional efforts at humanity—and second, that there was a requisite level of honesty and bluntness in dealing with her. Do her credit, truth was one of her virtues. "My apologies, captain, my personal and profound apologies for what you're going through at the moment. To this moment I don't know if it was intentional. Atevi custom can be arcane. But the dowager's attendance here—" He gestured with a glance toward the dark wall of atevi. "—Her attendance on you is an extreme statement. She's saying she views you favorably. She respects you. She respects your strength." Ego repair seemed in order, and there were qualities he knew Sabin respected. "Because you haven't buckled, captain, *therefore* she'll be able to cooperate with you, the same way she cooperates with the Mospheiran president and the aiji himself. There *are* very few authorities that she remotely respects. There's only one authority on earth she halfway abides, but she allows a very few equals. *Therefore* you were at her table; therefore she sat through—let me very bluntly refresh your memory, captain—your pushing her very, very hard to see what she'd do. And you know you did that. You meant to do it. You wanted to provoke her to push back. Well, now you've both proved something. So can we get beyond that, if you please, and walk through that fire, and get to what both sides really want out of this voyage?"

Sabin had been lucid, and listened to him, her mouth set to a thin line. She wasn't ready to speak, but she was holding on to arguments as they sailed past her doubtless aching brain.

"I'm mobile," she said, "as long as we're in zero-g. I've got my tubes. Everything floats. Give me a headache-killer. *Damn* you and your schemes, Mr. Cameron, and damn your atevi friends. I'm going to the bridge. Graham *isn't* in charge."

"Yes, captain." The chief medic made a move to bundle the tubes and the fluid-delivery apparatus—wrapped them together in plastic and tucked them toward Sabin, still pumping their stabilizing content.

"Sabin declares she will go to the bridge, nadiin-ji," Bren said in Ragi, knowing what he was throwing into motion—and avoiding names. "She is challenging. Advise the bridge."

Sabin looked at him, quietly rotating toward level, toward that eye contact that human beings wanted with each other, that contact of souls, and it was a blistering, burning contact—momentary, as Sabin sought, with the help of others, to leave.

There was nothing he could do. Absolutely nothing. Jase might try to prove she was out of her head and seize command by virtue of the senior captain's incapacity, but treatment and sheer dogged determination was overcoming the substance in Sabin's bloodstream, and she was going to get to the lift, and she was going to challenge Jase, and call on her own bodyguard in the situation . . . Jase's bodyguard all being *here*.

That, he could help.

"Mr. Kaplan," Bren said. "Assist the captain."

Kaplan looked at him, Kaplan with doubtless the same desperate set of thoughts going on behind that distressed expression, Kaplan knowing he *shouldn't* be taking orders from an outsider, in support of a captain hostile to his captain. But there was a level of trust between them, of long standing, and Kaplan did move, and the rest of the human escort did, willing to assist Sabin . . . least of several evils. Kaplan himself offered a hand to assist Sabin's movement.

And an alarm siren went off through the ship.

And stopped.

"This is Captain Graham. The Mospheirans are now aboard. We're going to release the hookups and stand off,

preparatory to spin-up. Take hold. Take immediate precautions."

Jase repeated the same advisement in Ragi and Sabin fumbled after her communications unit, struggling for composure. "C1! Captain Graham is *not* in charge. Put this to general address! Captain Graham is not in charge. First shift take stations."

Humans in the medical facility stood as if paralyzed.

It didn't come over the general address. Sabin's advisement hadn't gone out.

C1, on a decision C1 probably hadn't made alone, *hadn't* cooperated.

The motion warning sounded, staccato bursts, warning anyone who'd ever studied the emergency procedures not to be moving from secure places. The warning went on for over a minute, and medical personnel scrambled, securing loose lines, bits of equipment, checking latches.

The warning stopped.

Almost immediately a crash resounded through the ship frame.

Lights dimmed and came up bright again.

"We have released," Jase's voice said. *"Stand by."*

As if Sabin hadn't said anything. Lights on the intercom panel strobed yellow: *caution, caution, take care.*

Medics moved to take Sabin. Atevi shifted position. Bren grabbed a safety-rail, heart pounding.

"Damn you," Sabin shouted.

The world moved, slowly, subtly, the same feeling as the shuttle had. *Strange,* Bren thought. Strange that something so massive as *Phoenix* could move like that, just so softly.

"*This is Captain Ogun,*" the intercom said, "*speaking from station offices, wishing you a safe voyage and a safe return. Our hearts go with you. Be assured that the cooperation of world and station will continue, preserving and building a safe home base for this ship and others. We have been very fortunate in our welcome here.*"

"*Stand by,*" the intercom said then, this time in Jase's voice.

Muscles tensed. Medics cradled their unwilling charge.

"*Have no doubts,*" the intercom said, again in Ogun's voice, "*of our faithful keeping of this port. We will keep you in mind until you're safely home, with, we hope, all our missing crew, and all our citizens.*"

Recorded message, Bren thought desperately. God, it was going bad. Sabin was never going to forgive the dowager, or Jase, who he was sure had just played a departure message out of context.

Sabin damned sure wouldn't forgive him, once Sabin knew the truth.

But Sabin, hazed and hurting, didn't fight any longer. She'd made a valiant effort, a heroic effort. Bren knew, in his own gut, what it cost, and wondered at an old woman's stamina and will . . . even to contemplate traveling up to the bridge in her condition. Gravity was the trump card, gravity, that pulled bodies down to decks and reasserted ordinary capacities. Sabin couldn't make it—couldn't reach the lift. Couldn't stand, or walk. And knew it.

Motion started. A bulkhead came toward their

backs at glacial speed, so, so slowly, while at the same time bodies and objects moved as slowly toward the deck. Small loose items simply drifted across the room, a bundle of tubing, a handful of tissues, a towel, and Bren felt the bulkhead against his shoulder as he felt his feet contacting the deck.

Sabin went rackingly sick. The medics contained the situation, and there went the delicate chemical balance, both positive and negative. She could not hold herself on her feet, that was the plain fact, as objects slowly acquired weight to go with their momentum. The pressure of feet against the floor equaled and then exceeded that against the bulkhead.

The bulkhead pressure stopped. There was a very queasy moment, and then Bren became aware he was standing as he would on the station, with the ship drifting inertial.

And themselves sideways on the inside of a torus. There were things the mind didn't want to know or reckon with.

Sabin was convulsively ill, and the medics, protective of her, saw a cot let down and Sabin bundled into it.

"Mr. Cameron," the chief doctor said, "I'll ask you to take this occupation force out into the corridor. Captain's orders."

"No, sir," Bren said quietly. He had a dozen arguments, but only one matching Sabin's order: "We're here at the *sitting* captain's orders, and we feel we should regard that instruction until Captain Sabin's recovered."

The doctor wasn't happy. "Watch them," the doctor

instructed a subordinate, "and don't let them touch her. Don't let them touch *anything.*"

Oh, what a happy situation.

But there they sat. Or stood.

They could all end up under arrest, once the matter shook out—God forbid Sabin should die, though that would solve certain things at a stroke, and it could happen very, very fast if Ilisidi so much as flicked a finger. Bren walked over to her, bowed, and explained quickly, in a low voice.

"Aiji-ma, Sabin-aiji is furious and takes it that she was poisoned, on which I have not been so forward as to claim any knowledge. . . ."

Ilsidi smiled—was it a smile?—and rested a hand on Cajeiri's shoulder. "She is alive and quite well. It was a very small dose. But we will *not* be constrained in movement or access, and that you may tell her."

There was an arrival at that point. Ginny Kroger walked in, with a handful of the station's security guards, and the room . . . already crowded . . . became very crowded indeed.

"Bren," Ginny said, and gave a little bow toward the dowager. "Dowager." She said it in Ragi, a courtesy. Only a few years ago *no* human but the paidhi ever addressed an ateva, and it had become gingerly matter-of-course that one *should* do so. "We understand there's been a little question of our freedom to move about. We also understand the captain's taken ill. We're here. At your service."

Ginny, of all people. Bren's heart gave a thump; and he had to ask what the hell was going on.

Jase, he thought then. Jase, on the bridge, with freedom of communications.

"I'd like to keep this civil," he murmured, trying to keep it out of Sabin's drugged hearing. "The captain pushed the dowager, hard. We've had a bit of a blow-up and the dowager's willing to have it be settled, tit for tat. Given the freedom from restriction. That's how things are."

"Mr. Cameron." The doctor was irate. "I'll thank you to take this mob *out*."

"We can move the captain to the dowager's quarters, where we can care for her," Bren said . . . not having consulted in the least, but he took a chance, high and wide. "We feel, given the nature of the reaction, that we ought to remain a resource for her . . . and we take our commitment to Captain Graham very seriously. We *will* remove her from the premises if we feel she's in danger, damned right we will."

"Get out of here."

"You can't enforce it," Bren said. "Nor should. This is *international politics* you're taking a wrench to, sir, and *my* patient is the agreement that pastes three species together and keeps your ship operational. In that capacity, I'm supported by two of your captains and both the planet's nations. And I'm not budging."

"Cameron."

That was from Sabin. He paid attention, and walked cautiously over to the bed.

"You damn bastard," Sabin said.

"Yes, ma'am. I am and please attribute the misunderstandings to me, with profound personal apologies. I know the dowager's limited in her conversation with you, but she'd much rather have an agreement and a civilized understanding. Her presence here is both an honor to you and an expression of her wish to have an agreement."

Sabin's scowling face was pale and beaded with sweat.

"You think I'm tracking?"

"I think you're hearing things, and they come and they go, rather like talking down a pipe. Am I right? But I think you know the essentials. I think you know you can have a voyage with allies—or maybe that voyage shouldn't take place at all. If we can't bring the peace we've reached—out there—then what are we bringing, captain? If the representatives of the world and the station have to be locked belowdecks and kept out of decisions, we're not bringing them damned much hope."

"Who are you going to poison next? The pilot? That will be useful."

"Captain, here's a simple question. Did you back Pratap Tamun in an attempt to get information out of Ramirez? Was that where it went wrong?"

"What in hell are you talking about?"

"That is a fairly reasonable suspicion, isn't it? You nominated Tamun. You generally supported him. Tamun wanted information on conditions at the station, because he was suspicious there was something withheld, and Ramirez wouldn't give it to him. If he'd had what Ramirez knew, he could have brought the whole crew in on the mutiny—but he didn't have it. And if *he* didn't have it, maybe you didn't have it.

Now every eyewitness but one is dead. And you just appropriated him to *your* staff."

Sabin blinked slowly, sweat beaded in the lines about her eyes. The expression was somewhat bewildered. It might be she'd lost the threads of the question. It might be bewilderment of a different sort.

"Jenrette?"

"All the others died in the coup. So there's Jenrette. And you wanted him away from Jase. And we know it."

A slow series of blinks. Sabin's face wasn't accustomed to bewilderment. The map of lines was better suited to frowns.

"Damn this headache." She seemed then to lose the pieces. And grope after them. "You've built a fairy castle, Mr. Cameron. And poisoned me because of it?"

"Only incidentally because of it, because if I'd believed you were on the side of the angels, or if you'd understood my position, Captain Sabin, you and I might have talked and the level of tension on this ship wouldn't have prompted you to restrict the dowager's movements and insult her at her own dinner table."

"You were the translator, Mr. Cameron."

"I can't ameliorate body language, Captain Sabin."

"You . . . and Jase Graham. Damn him."

"Damn us both, captain. Let's be fair. *Did* you know about the situation on Reunion?"

Sabin's hand wandered to her head, shaded her eyes a moment, shutting him out.

Then dropped.

"Where's Jules Ogun? Does your coup extend to the station?"

"Call him. I'm sure Jase can patch you through. What's on the station is what we agreed on, a cooperative power-sharing, Captain Ogun, Lord Geigi, and Mr. Paulson. And considering everything that's gone on, I'm not sure we're not all going back aboard the station."

"Things onstation are what they were." Ginny moved to the foot of Sabin's cot.

"Who's that?" Focusing clearly hurt.

"Ginny Kroger, captain. Our deep concern for what's happening here. This isn't the way we wanted to start the voyage."

"Not what I planned, either," Sabin muttered.

"So things onstation are secure," Bren said. "And we can bring the ship back in to dock and try to settle this—you, your crew, the station . . . everybody. It does admit a certain failure on our part. Maybe we can avoid that."

Sabin shut her eyes. There was a lengthy silence. Bren looked at Ginny.

"She's pretty damn sick," he said. "She'll be all right, but she's in no shape to make decisions right now. I don't think this ship should leave port right now. We've been lied to, by Ramirez or by the whole captain's council. We know there are records we weren't given. We know there's been deception on deception—whether it's the old Guild running this show or not, no one's sure."

"Guild, hell," Sabin muttered, eyes still shut. "We

never were sure. Just put a brake on it, Cameron. Don't speculate."

"Yes, ma'am," he said, and folded his hands and stopped where he was, listening, waiting while a very sick woman tried to gather her faculties.

"First off, tell the dowager she's a right damn bastard."

It was no time for a translator to argue. Mitigation, however, was a reasonable tactic. "Aiji-ma, Sabin-aiji has heard our suspicions regarding Tamun and received assurances from me and Gin-aiji that we have not arranged a coup of our own. She addresses you with an untranslatable term sometimes meaning extreme disrepute, sometimes indicating respect for an opponent."

Ilisidi's mouth drew down in wicked satisfaction. "Return the compliment, paidhi."

"Captain, she says you're a right damn bastard, too."

Sabin almost laughed, winced, and grabbed her head with a hand that shook like palsy. "God."

"Hurts. I know. I'm sorry."

"Damn your 'sorry.' Tell the dowager she can wander all over the deck and into the reaction chamber for all I care. What's Graham up to, up there right now? Going through files?"

"I think he might be asking questions."

"Of Jenrette."

"Among other actions. I know for a fact, captain, that he'd shoot me before he'd take an action that endangered this ship. Let's lay suspicions out in plain sight. He lived onworld with us for a number of years, he understands us, and *his understanding* of us has led him to do what he's done. Frankly, he in no way anticipated what happened at the aiji's table. He rather planned to invade the files by subterfuge and try to find out the truth without embarrassing you. And maybe just to ask Jenrette some direct questions . . . if *you* didn't assassinate Jenrette."

Blink.

"People *have* been assassinated in this affair," Bren said. "Not least of our suspicions—Ramirez."

Blink-blink. "Not unless you did it."

"You suspected us? We suspected you."

"Did you do it?"

"No. I investigated, and my staff investigated. No."

"That's constructive." Pain made Sabin shield her eyes and breathe heavily for a moment. "I'll tell you what, Mr. Cameron. Let's just assume this voyage *is* going to take place. Let's assume we can even proceed on schedule. I'm not looking forward to acceleration until this headache stops, but we all have our inconveniences. Did you tell the dowager she's a bitch?"

"Bastard, ma'am, and she called you one."

"Good. We understand each other. How long does this headache last?"

"A few days. I hope less, with human-specific medication, all the facilities here . . ."

"Days." Sabin winced.

"There are a few native antidotes . . . at least things that help. But I think the medical staff can do more for you than . . ."

"Hell. Tell Graham get this ragtag settled into cabins, secure the ship and get the pilot on advisement.

Tell Graham I'll see him when he's got a moment and don't push any buttons up there."

"Captain Sabin." He was, on the one hand, amazed. On the other—still suspicious. Years in Shejidan had all his nerves atwitch. And gave him the sure instinct to take what the captain offered and look it over very, very carefully. "I'll certainly pass that message. But we waited all this time. Your comfort—"

"Is not an issue, Mr. Cameron." Incredibly, she lifted her head and struggled up on an elbow. Bren put out his hands to catch her, knowing at gut level the giddy spin that effort created. But she stayed tremulously steady. "Get the hell out of here and tell Graham to move the ship. *Now,* hear me?"

She sank back. A medic crowded in to check the tubes and the vitals.

"Aiji-ma," Bren said, "she accepts explanations and orders the mission to proceed. She wishes us to go to quarters and leave Jase-aiji in charge of the ship's operations." He said it, and his Shejidan-experienced mind urged caution. "One might, however, provide atevi security."

Ilisidi's eyes sparkled. "Here, and with Jase-aiji."

"One concurs."

It was a peculiar difference dealing with humans, that one understood there was the possibility of an association with Sabin—and yet, among atevi, there would be an aiji ultimately in charge of that association. Where in all reason did they find someone to be in charge of this one, since neither Ilisidi nor Sabin admitted an overlord?

One had the thoroughly uncomfortable notion that

the paidhiin glued it all together, and that Sabin didn't forgive what Ilisidi had done, and Ilisidi didn't forgive the insults at her table, and they had Cajeiri looking nervously from one participant to the other in an atevi child's honest bewilderment. His instincts surely said this shouldn't work and adults surely weren't telling the truth.

But that was the whole problem with the atevi/human interface, and that was the problem with educating children of both species to get along without touching one another's aggressive instincts. And that was the problem of a ship-culture that had a strong feeling of *us* and *them* and went armed to the teeth. Letting atevi under the ship's armor was a hard, hard thing to do.

And just as well, if they had current ability to move about, that they move into the most sensitive areas and make the point they could do so without harm.

"The dowager wishes you a speedy recovery," Bren said to Sabin, saying nothing about the movement of atevi personnel. "She accepts."

"The captain of this ship wishes her in hell," Sabin said dourly, holding a hand over her eyes, and the chief translator foresaw a very, very difficult duty on this ship. "Get me communication with the bridge. Not you. *Kaplan*."

Kaplan threw a glance at Bren. Bren tried simultaneously to say go ahead and to look as if he wasn't anywhere in the loop.

"Good you're here," Bren said to Ginny with a touch on the arm. "Want to drop by my quarters when you're settled? Bring yourself up to speed?"

"That's in the atevi section."

"Atevi, Mospheiran . . . we're all deck five. It's going to be close quarters. We're going to need to secure for motion, imminently, I think. When it's stopped—when we're inertial again—" He struggled to revise his earth-bound thinking. "Drop by for drinks. Or I'll come to you. I'll present you to the dowager."

"Deal," Ginny said, and turned and took her own escort out of the crowded compartment. The dowager signaled her intention to depart.

Sabin was talking to someone, presumably Jase, on her personal com, hand over her eyes, wincing.

It seemed time to depart. Bren joined the atevi contingent on the way out.

"One will remain on watch, nandi," Jago said as they rubbed elbows in the doorway—feet on the deck, the whole world restored to ordinary.

Jago meant that *she* took this post, here, by the infirmary . . . logical choice. She would stand here claiming not to know a word of human language, in which she had a fair fluency.

There had been quiet words passed among atevi all the while he'd been talking to Jase and Sabin: bet that there'd been communications traffic and agents spread out through the ship, all of whom now formed an atevi network of presence. There always was, when an atevi lord moved into an area.

And Jase himself was an atevi interest. Absolutely he was under the dowager's guard, seen or unseen.

"One agrees, Jago-ji."

Banichi stayed with him. Jago stayed behind.

They reached the lift and rode it toward five-deck

with the dowager's entire party, and with Ginny Kroger and her crew. No one spoke. The dowager leaned on her cane with both hands, vastly content.

They reached fifth deck.

The door opened.

"Bren-nadi." The intercom in the lift-car, right in his face, scared him.

"Jasi-ji?"

"Will you mind coming up here?"

He drew a deep breath.

It wasn't over.

The dowager meanwhile had left the car, with young Cajeiri. Ginny Kroger and her crew debarked. Cenedi held the door open.

"I'm requested to come to the bridge, aiji-ma," Bren said.

"Escort him," Ilisidi said, and Cenedi with a rapid gesture detached two men.

Two. Infelicity. Unless one counted Jase.

"Need help?" Ginny asked, from outside the doors.

"No. Questions from Jase, likely. I'll give you a report. —Aiji-ma." One owed last, parting courtesies to the highest rank present. "I'll report."

"Go," Ilisidi said. The pair of men got in. Cenedi got out.

The door shut.

"Do you know what this regards, Bren-ji?" Banichi asked him.

"One isn't sure," he said. His mind conjured a dozen scenarios, most disastrous—even the bridge being held at gunpoint by Sabin loyalists. "I don't *think* it's a trap, nadi-ji. I think it's Jase."

18

There was indeed an atevi presence on the bridge when the lift let them out—two men, felicitous three, counting Jase, the object of their protection: a better counter, perhaps, could have predicted it, with their infelicitous four.

Exceedingly fortunate seven. One wasn't inclined to count the number of humans on the bridge, technicians and operations chiefs, and security . . . but Bren did. They were outnumbered, if not outgunned.

Jase stood amid the rows of consoles, reserved, serene, among crew at work. And spared him a glance.

"All quiet?" Bren asked in ship-speak, precisely because there *were* eavesdroppers.

"Quiet here," Jase said. "How is Captain Sabin?"

"Strong-minded."

Jase quirked an eyebrow.

"In favor of the mission," Bren amended that. "Anxious to see it underway."

"We have section chiefs going through the corridors now, final check on stowage."

"It's the pilot that does this, isn't it? All the technicals. I'll assume things will work."

"They'll work," Jase said. And shot him a less cheerful look. "Clear operations with me or with Captain Sabin. No installations we don't know about. And where I don't know the risks, I'll have one of the technical staff pass on it."

"Understood. We remember how humans got to this star in the first place. We've no desire to foul up navigation."

"You understand. I want to be sure your staff does. I want to be sure the *dowager* understands us."

"I'll attend to that."

"Do. —Banichi-ji."

"Nandi."

"There's hazard in moving about the corridors. Understand that, nadi-ji."

"One understands, nandi."

"There may be hard feelings. And suspicion, nadi. Very deep suspicion."

"There's something about being that sick, among strangers," Bren said in Ragi, "that makes one re-evaluate the world."

"I don't count on it," Jase said bluntly. And in ship-speak: "Mr. Hammond, take over while I make sure our guests reach five-deck."

Not the deepest cover they could imagine, but Jase put a hand on Bren's back and walked him to the lift, his bodyguard attending.

Jase punched five, inside. The doors shut between them and the bridge. The lift started into motion.

"Tell me this one," Jase said. "Did you know?"

"I didn't. I honestly didn't. I don't think it was sure until it went difficult at the table."

"Dammit, Bren."

"Dammit, indeed. But she and the dowager exchanged frank words. Very frank words. There may be communication."

"We're going out there in the deep dark with no agreement. With everything in flux."

"Not wholly our doing. This limiting the dowager to *fifth deck*. This niggling away at the agreements started long before the dowager even came up to the station." The lift reached bottom. The door opened. They couldn't delay in conversation without provoking human suspicions. "You know Ramirez expanded agreements: you know he expanded them and you know he *pushed*, and you know the danger in that. He pushed Tabini into haste, and when he died, damned right we had an emergency. We had a council of captains without a useful clue attempting to change pace on the course we'd been following breakneck for years, all on human promises—"

"It doesn't give you leave—"

"Not excluding Sabin all along being outvoted by the Ramirez-Ogun combination and Ramirez putting *you* in. That's going to be with us. No, I don't trust her, Jase-nadi. I don't see a woman who's open to strangeness, not now, not yet. I see a woman who shouldn't be in charge of foreign contact, and yet that's where she's ended, and you and I know we're in trouble."

"This is our *household*," Jase said in a shaken voice. "Do you get that, Bren? I'm willing to take an office I don't want and try to make things work in non-

technicals, in the things I *can* do. And hereafter—I
may speak the language, but *man'chi* is to the ship."

"You know how to sit in a two-species meeting and
get out of it with a civilized agreement. That's the
point, Jase. That's the very point."

"We can't have another incident like this."

"I expect the dowager will invite Sabin back to
dinner."

"I expect Sabin will invite the dowager first."

That, in fact, seemed very likely. "We're going to
have our hands full, Jase-paidhi."

"I'll get that tape," Jase said, and reached for the lift
control panel. "Out. Takehold's going in effect in short
order. I've got to drop by and talk to Sabin."

"Luck," he said, and got out, with his escort.
Cenedi had a man on watch by the lift—a precaution.
"Understand—no more restriction of our move-
ments."

"None," Jase said. "Not on my watch."

The door shut. The lift departed.

Bren cast a glance to the borrowed escort. "They
stand ready to move the ship, nadiin. I send you to
the dowager, with thanks. —Banichi."

Banichi walked with him. The escort walked behind.

"Jago should come back down, to ride through this
with us," Bren said. Maybe it wasn't wise, but things
were about to change on a large scale. They were about
to do something his gut insisted was dangerous—even
if it was only getting up to speed, to clear the vicinity
of the only world he'd known—and he wanted all the
people he cherished safe and taken care of.

"I'll pass that order," Banichi said.

"Sabin should be safe. Her own people will see to her."

"One hopes, Bren-ji."

They walked down the curve of the corridor, past the dowager's guarded door—two men there; and that place absorbed their escort.

They reached that area of hall that was the paidhi's establishment—his own quarters. Doors were all shut.

Banichi spoke to Narani on his personal communications, and the door very quickly whisked open on a room vastly changed since the explosion of baggage.

There was order. There was his bed, freed of baggage, lid down, sparklingly modern.

It wasn't Mospheira, it wasn't Shejidan: it was modern, it was stark, spartan and scary. He almost wished for the clutter. He very much wished for the halls of the Bujavid, those halls where every carpet was hand-worked, antique, convolute in design; where draperies had one pattern and half a dozen vases of carefully selected flowers had another.

But there, right above his desk, in strong light, hung three globes—like Ilisidi's banquet globes, transparent, and containing green leaves—growing leaves, he discovered, and then recognized them.

Fortunate three.

Living plants.

Bindanda had had a hand in this, he was quite sure. Had he not given Bindanda Sandra Johnson's cuttings to establish?

And here they were, green, growing, an oasis, Bindanda's little secret. He'd entirely forgotten. Some sort of medium, a hole to let the vines trail out—there being only a leaf-tip at the moment.

He'd never suspected Tatiseigi's spy of such kind sentiment.

"Bindanda offers these," Narani said. "They're just rooted. Would you care for tea before the ship moves, paidhi-ji?"

There were atevi established here. Of *course,* silly thought, be very sure there was tea, it was hot, and it could just be delivered before the warning siren.

He sat in the reclining chair, sipped his tea in a disposable cup while staff hurried about.

Jago appeared, right with the siren, on her way through to the quarters she shared with Banichi.

"Don't take such chances, Jago-ji!" he begged her. "Kindly be earlier."

"One hears, nadi." Jago wasn't inclined to argue.

And would do exactly as she had to do, he was quite sure.

"How does Sabin fare?" he asked.

"Asleep, one believes, nadi."

A verbal warning, over the intercom: Jase's voice. *"Acceleration in one minute. Count has begun. Take hold."*

"Go," he said to Jago. "Quickly."

He was belted in. Staff had gone to safe positions. He drank the last of the tea, wadded up the cup and held on to it . . . a physics experiment, he thought, once they were underway. Or he'd just hold it until there was an all-clear.

His heart beat faster and faster.

The first movement was a great deal like the lift's

acceleration, in the core. The illusion of gravity grew stronger and stronger, until the chair seemed horizontal.

He stared at the far wall that was, for the duration, the ceiling, scared, and with no useful place to spend a Mospheiran's long-cultivated fear of flying.

For no reason and out of nowhere in particular, he thought of his mother's apartment, and a lost cufflink, and the last visit before things changed in the family for good and all—

It was the last holiday they'd been together. He remembered that cufflink going down the heating register, in a room his mother constantly kept ready for him.

For the black sheep of the family.

He remembered breakfast in his mother's apartment . . . and didn't know whether she was still alive—a human attachment simply lost in the works of nations and captains. He'd had his one chance to go home, and hadn't even made a phone call.

He couldn't blame anyone else for *that* choice.

The ship went on accelerating

No way to call out *Wait!*

No way now . . .

In point of fact . . . fear reached a level and stayed there, and fell behind.

The ship traveled, and, different than a flight here, or there, separating him from a situation—*Phoenix* was leaving the station, leaving the whole world behind.

While his household, these people around him— they were here on his account, and because of their *man'chi*, and because their home was always where he was.

Even the dowager, be it remembered, had left the world she championed. There was no fiercer advocate for the old ways of the world, and here she was, outbound with the next generation of her household, to take on whatever humans had done at Reunion—to use *his* help, among others.

Jase only *thought* two captains ran this ship.

He drew one breath and two, having his bearings, with the world and the station behind him—or under his back, as the axis of the ship went—and getting further away by the second. It wasn't so bad. He could have drunk the tea more slowly.

No emergency, and they were *launched*.

They were going to go out to wherever the ship did such things and fold space, bizarre thought. He couldn't wait to explain that process to Banichi.

And his family, such as he still had back on Mospheira, would have to deal with things in his utter absence, as families could, and did, surviving somehow, and in their own way.

Another set of large breaths. He felt completely light-headed.

"Acceleration will continue at 1.2 G," C1 said over the intercom. *"Emergency movement only until further notice."*

They were on a ship hurtling faster and faster through the cosmos and away from all they knew.

And the whole ship was a place of only crew, only staff—inaccessible to strangers and random lunatics, a place where he didn't have to worry about assassins and vantages for snipers.

He drew two and three free breaths, in that heady thought.

He *was* free—for the first time in more than a decade. Give or take Sabin, no one on the ship wanted to kill him.

Wasn't that a marvelous thought?

Read on for a preview of

EXPLORER

the stunning conclusion to the
second *Foreigner* sequence,
new in hardcover
this month from DAW.

"Sir." Kaplan opened the office door for Bren.

Jase looked up from his desk and waved him toward a seat, there being no formality between them. And since it was a meeting of intimates, Banichi and Jago automatically lagged to talk to Kaplan and Polano outside, such as they could. Atevi security regularly socialized during their lords' personal meetings, if they were of compatible allegiances—as Kaplan and Polano indisputably were; so Bren discreetly touched the on-button of his pocket com as he went in, being sure by that means that Asicho, on five-deck—would have a record for staff review.

The door shut. Bren dragged one of the interview chairs around on its track. Sat.

Unlike Sabin's office, which had a lifetime accumulation of storage cabinets, Jase's office was new and barren, a desk, two interview chairs—no books, in all those bookcases and cabinets: only one framed photo, a slightly tilted picture of Jase holding up a spiny, striped fish. It was his most predatory moment on the planet.

What would you do with it? shipmates might ask; and if Jase wanted to unsettle them, he might say, truthfully, horrifying most of them, that they had had it for supper that night—a rather fine supper, too.

They shared that memory. They shared a great many things, not least of which was joint experience in the aiji's court, with all that entailed, before Jase had gotten an unwanted captaincy.

"Good you came," Jase said. "Sorry about the midnight hour. But I've got something for you."

"Got something." He had niggling second thoughts about the pocket-com, and confessed it. "I'm wired."

"I'm always sure you are." Jase two-sided the console at a keystroke and gave him a confusing semi-transparent view of a split screen.

Bren leaned forward in the chair, arm on the desk edge. With a better light angle, he figured it out for a view through a helmet-cam on one side and, on the other, a diagram of the walking route among rooms and corridors.

His heart went thump. He knew what it was, then. And he'd expected *this* revelation eight moves and eleven months ago.

Now they had it? Close to the end of their journey, this showed up?

"Sabin knows?" he asked, regarding the extraction of this particular segment out of the log records.

"Not exactly," Jase said.

There was the timing. There was the non-cooperation of the senior captain. That Jase called him up here to see it, instead of bringing it down to five-deck . . . he wasn't sure what that meant. Relations between the two on-board captains had been uneasily cordial since—well, since the unfortunate incident at undock, Sabin having insulted the dowager within the first few hours and the dowager having poisoned the captain in retaliation. The two women had gotten along since, wary as fighting fish in a tank. The two captains had gotten along because they had to: the ship regularly had four, and ran now on part of its crew, part of its population, and two of the three surviving captains.

And despite his conviction this tape existed and despite the dowager's demands and Jase's requests for the senior captain to locate it in log and produce it— Sabin hadn't acknowledged it existed, hadn't cooperated, hadn't acknowledged the situation they suspected lay behind the tape. In short, no, Sabin hadn't helped find it in the last number of months, and now that it had turned up, didn't know Jase had it. And what was the object of their long search? The mission-tape from the ship's last visit, the record none of the crew had seen, the record that Ramirez, the late senior captain, had deliberately held secret from the crew. A man named Jenrette, chief of Ramirez's personal bodyguard, had entered that station and met survivors—and those survivors had allegedly refused to be taken off the station.

But those survivors included, one suspected, the hierarchy of the old Pilots' Guild, an organization whose management had caused the original schism between colonists and crew—and managed the contact with aliens who'd already taken offense and launched an attack. Not a sterling record. Not a record that inspired confidence. Or love.

Captain Ramirez, during that strange port-call, had told his own crew that Reunion was dead . . . destroyed by the alien attack. He'd refueled off the supposedly dead station, and run back to Alpha, where that lie about Reunion's condition had held firm and credible for nearly a decade—until Ramirez' deathbed confession had blown matters wide.

But secrecy hadn't ended with one deathbed revelation. His suspicion of other facts withheld had made this particular tape an item of contention between Sabin, who'd been one of the captains nine years ago, and Jase, Ramirez's appointee, whose assignment to a captaincy had nothing to do with knowledge of ship's operations. Jase had been aboard that day they'd found Reunion in ruins, but he hadn't been on the bridge—he'd been twenty-odd, junior, and not consulted, far from it. Sabin wouldn't talk about that time at dock; no member of the bridge crews had talked to anyone they could access. Every member of Ramirez's personal security team except Jenrette was dead—killed in a mutiny against Ramirez—and Sabin had snatched Jenrette into her security team immediately after Ramirez's death, the very day, in fact, that Jase had wanted to ask him questions about this tape.

That was the state of relations between the ship's captains—Sabin, very senior, and Jase, appointed by the late senior captain, very junior—and a lot of data not shared between them.

"Anything entirely astonishing about the tape?" Bren asked. "I trust you've reviewed it to the end."

"The match-up with station plans is my work," Jase muttered, keying while the tape proceeded. The screen afforded them a helmet-cam view of airless, ravaged halls picked out in portable lights as Jase skipped through the venues, freezing key scenes. "For a long stretch, things go pretty much as you'd expect to see. Fire damage. Explosion damage. Outwardly, the kind of thing you'd expect of a station in ruins. But the boarding team doesn't wander around much. No exploring. Straight on."

"As if they knew where they were going?"

"Exactly." Jase skipped ahead through the record, and now, in motion, the exploration reached a section that looked far less ravaged. "Their entry into the station, which is a long, tedious sequence, was through the hole in the mast; but after they got in, the lift worked on emergency power, which saved them quite a bit of effort. Piece of luck, eh? Emergency generators back up a lot of functions. Fuel port. Critical accesses. No questions there. Now we're in the C corridor, section . . . about 10. Notice anything really odd here?"

The matching map had the numbers. If one could assume the station architecture as similar to the atevi earth station's structure, the investigating crew was on second level near the cargo offices at the moment. Lights were out. Power was down. Helmet lights still picked out walls and closed doors. Intact doors.

"It's not that badly damaged here," Bren observed.

"No, it's not." A small pause. "But we did see part of the station survived. What else do you notice? For God's sake, Bren . . ."

He was entirely puzzled. After a silence, Jase had to prompt him:

"They're *walking*."

God. *God.* Of course. They were walking. Walking was so ordinary. But he'd helped revive a space station. He knew better. Walking, in space, was a carefully managed miracle . . . and on a station with an altered center of mass? Not easy, was it?

He felt like a fool. "The station's rotating."

"As good as put out a neon sign," Jase said. "To anyone born in space."

A sign to tell more than the investigating ship. A sign to advise any alien enemies that this station wasn't utterly destroyed. That much beyond any small pocket of light or heat where a handful of surviving tenants might cling to life, as they'd assumed all through this voyage was the case—this huge structure was rotating and managing its damage in ways very suggestive of life, intact systems, and sufficient internal energy to hold itself in trim.

"Computer couldn't manage this on auto," he said to Jase, "could it?"

"Less than likely. A dumb system—possible, I suppose, but I don't believe it. I don't think crew will."

"But you can see rotation from outside," Bren said, confused. "The ship docked, didn't they? How can crew not have seen it?"

Jase gave him a dark look. "We've never left home. We're still sitting at dock at Alpha. The atevi world's below us. Can you prove differently? Can you prove we've ever traveled at all?"

Once he thought of it, no, he couldn't. There was no view of outside . . . except what the cameras provided the viewing screens. They underwent periods of inconvenience and strangeness that made it credible they moved, but there was no visual proof that didn't come through the cameras.

And had Ramirez somehow ordered a lie fed to those cameras? A simple still image, that crew would take for the station's lifeless hulk, when the truth was moving, lively, self-adjusting?

From when? God, from how early in the ship's approach had Ramirez faked that output?

"If Ramirez faked the camera images," he asked Jase, "how early did he? Did he come into Reunion system expecting disaster in the first place?"

"I'll tell you that niggling suspicion did occur to me. But long-range optics might have seen there was a problem, way far off. Down below, I assure you, we didn't get an image . . . we don't, routinely until bridge has time to key it to belowdecks. It's not often important. It's protocols. And if bridge is busy, if a captain's too busy, or off-shift, or in a meeting, we sometimes don't get image for a while. For a long while, in this case. We saw the still image. We saw the team entering the mast."

"Where it's always null-g."

"No feed from helmet cam beyond that. This section went straight into the log's black box and nobody belowdecks *ever* saw it."

Anger. No *wonder* this particular tape had stayed buried for nine years. No wonder the current senior captain had silenced the last living member of the group that had made that tape and challenged the technically untrained junior captain to find the log record—if he could.

"But the captains all knew," Bren surmised. "Sabin

was there. She had to know the station wasn't dead. Anybody on the bridge, any of the techs, they had to know, all along, didn't they?" *That* had been a question before they launched on this mission. It looked darker and darker now, damning all chance of honesty between executive and crew.

"It's all numbers readout on those screens," Jase said. "You get what the station transmits. Or doesn't transmit. Or if *it* feeds you a lie—you'd have that on your screen, wouldn't you? I'm not sure that all the ops techs on the bridge knew. Some had to. But it's possible some didn't."

More and more sinister, Bren thought, wishing that at some time, at any convenient time, the late captain Ramirez had leveled with his atevi allies . . . and his own crew.

"I'll imagine, too," Jase went on, "that the minute we got into the solar system and got any initial visual inkling there was trouble, bridge showed a succession of still images from then on out—in space, you can't always tell live from still. I'll imagine, for charity's sake, that Ramirez ran the whole thing off some archive tape and a still shot and nobody else knew. He might have been the only captain on the bridge during the investigation: you just don't budge from quarters until you get the all-clear, and it didn't come for us belowdecks for hours. Maybe he didn't tell anybody but his own techs. Maybe the other captains got his still image and *they* didn't leave their executive meeting to find out. I can construct a dozen scenarios that might have applied. But I'll tell you I'm not happy with anything I can imagine. The more I think about it, I'm sure Sabin had to know."

"You docked at the station, for God's sake."

"Tethered. Simple guides for fueling. We're not the space shuttle."

Not the space shuttle. Not providing passenger video on the approach. Not providing a cushy pressurized and heated tube link.

Entry through the null-g mast, where even a trained eye couldn't easily detect a lie.

"There's another tape," Bren said, on that surmise. "There's got to be some log record where the station contacted *Phoenix* and gave Ramirez the order not to let the crew know there was anybody alive."

"You know, I'd like to think that was where the orders originated," Jase said calmly. "And I earnestly tried to find a record to prove that theory. But I couldn't. My level of skill, I'm afraid. Took me eleven months to break this much out. I know a lot more now than I did about the data system. But you get into specific records by having keys. I've cracked a few of them. Not all. *Not* the policy level. Not the level where Guild orders might be stored. And the senior captain isn't about to give them up and I'm not about to ask."

"You can't *erase* a log entry, can you?"

"You'd think. But at this point—we've rebuilt a lot of the ship's original systems, over the centuries, and I'm not sure that's the truth any longer. At my level of expertise, no. Not possible. If there's a key that allows that—it rests higher than I can reach. Maybe it sits in some file back on old Earth, that launched us. Maybe Sabin has it. I don't."

Jase was *Ramirez's* appointment, and Sabin hadn't approved his having the post.

And the crew, the general, non-bridge crew—who'd all but mutinied to get them launched on this rescue mission—if they saw this tape, they were going to be far faster on the uptake than a groundling ambassador. There was a reasonable case to be made that the Pilots' Guild itself, in charge of Reunion Station, was behind all the trouble and all the lies and all the deception. There was a reasonable, even a natural case to be made that the alien hostility that had wrecked the station was directly the Guild's fault, and not Ramirez's. But believing the old Guild was the sole culpable agency required suspending a lot of possibilities, because the station wasn't mobile. The station wasn't gadding about space poking into other people's solar systems.

And the ship's executive hadn't talked. Hadn't breached the official lie that Reunion Station was dead.

Nine years without talking? Nine years for that many people on the bridge to keep a secret from their friends and relations among the crew?

Mospheirans never could have done it, Bren thought. Then: atevi . . . possibly. And ship-folk—

He watched Jase watch the tape, thinking that all the years he'd known Jase hadn't gotten him through all the layers of Jase's reticence. Even with friendship. Even with shared experience. In some ways ship-folk were as alien to Mospheirans as a Mospheiran could imagine.

And the ease of lies in this sealed steel world of the ship . . .